SACAR

S.M. STORM

Dedication

To my crew, you know who you are. And to my husband, my greatest supporter. Thank you for never letting me give up.

Content and Trigger Warnings

Because I care deeply about mental health and the well-being of my readers, I want to be upfront: this book contains explicit sexual content and potentially triggering material, including:

- Kidnapping and captivity
- Torture and medical experimentation
- Violence and bloodshed
- Death and grief
- PTSD and trauma-related themes

Prologue

I lay there, staring at the ceiling, counting the faint cracks that spiderwebbed across its surface. The mattress beneath me was hardly an improvement to the floor; the springs pressing into my back were almost as uncomfortable as the cold, hard ground. Sky's soft humming drifted through the air like a lullaby, weaving into the rhythmic rustle of flipped pages as she read her book. It was a comforting melody, one she'd made up long ago, but it reached me now as though carried by a threadbare whisper.

Counting the cracks had become my ritual, my only way of passing the time.

Ten. Eleven. Twelve.

"Mmm-mmm, mm-mm-mmm, mmm-mmm-mm-mm…"

Her humming was my anchor. A balm against the suffocating monotony. It was a reminder that she was near, even if I couldn't see her. She could see me, though, and I knew that brought a small amount of comfort to us both.

I was at crack number twenty-five when the distant sound of a door opening and slamming shut echoed through the hallway. The sound cut through the space like a whip, ricocheting off the concrete walls and sending my pulse racing.

I knew what that meant.

Visitors.

And not the kind you welcomed.

I struggled against the restraints that pinned me to the thin mattress, the familiar bite digging into my wrists and ankles. The heavy muzzle over my face made it difficult to breathe, as the stale, metallic tang of the air filled my nose. But none of that mattered. My focus was on the footsteps thudding down the corridor, each one a harbinger of my future pain.

The humming stopped, and the silence was jarring. Sky must have heard the footsteps, too.

One. Two. Three.

"Time to get up," I murmured, the words hollow and dry. No one could hear me, as my voice was muffled by the muzzle. Still, saying it grounded me, helped me hold onto what little control I had left.

The lock on my door clanged, the sharp metallic sound cutting through the quiet like a blade. My body tensed instinctively as the door groaned open, flooding the room with harsh fluorescent light. Shadows stretched across the floor, long and jagged, heralding their arrival.

They always came together; their movements deliberate and mechanical. I didn't have to see them to know who they were. Their footsteps, their breathing, their scent, even their silence, I had memorized it all.

"Move her," one of them ordered. No, not just one of them. It was *his* voice — the one that stood above all others.

What would it be this time, a lung removal? Followed by endurance training? Can't wait to see what type of torture they have in store for me today.

As my hands gripped the edges of my mattress, my only source of mobility, the restraints around my wrists and ankles tightened, and I let my mind wander back to Sky.

"Mmm-mmm, mm-mm-mmm, mmm-mmm-mm-mm…"

Almost on cue, her humming picked up again, as if she realized I needed the reassurance that she was okay. She was, after all, my only constant here — my only proof that I was still alive. My only totem of existence.

They lifted me from my mattress onto the gurney. They tightened the straps across my chest before I heard their footsteps retreat from my cell.

Then —

The sound of another lock and metal door opening. The humming stopped abruptly this time.

No.

No!

Not her. Please, not her.

A slow, mocking *tsk* cut through the silence. "Ah, there she is." I thrashed against the restraints, panic surging like wildfire. "How nice of you to join us."

I tried to scream, but the muzzle was tight and distorted the sound, reducing my terror to a muffled, useless noise.

The bastard feigned a look of concern. "I'm so sorry, my dear, but I can't hear you." His voice dripped with insincerity, feeding off my helplessness.

He loved this game. The taunting. The belittling. The way he could strip away every last shred of my control.

"Did you really think there wouldn't be consequences for killing one of my employees?" he mused, patting my arm like some disobedient pet.

His fingers tightened, nails digging in as his tone turned cold. "We both know there's no punishment that would break you into submission." His breath brushed my ear, sending ice down my spine. "But what about your sister?" His tone turned dark as he leaned to whisper in my ear, "I can't wait for you to see what we have in store for her."

I thrashed harder against my restraints, feeling them dig into my skin until a wetness coated them. Pain followed, but I didn't care. I kept fighting until I heard it.

The soft shuffle of Sky's bare feet against the cold floor, moving down the corridor.

Toward the central lab.

Toward the place where they conducted their *tests*.

A ragged, muffled scream tore from my throat. I fought harder. My pulse pounded in my ears, my vision blurring with sheer desperation. I felt the familiar pinch of a needle in my arm as I traced my eyes up to the bag hanging above me. The silvery liquid was basically laughing in my face. Well, the joke was on him because it wasn't going to work this time.

"Time to watch," he goaded, a sick amusement lacing his words as I felt the wheels beneath me begin to roll.

I was being moved.

I wouldn't cry. I wouldn't give him the satisfaction.

I will get out of here. We will get out of here.

We had to.

Chapter 1

Onyx

One year later...

Branches lashed at my face, tangling in my hair, but my thoughts had never been clearer.

Run.

Duck.

Keep her safe.

Run.

"Sky, are you alright?" I called over my shoulder, struggling to catch my breath.

"Yeah," Sky replied between exhales that were equally, if not more, winded than my own.

Breathe.

Run.

"Almost there," I panted, leaping over a fallen tree. My every move was as instinctive as a deer running from wolves. That's what we were now. Prey. Being hunted by humans.

Humans...

When they don't understand something, they dissect it, experiment on it, and tear it apart to see what's inside.

Two decades. That's how long we'd been locked away — studied, broken, left to rot. And now, for the first time, we were out.

Our bare feet bled from the pine needles and sharp twigs that stabbed our soles as we ran. Yet, the searing pain was nothing compared to the horrors we just escaped. Still, the scent of blood signified we were leaving a potent trail for our captors to follow. Fortunately, speed was on our side.

I had just cleared another fallen tree when I heard
Sky hit the ground behind me, hard enough to knock the
breath from her lungs. I turned to see her struggling,
hands planted in dirt and dead leaves, face pale and
bruised, her chest rising and falling in desperate gasps.
She looked broken.

Was this too much for her?

"Come on, Sky, you can do it," I coaxed.

Sky's only reply was her labored breathing. Deep,
frantic inhales, like she just reached the surface after
being trapped underwater.

"Sky." My voice came out harsher than I intended.
"You have to get up." Panic clawed at me as I knelt
beside her in the crumpled leaves, gently rolling her onto
her back. I pressed my fingers to her wrist, focusing on
her heartbeat. It was too slow, and her face was too
pale.

No.

She was fading.

She had only left her cage because I convinced her
we wouldn't survive another week. It was clear how
conditioned she had become to her fate. When she
stepped outside, it was with uncertain steps, flinching as
if the sunlight could shatter her. Our escape didn't erase
the damage they inflicted. They didn't just lock her up;
they broke her, making freedom feel like a threat. Now,
I had to help her heal while we were actively being
hunted.

I bent lower, speaking directly into her ear. "Sky, we
don't have time. You must fight. I don't think I can
carry you. If they find us…"

I didn't finish. I didn't need to. I heard a branch crack
off in the distance.

No. No!

We hadn't come this far, fought our way out of hell just to stop here: on our knees in the middle of a dark, damp forest — like the start of its own nightmare. The shadows pressed in around us, cold and suffocating. We moved faster than human eyes could see and were stronger than anything chasing us — but still, we kept running. Still, we were hunted. It made no sense. It felt impossible to be here, on the edge of freedom, only to be pulled back into misery.

With that thought, a fierce resolve surged through me, stronger than the ache in my bones, more piercing than any fear. I would not let them break us. I would not go back. I hoisted Sky up, lifting my younger sister onto my shoulder and gritting my teeth at the added weight. I'd be slower this way, but at least we wouldn't be defenseless while giving our enemy the chance to close in.

As I pressed on, the terrain changed, and the air grew sharper. The icy sting on my skin told me we were heading north — whether by choice or something deeper, I wasn't sure. But the shifting landscape, the advancing frost, and the thinning trees made it clear — we were being pulled north, not by plan but by instinct.

My shoulder protested loudly under the weight of my sister. Honestly, I had lost feeling in it hours ago, but adrenaline and my determination to get us to safety kept me going. Or at least as close to safety as I could manage. Sky stirred slightly, sparking hope that her exhaustion was fading and life returning.

"I'm okay," she mumbled from my shoulder. "I'm okay, I can walk, Ox."

Not willing to risk the chance that Sky was still too weak, I took a couple more strides.

"I'm serious. You can put me down now," she protested.

Before my brain could catch up, my shoulder complied by bending over and gently setting Sky on her feet.

"We're not out of danger yet," I added, needing her to understand the severity of our current situation. "We may have to steal a car or something. If they're tracking us with dogs, it'll throw them off our scent faster."

"And when, exactly, did you learn to drive?" she asked.

"I didn't." I scanned our surroundings, determined to ignore the thoughts clawing at my mind. "But we'll be fine."

She nodded, her calm focus steady as she followed behind me. "This way," I gestured, listening carefully. "I hear cars a few miles ahead."

We reached a small town with a sign indicating that we were about 31 miles from Champaign, Indiana. We slowed down and approached a mostly empty parking lot, looking for an inconspicuous car. We found an older, worn-out blue sedan, but it was locked. The next car was a different shade of blue, covered in dirt, but luckily, unlocked. Though a newer model, it would do.

I slid into the driver's seat and reached under the console, fingers searching for the opening that covered the wires.

To my surprise, instead of just the plastic panel, my hand brushed against something else — cool metal, tucked against the undercarriage — a gun holster.

I pulled it free, my pulse steady as I examined the weapon. Someone had stashed it here. A contingency plan they'd never get to use. Without hesitation, I set it in the cup holder between the seats — close and accessible — then got back to the real task: getting us the hell out of here.

Hot-wiring wasn't a skill I'd been taught. But I understood electrical currents — how they flowed, how they connected, how they could be redirected. That knowledge had been burned into me through forced experiments, where failure meant volts tearing through my body.

Electricity followed rules. Circuits needed to close.

Stripping the wires, I worked through the logic, twisting them together like completing a circuit.

A spark jumped. The engine roared to life.

Success.

This was a skill I was never meant to learn. A lesson they never intended to teach. But watching my torturers had paid off, and served as another reminder that we needed to move. Fast.

I kept one eye on Sky as I finished up my handiwork, tracking her movements while she rifled through a large green donation bin near the curb. She moved with quiet urgency, pulling out clothes and purses like she knew exactly what she was looking for. I kept my hands steady as I tucked the wires back in place and snapped the panel shut. The slight shake in my fingers wasn't from fear; it was adrenaline, thrumming through me like its own electrical current.

And for the first time in a long time, freedom felt within reach.

By the time the engine settled into an idle hum, Sky was already climbing in without a word, arms full of mismatched fabric and forgotten belongings. She was unbundling her findings as she scanned the lot again.

And then I saw it, that quiet strength in her eyes. The expression I expected to see on her face when I opened her cell door. I hated everyone who tried to take that from her.

We peeled off the facility-issued medical gowns in silence, tossing them out the window like the ghosts they were. The clothes Sky found didn't fit us well, but they felt more protective than anything we'd worn in years. A faded college T-shirt, a skirt that didn't match, sleeves too short, and hems too long, none of it mattered.

They may not have belonged to us, but they didn't belong to *them* either.

And that was more than enough.

I didn't need to worry about onlookers; we were in the middle of nowhere. But even if we weren't, a random human or two wasn't a threat. Their minds were fragile, no matter how strong they liked to think they were. Compared to human minds, mine was superior, and replacing their memories was easy… unless silver was involved. That changed everything, and I learned that lesson the hard way.

I could never manipulate someone like Sky, though. Not that I'd ever try. Our kind? We were different. Stronger. Our healing didn't stop at broken bones or severed limbs; it extended to our minds, too. I knew, because they tried to break mine.

Before they took us, there were signs of our differences. My cuts healed too quickly, and I never bruised like other kids. Sky never got sick, and early signs of our fangs made me feel monstrous. Eventually, we stopped asking why we were different.

Unfortunately for us, others started asking questions and tore us apart in their quest for answers. They left no stone unturned, performing countless tests in their relentless pursuit to uncover any hidden secrets.

On the surface, I appeared stable and complete, but internally, I was a fractured soul, held together by my sister and the will to survive.

We navigated the darkened roads as best we could when Sky's voice broke the silence.

"I need answers," she whispered, her voice trembling. "Why us? How did it happen, all of it… I need to know if Mom and Dad are still alive. If they're okay. There's a chance, Onyx."

Her words, so full of fragile hope, left a strange ache in my chest.

I knew our captors didn't spare them. They saw our parents as liabilities. But if hope was the only thing keeping Sky going, I wouldn't be the one to steal it.

"You really think that's a good idea?" I asked, tension creeping into my voice. "Everything out here feels… off. Like it kept moving without us. It's loud, fast, and too open. I don't know the rules anymore, and that scares me. I don't know how to protect you in this world yet."

Sky turned toward me, her expression unreadable.

"We have to," she said softly, but firmly. "If we're going to understand any of this, it has to start there."

I sighed again, resigned. Sometimes it felt like we shared the same mind. In that moment, I knew where we were headed: back to Michigan. We had a few days, maybe, before our pursuers could catch up. With my hearing, we'd managed to avoid main roads and slipped through the forests, far faster than they'd expected. But now that we had some distance, it was time to rest, gather supplies, and maybe, if we were lucky, feed.

I hadn't fed in so long that I had nearly forgotten how, and the thought of drinking blood again made me grimace. Fortunately, we only needed a single blood bag every few months to survive, as it was our only source of nutrients. In captivity, we barely received even that much.

I glanced at Sky as she sat quietly beside me, her gaze fixed and intense. I'd missed that look — her quiet determination had survived everything they'd done to us. We'd make sure that whoever had twisted our lives, ripped us from our family, would pay for it.

"Alright," I exhaled, as the car hummed. "Let's go home."

✳✳✳

As we drove, my sister fell asleep in the passenger seat, finally resting without fear. A wave of relief and joy washed over me — we'd escaped. I'd done terrible things to get us out, but it was over. At last, we were free, and I vowed never to return.

Seeing Sky's relaxed face and steady breathing, I realized she was the only reason that I hadn't completely lost myself over all those years. Her suggestion to return home seemed immature and naïve. I pictured our captors waiting for us there, guns ready. All I could do was hope I put enough distance between us to buy enough time to finally find some answers.

The drive was long. Hours passed, and Sky got some much-needed rest, but I was stuck with the seemingly endless highway and cornfields under the gray morning light. The monotony nearly lulled me to sleep, but as we got close, the familiarity kept me awake. I saw old shops and abandoned restaurants from our childhood. I noticed a small, vacant ice cream parlor as the car bumped over the railroad track that split the town. I remember it used to cause major traffic jams in the summer.

We were home.

Despite the nostalgia, the familiar landmarks stirred more anger than comfort. Memories of trauma surfaced, clashing with flashes of simpler times. It left me conflicted, emotions raw and jagged, a twisted blend of longing and rage. If it were up to me, we'd head north, deep into the forests and lakes of the Upper Peninsula, somewhere our past couldn't reach us. But I could never say no to Sky.

"Let's stop here," Sky pointed to an old house on a ragged patch of land beside a battered barn. I pulled the car over, and we both stepped out. I paused, scanning the area with my heightened senses. Having just fed, I felt like a computer booting up for the first time in years; everything was sharper, cleaner, alive. Sky waited beside me, knowing without words what I was doing. Moments like this, when we could communicate silently, felt... *powerful.*

Once I scanned the area, no strange movements, no off-notes in the wind, no whispers I couldn't place.

I gave a nod.

The late-morning gloom settled over us like a film, the kind Michigan specialized in. Chilly but not unwelcome. Sky led the way, stepping onto the porch first and knocking firmly on the door, knuckles rapping against the peeling wood. The paint flaked beneath our feet as we waited, tension thickening the air.

A man in his mid-forties, smelling of alcohol, opened the door and squinted at us with bloodshot eyes. "And who are you?" he slurred, leaning against the doorframe. His gaze lingered on my chest before he licked his lips slowly. The whiskey smell on his breath was strong. "If you're here for money," he said, still eyeing me, "you're out of luck. I don't donate to whatever you're selling... unless you're selling something else."

I almost told him he was staring at his worst nightmare, but how cheesy would that be? Instead, I snapped my newly acquired gun from its holster and aimed it at his face.

"Who I am isn't important," I said, voice low. "What matters is that we have questions, and you have answers." That definitely sobered him up.

You're welcome.

Sky shot me a warning glare. "Enough," she hissed at me. Then turned to the man with a soft smile, concealing her fangs as she spoke. "My apologies, sir. Let me introduce myself, I'm Brittany, and this is my sister, Nicole."

She cast me a sideways look before continuing, her voice smooth and calming. "What my… overly enthusiastic sister means is that we used to live here, in this town, on this very street, actually. We were just wondering if you might know what happened to the house up the road?"

The man stared down the barrel of my gun, frozen. Sky leaned in and hissed, "Lower your gun *right now*, ya menace."

Fine, fine.

I slipped the gun back into its holster with lightning speed, so fast the guy didn't even see it. The movement seemed only to terrify him more.

"Answer her," I said, crossing my arms.

He stammered, "Th-there was never a house h-here, ma'am."

Chapter 2

Onyx

My temper flared, and Sky must have sensed it. Before I could retort, she jumped in. "Sir, I can assure you, there was a beautiful white farmhouse on this road. We grew up in it," she said, her tone patient and coaxing. "We'd like to know what happened to it."

The man swallowed hard, eyes darting between us. "I, um, I bought this place almost twenty years ago," he said, voice trembling. "An-and I've never had neighbors. Haven't seen another house on this road since I moved here. I swear that's all I know — please... please don't hurt me!" *Ugh.* This guy was so rattled, he'd likely do something stupid, like call the cops. This was already spiraling out of control.

Sky stepped in smoothly. "Sir, I'm very sorry for the trouble," she said gently. "Thank you for the helpful information you've given us."

"Helpful information?" I huffed as we turned to leave. "He didn't tell us anything." You'd think Sky would know better than to play nice in this situation, given everything we'd been through.

She shot me an exasperated look. "Onyx, erase his memory, please? And be nice about it, for Pete's sake — you've already caused enough mental damage." With a firm look, she added, "And you and I are going to have a *long* talk once we get back in the car."

Great.

Nodding, I followed Sky's request, always doing whatever she asked of me. Our bond was so strong that it was almost its own language, enabling us to understand each other without needing words. We even looked alike, though we weren't twins. I was a few years older, with long, loose black hair. Sky's hair was shoulder-length, usually pulled up and out of her face. We both had strange, pale ice-blue eyes and animal-like fangs that showed when we smiled. Though it had been so long since I'd smiled that I wasn't sure I even remembered how.

But that didn't matter. My only duty now was to protect Sky, and I would endure a thousand deaths if it meant she could live peacefully again.

After wiping the man's memory of our visit and adding a sudden aversion to whiskey for good measure, we headed back to the car. Wiping memories was a simple parlor trick. It would leave him with a mild headache for an hour, nothing an aspirin couldn't fix, or so I'd overheard. It didn't take much effort. Just eye contact, a connection to the person I was wiping, and with a single thought sent their way, the memory was gone. I once heard a nurse say I'd 'hypnotized' her — like it was some kind of trance.

Maybe it was.

"Are you insane?" she asked as soon as we sat back in the car.

"Probably. But that man was an idiot." I shrugged. "The look on his face said it all. He was lucky I didn't blow his brains all over the door, the way he sized me up like a piece of meat."

Sky shot me a withering look. "You're an attractive woman, Onyx. Sometimes men react like that. The sooner you accept it, the sooner we can get answers from people without getting the cops on our trail."

"And another thing," she added with exaggerated dramatics, "have you ever considered just giving people the benefit of the doubt? I don't know… maybe even trusting people for the sake of new beginnings?"

I said nothing. When Sky got this worked up, arguing was pointless. I'd postpone the lecture on never letting herself be degraded for another day, not to mention all the anxiety that comes with the word *trust*. Instead, we sat in silence, each of us processing what we learned. The man said he had lived there for almost twenty years, confirming it had indeed been that long since we were taken. Twenty years of being dissected and tested like animals, after every trace of us had been scrubbed from our hometown.

But why?

It was another answer we'd have to find. Unfortunately, we'd just hit our first dead end.

"I think we need to go into town. House calls aren't going to cut it," Sky said finally. "And you need to try to control yourself. These are different times, Onyx. Technology isn't what it used to be. You know that much, at least."

Frustrated and exhausted, I was ready to call it a day. "Why bother?" I muttered, rubbing my face. "We can't stay here. It's only a matter of time before they find us, and this is the first place they'll look. Why wait like sitting ducks?" I glanced out the window, the question masking my unease. Despite my curiosity about the house and our parents, it didn't feel safe to stay.

"Don't you want to know if Mom and Dad are out there somewhere?" Sky's voice softened, breaking slightly. "We need to find them and let them know we're alive. Show them we're no longer helpless girls, that we can defend ourselves. Then they won't have to live with the belief that they failed to save us." Her eyes filled with tears, adding shimmer to the pale blue.

"Sky…" I began, but she held up a hand.

"I know what you're going to say. But *I* have to know." She dabbed at her eyes with the sleeve of her stolen shirt, her voice quiet. "I have to know if what they told us was true. If they really killed our parents… I don't want to be alone, Onyx."

A pang of helplessness hit me, tightening my chest. I hated to see her in pain, seeing her in tears, and knowing there was nothing I could do. Protecting her, keeping her safe, that I could handle. But soothing her, making it all okay… that felt impossible.

"We were never alone," I scoffed, the words coming out sharper than I intended. "We've always had each other." I took a breath, trying to soften my tone. "Sky, I've already grieved our parents. You need to do the same. Wandering around this town, opening old wounds, it isn't safe."

She looked at me, tears still shimmering in her eyes. Ignoring my sincere acceptance of our parents' deaths, she softly cried, "Please, Onyx? Just a few more places. We might find someone who knows what happened."

I groaned, defeated. There was no way I could deny her closure. "Fine. But if this goes south, prepare yourself for the loudest *I-told-you-so* you've ever heard."

Sky's face lit up, excitement replacing her sadness. A smile amongst the tears. "Thank you, thank you!" she said, as she squeezed my hand. "You don't know how much this means to me."

"No, I do," I said quietly, giving her hand a quick squeeze back. "That's the only reason I'm agreeing to it."

As we headed into town, I remembered the last time I saw these roads. They were now lined with neon signs, but my mind took me back to when I was nine, just before we were taken. That night was etched in my memory in vivid, merciless detail: my mother's screams, my father's gunshot wound, Sky crying. The smell of death was thick and sharp, lingering and crawling under my skin. I focused on the road, gripping the wheel tightly. Dwelling on the past wouldn't help, and Sky would soon sense my mood. I didn't want to upset her more than I already had.

Chapter 3

Dayken

I sat at the edge of the table, rolled sleeves, pen in hand, sorting through land titles and property transfers. A map was spread out beside me, marked in red ink, old borders, and new claims. Deeds, permits, and digital copies of agreements dating back decades. Quiet work, but vital. Territory meant power. Protection. Stability for the clan.

I signed the next form, barely glancing up.

Thum-dmp. Thump-thump. Thubmp. Thump.

It felt like something was physically hitting me.

A jolt — hot and sharp — spiked through my chest. The pen dropped from my hand as a feverish wave rolled over me, fast and disorienting. My skin went cold, then burned. I gripped the edge of the table, heart pounding, breath locked in my throat.

Thum-dmp. Thump-thump. Thubmp. Thump.

The sound crashed through me — inside me — a pounding, erratic rhythm, deeper and heavier than my own heartbeat.

Nothing about it felt normal.

Holy shit. What is this feeling?

Something was seriously wrong. I know it wasn't an illness; sicknesses didn't touch us. But as I rubbed my chest, trying to soothe the lava-like heat coursing through my veins, I could feel my instincts kicking into overdrive, sharpening, going haywire. The familiar urge to hunt and track, usually so controlled, now became a demand, clawing at the edges of my mind. This wasn't right.

Thum-dmp! Thump-thump! Thump-thump-thump!

I pressed my palm against my chest, as if that could smother the drumming, but it only seemed to grow louder. *Faster.*

I barely recognized the rough edge in my voice when I roared, "Aurora?!"

I heard her footsteps pounding down the hall before she appeared in the doorway, golden-brown hair falling over her shoulders as she stopped short.

Thum-dmp! Thump-thump! Thubmp! Thump!

Her eyes flicked to my chest, her brows drawing together.

"What happened?" she demanded, stepping inside. Her gaze darted around before landing on me.

I forced myself to sit up straight, but the motion only made the heat and nausea worse. "I know this sounds crazy, but… I think there is something wrong with my heart." The words felt wrong in my mouth. It wasn't like our kind got heart attacks, and we were immune to human diseases. But this… this was something else.

"My chest feels like it's about to explode, and I'm burning up." I inhaled deeply, struggling to stay calm. "My head's spinning, and my senses are all over the place." I rubbed my sternum, trying to ease the relentless pounding beneath my skin.

Aurora's eyes narrowed. "You *look* like a human with a fever… but that's impossible."

She hesitated, her mind racing, then she snapped into action. "Hang on. I'll get a cold towel." There was an edge of fear in her voice — rare for her. If *she* was scared, I should be terrified.

She returned within seconds, moving quickly and efficiently. "Lean back," she instructed, dabbing the cold compress to my forehead. The relief was fleeting as the towel's temperature promptly rose to match my own.

When she felt the towel warm beneath her fingers, her brow furrowed.

Thum-dmp! Thump-thump! Thubmp! Thump!

My skin was becoming clammy. I lifted my gaze to tell Aurora as much, but when I looked at her, something flickered across her face.

Recognition?

Like she'd just pieced together a puzzle only she could see.

Her eyes widened.

"Dayken… can you hear that?" Her voice carried a new urgency. "The drumming?"

THUM-DMP! THUMP-THUMP! THUMP-THUMP-THUMP!

"Y-yes," I choked out. The sound pounded in my skull, relentless, rhythmic. Coming from my chest, rattling my ribs, shaking my bones. "And it's making me nauseous. I need it to stop."

The color drained from Aurora's face. She took an instinctive step back, like she was trying to escape the sound… except it wasn't *around* us. It was *inside* me.

She pressed her hand over her mouth, but I could still hear it, still feel it.

Her voice barely came out. "Oh no… I *shouldn't* be able to hear that, either. It's too loud. No. No." She shook her head, horror dawning in her gaze.

"Dayken…" Her breath hitched.

"You're being *summoned.*"

The words hit me like a thunderclap.

Summoned.

Only one person could do that.

My mind roared, instincts flaring to life. I stood so quickly that the chair flew from behind me, already moving before she finished speaking.

My Sacar.

The words resonated within me like an alarm, bringing everything into focus. It had been years since I last heard it — since I last dared to believe. The title was reserved for those we were born to protect. The ones who chose us, marked us, and bonded us for life.

For years, I searched for her. I scanned every crowd and chased the faintest whisper of familiarity, hoping and praying I would find her. But I never did.

Until now.

Now, after all this time, I *felt* her. The bond pulsed through me, deep and undeniable, an echo of something ancient. Why now, after all these years? That didn't matter. The only thing that mattered was getting to her. Quickly.

I yanked a shirt from the closet and pulled it over my head; my movements deliberate and intentional.

Aurora stood frozen, eyes glistening. She knew what this meant and knew there was no stopping me. Her lips parted like she wanted to say something to plead, warn, or beg me to be careful. But she didn't.

Instead, I crossed the room and pulled her into a quick hug, a silent promise.

Then I bolted out of the house.

Once in the car, I rolled down the window and took a deep breath, filling my lungs with fresh air and steadying myself. I wiped my sweaty palms on my pant legs so I could grip the steering wheel properly.

She's alive?

She had only been a child when she and her sister disappeared. Did she know what she was?

Did she know about the bond between Sacar and Guardian? Did she know about me?

I held out hope that maybe, just maybe, she'd remember.

Failure wasn't an option. I had to approach this carefully and keep my head clear, which was damn near impossible with the constant thumping throughout my body. My bones felt ready to exit my flesh.

It took me twenty minutes to drive from my house to town. I parked near the outskirts on an abandoned dirt road, unsure how far into town she actually was. As I prowled through the streets, I could feel her, feel the summoning pulse through me. It had changed. The closer I got, the less it burned and the more it thrummed, like the bond had shifted from a scream to a signal. Each of my steps sharpened the connection, making it stronger and clearer, like tuning into her frequency through static. Stores, buildings, restaurants, all of it faded beneath my instincts. There was a distance to the bond. I could feel it. And I planned to figure out exactly how much had separated us after all these years.

Just then, my consciousness snapped into something primal. I swore I could hear the heartbeats of the humans nearby. Like being guided by sonar, but through all my senses at once.

I was drawn to a small, overlooked bar near my favorite coffee shop. I never understood its appeal and never felt the urge to enter. Yet now, this place called to me like it held the answer to my entire existence.

I stopped just outside, forcing myself to breathe. Steady. Focus. The drumming in my chest had dulled to a whisper, but its presence still lingered, a ghost of urgency beneath my ribs.

One last deep inhale.

I pushed open the door and stepped into the dimly lit room.

Immediately, I looked for her, desperate for a sign.

My eyes swept the space, cutting through the haze of cigarette smoke and the murky yellow glow of overhead lights. The scent of stale beer, sweat, and aged wood settled over me, but I ignored it. Those were not the scent I searched for.

There was no sign of her.

I shifted my focus, scanning for threats. I tuned into conversations, movement, and the scent of adrenaline in the air. Over the years, my instincts became an alert system for sensing danger — a raised voice, sudden movement, or the sharp tang of aggression.

Nothing. No immediate threats.

I exhaled slowly, steadying myself. She *was* here. I could feel it.

Pushing past one of the patrons, I stepped deeper into the bar.

My heart stilled, and everything around me sharpened as my senses hit overload. Time seemed to slow, each beat in my chest synced to a new, electrifying awareness.

It's her.

There was no doubt about it. There she was, sitting at the bar, her figure bathed in the dim glow of the bar lights. My Sacar. She was no longer a little girl…

She was talking to a friend, occasionally glancing at the news playing on the TV above the bar. Her companion — a smaller, softer-featured female — was completely engrossed in the screen. But my Sacar was different, on edge. Her gaze flicked around the room, mirroring the same alertness, which caused my muscles to tighten in response.

To anyone watching, she looked like just another woman grabbing a beer with a friend. Ordinary. Truthfully? She was anything but. If these people knew, if they understood what she was born for, what truly sustained her, they wouldn't sit so close. Realizing I was standing there staring at her like an idiot, I shook myself and moved closer. As I neared, I finally saw her clearly: her pale, porcelain skin seemed to glow against her dark hair, which fell like black silk over her shoulders. I caught a hint of vanilla in the air, making my heart race again. Her naturally red lips were shaped perfectly, sending chills down my spine.

She must have sensed me watching because her eyes snapped to mine, freezing me in place. Those ice-blue eyes pierced right through me, leaving me breathless. Relief flooded me — she was alive, right here, healthy and more breathtaking than I could have ever imagined.

Her glare deepened, making me feel exposed in a way I wasn't prepared for. There was no recognition in her eyes. I tried to compose myself and flashed a smile that worked on almost anyone. But she just stared, unimpressed, ready to discard me like a piece of trash.

Okay, plan B. I blurted the first thing that came to mind. "H-Hi. Hey."

Smooth, Dayken. Really smooth.

I cursed inwardly, still unable to tear my gaze away from her. Rattled to my core that she clearly had no memory of me.

She turned slightly, clearly annoyed, with a spark of frustration in her eyes.

"Wait," I said quickly, holding my hands up in surrender but keeping them to myself. I knew better than to touch her without permission; everything I knew about her kind demanded caution. "Can I buy you and your friend a drink? I really need to talk to you."

"No." That single word sent my heart dropping. It wasn't what I wanted to hear, but just the sound of her voice held a strange power over me.

"Can I at least introduce myself?" I tried again, now speaking to her back after her obvious dismissal. "I'm Dayken. And as strange as this sounds, you and I have a lot to talk about."

She reached into her coat, her eyes narrowing. There was no doubt in my mind that she was reaching for a weapon. That long black coat wasn't exactly casual attire around here. With a spike of adrenaline, I decided to clarify things.

"I know what you are," I whispered, my voice so low that only she would hear. She froze, and I knew she'd heard it.

Her friend's head whipped toward me, and in her face, I saw it, a softer version of my Sacar, yet strikingly familiar. A replica, smaller and somehow more delicate, with almond-shaped eyes and defined cheekbones. I knew her instantly.

"Sky…" I breathed, barely realizing I'd said it aloud.

That was a huge mistake on my part.

Chapter 4

Onyx

I saw the shock on Sky's face before my body automatically moved into action, twisting to shield her from the intruder. I faced him, and my eyes locked on his, steady despite my pounding pulse. He reacted with a quick beat of recognition when he saw my slitted pupils and glowing irises. My body shifted, senses sharpening, clutching the knife I took earlier. He was frozen by my gaze, caught in that heartbeat of hesitation, just long enough for me to slip the tip of my blade against his gut.

He didn't notice the blade until I had it against him. The hilt rested firmly in my grasp, the angle precise, a killing strike held at bay by nothing more than my restraint. One flick of my wrist, and his insides would spill onto the floor before he could take another breath. The bar around us carried on, oblivious, laughter, the clinking of glasses, conversations weaving through the air. No one saw the moment hanging between life and death.

His gaze flicked downward, finally acknowledging the knife pressed against him, but when he looked back up, his expression remained unnervingly calm.

"Now hold on, Onyx," he said, his voice steady.

My name.

He knew my name, too, and hearing it from his lips made my grip tighten. The blade pressed a fraction deeper, just enough for him to feel the warning. He didn't flinch. If anything, he forced himself to stay perfectly still, as if he understood just how thin the line was between breathing and bleeding out.

"I'm a friend," he said carefully, as if the words alone could hold back my blade.

Friend. The word felt foreign and useless. I'd heard it before, but it never meant what it was supposed to. He might be deceitful, threatening, or even dangerous. Yet, something about him scratched at my memories, an unformed thought, a familiarity I couldn't place: his scent, presence, something just out of reach.

"We don't have friends," I said, my voice laced with animosity.

He wasn't afraid; that much was clear. If anything, a hint of a smirk played at his mouth despite the tension rolling off him. I should gut him, just to be safe. It would be easy, but I didn't. Not yet.

Instead, I let the silence stretch, let the weight of the knife speak for me. If he were smart, he'd give me a damn good reason not to spill his blood here, because I wasn't feeling particularly merciful right now.

I also wanted to know how he knew our names. He didn't carry the reek of the facility, but maybe those bastards were getting more clever, sending ignorant civilians to find us.

Highly unlikely.

He didn't look like a random civilian. Maybe a mercenary? Regardless, the man was enormous. His T-shirt stretched tight across broad shoulders and biceps. They were thick enough to make me wonder if he was training for something. If he challenged me to a fight, it would be a tough battle, but I knew I'd win. I wasn't just stronger — I was immortal. I shot him a look that dared him to make a move.

But as I looked closer, I realized I was getting irritated and distracted. He was tall, about 6'4". He had tousled brown hair, emerald green eyes, and a chiseled jaw that only made his smirk more frustrating. I was annoyed with myself for noticing — since when did I have time for something as silly as looks?

Snap out of it.

I pressed the knife just a little closer, the blade kissing his hard abdomen. I could see his muscles tense through his shirt, taut against the steel. Muscles I was suddenly picturing bare, without clothing… *fucking hell.*

"Look, I'm Dayken Danielson," he said, his tone calm, snapping me out of my mental warfare. "I came here for you."

I froze, just for a second.

His steady, intentional tone sent a prickle down my spine. His unwavering eyes showed quiet confidence, but beneath, a familiar feeling tugged at me… something I couldn't place. And I didn't know what to do with that.

"I swear on my clan that I'm no threat to you or your sister."

On his clan?

He sounded sincere, despite the odd word choice, and while my instincts told me he wasn't lying, I had no plans of lowering my guard, not with a stranger who knew our names.

"Clan?" Sky asked, mirroring my thoughts. Tilting her head with that relentless curiosity of hers, her gaze flicked between me and Dayken as though she'd already forgotten that I was one word away from gutting this man.

"Yes, clan," he glanced at Sky. "Like I said, there's a lot to talk about."

Sky looked at me. I kept my blade exactly where it was, not moving an inch. Dayken's gaze flicked back to me, his expression calm but unsettling. There was something in his eyes — reverence, maybe. Affection. It shook me to my core, and I didn't like it one bit.

Sky leaned in to whisper, "This could be the real deal, Onyx, like a lead on our parents or something. He clearly recognizes us and isn't giving that nasty facility vibe. Let's at least hear him out."

I had similar thoughts myself. I quickly weighed my options. Option one: kill him. Option two: hear him out. Or option three: I knock him out, and we make a quick exit. Option one would draw a lot of unwanted attention, and option three left us with no more answers than when we started. So, that left us with option two.

"You're going to go outside, down the alley to the left of this bar, and wait for us there," I instructed, my voice low. "We'll continue this conversation in private."

It wasn't a suggestion; it was an order. And I wanted to see if he would follow it. If he really was a 'friend.'

A smirk tugged at the edge of his lips, as if I'd said something amusing. His gaze lingered on me, unreadable, but with a flicker of something deeper, something I couldn't ignore. So, I dug the knife in just a touch harder before snapping it back to my side. He didn't even flinch. Instead, he gave a short nod.

"Alright," he chuckled as he turned and strode back out the door. I could have sworn I heard him murmur *bossy* and *goddess* under his breath, but that wouldn't have made any sense.

The moment he was gone, Sky turned to me, practically bouncing in place. "This is nuts!" she whispered, eyes wide with excitement as she tugged on my shoulder like she'd forgotten it was attached to my body.

I nodded once, keeping my voice steady. "Ready to see what this guy is all about?" I asked, placing stolen bills on the bar to settle our tab.

She nodded back, eyes gleaming, and together we slipped outside.

He waited by the damp brick wall, arms crossed over a solid-looking chest. The sour reek of a nearby dumpster burned my nose, sharp enough to make my eyes water, but I didn't let it show. He stood there as if carved out of the shadows; broad, steady, and undeniably good-looking, but I'd learned long ago that appearances were just another kind of weapon. All men wanted something. The only question was, *what?*

I cocked my gun, making a show of it. The racked chamber echoed off the wet bricks and mingled with the stench. "How do you know us? Explain, and make it quick," I ordered, raising the barrel until it was eye level with his chest. Kill shot, straight to the heart.

He arched a brow, glancing down at the gun in my hand, then gazed back up to lock eyes with me. There was a mischievous challenge in his eyes as he said, "That won't kill me, you know. It'll hurt like hell, but it won't kill me."

The fact hit me like a shockwave, making Sky and me tense in unison. I kept my gun aimed, refusing to lower it, but he smiled, observing my stance. "I'll give you this, you're impressively prepared," he said with a nod of approval, as if my hostility amused him. Sky's eyes narrowed.

"Ah, you're not human," she said thoughtfully. "But you're not a vampire either. So, let's skip the games. Explain who you are and how you know us."

Dayken's gaze softened at Sky's polite tone, and he gave a slow nod. "Yes, I'm not a vampire nor fully human. I know both of you well. It's a long story. On my way here, I wondered how much you might remember from before, but I will try to make it quick." He paused, as if contemplating how much detail to give. His brows furrowed as he chose his next words. "When I mentioned 'clan' earlier, I was referring to my wolf clan and the bonds we protect."

Sky's eyes widened, her light blue gaze locking onto Dayken with sharp intensity. "Wolf…" she murmured, the word carrying an almost reverent weight, as if she were tasting its significance for the first time. "Bond?" she added, her tone edged with wonder, like a puzzle piece finally clicking into place.

She looked at me briefly, her eyes bright, alight with the thrill of discovery. For a moment, it was like she didn't need reassurance, only more answers. This was Sky at her core: relentless, inquisitive, and hungry for understanding. And yet, even as her fascination grew, I kept my guard firmly raised along with my gun.

Dayken glanced back and forth between us, his face unreadable, but I caught the flicker of determination in his eyes, a sign he'd been waiting for this moment for years. "Yes," he said confidently. "I'm part wolf. I'm here because I'm bound to protect you, Onyx." He raised his hand, pointing straight at me, then placed it over his heart. "This is my identity — my purpose. This is what the bond means."

I scoffed aloud, even though his words hit like a blow, leaving me speechless. He believed every word he spoke. But belief alone wasn't enough to earn my trust. My gun stayed raised, my stance firm, as I waited to see what else he dared say.

"Like I said," Dayken continued, as if plucking the thoughts straight from my mind. His voice was steady, unwavering. "I'm Dayken Danielson, from the Danielson Clan. My clan is mostly wolves, though we have a few other species among us." He paused, his gaze shifting between Sky and me, his words deliberate. "I'm a Guardian of the Sacar. And you, Onyx," — his eyes locked onto mine, sharp and unyielding — "are my Sacar."

The declaration hit me like a lightning bolt — sharp and sudden. I hid my reaction, creating a mask of indifference, as he waited for me to show some recognition. An overwhelming urge to rub my heart pressed me, but I kept my hands on my gun. *Sacar*, that word, filled my mind, stirring questions I wasn't ready to face.

His voice was quiet but steady as he said, "I realize this is a lot to unload on you, especially here." He gestured vaguely to the damp, shadowed alley around us. The flicker of a distant streetlight cast uneven patterns on the cracked pavement, shadows stretching and curling like they wanted to listen in.

"But you need to know, I met you both when you were young. Sky was just a little thing, and you, Onyx, you were eight." He paused, his expression tightening as though weighing the burden of his next words.

"I didn't understand why our parents made it seem so important, almost ceremonial in a way." He took a deep breath, his chest rising with effort. "It wasn't until later that the full weight of that meeting hit me," he admitted, his tone dipping into something quieter, almost ashamed. "But by the time I did understand, it was already too late. Everything was gone. I've spent years searching… but there was never a sign of you. No trail. Just… nothing."

His gaze locked onto mine, sharp and unrelenting.

"You have to know, though, my purpose — my *only* purpose—has always been to protect you," he said, his voice resolute, again pointing at me. Not Sky.

It came as no surprise when I broke eye contact with Dayken to glance at Sky. Her face was bright with excitement, her fangs barely escaping the curve of her lips. Her expression was almost childlike in wonder. I could see her mind racing, piecing together fragments of the answers she longed for. Meanwhile, I kept my emotions hidden, every instinct demanding control. I refused to let my face show anything but indifference.

This all felt too much, too fast, a tidal wave of revelations I wasn't ready to face yet. I needed time to process, to sift through the chaos in my head. And more than anything, I needed to keep my cards close to my chest.

"Okay, Dayken Danielson," Sky said, attempting to rein in her excitement, "a couple of questions. First, what exactly is a Sacar? Second, why should we believe a word you're saying? And lastly…" Her tone sharpened slightly. "While I've read enough folklore to know about shapeshifters, are you seriously expecting us to believe that's what you are?"

I suppressed a wry thought… *werewolf?* But I held my tongue, leaving space for Dayken to address Sky's rapid-fire questions.

Dayken met her gaze, his tone softening as he spoke. "A Sacar is a vampire. They are sacred to clans. But your parents…" He hesitated, gauging our reactions. "They were so excited about the bonding marks, they must not have had a chance to explain any of this to you before the fire."

Chapter 5

Onyx

Marks? I thought at the same time Sky asked, "Fire?" in a breathless tone. All her prior excitement faded, as if the wind had been knocked out of her.

Dayken nodded slowly. "Yes… the fire. Four sets of remains were found in the ashes, but I knew. Call it my instincts, the bond, or whatever you prefer, but I was certain it wasn't you." He inhaled deeply before continuing. "But I also knew something wasn't right." He looked at us for confirmation, searching for a look of realization to dawn on our faces, but that didn't come. There was a trace of warmth in his eyes, as if he could still see the little girl I once was.

"I searched for you." His deep emerald gaze pierced straight through every shield I had ever built. I didn't know how to feel about this. He seemed to have a blind devotion to me, which stirred unwelcome emotions.

Not wanting to expose my unease, I broke away from the look in his eyes and turned to Sky. My stomach twisted. She looked like the world had crashed down around her. She never fully accepted that our parents were gone, not like I had, and her last bit of hope was just shattered to pieces.

Dayken's expression shifted, a look of remorse crossing his face. "I'm sorry," he said, looking at Sky. "I thought you knew."

"We knew you were hiding from whoever burned your house down, that you wanted to disappear. But I didn't realize how completely cut off you were."

"Hiding?" I said, voice edged with frustration and disbelief.

Dayken sighed and looked me in the eye. "I'm sorry. I'm not trying to upset you, but I just don't understand what happened. There was no trace of you anywhere. Not for years."

Fury burned inside me, and the memories surfaced in a violent rush: the shouting, the terror, the SWAT team storming our house, the sounds of crying and chaos before everything went black.

Sky's voice cut through my anger, soft but unyielding. "We didn't just disappear." She took a deep breath, her gaze steeling as she looked at him. "We were taken. Operatives stormed our home. They somehow heard that we were 'unnatural' little girls and came ready to eliminate the threat. When they realized they couldn't destroy us, they did the next best thing — took us. Locked us in a facility. Treated us like test subjects." Her voice trembled, but only for a moment.

"They cut into us," I said as I took over, my voice growing colder with each word, "ripped us open to see how we worked. Stuck things in us just to see what would happen. Over and over — for twenty years." Dayken's jaw tightened, his fists clenching. "They called it dissection and restoration. Studying our regenerative patterns. They'd carve us up, sever limbs, then sit back and take notes while we went back to normal, as if none of it had happened. No scars. No evidence of the torture. Just a clean slate for them to violate all over again."

I felt my face harden, the weight of invisible scars pressing down on me.

"I spent years locked in a muzzle and straitjacket. And when our healing began to outpace most of their experiments, they found something better. Liquefied silver. They pumped it into our veins like it was saline — keeping us too weak to fight back."

I met Dayken's gaze, unflinching, "So no, we didn't run away, didn't hide. We were taken. Erased."

Dayken's expression darkened. His eyes briefly flashed black before returning to green, something primal flickering there. His fists clenched, trembling with rage. He looked ready to pounce. I couldn't understand why he cared so much or why this was so personal to him, especially since he didn't know us, no matter what he claimed.

"Onyx," he began, voice low and steady. "Now that I've found you, I swear I'll never let you out of my sight again. I am your chosen Guardian, and as long as I'm breathing, nothing like that will ever happen to either of you again." He dropped his gaze and turned inward, as though he was fighting against a memory, or something darker. "The thought of my Sacar being cut into like… like an animal… it makes me sick!"

His fury sharpened, and his expression went tight with the weight of what we had told him. He looked as if it were up to him; justice wouldn't wait. It would be personal. Brutal. Immediate.

"I know this probably doesn't make much sense," he continued, his tone softer, "and I know it's a lot to take in. But my people exist to guard yours, and I will not fail you again. That's a promise, Onyx. You can trust me."

I kept my expression unreadable, letting the silence hang between us. *Trust?* After everything we'd been through? Trust wasn't something I handed over to some stranger in an alley. That was the stuff of fairy tales, and I wasn't living in one.

"I don't want or need your protection," I said flatly, daring him to challenge me.

He cursed under his breath, frustration crossing his face before he inhaled deeply and ran a hand through his hair. But I could see it, his determination. He wasn't giving up. He squared his shoulders, gaze steady.

"Please," he said, voice soft, but insistent. "You have to let me stay by your side. It's my duty and our bond requires it."

Bond?

I felt a strange irritation at his pleading tone, though I couldn't pinpoint why.

"And why do I *have* to do that?" I challenged. "Because *you* said so?"

"Listen, we're linked," he replied, hesitating slightly. I could tell he was weighing how much to reveal with his next words. They came out almost desperate as he tried to reason with me. "I know you have a flower marking above your heart. Dark tan color, eight petals, about the size of a fist." He paused as my hand moved instinctively to cover the mark.

How does he know about that?

"I know, because I have the same mark on the back of my neck." He turned, pulling back his shaggy hair to show it — a perfect match, identical in every way.

I just stared, completely caught off guard. My heart pounded so hard it felt like it was trying to climb up my ribs and lodge itself in my throat. People might have assumed the mark was just a tattoo, but I never understood why mine appeared or why it looked the way it did. How did he know, and why did his match?

Now he had my full attention.

"One night," he continued, dropping his hair back down and turning to face me. "I came to your house with my parents. We were there to see if I was worthy of being your Guardian. You picked me. I don't know how or why, but something in you saw something in me. We bonded, Onyx. This is how it's been for our people since the beginning."

He paused, and his voice was almost a whisper when he said, "Please, don't deny me this. Don't deny me my entire purpose." There was so much desperation laced in his quiet tone.

I was speechless. A memory flickered to life in the back of my mind. I almost remembered him — a boy visiting for dinner, a rare thing in our secluded home. The scene was hazy, but it was there. As quickly as it appeared, it left my mind. I tried to cling to it, but it was too blurry.

"I don't believe it," I murmured, the words slipping out.

So, the mark appeared after I met him.

"If you don't have a place to stay, you can come with me," he offered gently. "I have plenty of room for both of you."

My gaze hardened. "I barely remember you, and we've been on the run for days. Now, we finally have a chance to start over, and you're telling me you can help because of some buried history? That's hard to believe, Dayken. We've been through twenty years of *hell*, with no sign of help. So, your pretty words are just that… pretty words. What you're asking for is a lot, don't you think?"

"Yes, I know it's a lot," Dayken said, nodding his head in agreement, his tone resolute. "But if you can just trust me, Onyx. I am your Guardian. No harm will ever come to you again." He placed his hand on the back of his neck, quietly reminding me that we were linked.

There he goes using that trust word again.

"Then why doesn't Sky have a Guardian?" I demanded, narrowing my eyes as the thought hit me. "She has a mark too." Hers was slightly darker and a little smaller — not an exact match to mine, like his.

Dayken's gaze flickered to Sky, his face softening with an apologetic look. "She does. His name is Kolton. He went missing shortly after coming into his abilities. His clan lived near mine until they were eventually absorbed into ours. From what I've heard, Sky and Kolton bonded right after birth. It's rare for a bond to happen so young, so there was a lot of talk about it. You've probably met him but were too young to remember."

"Kolton…" Sky murmured, her fingers tracing over her chest where her mark lay, as if it ached.

"Is he still alive?" I couldn't help but ask.

Dayken gestured to Sky, "If she still has her mark, then yes." Sky's face was about to light up, but then, she froze, nostrils flaring as she scented the air. She turned to me, eyes sharp. I felt it too, a chill that prickled through my senses.

"They're here," she said in a flat, emotionless tone. My gaze darted to the bar's rooftop, where the moon cast its pale light.

"The roof," I said. Sky nodded, and in one leap, we vaulted from the alley to the rooftop, our footsteps silent as we crouched near the edge.

I peered over to see Dayken, still below. Part of me wanted to jump down and grab him, but my attention snapped to a new sound, a car engine. Bright headlights sliced through the darkness as a black sedan rolled into the alley. I watched Dayken raise his hand to shield his eyes from the light.

"Where are they?" a voice demanded, echoing off the brick walls, as a stranger emerged from the car and slammed the door, storming towards Dayken.

Dayken's calm reply came quickly, his face betraying nothing. "Where are… who?"

"We received an anonymous tip that two very dangerous fugitives were spotted in the area."

Dayken frowned. "Fugitives, huh? Got a description?"

The agent's jaw tightened. "That information is classified."

Dayken crossed his arms, unimpressed. "Uh-huh. Seems legit."

Another man stepped out from the passenger side of the car, as three more cars pulled in behind him. More men emerged, their silhouettes dark against the headlights. "Search everywhere," the leader barked.

One of the men muttered, "Sir, they could be miles away by now." His voice was low, but with my hearing, it was crystal clear. Dayken must have caught it too; his entire body went rigid, muscles tensed, still as stone.

"I don't care," the leader snapped. "The grid showed them here minutes ago. Search! That's an order." He turned his attention to Dayken, eyes cold and demanding. "Step aside, son. This is official government business."

I saw the subtle shift in Dayken's stance, and his look of calm was replaced by something darker. Without a word, he moved faster than I could track, spinning and clamping his hand around the man's throat. Before the agent could react, Dayken's hand twisted, and with a swift motion, snapped his neck.

Gunfire erupted in the alley. I watched as Dayken blurred into motion, dodging bullets with deadly, precise movements. He growled, lunging at the nearest agent, grabbing his hair, and slamming his fist into his face. The agent tried to strike back, but his blows seemed to bounce off Dayken's frame.

With brutal efficiency, Dayken spun his opponent around and slammed him into the wall, the force knocking him out cold. Before Dayken could turn back, another agent stepped from behind his vehicle and aimed his gun squarely at Dayken's head. Three shots rang out in quick succession, echoing sharply off the walls. I didn't even see Dayken move. I only caught glimpses of his blurred figure as he twisted out of the bullets' path with unnatural grace. He flowed like shadow and instinct, dodging effortlessly. His movements were impossibly precise, as if he'd sensed the shots before they even left the barrel.

I didn't know what came over me, but I suddenly felt the need to help him. Something stronger than instinct propelled me from the rooftop. The wind whipped my hair around as I dropped into the alley, my feet hitting the ground with a force that seemed to ripple through me. Giving in to the inexplicable pull toward this stranger, I launched a roundhouse kick at the man closest to Dayken, striking his head with deadly precision. He crumpled instantly, his body hitting the cold, damp ground with a lifeless thud. I kicked the gun that had been aimed at Dayken's head, sending it skittering down the alley.

Sky arrived a moment later, silently sneaking behind the man now aiming his gun at me. Before she could disarm him, his gun fired, and the shot hit my chest. Pain seared through me, but it was nothing compared to what I had already survived. I clenched my teeth, steadying myself. I barely had time to react before Sky's anger flared. With a chilling calm, she seized the man by his head, twisting until an eerie snap echoed through the alley. She looked like an avenging angel — until you saw the cold calculation in her eyes. We had been treated the same way, which meant we both knew how to end a life when necessary.

The men quickly realized that they were outmatched and scattered, running in different directions. Sky, Dayken, and I exchanged a look, silently agreeing not to chase after them. Since this was a small town, it would be too easy to draw attention to something unusual happening here.

I turned as Dayken walked toward me, his face tense with worry. But Sky reached me first, examining me from head to toe. Her hand hovered over the bullet hole in my chest, which was already healing. Her concern was genuine, but unnecessary. I'd been through worse.

"You okay?" Dayken asked as he reached us, his voice low and tense.

"She'll be fine," Sky answered before I could, her voice cool as she examined the wound.

I swatted Sky's hand away, lifting my gaze to meet Dayken's, and froze. It took a lot to shock me, but the sight left me speechless. Dayken's face was no longer the handsome, chiseled one from before. It was wild and otherworldly, as if something primal had surfaced. His canines and incisors had grown into sharp, gleaming fangs, and his eyes… They were no longer the vibrant green I remembered. They were pure black, with the whites completely gone, an endless, inhuman darkness.

He was breathing heavily, his gaze unfocused. He looked like a beast fighting to rein itself in. Electric energy filled the air, and I realized my pulse was racing. I didn't know why, but I stepped closer, compelled by something beyond reason. Every instinct warned me to keep my distance, yet his intensity drew me in, like a tether I couldn't shake.

He looked both monstrous and beautiful, savage and restrained, all at once. My fingers twitched, reaching out before I could think better of it. I needed to know if he was real, if the bond he'd mentioned had somehow pulled me here, to something I couldn't fully understand. I moved closer, my breath shallow, my hand lifting, until I felt the warmth of his skin beneath my fingers.

The moment my fingers brushed his cheek, I felt it — his rage easing like the tide ebbing. The fury that had been radiating from him just seconds before softened beneath my touch, like I'd reached inside him and smoothed the edge of something raw and unhinged. It wasn't a part of me, but I felt it like a caress beneath my skin.

I hadn't meant to touch him. But now that I had, I couldn't seem to stop.

He stood still, eyes closed. It felt like even a single breath might shatter whatever just passed between us. And for one disorienting second, I didn't want to move either.

Then he opened his eyes — and the look in them almost undid me. Not hunger. Not power. Something steadier. Like I was something he recognized. Something he *needed*.

"What are you…?" I started, but the words tangled before they formed. I didn't know what I was asking.

"Come with me," he said, his voice quiet but sure. "I'll explain everything — everything you've ever needed to know about our kind. But it's not safe here anymore."

I dropped my hand. Immediately, I felt the loss of that strange tether. And I hated how much I missed it.

Sky stood close, her eyes flicking between us. She didn't speak; she didn't need to. Her gaze held a question, but also that quiet trust only she could give me. I could feel her energy reaching out for me, steady and silent, conveying everything she wasn't saying. She was asking if I was ready… ready to trust someone. And worse, she was leaving the choice up to me.

I looked back at him.

"Fine," I said at last. "But we're clearly being tracked. Taking us with you might put everyone around you at risk."

He grinned like he'd already accounted for that. "Already way ahead of you."

Chapter 6

Onyx

Sky looked at the lifeless bodies, then met my gaze, pain shadowing her face. We exchanged a quick look, just enough to know she didn't want more lives lost, each death weighing on her quietly. We understood what I needed to do to escape that facility, felt the unspoken burden, but she didn't want to keep killing. I nodded silently, promising to make things right. Then, we turned to Dayken.

"Let's get out of here before those other three come back," I said, breaking the silence.

Dayken's shoulders relaxed. His eyes cleared, and then — there it was — that maddening smile. Something twisted in my chest. I didn't like it.

"Aurora's going to lose her mind," he said, his face lighting up.

Aurora?

I paused. The name struck me harder than it should have. I didn't ask, but the image bloomed anyway — some gorgeous woman waiting at home, arms wide open. I told myself it didn't matter. And it didn't. But something about it gnawed at me.

"Can't help but notice you're good with a gun…" he said, leaving the unasked question hanging in the air.

He didn't need the story.

In the beginning, before the muzzle, before the straitjacket, I was trained. Part of their research involved pushing me past my limits: pain thresholds, muscle conditioning, reaction times with every weapon they could throw at me. It continued even after the restraints were put in place, just not as often. They still needed to break me. Still, let me fight, only to be torn down again with silver. Then they'd start over. Again. And again. And again.

So, I just nodded.

He let it drop, for now, and gestured toward the woods. "Car's just north of here." Then he glanced back at me, smirk deepening. "Think you can keep up?" And with a wink, he was gone, already fading into the trees.

I stared after him, jaw tight. That damn smirk was still etched into my brain. I exhaled sharply and turned to Sky.

We exchanged a quick nod.

Let's go.

***

We got into the car, Sky in the backseat, Dayken driving, and me riding shotgun. I still wasn't convinced that this wasn't a trap. Perhaps it was a survival instinct or a case of trust issues; either way, it felt wrong. As the engine started, I glanced at Dayken's hands on the wheel. Steady. Too steady for someone who had just committed murder. He didn't look shaken — if anything, he looked… practiced. *Calm.* I tracked his choices: parking off the main road, using the trees for cover. Not random. Not panicked. I was reluctant to admit it, but his measured and deliberate way of thinking was beginning to pique my curiosity.

"That reminds me," Dayken said, breaking the silence. "You said you were locked up all Hannibal Lecter style. Why?"

"Hannibal… who?" I asked, genuinely confused.

Sky laughed gently from the backseat. "Pop culture reference. He's asking about the mask and straitjacket."

"Oh. That." I leaned back into the seat. "When I came into my full powers, I found ways to hide them. After I took out a few facility workers, they ran out of effective ways to contain me. An IV bag of silver and restraints were the final solution."

Dayken stiffened. "Jesus. That could've killed you."

"It didn't." I didn't offer anything more.

He glanced at me, then at the road, then back again as if he wanted to ask something but couldn't find the words. Finally, he caved. "I'm sorry, I'm still stuck on this, so silver doesn't kill you? Like you're immune to it?"

Sky answered for me, like the savior she was. "I wouldn't say *immune*, more like *tolerate*. And I can a little, but not as much as Onyx can."

"Wow, that's unheard of. And the muzzle?"

"She bit off a nurse's finger once. That's when they added the muzzle."

His jaw clenched, knuckles whitening around the wheel. "You were just kids," he said quietly. "You shouldn't have had to survive like that."

"You grow up fast when every day might be your last," I muttered, eyes on the passing trees.

A beat of silence followed, stretching long enough to feel heavy.

"And you?" Dayken asked, catching Sky's gaze in the mirror. "They didn't put you in a jacket?"

"No. I figured out pretty quickly that we weren't going to get out. Onyx never subscribed to that theory. I always told myself, at least we had each other. When she ended up getting fully restrained, I could still see her through my cell, even though she couldn't lift her head to see me. I still thought, *at least they didn't take her to a different cell*; we could still talk. It was my biggest fear that they would move her… so," her voice was soft. "I kept my head down. Followed the rules. And in return, they didn't take my sister from me, and they let me read."

Magazines. Novels. Instruction manuals. I'd watched her devour words like they were oxygen until I was no longer able to see her.

They gave her stories.

They gave me straps and steel. The memories hurt because they broke her gently, not violently; having to coax her out of her cage might haunt me more than anything else we endured.

Dayken was quiet for a moment, like he noticed that the space between us wasn't just physical. Then, gently, like it had just occurred to him, he asked, "So… how did you get out?"

My hand clenched around the hem of my shirt. I didn't answer right away. Sky shifted in the backseat.

"Onyx—" she started, but I cut her off.

"I don't want to talk about it." My voice came out sharp, clipped.

It was a fair question to ask, and I knew that. I wasn't sure if I respected him more for caring… or hated that I wasn't ready to answer.

He didn't push. Just nodded, eyes back on the road. The silence that followed wasn't awkward; it was heavy. And for once, I was glad for it.

Eventually, we pulled into a long dirt driveway, tires crunching over gravel as we continued up a slow incline. A house appeared through the trees — tall, old, two stories, with a wide wraparound porch. Warm yellow light spilled from the windows.

It looked… peaceful. Cozy, even.

That made me nervous.

The car came to a stop, and we got out. I palmed the gun tucked into my waistband, eyes scanning the tree line — one road in, one road out. No fence. No cameras. Dayken was either reckless or confident. I wasn't sure which was worse.

He gestured toward the porch. "This way." I was about to follow, but paused when I heard wolves howling in the distance.

Before Dayken could reach the front door, it flew open. A blur of movement. Long golden-brown hair and a small frame. My hand went instinctively to the blade inside my jacket.

Then she threw her arms around him.

"Are you okay?" the woman asked, running her hands over his chest and arms like she was checking for broken bones.

I froze. My instincts didn't know how to classify this. Threat? Affection? I didn't move, but the tension in me coiled tighter.

Dayken gave a soft laugh. "I'm fine," he said and took a small step back. "Actually, I brought someone."

He glanced over his shoulder, and the woman's eyes followed. They landed on me, then Sky. Her hands went to her mouth.

"Oh my gods, Day — they're here. They're alive." She stepped forward like she couldn't quite believe what she was seeing. "And they're… beautiful."

Her voice was warm. Genuinely thrilled. She moved as if she were going to hug us.

"Onyx, Sky," Dayken said quickly, catching the look in my eyes. "This is my sister, Aurora."

Sister.

The tightness in my chest didn't go away, but it shifted. I hadn't realized how tense I'd become until the word 'sister' delivered a sliver of relief.

Aurora's smile softened even more. "Welcome home."

Home.

My grip on the knife loosened, but I didn't let go.

We stepped inside. I looked around as we moved through a spacious foyer, long hallways, and soft lighting. The walls were unfinished wood, creating a strange mix of openness and enclosure. Elegant furniture, welcoming warmth. Too peaceful.

It was everything my cell hadn't been. And yet, somehow… I still didn't breathe easily.

I glanced at Sky. Her expression was calm, almost hopeful. I gave a slight nod, the kind that said: 'Don't get too comfortable.'

"Hey, sis," Dayken said, nodding toward us. "They'll need to catch up — might want to point them toward the library. Maybe start 'em on the basics," he added, flashing Sky a grin. "Like how not to pass out while reading ancient text."

Sky's smile was mischievous as she tilted her chin. "I'll be fine."

Aurora smiled, eyes on Sky. "I'll give you a tour first, then take you to the guest rooms to settle in." Her warmth was disarming, clearly drawing Sky closer, like a moth to a porchlight.

Not me.

"I don't need a tour," I said flatly. "Basement's that way." I pointed to a closed door. "The library is to the left. The kitchen smells like garlic and vinegar, which means someone cleaned it recently. Five bedrooms. Three bathrooms. The house sits on about three acres."

They stared at me.

I tapped the side of my nose. "I have this."

Sky smirked. "Her senses are extreme. She probably smelled the books, the old food, the fabric softener in the sheets."

Dayken blinked. "That's impr… I'm truly impressed." His voice carried a certain weight, not admiration, but astonishment.

I shrugged. It wasn't impressive; it was just survival. But Aurora was watching me now, too closely, as if she was taking notes.

I averted my gaze, feeling uncomfortable with the attention.

"I'll take the guest room down the hall to the left, and you can take the one across?" I asked Sky.

When she nodded, Aurora added, "And just so you know, most of the rooms are reinforced — sealed windows, soundproofed doors. It's meant to help with sensory overload."

Or isolation, I thought.

The idea of losing my senses — my edge — stirred something primal inside me. I clenched my fists and headed down the hall before I said something I'd regret.

"Onyx," Aurora called after me, still cheerful. "I think my clothes will fit you. Sky… I have a dress I can alter. I'll grab my sewing machine from the basement."

I didn't stop walking. I just nodded once

"Can I watch? I've always wanted to learn how to sew!" Sky's voice, filled with excitement, reached me from behind.

"Of course," Aurora replied, her voice sweet and inviting.

I glanced back once. Sky was glowing, animated as she engaged in conversation about fabrics and recipes with the others, as if we weren't still being hunted.

It felt like a fine line was forming between us, small yet growing by the second.

With one last look, I turned away and kept walking.

As I moved through the house, I took in the surroundings — this place felt heavy with history. Old family photos and books filled the corners; animals were carved into dressers, frames, and even the art on the walls. Framed parchment bearing signatures hung on display, as if these names were something to be proud of. All of it left me with more questions than I had before arriving.

After sweeping Sky's room and mine, I stepped back into the hallway to find Sky and Dayken talking. Aurora wasn't joking about the soundproofing; their conversation sounded like a dull murmur.

Dayken saw me, and his face brightened. I couldn't explain why, but it felt odd to be looked at that way after years of being seen as a specimen. "We should hit the library," Dayken said. "I've heard how much Sky loves books, and we've got plenty."

As we walked down the hallway toward the library, a series of paintings caught my eye. They weren't just generic landscapes or dull still lifes — each frame showed the same two figures, painted in different styles. Sometimes they looked like warriors, sometimes like brothers, and sometimes like opposites — a pale man with fangs and another with wild, golden eyes.

I paused in front of one, studying how the artist had painted them shirtless, showcasing a familiar eight-petaled flower over one's heart, its petals spreading out, making it look much larger than my own.

"Who are these?" Sky asked, unable to hide her curiosity, saving me from having to reveal mine.

Dayken stopped beside her, eyes eager as he explained the display. "That's the first Sacar and Guardian, the brothers Avont and Lunce," he said, almost grinning, clearly excited to finally share a piece of their history with us.

The revelation made something twist in my stomach. Sky, always the enthusiast, leaned in to examine the painting, her eyes bright.

"We should research more," I said, tearing my gaze away. Despite the unease, this was the closest we had come to answers in many years. I was beyond impatient.

Chapter 7

Onyx

The heavy door groaned as I shoved it open. Warm lamplight spilled across shelves and polished oak, cutting through the darkness outside. The air smelled of old paper and something faintly sweet, almost like smoke.

Dayken went straight to the window, broad shoulders framed in silver moonlight, every line of his body relaxed as if the moon belonged to him. Aurora was at the oak table, flipping through a magazine. The room felt like the heart of the house, and to Sky, it was heaven.

"Where should we start?" I asked, but my question was ignored. Dayken's eyes shifted to mine, that damn smile curling as if he was guarding a secret meant only for me. My breath caught before I forced myself to look away. He moved with quiet purpose to a glass case, unlocking it before drawing out a worn leather book.

"How about this? Our Bloodline Journal," he said, handing it to Sky. "My mother passed it down to me."

Sky accepted it like a relic, its edges frayed with age, her voice dropping to a hush as she opened it, as though afraid to disturb its sleep. "Decima Anu Otacilia… a widow with one son, Augustus Otacilia."

I tried to listen. I really did. But Dayken hadn't moved back to the window. In the library's glow, his profile looked sculpted, cheekbones defined, his hair rimmed in pale light. His towering frame seemed to swallow the space around him, a presence too large to ignore. I caught myself staring. *Again.*

"…she tampered with sacred rites," Sky read, eyes shining.

Aurora murmured something about 750 B.C., and Sky kept talking, too fast, too eager. I tried to follow every word, but my ears kept straying to the steady rhythm of Dayken's heartbeat. I forced myself to push it aside and bask in the moment; my sister was glowing with pure joy.

This history lesson went on and on, Something about a dying boy. A flower. A ritual.

My hand drifted over the mark on my chest. Sky's voice blurred until a single line sliced through everything else.

"One heartbeat between them."

My pulse faltered, then steadied, as if it wasn't beating alone.

Thump.

Thump.

I went still. Dayken shifted, the slow roll of his massive shoulders dragging the air out of my lungs along with it. His eyes found mine, locking me in place. The green in them wasn't just green anymore — it glowed, catching the lamplight like glass.

Heat unfurled low in my stomach. A pull. A dangerous, hungry pull I didn't understand. My body almost swayed forward, instinct leaning toward him even as my mind screamed to stay put.

Thump-thump.

Thump-thump.

The air thickened, sharp with the scent of him, like cedar and something wild. I wanted to move closer, to press into the pull, to test if his heartbeat truly matched mine against his chest. The thought startled me, shameful and electric.

He tilted his head just slightly, looking at me as if he already knew, as if he was expecting something.

Aurora cleared her throat, and the spell shattered.

I tore my gaze away, my pulse stumbling and racing ahead of his again. But the echo of that shared rhythm lingered, hot and unshakable, thrumming against my ribs.

What the hell was that? One heartbeat with him?

Sky's voice cut through, oblivious. "The boy lived after his mother forced the sacred flower mixture down his throat, and into the hound's as well. But the act bound them together, one soul split in two."

Aurora laughed softly. "Hound? More like a wolf."

Dayken chuckled at her teasing, and the sound twisted inside me, low and rough and far too close to the heat still crawling my skin.

One heartbeat.

Sky turned the page. "Augustus's children bore the consequences of their grandmother's choice. Twins. One with the wolf's blood. The other…" Her eyes flicked toward me. "The cursed one. Pale. Fanged.

"Augustus never showed favoritism; he protected both equally, forging a unique bond: Avont the Guardian and Lunce the Vampire. One legacy, two halves. The brotherly bond forged between them ran deep — spiritual, intellectual, unshakable." Aurora's voice carried the words like a chant, then softened into background hum as she recited the rest of the tale, the brothers' adventures, even how Lunce discovered a way to make others like him.

But none of it mattered. The history, the lineage, the curses and rituals — it didn't ease the weight pressing on my chest. Knowing the origin of my mark didn't make it feel any less like a chain.

I pressed my palm flat over my mark again, as if I could smother its burn. "Feels surreal. I'm chained to someone and branded with a mark I never asked for, all because someone broke a rule centuries ago."

Aurora met my gaze without flinching. "It's more than a mark. And you did ask for it—"

"I don't remember—" I bit out, sharper than I meant.

But Sky kept reading, her voice rushing forward, breaking apart the tension strangling the room. Maybe that was for the best.

Chapter 8

Onyx

Sky read on, but my mind kept faltering. This time, my thoughts raced back to that place — our personal hell. I tried to stop the intrusive thoughts, yet I couldn't help remembering how I would look out from my cell and see Sky sitting cross-legged on the floor, fully absorbed in a book, just like she was now.

The sight pulled me straight into memories I couldn't escape. She always sat on the ground because they never gave us chairs or tables, just concrete. When the agents handed her books and magazines to pass the time, Sky would sit right there on the floor, legs tucked beneath her, as if that were the only place books should be read.

Even now, she still sat on the ground out of habit.

And seeing it — *seeing her* — like that again, it was like a punch to the chest.

The agents always attached strings to their gifts. If she didn't meet their standards, if she so much as flinched out of line, they'd rip those books from her hands and burn them in front of her.

I'd hear her scream, cry, and beg as the pages curled and blackened in the flames. They knew how much each book meant to her and exploited that weakness. Her reading was a way to escape hell, and witnessing her suffering was torment for me.

I swallowed hard, dragging myself back to the present, but I could still hear the echoes of Sky's screams in my mind.

I almost raised my hands to my ears to block the sound before remembering where I was. "Sky," I managed, trying to hide my anxiety, "why don't you sit at that table with Aurora?" I forced a calm smile and motioned for her to move.

For a second, I was half a breath away from pulling her to her feet, just to make the images stop flashing through my mind.

But Sky didn't hesitate. She gave me a calm, steady look that conveyed everything. We didn't need words; she understood. That simple gesture was a quiet comfort to my unraveling mind.

With a reassuring nod, she rose and took her place beside Aurora.

Aurora scooted back in her chair with a soft scrape. "Here, take mine, it's the only one with a cushion."

"Oh, thank you!" Sky lit up beside her, practically glowing. There was something magnetic about Aurora's energy, welcoming, calm, quietly observant.

I hated how much I wanted to be part of it.

Across the room, I noticed Dayken watching me with an intense gaze, as if studying me. Aurora also looked my way, then quickly back at Sky, pretending she hadn't. They seemed comfortable and familiar. I wasn't used to seeing Sky relaxed and smiling, surrounded by people who understood her, people who hadn't spent years hurting her. I noticed Dayken still staring at me.

"Got something to say?" I snapped, my voice piercing the quiet.

He just flashed that infuriating smile, innocently shaking his head. I felt my guard go up, even as a frustrating part of me noticed how disarmingly handsome he was and how his eyes crinkled in a way that was hard to ignore. I didn't need those kinds of distractions.

Without saying a word, I turned and exited the room, trusting Sky to handle it if anything went awry. Oddly, I didn't expect that to happen... which felt unusual. The calm atmosphere of the library, at least until I disrupted it, was unfamiliar to me. It unsettled me more than any danger could. As I headed down the hallway to my temporary room, I was once again reminded of Lunce's chest marking. I looked at it anew, trying to see it differently now that I had more context. Yet, I only felt more... caged.

***

Once inside the quiet of my own space, the room Aurora so kindly kept ready for guests, I flopped onto the bed with a heavy sigh. So much happened tonight that my thoughts felt tangled and raw. Sky seemed to be handling everything with a strange ease, but for me, this flood of new information and 'answers' just felt hollow. I was restless. Angry, even. We were still being hunted, and to make it worse, now we needed the help of an actual animal. A Guardian. And not just any Guardian — one I was apparently bound to for the rest of my life.

A permanent bond.

Because, according to Sky, a woman tied her son's life to a hound.

Although I disliked admitting it, my Guardian was nice to look at, attractive even. My mind wandered to his smile and how he appeared to connect to my heartbeat almost effortlessly. I quickly dismissed the thought, reminding myself that good looks don't necessarily mean trustworthiness.

And, of course, Sky's Guardian was nowhere to be found. Not that it mattered. One story would not dictate who could stand by Sky's side; I would be the one to protect my sister. No bond, no ancient text, would change that.

A soft knock at the door shattered my thoughts. My heart jolted. I hadn't sensed anyone approaching.

"Damn this room," I murmured. Clenching my jaw, I steeled myself. Whoever it was had better have a good reason for disturbing me.

I forced myself to mutter, "Come in," with as much *'fuck off'* in my tone as possible.

The door opened, and Dayken's massive frame filled the doorway. Disheveling his shaggy hair, he rubbed his temples like he was in serious pain.

"Were you… calling for me?" he asked, his voice tight, eyes narrowed like he couldn't quite focus.

"No," I replied, thrown by the question. Was he out of it? Maybe one of those guys in the alley had managed to land a good hit to his head.

"Oh. Never mind, then." He moved as if to leave but paused in the doorway. "Just so you know, my clan is nearby, patrolling the area. You're safe here. I promise."

There was no pressure in his tone, just a quiet certainty that settled in the air. Then he stepped back and started easing the door shut. The instant he did, I felt a strange, urgent tug, as I watched the door close and felt the distance between us widen. Something tightened in my chest. Why did it almost hurt for him to leave? All my instincts screamed to push him away, but I felt compelled to reach out, to make sure he was okay, to ask… something.

"Hold on," I heard myself say, almost in a whisper. The words surprised me. I rose from the bed, standing there, dumbfounded, but trying to mask my astonishment.

Dayken paused, and when he turned back, his eyes met mine. The pain in his face was gone, replaced with something that looked almost… hopeful. A smile flickered across his face, there and gone, replaced by that casual, unreadable expression that drove me mad.

"I…" I hesitated, swallowing against the knot tightening my throat. "I never thanked you… for earlier… in the alleyway," I managed, the words feeling heavier than they should.

He inclined his head slightly, his voice quiet, almost reverent. "It was an honor. My duty. You don't have to thank me."

Of course. *Duty.* I should have expected that answer.

No one risked their life fighting government agents for two strangers unless absolutely necessary. I knew that. *I knew that.* And yet… I couldn't shake the sting of disappointment.

What a strange thing, to be saved not because someone wants to, but because they're obligated to.

I should get used to that concept, I supposed.

"Oh." I nodded, my mind suddenly blank. I didn't know what else to say, and I felt more ridiculous with every second that passed.

"All right then. I'll see you in the morning." He turned to leave, his voice polite but distant, and just like that, he was almost gone again.

Wait — I needed to understand this…

I tried to convince myself that it was the lack of conversation and companionship from my twenty years of imprisonment, but deep down, I knew I just wanted to know more about *him.* "Are you hurt?" I blurted out, fumbling to sound casual. "You know, from earlier?"

Just let him leave the room already.

Dayken looked a little stunned by my concern, though he covered it quickly. "No, I'm fine," he said with a slight smile. "But… since you asked, my sister did tell me that when you need me, I'll feel this… pull. And if I resist or ignore it, I start to feel kind of ill. I wanted to check and make sure you didn't need anything, because, honestly, I was starting to feel pretty shitty." He paused, looking at me intently. "Are you sure everything's okay?"

"Yeah, I'm fine," I lied. I felt like I was losing my mind. It was different, but almost as bad as when I was locked up. He didn't need to know that, though. And it didn't help that I barely understood what he meant about this 'pull.'

Dayken's brows pulled together in an adorable scowl as he processed my answer, almost pouting as he mulled something over.

"That's so strange… I felt it earlier too, but it was a false alarm both times, then." He thought a moment longer, then asked, "Would you mind if I asked what you were thinking about earlier tonight, before I found you at the bar?"

I sat on the bed, and Dayken took it as an invitation, entering quietly and closing the door softly behind him. My heart skipped a beat as I realized we were alone, and he probably sensed it. He paused before sitting beside me, as if he could hear my heartbeat. When he sat down, the bed sank under his weight, and I leaned toward him, suddenly aware of how close he was. His back muscles tensed as he straightened and turned to face me. Everything about him was so large. He looked at me, expectant, as if I held the answer to an unspoken question.

When I stayed silent, he finally spoke again, his tone careful. "I'm only asking because of how I felt just now, before I knocked… it was the same as how I felt on my way to the bar. It was as if it led me right to you. I thought maybe if your emotions are tied to this bond, we might understand it better."

I sighed, realizing I'd have to explain myself. While I didn't relish the idea of exposing myself to him, I would be lying if I didn't admit I was a little curious about how this bond worked as well.

"I am worried about Sky. I'm doubting myself… and I have no idea if I can protect her from whatever's still out there. I keep it together for her, but inside, I'm stressed. I don't ever want to go back to that place. But at the same time, I don't know how I'm going to keep her safe." I took a deep breath, and my voice dropped to a whisper. "She's all I have, Dayken."

His expression softened, compassion filling his gaze. It was almost too much to bear. He looked like he wanted to comfort me, but held back, maybe unsure of what I'd allow. He settled for running a hand through his tousled hair.

"I understand," he said, his voice so sincere it took my breath away. "I know you don't *need* me, but I need you. Like I said before, in the alley, I've searched for you for a very long time. And I was close to losing hope of ever finding you. There's this need in me that drives me to protect you. So, I know it's not the same, but Sky isn't all you have — you have me, too."

My heart wouldn't stop pounding, and a thousand responses spun through my mind: tell him to leave, tell him 'thank you', tell him *okay', at least*. But in the end, I just stared at him, unable to say anything at all. Having just learned about this connection, I needed to not read too much into it.

"So, anyway," Dayken said, pulling me out of my tangled thoughts. "Now that we've got that out there, what were you thinking about just now?"

"Um…" I glanced down. "I've been thinking about how overwhelming this day has been, and I'm still scared for Sky. She's the one who needs protection, Dayken, not me. She's the one who needs a Guardian." I hesitated, feeling something like guilt, as I forced out, "I wish you could look after her instead."

For a second, something shifted in his expression, and I could have sworn he looked disappointed. But he turned his gaze to the window before I could be sure.

"I'm sorry, I can't protect Sky the way I can protect you," Dayken said, his voice low. "I honestly don't know what happened to Kolton. He went off the grid a long time ago. He was… going through a lot when he was still with the clan." His jaw tightened as he continued, "But regardless, I can't be her Guardian, Onyx. I'm yours. You chose me that day, no matter how long ago it was." He turned back from the window, and his eyes held an intensity, almost a plea, for me to accept him. I could see it — and, somehow, I could even feel it.

But I just kept looking at him, unsure of what to say. What would happen if I refused to let him guard me? I wondered if it would be a first, something that would end up in history books someday.

"Well…" I trailed off, reluctant to break the silence, "I just… wish things were different." The tension thickened between us. I didn't think I said anything wrong, but his expression suggested otherwise.

"Is that really how you feel?" he whispered, his eyes searching mine. I locked eyes with him, suddenly aware of my heart hammering, almost betraying me. Did he hear it? Pounding as if it were beating just for him.

"Look, I'm tired. It's been a long day, and I need to go to bed," I sighed, trying to put a barrier between us.

Dayken nodded, seeming to let it go, at least for now. "Alright," he said with a sigh, running a hand through his hair again. It made his arm flex and left me wondering about his workout routine again. "But I think when you're in distress, mentally or emotionally, you're unintentionally calling out to me. I don't mind, and I'll be right down the hall if you need anything." He gave me one last, intense look. "Good night, Onyx." And with that, he ducked out of the room, softly closing the door behind him.

Distress…

I pondered his words, trying to calm my thoughts so I wouldn't 'call out' to him, whatever that meant. It was unsettling to be so deeply connected to someone and not even understand it. The history lesson helped, but we still had much to figure out. I sighed as silence settled around me, but sleep evaded me. Thoughts and questions raced through my mind, Dayken's words lingering, making this new reality feel heavier.

Did the facility know about this ancient history? Had they already uncovered all of it? Was that what they had been trying to solve all these years? Eventually, the whirlwind of thoughts calmed, and exhaustion pulled me under. My mind was at ease with the thought of Sky safe across the hall, and with that small comfort, restless sleep finally took hold.

Chapter 9

Onyx

The next morning, sunlight was already creeping through the curtains when I woke, warming my skin in a way that felt almost foreign.

Unlike the fairy tales where vampires turned to ash, the natural heat of the sun was a welcome change.

For years, I'd woken to cold, artificial light, or worse, complete darkness.

For a split second, my mind lurched into panic, instinct telling me to check on Sky. I had to remind myself, *we're safe now.*

She's safe.

Blowing out a slow breath, I let my body sink into the mattress, grounding myself in that single thought: *safe.*

It wasn't a word I was used to, not even after running through my usual mental checklist of potential threats.

But still, it lingered.

Safe.

Blinking against the light, my eyes adjusted to the room. That's when I noticed the pile of blankets and pillows on the floor, just a couple of feet away from my bed.

What the hell?

Rubbing my eyes, I sat up and examined the lumpy mess. Then I froze. I could hear a faint heartbeat. And then the scent hit me. "Dayken?" I called, frustration in my voice. No response, just the soft rustling of blankets. But then an enormous muzzle emerged from the pile, followed by pointed ears and piercing black eyes staring right at me. The creature tilted its head, as if to say, *'What?'*

I felt my frustration vanish, replaced by awe and fascination. The animal facing me was magnificent, covered in shaggy, chocolate-brown fur, rippling muscles, and paws larger than my hands. Built to hunt and protect, he was lethal and beautiful.

"Dayken," I whispered, pulling off the covers and moving closer. "Is that you?"

The animal nodded, a slight, almost human gesture. *Wow.*

Realization hit me, and I felt a flicker of disbelief. I had no idea he could fully transform into a wolf. I climbed down from the bed and knelt on the blankets in front of him, studying him closely. Slowly, I reached out and let my fingers brush through the thick, soft fur on his neck. A deep rumble, almost a purr, vibrated through his chest in response, and I couldn't help but smile.

A genuine smile hit my face. This felt unreal. However, as the amazement began to fade, reality set in. My hand dropped away, and concern crept into my mind.

How had he snuck in here without triggering my senses?

"Wait. What the hell are you doing in my room?" I demanded.

The wolf blurred, shifting into Dayken in one seamless motion. The transformation was so quick, it felt like he'd been sitting there the entire time. He reached for the nearest blanket, pulling it up to cover himself, but not before I caught a full view of his chiseled chest and shoulders — muscles sculpted as if they belonged on a statue. My gaze lingered longer than I intended, tracing the broad, defined expanse of his torso — the sculpted lines of his shoulders and the deep ridges of his abdominal muscles. I couldn't help it; he was built like nothing I'd ever seen.

Focus, Onyx. I told myself, struggling to keep my thoughts straight.

He was clearly amused that I'd been caught checking him out, a signature smirk appearing on his sleepy face. I, however, was not amused, or at least, I didn't want to be. I cleared my throat and motioned for him to explain himself.

"Oh." He looked down briefly before meeting my eyes again. "You must've had some intense nightmares last night because you were calling out for me, at least, that's what I thought. But whenever I checked, you were sound asleep." He rubbed the back of his neck, seeming a bit embarrassed. "So, I decided to just stay here instead of waking you up constantly." He patted the nest of blankets on the floor, his muscles flexing with the movement. He watched me with an expectant look, as if waiting for me to yell at him.

But I didn't. Instead, I looked down and placed my hand over my heart, feeling it pound beneath my fingertips. What was happening to me? Dayken could probably hear it too. When I looked back up, I saw him watching me with that same intensity, and I felt it, a pull, like a rubber band stretched to its limit, ready to snap.

"You slept on the floor… to look after me?" I asked, still trying to piece it all together.

Dayken nodded.

A strange warmth stirred in my chest, but before I could dwell on it, a rhythmic pounding filled my ears. My hand instinctively pressed more firmly against my bonding mark. "Can you hear that?" I murmured, glancing up at him.

"Yeah," he said, leaning in from his position on the floor. "I hear it."

The sound intensified, deep and insistent, as if it were trying to convey something.

"Is this… normal?" My voice wavered with genuine confusion.

His eyes held mine, dark and steady. "I don't know," he admitted, his voice low. "But I hope you're starting to understand how important you are to me." He nodded toward the makeshift bed on the floor. "Sleeping here wasn't a huge sacrifice. I'd do it a thousand times if it meant you felt safe."

I swallowed, unsettled in a way that had nothing to do with his words. "I'm… starting to get the picture."

But my thoughts refused to settle. Why was I suddenly wondering how his hair would feel between my fingers? How his lips might feel against mine if—

No.

I shoved the thought away. Clenching my jaw, I forced my focus elsewhere.

"But I'm not okay with you just barging into my room," I said, still rattled by the fact that he'd managed to slip past my sensitive hearing and sense of smell.

Dayken held up his hands in mock surrender. "I had the best intentions, I swear." His voice was light, but there was no mistaking the sincerity beneath it. "I can only imagine what you've been through. I want you to know I'm here — and I've got your back."

I studied him, trying to stay guarded, but my attention was caught by the slight quirk of his lips — smooth, well-shaped, and maddeningly distracting. He had no facial hair, just sharp angles and tanned skin that looked inviting to touch. And he smelled good. Not overpowering, not artificial, just... fresh, like cedar and something uniquely him. For a moment, I forgot why I was even annoyed.

Then reality snapped back into place. *Focus, Onyx.*

I cleared my throat, forcing my thoughts back on track. "Fine. Just... don't make a habit of it."

His lips twitched again, like he knew exactly where my mind had wandered, but he only nodded. "Noted."

Taking the momentary lull as an opening, I exhaled sharply. "I did think of something I wanted to run by you."

"Anything," he said without hesitation.

I paused for half a second before continuing. "I was thinking a lot last night, and I have this theory that Sky and I are being tracked somehow. I can't prove it, but there's no way they could have found us that fast."

Dayken's amusement vanished, his expression sharpening.

"Tell me everything," he said.

So, I tried.

I couldn't bring myself to share everything... memories of the escape itself still clawed at the edges of my mind, too heavy to say out loud.

But I told him what I could. How I carried Sky, how we stole a car, clothes, and weapons, and how we stopped, desperate for answers, only to come up empty.

I laid out every piece I could bear, and the entire time... he just listened.

But it was more than that.

There was something in his eyes that made my stomach tighten, something soft, steady, almost reverent.

He looked at me like I hung the damn moon. Like every brutal, necessary choice I made was carved from courage, not shame.

And I couldn't, for the life of me, understand why.

What I described wasn't noble; it was survival. Messy and wrong, but he didn't flinch. Not once.

I left out the parts I couldn't bring myself to say.

The escape.

The kills.

Dayken finally exhaled, already shifting into problem-solving mode. "You're probably right about the tracking," he said. "I'll make a few calls, see what I can dig up."

I nodded and took a steadying breath, regaining my usual composure. And when I did, a sudden realization hit me like an anvil.

I had just unloaded a ton of baggage onto a *naked* man in my bedroom.

My stomach tightened. *Great.*

"I'm going to get dressed, and I suggest you do the same." My voice was steady, but as I let my gaze sweep over him, I instantly regretted it.

The blanket had slipped from his shoulders, leaving his chest completely bare — broad, sculpted, every muscle shifted subtly with his breath, as if designed to catch my attention. And unfortunately, it did.

I should not have been looking.

But I was.

Heat crept up my neck; I shot up abruptly and moved faster than necessary. I turned toward the private bathroom, pulled the door mostly shut, leaving a sliver. I should have closed it completely to break his hold.

But I didn't.

I was too intrigued.

Intrigued by his sheer size. The way every movement seemed deliberate. The quiet confidence in his smirk — the same damn smirk that disarmed my temper far too easily.

He was... unique.

And I was allowed to be interested in uniqueness. *Right?*

I continued watching as Dayken stood, wrapping one of the blankets around himself. For a brief moment, I caught a glimpse of a perfectly sculpted — and very firm — ass cheek.

The sight did things to me.

Heat curled low in my stomach, sharp and uninvited, and suddenly, I craved blood despite having no need to feed.

I groaned, clenching my jaw, and I forced myself to look away. But not before I caught a glimpse of Dayken opening the door just as Sky stepped out of her room.

"Whoa," Sky gasped, covering her mouth. Her eyes flicked over Dayken's half-dressed form, filling with amusement. "Oh. My. Gods."

My stomach dropped.

No. Absolutely not.

Dayken raised his hands defensively, then caught the blanket just in time to keep it from slipping. "This is not what it looks like!"

Oh, for the love of —

I swung open the bathroom door, glaring. "Damn it, wolf," I muttered. Turning to Sky, I said, "He just fell asleep in my room. That's it."

Sky raised a brow, unconvinced. "Right... naked," she said, eyes glinting. "I don't care. Just surprised and happy you let someone get close. Good for you," she winked.

I narrowed my eyes. "Sky." Then, noticing the triumphant smirk on Dayken's face, I turned to him instead. "You're not helping," I said, jabbing my finger at him. "Sky, seriously, he just fell asleep in wolf form. He shifted. That's why he's…" I gestured at him, my hand sweeping up and down as if presenting evidence at a crime scene.

Dayken, to his credit, took that as his cue to leave. "I have to go call in a favor," he said quickly, slipping past me toward the hallway. "I'll check on you later."

I yelled at him, my voice echoing down the hallway, "I'm not a child, Dayken! I don't need to be checked on!"

He chuckled. I could hear it — low, amused, and absolutely infuriating.

As his footsteps faded, I let out a long breath and turned to Sky, who was still watching me, her head tilted as if she were examining an exotic animal at the zoo.

"What?" I snapped.

Sky just smiled knowingly. "You like him."

I groaned and walked back into my room, huffing dramatically as I plopped on my bed. I was never going to live this down.

Sky followed in after me. Her pale eyes alight with excitement and mischievousness. It looked good on her.

"Isn't this so cool?" Sky spun in a slow circle, arms outstretched as she took in the space. "We have this whole place to ourselves!" She stopped and turned to me, her expression unreadable for a second before she smiled. "Well, Aurora and Dayken are here too, but still — it's just us four. We can do… sister things."

I raised a brow. "Like what?"

She hesitated, glancing down as if embarrassed. "I don't know. We never really got to be normal sisters, did we? Maybe we should try. Like… braiding each other's hair or — a hug?"

I stiffened at the word. "A hug?"

Sky nodded, stepping closer. "Yeah. I mean, it's a normal thing, right? Sisters hug."

I stared at her, unsure how to respond. We had been together our entire lives, yet physical affection had never been part of our relationship — not in the facility, with concrete walls and bars always separating us. When given the chance, we fought for each other. We killed for each other. That had always been enough.

If we had ever been affectionate before our capture, that memory was long gone, buried beneath the pain, the need for survival, and the years lost.

Sky was still looking at me, waiting. Hopeful.

I took a deep, stabilizing breath through my nose. "Okay."

She barely contained her excitement as she reached for me, and before I could even brace for it, she wrapped her arms around me. It was awkward at first — stiff, hesitant. I didn't know where to put my arms, and she seemed just as unsure, like we were both figuring this out in real time.

Then, something inside me cracked.

Maybe it was the warmth of her body, or the way she let out a shaky breath, like she needed this more than she wanted to admit. Perhaps it was the realization that we had gone too long without this. Without the reassurance of a touch that wasn't meant to harm or control.

I exhaled, my body relaxing, just slightly, and I let my arms tighten around her.

Sky buried her face against my shoulder, gripping me harder. "You're really hugging me," she murmured, almost in disbelief.

I swallowed against the tightness in my throat. "Yeah…. I am."

She let out a watery laugh, and for once, I didn't mind the closeness.

For once, I let myself have this.

Chapter 10

Dayken

I was halfway down the hall when I heard their voices, soft, urgent. The kind of tone people used when they thought no one else was listening. I paused, letting the soundproofed walls swallow most of the noise. But every so often, a word or two would slip through the cracks, just enough for me to catch the rhythm of the conversation.

Sky's voice, excited and breathless: "So I stayed back to study that flower that was mentioned in that history book. And it is extinct now. So, it looks like that will be a dead end. But it seems to hold the key to our life force and creation."

Sky was right. If Decima had never performed that forbidden ritual, binding her son Augustus to a hound, his twins would never have existed.

It all came back to the flower.

"I have to show you what else I found… I think Dayken left out something kind of important."

I tensed up, recalling a lifetime of lessons in school; some history was better left as myth.

Onyx, always wary, sounded skeptical. "What do you mean?" she asked.

I edged closer, guilt gnawing in my chest. I didn't want to eavesdrop, but I needed to know what Sky had learned.

"Right here. It says the mark only appears when a Sacar chooses their Guardian and shares their essence; the magic comes from the Cosmos atrosanguineusthis, this vanilla-scented, eight-petal flower we learned about." I heard her tap a page on the book she must be holding, "That much lines up. But listen to this… the bond is a one-way imprint. If the Guardian dies, the vampire's mark disappears. But if the vampire dies, the Guardian keeps the mark. Forever. It never fades."

I shut my eyes. So, now she knew. I'd always meant to tell her — just not like this.

Onyx whispered, but the words struck like a blow. "If Dayken dies, my mark disappears. If I die, he carries it for the rest of his life?"

I missed most of Sky's answer, something about her relief that her Guardian still lived. The same couldn't be said for everyone.

The silence in the next room felt heavy — almost suffocating. I envisioned Onyx pressing her hand to her chest, feeling the mark that connected us. I wished I could step in and ease the heaviness. But I somehow knew she'd resent the comfort.

Sky's voice: "I wonder why Dayken never mentioned that."

A knife-twist of guilt. Because some truths were too heavy to lay on someone you cared about. I was trying to ease Onyx back into this world, not dump every detail on her at once.

I heard Onyx's sharp inhale, sensed her discomfort, and suddenly I couldn't stay in the shadows any longer. My feet carried me to the doorway. My need to say something outweighed my instinct to give her space.

"Because it wouldn't matter," I said, voice steadier than I felt. "If you were gone, I'd already have lost everything."

The room stilled. Onyx faced me with wide eyes. Sky stood between us, caught in the truth we all shared. To avoid prolonging Sky's mortification, I decided to ease the tension by explaining why I was there.

"Join me on the porch. I've got a friend coming over who is going to help us."

***

Everyone gathered on the porch, waiting for our guest to arrive. The weather was quickly turning from fall to winter in a way that only Michigan could.

Aurora kept a cheerful mood, serving drinks and snacks as if preparing for a fun evening with friends instead of something much more serious. Sky sat quietly, softly reminiscing about her parents and sharing small, meaningful times together to honor their memory. She would glance at Onyx, quietly asking for details to help fill the gaps from her young memories. It was clear that Sky was grieving in her own way after I dropped the news on them last night. Catharsis was crucial now that they were back in their hometown, where it all began.

Eventually, Onyx must have sensed that the visitor posed no immediate threat because she and Sky went back inside. After a few minutes, I followed them, settling by a window in the library, where I could see the driveway stretching down to the road.

The low hum of a car engine reached my ears before the vehicle itself came into view, winding its way up the long driveway. From my vantage point, I recognized the driver immediately, Alicia. Her expression mirrored the one Onyx had worn upon arrival: deeply unamused. A permanent crease marred her brow as she pulled to a stop and stepped out, her red curls bouncing with every movement. My sister greeted her at the door, and I saw Alicia's face shift from mild annoyance to outright anger.

I couldn't blame her. I'd barely given her any information over the phone — just enough to let her know that it was clan business and she needed to hurry. Judging by her reaction, Aurora must have filled in the key details I'd conveniently left out.

The library door creaked open, pulling my attention that way. I glanced up from where I was perched on the windowsill and found myself staring at a storm of fiery red curls. Alicia looked every bit as furious as I'd anticipated. Her curls stuck out at odd angles, her wide brown eyes burning with irritation, the kind of look that made me consider running while she worked through whatever rage was boiling inside her.

But that was Alicia. All fire, all heart. I trusted her with things I didn't trust most of my own clan members with; I had since we were teenagers. She didn't flinch at the ugly parts; she never had. And right now, I needed that kind of support. That, and someone who wouldn't sugarcoat it if she thought I was screwing this up.

"Hey, pighead," she greeted, tone sharp but tinged with a familiar amusement. A smirk tugged at her lips, despite the heat in her eyes. "Your sister told me Onyx is alive. You could've mentioned that on the phone, ya know."

"I couldn't risk it," I said, hopping down from the sill. "Phones can be tapped."

She raised an eyebrow but didn't push. Just folded her arms and waited. She was always good at letting me get there in my own time. I motioned for her to sit. She didn't. Just stepped into the room, shut the door, and planted her hands on her hips.

"I'll make this quick since I know you've got Peach waiting on you." I paused, just long enough to let her know I hadn't forgotten. "But I need your head in this, okay?"

That softened her, just a fraction. Peach wasn't just her bonded Sacar; she was also her best friend. Two stubborn teenagers who picked each other early in life and never looked back. They'd been inseparable ever since.

"Everyone thought the sisters were killed in the fire or that they ran. But I think the fire was staged. A cover-up to throw everyone off."

Her face paled. "A cover-up?"

"Yeah. For their kidnapping." My fists clenched on instinct. The rage was always there — quiet, seething, waiting. "Someone took them. Someone who knew exactly what they were."

"Who would do something like that?" Her voice was tight, and I could see her struggling to understand the depths of it.

"They called it 'the facility'… I don't know what that actually means, but from what they described, we're up against something big, Alicia. Humans ran experiments on them, tortured them, for twenty years. Now they're being hunted."

Her hand flew to her mouth, eyes wide. "Oh… my gods." But the shock didn't last long. She blinked hard, shoved the horror aside, and straightened. "What exactly do you need?"

"I need a place. Somewhere safe for them. Like the one you have for Peach. Somewhere they'll be protected."

Alicia's face softened. "I'll see what I can arrange. I know a place, but it won't be easy to convince my clan to open it up."

"Thank you, Alicia. Just name your price."

She gave me a long, hard look. There was a familiar glint in her eye. "No price yet," she said, adding a playful wink. Then her tone grew serious. "But I can't help but notice, you keep saying 'they.' I know Onyx is your Sacar, but why are you protecting both of them? Where's Sky's Guardian?"

I sighed, running a hand through my hair. "Kolton's gone. Has been for a long time. And Onyx would never leave her sister's side. Not after everything they've been through."

Alicia nodded. She clearly had more questions, but I could see a flash of understanding in her eyes. She had always been a fierce protector of those she cared about, so I knew she understood what this meant to me. But there was something else I needed to know, something that had been gnawing at me since the moment I found Onyx.

"Hey, um, one more thing." I hesitated, feeling a little foolish for even asking. "I need to know how this bond works. Ever since I found her, I've felt… strange."

Her brow furrowed as she leaned forward, studying me. "Strange how?"

"Just… strange," I started, struggling to put the feeling into words. "Whenever I see her, my heart pounds, and it's like I can't breathe. She's all I can think about, and the thought of failing her again — it's unbearable. I want to keep Sky safe, too, but with Onyx, it's different. It's like… like I can't imagine my life without her safe, or without her, period. This bond thing—" I shook my head, trying to brush off the intensity of my words. "It's overwhelming."

Alicia chuckled, and I could tell she chose her words carefully when she said, "Dayken, I'm going to be honest. Yes, the bond does heighten our need to protect our Sacar, but what you're describing sounds like it goes a bit beyond duty."

I stared at her, confused. "What do you mean?"

She gave me an amused look. "I mean that you might be attracted to her… you know, like actual, human feelings, not just Guardian instincts. I'm talking admiration, attachment, maybe even something stronger."

I nearly laughed. I couldn't remember the last time I had thoughts like those. "That's ridiculous. I've just gotten her back, and I barely know this version of her. And besides, I've trained my entire life to protect her. It's just a stronger sense of duty." I tapped the back of my neck where my mark was. "I'm bonded to this," I said, almost as if I'm convincing myself of something.

Alicia tilted her head, unconvinced. "True, but duty doesn't usually leave you feeling breathless. Look, I'm bonded to Peach, and yeah, she means the world to me. But it's never been more than a deep kinship and me sensing her when she's in distress. Yes, what you're feeling might be the bond, but it sounds like it's also something more… *personal.*"

I shifted in my seat, uncomfortable. I wanted to end this conversation immediately. "Maybe… I don't know. At the end of the day, I just want her to be safe, and I'll do whatever it takes to make sure that happens."

She softened, nodding. "You will, Dayken. And you're right — I've known my Sacar for years. I've had time to learn about these feelings and sort through them. You're still adjusting, but the main thing is that you're trying, and you're here for her."

We fell into a lighter conversation after that, discussing clan politics, strategies for unclaimed properties, and potential options for a secure location for Onyx and Sky. When she finally asked to meet the sisters, I nodded, not seeing the harm in a quick introduction.

I led the way down the long hallway, stopping in front of Sky's door. I had barely lifted my hand to knock when her soft voice floated through. "Come in."

Alicia's face immediately softened as she stepped inside. Sky sat on a chaise, reading, her delicate fingers turning the pages with a natural elegance. As she looked up, her eyes were so light they looked almost white. I watched Alicia's grin widen, unable to contain it.

"Hi! I'm Alicia," she said, stepping forward to shake Sky's hand. Sky set her book aside, rising gracefully, and took Alicia's hand in hers, her small frame radiating a quiet power I knew well.

"Hello, Alicia. I'm Sky. It's a pleasure to meet you," she said, her voice as gentle as ever.

"Alicia is a childhood friend of mine," I explained. "Our clans are allies, and she is going to help us find a safer place for you."

Sky's face lit up. "Well, any friend of Dayken's is a friend of mine."

Alicia's voice brimmed with warmth as she responded, "Can I just say how stunning you are? I heard stories about you two when you were younger, but they don't do you justi—"

The door burst open with a crash, slamming against the wall hard enough that I half-expected to see drywall on the floor. Alicia jumped, startled, but Sky stayed calm, her expression neutral.

"What the hell, dog?" Onyx's voice was sharp, her gaze piercing as she took in the scene. She stood in the doorway, arms crossed, with an unmistakable ire in her ice-blue eyes. She looked fierce, standing tall with her black hair tumbling over her shoulders, and a fire in her gaze that could burn down the room if she wanted.

I opened my mouth, but Sky cut me off, her tone unexpectedly firm. "Sister, this is Alicia. She's one of Dayken's friends." She gestured my way before she leveled a look at Onyx, her voice taking on a low edge I hadn't heard from her before. "Be nice. She's here to help us."

Onyx's stance softened a fraction, but her gaze stayed locked on me, unyielding. "And why, exactly, did you bring a strange visitor into my sister's sleeping quarters without talking to me first?" Her tone was biting, each word laced with a challenge, as if daring me to make excuses.

"It was a last-minute call," I replied, fighting to keep the grin off my face. There was something so fiercely protective about her that, I'll admit, I found kind of… hot. And the way she called it 'sleeping quarters'? Adorable. "But this is Alicia Mack, from the Mack Clan. Our clans have an alliance, and she is a highly trusted friend." Then I realized they probably couldn't sense other Guardian types like I could, so I added, "Her clan is made of all bears."

"You're a bear?" Sky all but squealed. Alicia proudly smiled as she nodded yes. When she met Onyx's eyes, though, it was clear she wasn't as impressed with the news as Sky.

To Alicia's credit, she moved the conversation right along. "Well," she said brightly. "Now that we're all here, I'd like to go over the plan. There's an old compound I have access to — a bit of a historical hub for our kind. Think of it like an 'Office of Public Records' but for vampires and Guardians. It's very secure and in a remote location. Safe from unwanted visitors." She paused, putting on a sly smile. "It hasn't been touched in years, and with the right nudge, I'm sure my clan will let us use it."

"Now that we have a potential place lined up," I added, turning to the sisters. "The first step is getting rid of any potential tracking devices. We'll go over all your gear and anything you've picked up along the way. It's better to be sure before we go anywhere."

Chapter 11

Onyx

As this Alicia woman kept going on about tracking devices, I couldn't stop thinking about how easy it would be to snap her neck. Who did she think she was, giving orders? And why was she standing so close to Dayken? It's not like those ridiculous spiral curls were anything special. Quite the opposite, actually. She looked like a big, stupid clown with a red wig on, especially with her overly friendly doe eyes. Not remotely threatening. Yet I couldn't shake this strange, simmering irritation.

I don't like her.

Trying to pull myself out of it, I finally interrupted her. "So, when are we getting started?"

"Just a sec." She held up her phone and stepped out, mumbling something about making a call. Sky, always the empath, sensed the tension radiating from me and quickly excused herself as well.

"I'll be right back," she murmured, slipping out with an unreadable look.

Fantastic. Just Dayken and me, alone.

I could barely keep myself from snapping at him. "Next time, if you bring a stranger here, keep them out of my sister's room. If you expect me to trust you, you can't just be bringing random women into the house." The words tumbled out before I could stop them.

Dayken raised an eyebrow, smirking as he leaned closer. "My keen wolf senses are telling me you're not a big fan of Alicia… Is it because of her unwavering loyalty to me?" He sniffed the air for effect, his smirk widening. "Or is this… jealousy?"

I could feel my face heating up. "I am not jealous!" I nearly shrieked, feeling a twist of annoyance at myself for how it came out.

He chuckled, crossing his arms. "Oh, you absolutely are. You're practically fuming."

"Listen, Wolf Boy, if you don't quit fucking with me, I'm going to kick your nuts into your throat."

His laughter only deepened, and I was seconds away from wiping that grin off his face when Alicia stepped back in, looking surprised, as if she'd interrupted a moment between us.

It was *not* a moment.

"So, my clan has agreed to lend the space," she said, an awkward smile flickering on her face. "Under one condition."

"Of course there's a condition," I muttered, crossing my arms just as Sky reentered the room, managing to stomp down on my bare toes. I swallowed the pain, glaring at her. She just raised an eyebrow, clearly promising we'd talk later.

"What's the condition?" Dayken asked, ignoring our exchange.

"They want to throw a formal welcome-home party for the sisters," Alicia announced, glancing between us.

Sky gasped, clapping her hands. "A party in our honor?" She looked at me, her eyes wide with excitement.

"No." I crossed my arms tightly. Then, I focused on Alicia. "And no. Absolutely not."

Sky's excitement barely wavered as she continued, "I just read about these in the library! It's a huge honor, Onyx — more like a ball than a party!"

"A ball?" I stared at her. "Not happening. We'll leave at first light." I turned to Dayken. "I'm gonna need a vehicle." There was no way I was going to let a ridiculous event put her at risk.

Sky's face fell, and her voice turned pleading. "Wait… no… Why not?"

"Oh, I don't know," I said, my tone dripping with sarcasm. "How about the little fact that the facility, run by war-mongering cretins of the United States fucking government, wants our heads in a jar of formaldehyde? How about that for a reason, Sky?"

Sky rolled her eyes and pointed at Alicia. "You just heard her. We'll be safe and secure. They won't be able to get to us."

I wanted to tell her I trusted this curly-haired stranger about as much as a starving dog in a butcher shop, but Dayken stepped in, placing his large, unreasonably steady hands on my shoulders, turning me to face him. My first reaction was to swat him away, which he dodged with that irritating calm of his.

"What?" I bit out.

Dayken didn't so much as blink at my harsh tone. "How about I introduce you to Derek?"

"Derek? Who the hell is that?"

Alicia's face lit up. "Yes! That's a great idea, Day! Onyx, if you're feeling uneasy, Derek will help put your mind at ease."

What would put my mind at ease was if everyone took my sister's life and freedom as seriously as I did and stopped talking about a stupid party. My sister's life, and mine, were hanging in the balance.

I crossed my arms. "I don't care who this Derek guy is. The answer is no."

Chapter 12

She was so beautifully stubborn; it was truly remarkable. But that was fine, I was stubborn too, and I wouldn't be satisfied until she agreed to the new plan and its contingency. I'd do whatever it took to keep her safe at Alicia's compound, and if convincing her meant pushing a little further than I cared to, so be it. I had a feeling I knew exactly what she needed to hear.

"Look, just meet him," I said. "We'll drive over to where the event will be, and you can check the place out yourself. The security system won't be up yet, but you'll get the lay of the land. You have to know I'd never put you or your sister in harm's way."

She was thinking about it. I could tell by the way her expression softened just a fraction, her eyes flicking from me to Sky and back to Alicia, time to play my ace.

"Plus, Sky wanted to meet other Guardians, right?" I added. "I'd only invite a few of the clans, so it'd be a small event. A hundred people, maybe, tops." I watched her eyes flash to Sky, and right on cue, Sky started pleading again, eyes wide and hopeful.

I've got her now.

Onyx narrowed her eyes at me, knowing what I'd just done. Sizing me up, she said flatly, "So what you're basically asking is for me to trust you?"

It was a big ask; I knew that. I didn't expect her trust to come easily. But yeah, basically, I was asking her for blind trust.

"Can you two give us a moment?" I asked, glancing over at Sky and Alicia. They both nodded, stepping out of the room and leaving us alone.

I moved closer to Onyx. She stiffened and set her jaw defiantly, probably thinking it was some intimidation move. Her resolve only made her more striking. I placed my hands on her face, tilting her head up so our eyes met. Her hand moved to smack mine away, but I held firm, refusing to let her push me back.

"Let. Go," she growled.

"No," I replied evenly. I knew I was playing with fire, but I didn't care. Her gaze, fierce and assessing, locked onto mine. I could stare into those light blue eyes for hours if she'd let me. "I'll beg if I have to. Please, Onyx. Trust me."

I watched as her guard slipped, bit by bit, and for a second, the fire in her eyes softened. Her breathing grew uneven, almost like she was holding her breath. I lowered my gaze to her lips, wondering if she could hear my thoughts, wondering if she felt what I was feeling.

Finally, with a sigh, she let out a quiet, "Fine."

I lifted my gaze from her lips back to her eyes, hearing her say, "Just a quick visit," in a soft murmur.

For a split second, I had an intrusive thought, telling me to close the distance between us. Instead, I loosened my grip on her face, slowly stepping back. Just as I was about to speak, she cut me off.

"Hang on," she said, raising a finger as if to pause me. "I just want to show you something real quick, okay?" I could almost see a smile forming at the corners of her mouth.

Before I could eagerly nod, the air rushed from my lungs as something slammed into my chest, and my back suddenly hit the floor hard. The thud echoed through the room, and I just lay there, staring up at the ceiling, dazed. It felt like I'd crashed through the floor and landed in the basement.

"Ughh. Jesus, woman. Was that really necessary?" I hadn't even seen it coming. She was lightning fast.

She stepped over me, planting her foot on my chest and applying just enough pressure to keep me pinned. The look on her face was one of pure triumph as she stood over me, like the goddess she was. I couldn't help but notice her long, toned legs in that victory stance.

"Yes, it was," she said, beaming. "I just thought you needed a little reminder to never fuck with me."

All I could do was stare, absolutely captivated. Hell, I'd start a fight with her just to see that smile again. "All you've done is make me want to piss you off again," I laughed.

The door flew open, and Sky and Alicia rushed in, stopping dead at the sight of me on the floor, pinned under Onyx's foot.

"I poked the hornet's nest, apparently," I said, grinning, as I tried to push her foot off. She held firm for a moment before finally letting me up.

Sky started, "Onyx! Oh my gods, what—"

"We'll go check it out in the morning," Onyx cut in, and I heard Sky's sigh of relief as her face lit up, forgetting whatever she was about to say.

"Are you serious?" Sky asked, eyes wide with excitement.

"Yeah." Onyx looked down at me, her expression letting me know exactly how she felt about trusting me.

"All right, then," Alicia said. "I'll meet you at the compound so you can check it out. I'll make sure Derek brings his equipment." She turned to leave, waving as she walked out.

***

The following morning, Onyx, Sky, and I climbed into my car, heading toward the compound. "I know I've asked this before," I said, keeping my eyes on the road, "but you're positive you didn't bring anything with you from the facility?"

From the passenger seat, Onyx let out an exasperated groan. "I'm not an idiot, Dayken. Of course, we didn't bring anything. Like I said, we dumped our small bit of clothing back in Indiana."

Her irritation was clear, but I pressed on, the weight of my thoughts too heavy to keep quiet. "You know that only leaves one other option for how they tracked you so fast..." Saying it aloud felt like a physical blow to the chest.

The car fell into a tense silence, broken only by the hum of tires on the empty road. I glanced at Onyx out of the corner of my eye and caught her nod in understanding. She had her window cracked open, allowing the crisp morning air to enter. I knew what she was doing — sensing for anything unusual. Every inhale was a check for danger long before it could reach us.

Still, I couldn't help but check the mirrors every few moments. Sky sat in the back seat, turned sideways with her feet stretched out beside her, keeping an eye on the rear and left side. Onyx scanned the right, her sharp gaze unrelenting. As requested, Alicia's car followed closely behind, and I took some comfort in the vigilance between the three women. No one was sneaking up on us, not a chance.

After what felt like an eternity of silence, Onyx finally spoke. Her voice was low, steady, but with an edge that mirrored the tension we all felt. "I don't like the idea of everyone knowing where we'll be living."

I glanced at her, meeting her wary gaze. "I told you, you can trust me, right? I have no choice but to protect you," I said, hoping she could hear the conviction in my voice. "I'd never let anyone near you who could even be a *potential* threat, let alone invite them into your home."

I wanted to reach over and brush the dark hair from her face, anything to see her expression more clearly. It felt strange to be so drawn to her, wanting to understand her. To know her moods and thoughts.

As the silence lingered, I tried again. "Everyone who'll be there is either part of my clan, affiliated with it, or vetted through generations of clan alliance. It's important, Onyx. Any Sacar tied to the clan isn't just a show of power, it's a symbol of unity, of strength."

I paused, watching for a reaction, any flicker of acknowledgment in those intelligent eyes of hers. I could only hope my words were enough because her guarded expression gave nothing away.

Sky's voice drifted forward from the back seat, her tone endlessly optimistic. "Everything's going to be fine, Onyx," she said softly, her energy warm and reassuring. I was amazed at her ability to radiate hope after everything she'd been through.

When we finally pulled up to the abandoned structure, I watched Onyx take it all in. Her gaze was calculating, cataloging every detail, as if she were making a mental blueprint. To anyone else, the place looked as if it had been left to the elements — vines climbing over every wall, weeds breaking through concrete, and the structure itself was worn and weathered. But I knew what was waiting inside. This place didn't need to look flashy to be safe.

Chapter 13

Onyx

We parked by the overgrown lot and stepped onto the cracked pavement as Alicia's car pulled in behind us. The building was run-down, overgrown with ivy and weeds. It looked abandoned and neglected. Sky looked around cautiously while Dayken entered a code into the heavy door. It groaned open, revealing a shadowy interior. We walked inside silently, the air thick with anticipation, as if the building was holding its breath. I inhaled deeply, extending my senses like sonar — a talent uniquely mine. I once explained to Sky how I could detect people inside the facility, each guard's movements echoing through my senses like a map. When she couldn't relate, I realized this was a special gift only I possessed. Sky had her own abilities; I often wished I had her skills, but I was thankful for my superior senses.

I examined our new home as we walked deeper inside: shadowy corridors, empty offices, open spaces where old machines once sat, and tunnels winding beneath the main level. This place would do for now — safer than the farmhouse and far from the main roads. Plus, I wouldn't have to deal with Dayken's constant presence, though the place was a bit unsettling. A loud clang from the metal doors suddenly pulled me from my thoughts. A man entered, carrying a blue cooler, two cross-body bags, and a backpack. Lean and muscular, he seemed to prefer cardio over muscle training. His sharp brown eyes quickly assessed the space. I might have found him attractive, but then he opened his mouth.

"Damn, Dayk, you didn't mention you'd have two smoking-hot babes here. I might've actually showered for this!"

Dayken looked at me apologetically. "He's joking." Then he thought about it. "Right, Derek?"

Derek shrugged, unloading his gear and glancing over with a grin. He nodded to Dayken, then made a show of placing his fist over his heart, as if performing some sort of salute. But then he dropped to one knee in front of Sky, reaching for her hand.

"Oh, wow," he said reverently, holding her hand just inches from his lips. "You must be Sky. I'm Derek Avery, of the Avery Clan." His voice took on a dramatic, regal tone, and I nearly lunged at him before Dayken reached out to grip my forearm, halting my attack.

"You look like a parking ticket," Derek continued, "because you have fine written all over you." He glanced over his shoulder, throwing Dayken a smirk. "So, Kolt's gone, right? Can I protect her?"

Dayken's jaw clenched, but he kept calm. "Derek, if you value your life, get off the floor and quit messing around."

"Who said I was messing around?" Derek winked, finally letting go of Sky's hand and rising to his feet. Sky was nothing but giggles over the whole show.

Dayken rolled his eyes. "You can't even keep a houseplant alive, man."

Derek just shrugged, unbothered. "Please, who knew they needed water weekly? That's a lot of commitment for a 'plant.'" He turned to me, offering a lopsided smile as he extended his hand. "And you must be Onyx."

I took his hand and gripped it hard, making a point. He winced immediately, face twisting in pain. "Ow! Okay, got it — iron grip. Nice to meet you, too."

Sky raised an eyebrow, giving me a look. "Onyx, let go! He's here to help us."

I released him, and he staggered back, rubbing his hand with a pained grin. "Geez. You two are like night and day. I mean, you look alike, but... holy hell." He chuckled, shaking out his hand.

"Everyone, this is Derek. I was going to apologize in advance, but it appears I was too late," Alicia said with a smirk, as she entered the main room. "He'll be the one to perform the X-rays, remove any devices we find, and set up the security systems — inside the building and around the perimeter."

"What?" I snapped. "No way is this buffoon operating on us!"

"Hey, I'm not a monkey! I'm a—" Derek began, but Alicia cut him off.

"Derek," she warned under her breath, her doe eyes narrowing at the nuisance.

"Onyx, I promise he knows what he's doing. It might not seem like it, but he actually has a doctorate and specializes in advanced medicine. Plus, he's one of us, so he understands firsthand how we heal and regenerate," Dayken said, his tone steady, clearly hoping to ease my apprehension.

"Yeah, I got this! A little snip-snip here, snip-snip there," Derek said, holding up his fingers like scissors and snipping the air with a grin. "I could even throw in a BBL while I'm at it — wait, you probably don't know what that is. Brazilian Butt Lift! No?" He looked at Dayken. "Dayken, can I interest you in a BBL?"

Outraged, I turned to Dayken. "This was supposed to make me feel better?"

Alicia took that moment to exit the room. Clearly wanting nothing to do with this anymore.

Dayken turned sharply to Derek. "Derek, quit screwing around, man. You're seriously missing the weight of this; it's not a joke. We need you focused. Got it?"

Derek straightened, instantly dropping the act. "Right, got it." His tone suddenly all business. "Chase, my twin brother, will be here shortly with the rest of our equipment, but here's the plan…" He leaned casually against a concrete wall, arms crossed, and all I could think was, *great, there's two of them.*

"Dayken and Alicia filled me in. Someone's tracking you both, and they found you almost immediately after you surfaced, right? Everyone's guess: you're both implanted with some sort of tracking device. This is how we find out." He paused, pointing to the equipment he brought, then continued. "If I find something, I'll remove whatever's inside you and fly it to a remote location — a little hunting cabin on Beaver Island, maybe. Which, sadly, is completely devoid of beavers, I might add." He snapped out of his own chaotic tangent as quickly as he'd entered it.

"My brother and I will bury the trackers, riddle the area with silver bullets, light a couple of explosions — bada-boom — staged vampire death." He finished with a mock flourish; hands spread like he'd just performed a magic trick.

"Did you say fly?" Sky asked, her excitement barely contained.

"That's right." Derek grinned widely. "You're looking at the sexiest falcon to have ever walked… er, flown the face of the earth." He puffed out his chest proudly, sticking a thumb toward himself. "My brother's one too, but trust me, I'm the good-looking one."

I rolled my eyes. Leave it to Sky to latch onto the irrelevant details. "Great. But why silver bullets?"

Derek gave me an incredulous look. "Um, silver kills your kind. Duh."

I ignored him and glanced at Sky, wordlessly checking if she knew about that. She shook her head, clueless as I was.

"Newsflash: it doesn't," I said flatly.

"My lady, I promise it does," Derek replied, suddenly more serious. "I've seen it take down plenty of your kind."

The surprise hit hard. I was stunned. I'd had liquid silver repeatedly injected directly into my veins and survived. Before I could dwell on it, Sky said, "You don't understand. My sister—"

"Sky, that's enough." I cut her off, realizing Dayken hadn't disclosed that little detail. My clever wolf.

Wait, no, not mine.

Dayken chose to keep the fact that Sky and I were immune to silver under wraps, possibly to prevent Derek from suggesting any invasive tests. Maybe he did have my best interests at heart. I caught Dayken's eye, noticing a hint of a smile tugging at the corner of his lips.

"Well, Derek," I finally said. "I hate to break it to you, but your plan has some flaws."

"I don't see how," he replied, sounding all too confident.

Of course, he wouldn't. Any agent investigating the site would see right through his 'staged death' plan, but he didn't need to know why. "Doesn't matter," I said curtly. "Just get whatever you find out of us and take it far away. I don't care where to."

I couldn't deny that they were putting a lot of thought into our safety. It was touching, maybe, but I wasn't about to show gratitude until we were truly in the clear. I didn't know these people. And I didn't trust anyone who hadn't proven themselves, Dayken included.

The sound of the large doors opening snapped me out of my thoughts.

"Ah, finally! The weaker sperm has arrived," Derek called out.

"I heard that, you feather-brained degenerate," a deep voice retorted, echoing through the hallway. In walked a tall, shadowy figure with striking looks. He was nearly the same size and build as Derek, but he was dressed head-to-toe in black and sported several piercings across his brows, lips, nose, and ears. He wore a dark knit cap over his shaggy black hair.

He nodded to us briefly before he began hauling Derek's equipment over to the table, but he suddenly froze when his eyes landed on Sky. Sky, ever oblivious, just gave him a cheerful wave.

Derek noticed his brother's reaction immediately. "I know, right, bro? She's smokin'!" Then, pointing at me, he added, "This one's hot too, but man, is she mean."

"Alright, enough." Dayken straightened up, stepping in just enough to shield me from their stares.

The newcomer walked up to Sky, extending his hand. "Hey, I'm Chase."

"And he has a spoon collection, one from every state *and* the District of Columbia!" Derek added with a mischievous grin.

"Goddamn it, Derek, I do not!" Chase shoved his brother, and Sky just laughed at their back-and-forth.

"Can you two please focus?" Dayken huffed, visibly losing patience.

"Whenever you two children are done, I'm ready." I crossed my arms, staring Derek down.

He smirked. "You're first, then?" As he began setting up, unfolding a medical table and pulling out wires and equipment, Chase started plugging cables into outlets and organizing the array with surprising efficiency.

I held back a sigh, meeting Dayken's gaze, the weight of the situation hitting me hard. There was a small but very real possibility this wouldn't end well for me. And if something happened to me, that meant Sky would be alone, a thought I'd never truly allowed myself to consider before.

The words slipped out before I could think better of it. "If the device in us is dangerous… like a bomb, or something, then you do not let them touch Sky. Understand?" I hesitated, the next words catching in my throat, as I hoped, prayed, that this bond could extend to my sister, too. My voice cracked as I added softly, "You keep her safe."

Dayken gently placed both of his massive hands on my shoulders, completely engulfing them. The weight kept me grounded and made me look up to lock eyes with him. "Hey, don't even talk like that. You're going to be fine. I'll be right here with you, and Chase will keep an eye on Sky."

I hated how much I needed to hear those words, hated that I was trusting someone else to keep Sky safe when it should have been me. I glanced over at Sky, who was smiling up at Chase, looking completely at ease. He seemed nervous, like he was trying too hard to keep her attention, but Sky didn't seem to mind.

Watching her laugh, I reminded myself that she could handle herself if he stepped out of line.

Turning back to Dayken, I took a steadying breath. "Okay, you're right. Let's get this over with."

Chapter 14

Dayken

After reassuring Onyx, panic struck me. The thought of any harm coming to her, gods, it was unbearable — and all she cared about was Sky. Brave and selfless, she made my heart ache in the best way.

"Alright, let's do this," Derek said, clapping eagerly. "Lie down, Ms. Onyx." He motioned to the exam table and began attaching electrodes to her temples, wrists, and chest. I tried not to look concerned. "Stay still," he said, eyes on his laptop. "This test sends signals through your body, like advanced echolocation, to detect anything foreign." He grinned. "It's fancy, trust me."

Derek's way of reassuring my Sacar was unique, but the alliance with him, Chase, and their clan was invaluable. The twins split responsibilities; Derek handled fieldwork, medical, and combat, while Chase handled tech and logistics. They were the most skilled Guardians I'd seen. Tension grew as Derek studied the screen, muttering while we waited in uneasy silence. My wolf stirred inside me, agitated as time passed.

"Hmm," he finally said, adjusting wires and leaning closer to the screen. "Aha! I'm picking up something," he murmured seriously. He spun the laptop to show a faint image of Onyx's hip and femur, with a small, dark, round shape near her hip bone.

"That," Derek said, pointing to the image, "is embedded on the inside of your hip bone. I don't know how they managed it, but it looks like they somehow opened you up to implant it."

The blood drained from my face. *Opened her up? Fucking hell....* The details of her horrors still shocked me.

"Chase, get over here," Derek called, motioning for his brother to join us. "Look at this, it's right on her ilium." Chase came over, squinting at the screen.

"Damn… that's dangerously close to the iliac artery. How did they even reach it?" he asked, hesitating as he recognized her captors' skill. His gaze moved to Sky, realizing she must have endured similar horrors, his face hardened with pure rage.

I moved to the end of the table and met Onyx's gaze. Her eyes looked almost white under the harsh fluorescent lights, but hauntingly beautiful. With her examination complete, I offered to help Onyx down, but she declined.

"Sky, my precious," Derek said creepily, making her laugh. I was relieved he distracted her before attaching the electrodes and other sensors.

Derek surveyed Sky, but after a lengthy examination, he leaned back, puzzled. "That's weird," he muttered, making a few adjustments. "There's nothing there." He double-checked the settings, but still nothing. "Chase, look."

Chase looked over the screen — nothing.

"They didn't think Sky was a flight risk," Onyx said softly, distant. "Just me." I felt the weight of her words but stayed quiet; she wouldn't want comfort.

Sky smiled gently. "It's okay. I gave them no reason to track me; Onyx was the bigger threat." She nudged her sister. Both brothers nodded, rattled but obviously smitten.

"Hey, Day," Chase asked, still staring at Sky. "Who's looking after her now? Kolton hasn't been seen in years."

"I—" Derek started.

"I am," Onyx cut in, sharp and final.

Chase shrugged. "Then I'm staying by her side."

"No way. I called dibs," Derek argued, full-on pouting.

"You?" Chase scoffed. "She doesn't need an overgrown frat boy hovering." They bickered — Sky caught in the middle. She tried to assure them she was fine, but neither listened. When Chase looked ready to throw a punch, I stepped in.

"Enough," I said firmly. "Is she clear or not?"

They paused. Chase spoke first. "Yeah. She's clear."

Derek nodded. "Agreed."

Behind me, Onyx let out a quiet breath of relief. I didn't turn, but I felt it like a ripple through me.

"Alright," I said, glancing back at the brothers. "Just one tracking device, how do we go about getting it out?"

"Yeah," Derek replied, scratching his head. "It's not going to be pretty. And, uh, I'm going to need a bigger table."

***

I started pacing, overwhelmed as they prepared to cut into my Sacar, feeling helpless. I knew it was necessary, but standing by felt wrong. My instincts urged me to protect her. I kept telling myself, *this is good,* to calm my wolf. It had to be, because she was safe, in the best hands, and here with me.

Onyx leaned against the nearby stone wall, arms crossed, her sharp gaze fixed on me. She let out an exasperated huff. "Calm down and stop pacing," she snapped. "I'm the one getting dissected, not you."

I ignored her comment, which frustrated me more than I expected. I wished she understood how unbearable this was — that I'd gladly take her place if I could, but I knew better than to say it aloud, as it would lead to an argument. Neither of us had the energy for that right now.

I kept pacing. She kept staring. I could feel the annoyance radiating off her. When I thought we'd finally reached a silent understanding, she muttered, "Just get over it."

I stopped, wheeling around to face her.

"No. I will not get over it," I threw back, dropping my voice to match her flat, unbothered tone. "I care, Onyx. Just let me give a shit about you already."

The room went completely silent. I'd never spoken to her that way before. I instantly regretted it, but a part of me didn't. I needed her to understand that I wasn't going to stop caring. The sooner she accepted it, the better.

Derek clapped loudly, breaking the moment. "All right, let's get this party started," he said cheerfully from his makeshift operating area. His enthusiasm baffled me, given that he was about to perform invasive surgery on my Sacar. The setup was laughable: a sheet across two desks, IV bags hanging from an old coat rack. It resembled a medical tent in the middle of a war zone. My stomach twisted, and I felt the color drain from my face as Derek prepped Onyx.

Sky sensed my unease and touched my forearm. "She's been through worse," she murmured sadly. If she could stay calm, I could try too. But when Derek started the injection, my wolf went wild at the scent of Onyx's blood mingling with whatever was in the IV.

Stop him.

He hurt her.

Sky squeezed my arm. "She'll be okay," she whispered. "Don't stop caring, keep chiseling at the ice around her heart." Her words gave me hope, but the sight of Derek placing an oxygen mask on Onyx, so still and vulnerable, hit me hard. My instincts screamed to save her, but I couldn't. Wolves weren't logical, so I fought mine to stay grounded.

Onyx was mine to protect.

Mine.

"Maybe it would be better if you left the room," Sky suggested softly.

As if on cue, the sharp, metallic tang of Onyx's blood thickened the air, slicing through the room like a blade. The scent was potent and electric, sending tingles down my spine and making the hairs on my bonding mark prickle.

Stop him.

But I shook my head, slumping to the ground. I pressed my back to the cold wall and crossed my arms tightly over my chest to steady myself. I couldn't leave. Not now. The ache inside me burned like fire. It consumed me, left me speechless.

Derek wore a small camera on his glasses that projected a video feed to the laptop propped on a nearby desk. I couldn't tear my eyes away from the screen.

Through a haze, I watched as the twins worked. Before I knew it, Derek was elbow-deep into the procedure, Chase beside him, passing instruments like they'd done this a hundred times.

Still, I felt like I was crawling out of my skin.

Chase glanced over and said, "Shift." I nodded and quickly shifted into wolf form, relief filling my chest. My instincts became alert and focused as my vision sharpened, allowing me to watch the screen while pacing. Everything seemed fine, until it wasn't.

I caught a foul scent. The monitor flatlined and then screamed. Onyx's vitals dropped rapidly, and I lost control, shifting back and lunging at the screen, hands on the table.

I growled, "What the hell just happened?" as I pulled on my pants while Derek barked orders.

"The damn device was rigged," he snapped. "It had a capsule behind it. When I pulled, it was like popping the top off a milk carton; now it's leaking something."

The beeping intensified.

"FUCK! Chase, suction now!" Derek roared, voice breaking.

A sickly gray fluid oozed from the jagged metal fragment he'd pulled from her bone.

Her bone.

I watched as the toxin spread like wildfire, seeping through muscle and curling toward her ilium.

"No, no, no—" Derek was already moving fast. "It's reacting with the bone marrow. This thing was designed to poison her from the inside out if removed."

Alicia's voice broke through the chaos. "I heard her vitals spike. What's going on?"

"Toxin release," Derek snapped. "I need clean blood. Fast. I don't have enough here. We're losing her."

I heard Alicia's boots pounding down the hall. Seconds later, she burst back through the door. "Here! I've got Peach's cooler from my car!" she called as she started pulling out blood bags.

Onyx convulsed. Black veins snaked across her skin from the wound. Her skin turned pale, almost translucent, and her lips darkened to bluish-black.

My chest cracked open.

I didn't just see it, I *felt* it.

The bond between us flared like it had been slashed open. I could feel her life force slip through my fingers, and I wasn't even touching her. I couldn't breathe.

"No."

I shoved forward.

"Dayken—" Sky started.

"She's dying," I growled. "She needs me."

Derek didn't argue. He was still working, still fighting, but his eyes revealed everything. While Alicia fumbled with the cooler, I took matters into my own hands. I bit into my wrist with both fangs and pressed it to Onyx's lips. At first, nothing happened. I tilted her head, trying to get the blood down her throat. Still nothing. Then, a tremor. A twitch in her fingers.

"Come on," I whispered, blood still running down my arm. "Come back to me."

My vision narrowed. I could sense her, her essence. It felt as if I was standing at the edge of a cliff, witnessing her descent.

And then...

Warmth.

A spark.

Her essence flared against mine like a pilot light reigniting.

Her chest jerked. Her breathing deepened. Color bloomed beneath her skin like fire catching paper. I nearly collapsed with relief.

"She's fighting it," Derek said. "Her body's burning the toxin faster than it can spread. Keep going. I'll hook up a blood bag to the IV."

Alicia arrived at my side. "You saved her," she whispered. No. *We* did. The bond, the blood, the connection she'd been avoiding. It wasn't just there; it had flared to life inside of us.

"Chase, we've got to get this out of here," Derek said, handing the device over. Chase sprinted out of the room, and I heard the front doors slam open. A screech signaled his transformation as he took off for the hunting lodge, just as planned.

I took a deep breath, feeling a mix of relief and exhaustion. My eyes stayed on Onyx, still under the sheet. When Derek was sure the poison was gone, he carefully stitched her up. I turned away, unable to watch. The device was gone. Now, I just wanted her to open her eyes.

I was gently running my fingers over her temple when her eyelids fluttered. Heavy. Slow. Then those pale blue eyes, fogged with exhaustion but undeniably hers, met mine. The connection hit like lightning. Raw. Unfiltered. She didn't speak. She didn't need to. I felt it.

I know what you did.
Thank you.

Her gaze lingered for a heartbeat longer, like she was memorizing me. Then her eyes slipped shut again, pulled back into sleep. But I felt it. She was still in there.

She knew.

We decided it would be best to take Onyx back to the farmhouse to recover, as the compound was nowhere near ready, with wires hanging everywhere and equipment waiting to be installed.

We settled Onyx in the car, and Sky insisted on riding next to her in the backseat. She fussed over her with a quiet, determined care that even Onyx didn't bother fighting.

The drive was quiet, with only the engine and Sky's soft humming. When I checked on them in the rearview mirror, I saw Onyx resting her head on Sky's lap as Sky gently ran her fingers through her hair. It was a raw, intimate moment of sisterly vulnerability that made me feel like an intruder. I focused on the road, loosening my grip and slowing down, trying to extend their peaceful moment for as long as I could. They deserved it.

I gently pulled into the driveway to avoid jostling Onyx's wound. Once parked, Sky helped Onyx sit up. I opened the back door and offered my hand to a groggy, adorable Onyx, but she swatted it away. I'm glad; it proved her fighting spirit was still there.

She exited the car slowly, clearly in pain. I finally had enough and swooped her into my arms. Her protest was instant.

"Put me down," she said, barely putting up a fight.

"No." I tightened my grip on her, effortlessly securing her to my chest. She stopped struggling, and I could feel her relax in my arms ever so slightly.

I carried her to bed and gently placed her on the mattress. Her eyes were closed, but her furrowed brow and annoyed expression showed she wasn't asleep, just ignoring me. I stepped back, resisting the urge to brush her inky hair from her face. I waited for Sky to come in so she could care for her sister, then I left. After a few hours, Onyx stubbornly joined us for dinner, quiet but listening closely. Her silence made me uneasy, though I couldn't say why.

Later, restless in my room, I replayed the evening in my mind. Was she really okay after the procedure? She seemed fine, but I worried she might still be in pain. I didn't want to bother her, and I couldn't ask Alicia about the bond without her teasing me again, so I stayed put.

But eventually, I had to see her. I walked to her door but hesitated.

What am I doing?

Her sharp voice suddenly called out, "I know you're out there, Dayken. Just come in if you're going to linger like a creep."

Great. I look like an idiot.

I took a deep breath and opened the door, unprepared for what I saw.

Chapter 15

Dayken

Onyx sprawled across the floor, lying on her back with her hands tucked behind her head, her hair spilling out like a sea of pitch black. Her vanilla scent hit me immediately, sharp and sweet, the same scent that had haunted my line for centuries. The flower. The curse. The bond that had started with a ritual long before either of us had taken our first breath.

I tried to ignore the ancient pull it carried, but the weight of it pressed against my chest, reminding me that every thread of history still lived in us.

So I looked instead at what she was wearing, which was barely anything. Black gym shorts, a thin-strapped tank. One leg bent, the other stretched long, leaving her pale porcelain skin exposed, gleaming like moonlight poured over steel. Lethal legs. A body carved for survival, for war.

My pulse stuttered. Froze. I couldn't move. Couldn't look away.

"What is it?" she demanded, her gaze meeting mine.

Hang on… she's really on the floor?

"Wh-why are you on the floor?" It was all I could think to say.

She inhaled a deep breath and looked as if she was fighting the urge to roll her eyes as her expression turned annoyed. "That's why you came in here?"

"No." I cleared my throat, trying to gather myself. "Actually, I wanted to see if your wound had healed."

"I'm fine," was her only response.

"Show me," I said, knowing she'd probably rather kill me than be vulnerable for even a moment.

She glared. "Seriously, Dayken, I'm a big girl. I don't need you hovering every time I get a scratch."

As expected, but this had been much more than a scratch. I wasn't leaving until I knew she was okay. The thought that some part of that device might still be inside her made my blood boil. I wanted to wipe every one of those twisted bastards off the face of the earth, for touching her, for branding her, for embedding something that lethal under her skin like she was nothing. She must have noticed the turmoil written all over my face because her expression softened, just slightly.

With a long, exasperated sigh, she muttered, "Okay, fine."

She reached down to the hem of her tank top and lifted it, showing me her side. Holy — she'd just exposed her entire midsection, and it was... perfect. My mind scrambled. Her abs flexed as she pointed, just above her hip, to the now faint, slightly pink line that marked the incision. She was saying something about how the wound was 'completely healed,' but the words were just background noise as my brain short-circuited.

"See?" she said, fingers tracing the line. "I'm fine, so now you can rest easy—"

The combination of her voice, scent, and exposed skin drew me in, and before I could stop myself, I dropped to my knees beside her. The motion was almost instinctive. My hands moved with a will of their own, slow, deliberate, and purposeful. They knew what they wanted: to feel the puckered skin, to confirm for myself that it would heal as seamlessly as the rest of her. That she would be okay, just as her kind was meant to be.

I thought she might flinch away from my touch or quickly pull her shirt back down, but to my surprise, she didn't. Instead, she just lay there, her gaze locked onto mine, so intense that it felt like a warm embrace.

She's okay.

And I was going to make sure she stayed that way.

I exhaled slowly, forcing myself to pull my hands back, despite the undeniable urge to let them linger, to explore more of her. When I glanced up from her stomach, I wasn't surprised to find her watching me intently, her eyes glued to me like I was a wild beast.

Keeping my tone light but laced with earnestness, I said, "But, seriously. Why are you on the floor?"

She paused, her brow knitting as she examined me. "Why is it so important to you, Dayken?" Her voice held a challenge, yet underneath, there was a gentleness — an almost vulnerability — unlike anything I had heard from her before.

"What do you mean?" I asked cautiously, my eyes never leaving hers.

She hesitated, then motioned between the two of us, as if searching for the right words. "…Is it the bond we share that makes you…" She paused, choosing her next word carefully. "…care? About my sleeping arrangements of all things?"

Her question was pointed, but there was something deeper lurking behind it — something she wasn't quite ready to reveal yet.

"Well, yes," I said slowly. "But also… there is nothing comfortable about lying on a cold, hard floor… especially after recovering from surgery." The look on her face told me I'd said something wrong again. Her gaze sharpened, and I could tell I was seconds from getting told to leave. But part of me was thrilled just to be this close to her, and if she was going to kick me out anyway, I might as well make it worth my while.

I lay down next to her with dramatic flair, and without a second thought, I reached over to pull her on top of me. In one quick motion, I flipped her, forcing her to hover over me. She planted her hands firmly on either side of my head for balance, her body tense against mine.

I prepared for a deadly glare, but instead, her wide-eyed, stunned look left me speechless. Her hair cascaded around her face, accentuating her features as she steadied herself with flexed shoulders. Time stood still, her presence enveloping every inch of the space between us.

"I'm softer than the floor, and I know how much you love sleeping with my wolf," I teased. It was dangerous territory, but I loved watching her mask slip. I craved it. Lived for it.

"Dayken…" Her voice was barely a whisper, almost more of a warning to herself than to me. Her guard was still up, the walls she held high and thick, but I could tell she was wavering.

As we lay there, face to face, I couldn't resist taking her in. She was dangerous — fierce — yet delicate in ways I'd never seen. She had the kind of beauty that could command a room, even when she was scowling. And here, inches from her, I was helplessly drawn in.

"You are so beautiful," I murmured, letting my gaze trace her face, every line and shadow, as if memorizing it.

Her mouth parted slightly, as if she wanted to speak but couldn't find the words. Each second our eyes held, my heart pounded louder, an insistent beat I couldn't ignore. She looked...entranced, like she thought I'd lost my mind for pulling her close, but there was no anger in her gaze. Her usual wariness had softened, just enough for me to glimpse a part of her she rarely let anyone see. She didn't push me away. She could have, easily, but she didn't.

It felt like, in the charged silence, she was allowing herself to feel for the very first time.

Her hand rose, shifting her weight and lowering her body so that it pressed flush against mine. She braced herself on one arm, her free hand drifting toward my face. I held perfectly still, barely daring to breathe, like I was watching a feral — but beautiful — creature inch closer. Untamed, unpredictable, the kind of wild that made your blood stir. Her fingertips hovered inches from my cheek, suspended in hesitation, as though one touch might burn her or break whatever spell had drawn us together.

Then, just when I thought she might pull away, her fingertips brushed against my skin. The touch was electric, jolting every nerve awake. This wasn't like the moment in the alley; this was pure, unadulterated desire. Her fingers trailed from my cheek to my chin, and I closed my eyes as a low growl rose from deep in my chest.

She chuckled softly, the sound like music meant only for me. My eyes snapped open, locking onto her mesmerizing gaze. She parted her lips to speak, but whatever words she intended to say died on her tongue as a sudden knock on the door shattered the moment.

Damn it.

In a blink, she was off me, across the room by the nightstand, glaring at me as I lay flat on my back.

"Get out," she said. Her voice was low, almost hesitant, as if the words surprised her.

I got up without a fight, feeling oddly triumphant. She'd let her guard down, just for a moment. That sliver of vulnerability was enough to keep me hoping she might let me in again.

I couldn't resist a small smile. "Stay off the floor," I said softly, heading towards the door before she could argue.

Her glare was back, familiar and fierce, though her silence told me she wasn't entirely unmoved. I opened the door to find Sky standing there, her wide, innocent eyes darting between us.

"Sorry, Dayken," she said, sheepishly tucking a strand of hair behind her ear. "I didn't realize you were in here."

"It's fine. He was just leaving," Onyx cut in, her voice ice-cold.

I stepped past Sky, with a satisfied smile lingering on my face. "Goodnight, ladies. Sleep well."

With one last look, I closed the door behind me.

Chapter 16

Onyx

What the fuck.

I kept repeating it in my head, over and over, trying to process what had just happened. Had I seriously just been on top of Dayken, looking down at him like he held all the answers to my problems? Had I really given in to the urge to touch him? And had he… growled? For me? Or maybe *at* me?

His eyes had dilated, making the green vanish and leaving only deep black behind. The way he looked at me felt raw, primal, as if he saw me in a way no one else ever had. I couldn't understand why I was so drawn to it, why he distracted me so much, and why my body responded to him without even meaning to. I'd let my guard down, feeling... something I couldn't even name. Maybe it was because I drank so much of his blood.

I was so lost in my thoughts that I almost forgot Sky was still in the room. Her lips moved, words spilling out, but I didn't catch any of them.

"Wait. What?" I muttered, barely pulling myself back to the present.

Sky held up three thick, hardcover books, each one heavy enough to make a table sag. "Etiquette books," she explained, her voice chipper. "I figured you could read up on how to interact with people. Hopefully, it'll help you behave yourself. And hey, what better way to learn than from a book?" Her smile was wide and genuine. It hurt knowing I'd be the reason for its disappearance.

"Sky… I never agreed to a party. I said we could check out the building," I said, my tone careful.

"And?" She raised her eyebrows, waiting for me to finish. When I didn't, disappointment clouded her face. She held up one finger. "Dayken has proven he has excellent resources." Then a second finger. "Alicia has secured us a safe location."

"…a rundown, abandoned factory," I muttered under my breath.

She ignored me, raising a third finger. "And the twins successfully removed your tracking device — despite it trying to kill you, might I add."

She then held up four fingers, adding, "And lastly, they flew that same device to a hunting lodge in the middle of nowhere to get those agents off our trail."

She paused, waiting again. When I stayed silent, she threw her arms up in frustration.

"Onyx, I get it. It's scary. I'm scared too. But we have a chance here. I know it. We can trust these people." Her voice softened as her hand rested over her heart. "I feel it."

So, this was what it felt like to stand at a metaphoric crossroad. Part of me wanted to run away into isolation, just my sister and me against the world. But Sky… she wanted to stay with these people. And as much as I tried to hold onto my desire for isolation, I couldn't lie to myself; it didn't have the same appeal it once did.

I sighed, extending my hand for the books. "I don't necessarily share your feelings, but I want to try for you. I can't blindly trust them, but I can at least see what this is all about."

Sky's eyes grew glassy, as if she were fighting back tears. The sight made my chest tighten, so I quickly changed the subject, taking the books from her.

"Seriously, Sky, I think this is overkill. We're just going to say 'hi' and leave. I don't think reading all of this" — I waved the books for emphasis — "is going to prepare us for what's coming."

Her smile returned, soft and hopeful. "Everything is going to be okay. I just know it."

I wished I could share her confidence. The thought of being on display made my stomach twist, and trusting Dayken, a ghost from a forgotten past, didn't help. But I couldn't take away her dream of normalcy, especially when her eyes sparkled with such joy. She deserved this moment after decades without friends or healthy attachments.

"I'm only doing this for you, you know," I muttered. "I couldn't care less about these people."

Sky's eyes softened, her giddy energy making her glow. It moved me in a way I couldn't explain. She leapt into my arms, hugging me, and I smiled as I hugged her back.

"Thank you," she whispered.

"Go to sleep, sister. We'll talk more about this tomorrow."

She let go, turning toward the door but pausing to glance back over her shoulder. "I love you, Ox. Goodnight."

"Love you too," I replied, watching her walk away. My heart swelled with pride as I savored moments like this, moments I once feared we'd never have.

With the door shut, I was alone again, left with my 'entertainment' for the night. I glanced from the floor to the bed, then back again, my mind replaying how Dayken's hands had grabbed hold of me, pulling me over him with such ease. And that noise from his chest, that deep, raw sound would haunt me for days. Why did he affect me like this? Why couldn't I stop thinking about him?

No. Focus.

This wasn't about him; it was about Sky. She became a beacon of joy when she handed me the books, glowing with excitement. I settled onto the chaise and opened the first one. For me, reading was a completely different experience than for Sky. She could blaze through books in minutes, her mind absorbing every word. The facility tested her constantly, amazed by her speed and memory. For me, it took a lot more patience.

About halfway through Chapter 7, "Formal Dining and Attire", I heard a knock at the door, sharp in the still quiet.

"Come in."

The door creaked open, and Dayken stepped inside, shutting it softly behind him. His movements were restless. Tension radiated from him as he raked a hand through his hair.

"You again?" I couldn't keep the irritation from my tone. I'd had more than my fill of him today.

"Yeah, sorry. I tried to sleep, but I couldn't stop thinking," he admitted, voice low. He began pacing back and forth from the door to the bed, an almost wild energy emanating from him.

"Try reading something." I waved the book in my hand, but he barely glanced at it. Instead, he stopped short and dropped to his knees in front of the chaise where I sat. His face was suddenly close. His bright emerald eyes locked onto mine with an intensity that made my stomach flutter.

"What is wrong with you?" I asked, my annoyance mingling with a pang of unease.

"I learned something interesting about the bond," he said, gesturing vaguely between us. "I need to test something. Just… promise you won't attack me."

Suspicion prickled at my thoughts. "What kind of test?"

"I won't hurt you," he said gently, as if trying to soothe a skittish animal. "Just promise. No hitting."

I narrowed my eyes, but his tone disarmed me. He looked so sincere, like he was mulling over so much information in his head, and he just needed me to agree… to something. Against my better judgment, I nodded. "Fine. I promise, bu—"

Before I could finish, he leaned in. His hand cupped the back of my neck, pulling me toward him. I instinctively put my hands on his shoulders to brace myself against the momentum as he yanked me forward.

I was immediately hit with his scent, clean and fresh. Like soap and something earthy, *sun-warmed*. Comforting.

Then, I felt his nose brush against the side of my neck. A shiver rippled through me, and goosebumps spread down my arms. Suddenly, I was *hyperaware* of every movement he made — every shift of muscle, every unsteady breath he took.

Then, he inhaled deeply at my neck, and his entire body *tensed*. It was as if he not only inhaled the air at my neck but the air from my lungs as well because I suddenly couldn't breathe.

A low, feral growl rumbled from his chest, his muscled shoulders going taut beneath my fingers. The cords in them strained against whatever internal fight he was having.

My heart hammered in my rib cage. I didn't dare move for fear it could ruin whatever *this* was.

"I lied earlier." His confession broke the silence between us. "It's not just the bond that makes me care if you're on the floor or the fact that you were just operated on… it's *you*." He spoke each word against my pulse, and his breath sent a tingling feeling down my neck to a very, very lower part of my body.

His words left my thoughts spinning. My pulse roared in my ears, drowning out reason.

Thump.

Thump.

THUMP.

"Dayken…" I managed, though I wasn't even sure what I wanted to say.

"You don't have to say anything," he murmured, pulling back from me, his gaze searching mine. "I just wanted you to know that I care about you. This isn't the bond speaking — it's me. No pressure, alright? I'm not asking for anything in return."

Before I could respond, he pulled away from me completely, and his body shifted with a burst of energy. Fur erupted as his form transformed into the same massive wolf from before. He leapt onto my bed without hesitation, curling into a mountain of dark fur and closing his eyes as if nothing had happened.

I stared, heart pounding, my neck still tingling from his touch. This was new. This was dangerous. And I hated how much I already wanted more.

"Hey!" I snapped, glaring at the wolf sprawled across my bed. "Get off. You are not sleeping in here again."

Dayken's tail wagged lazily, his giant head shifting just enough to give me a smug, satisfied look.

"No. Absolutely not. You don't get to just barge in here, and…." *How do I explain what just happened…* "and… then claim my bed," I said, crossing my arms. "So help me, I will kick your ass, wolf form or not." He flopped onto his back, paws dangling as he wagged his tail with exaggerated innocence. He was huge; there would be barely enough room for me on the bed. Not that I was even considering letting him stay.

Was I?

"This isn't funny, Dayken," I huffed, trying to ignore the traitorous warmth still blooming in my chest.

He let out a pitiful whine, covering his eyes with his paw like a guilty child.

I exhaled sharply, frustrated with him, with myself, and with the entire situation. "Fine!" I growled. "But you better just lay there and not make a sound, you hear me?"

Dayken snuggled deeper into the blankets, his massive form radiating smug contentment.

Muttering low curses, I turned away from him. "I can't believe this…"

Even as I tried to settle back into my book, my mind refused to focus. The scene replayed over and over, confusing me, infuriating me, and pulling at something I didn't understand.

Chapter 17

The next day, I avoided Dayken like the plague. Smug bastard. Who did he think he was, crashing into my space like that? Like he… just… *belonged.*

And worse?

I let him.

I hadn't slept that well in years, and he would never know that. Not if I could help it.

It pissed me off how safe I'd felt with him there, like it was normal… like *I* was normal.

Safety wasn't supposed to feel foreign. Or wrong. But it did. And it confused the hell out of me.

That's it. I'll stab him. Just once. To recalibrate.

But then I remembered his peaceful, adorable sleeping face, and the thought of hurting him, even in jest, made me uneasy. I rolled my eyes at myself. I needed the new security system at the compound to be operational quickly so I could create some distance from Dayken, who was disrupting my focus. I hated how easily he did it, too.

I wandered through the massive farmhouse like a caged animal, mentally plotting my escape. Where was Sky, anyway? She said to meet her in her room, but she wasn't there. She mentioned wanting to discuss the ball tonight. Her enthusiasm couldn't be more different from mine. With a sigh, I sat on her soft bed, which was edged with a delicate, pale blue lace. It suited her perfectly.

Lost in a frustrating cycle of thoughts, mostly about stabbing Dayken, Sky finally appeared in the doorway.

"Sorry, Ox! I was in the basement with Aurora, stitching these up." She lifted two, comically large, black bags that were almost as tall as she was and hung them in the closet. "Okay, so here's the plan!" Her eyes sparkled with excitement as she spun to face me. "We're going to have a girls' night! An actual night of just the girls! You, me, Aurora, Alicia, and Alicia's even bringing Peach, her Sacar. We'll all get ready for the ball together, right here in the house!"

She twirled around the room, her short, blunt bob bouncing with each spin, gravity seemingly powerless to her excitement. Her energy was contagious. She talked about the details, and while most of it was beyond my level of interest, I found myself drawn in anyway. Seeing her like this made me want to try. It made me want to lower my guard, let these people in, and just for one night, let go of the fear and pain.

For Sky, I'd give it a shot.

That evening, I was surrounded by women fussing over my hair, debating eyeliners, and comparing lipstick shades. It felt excessive for a simple meet-and-greet with Dayken's and Alicia's clans. But then I saw Sky, her short hair pinned back, her eyes full of awe, and I swallowed my complaints.

Peach introduced herself immediately. She seemed sheltered, maybe naive, but lovely. She was petite, with long, wavy, light blonde hair, pale skin like mine, and striking purple eyes… so captivating. I'd never seen anything like them.

Peach handed me a tube of lipstick that was at least three shades darker than my natural tone.

"Hmmm, maybe too dark. Alicia, what do you think?"

"Oh, come now, Peachy, you know I can't tell red from burgundy," Alicia chuckled. Which, honestly, made sense coming from her. Her hair was the same untamed, curly mess — wild but somehow perfect. No makeup, a beautiful dress, an effortless kind of stunning that didn't need fixing or fussing. It was like she didn't have to try because she was so naturally gorgeous, so she didn't.

"Fair," Peach sang cheerfully as she placed the lipstick down and picked up a different shade of red.

Aurora sat by the window, quietly hemming Sky's dress with her sewing kit. She was watchful and warm, her presence subtle but impactful. Occasionally, she made a dry comment or sharp observation that made Sky giggle and Alicia roll her eyes.

"You know," Aurora said at one point, not looking up from her stitching, "when I was little, I mashed up flowers from my mother's garden, trying to recreate the sacred mixture. Thought the bowl would shimmer like the lore promised."

Peach gasped and nearly dropped the lipstick. "Oh my God, I did that too! I would raid the kitchen for oils and herbs to mix in, just like the ancient text said."

They both laughed, swapping memories, and Sky leaned in, eager to hear more about the history.

I stayed quiet. I'd never crushed petals or stirred bowls of pretend magic — my childhood had been shackles, not gardens. Their laughter wasn't meant to exclude me, but it still did.

It was strange how easily Sky fell into rhythm with the other women. Like they'd all known one another far longer than they had. Like this wasn't temporary.

I watched from the edge of it all, unsure whether I was meant to join in or observe — and not entirely sure which one I preferred.

The group would ask me questions, but my one-word answers hinted at my disinterest. What caught my attention was Aurora's detailed questions about our captivity, blood consumption, escape, and my speed compared to Sky's. Sky answered casually, not minding. Occasionally, Aurora asked Peach something, and they chatted. I didn't know why it annoyed me.

After what felt like forever deciding on hairpins and eyeshadow, they finally led me to the car. I was apparently the one holding everyone up, even though I'd been ready for ages. I knew Dayken was already at the venue. He'd barely let me out of his sight and probably wouldn't have left if I hadn't made some kind of threat.

Once we finally hit the road, I settled in for the 45-minute drive.

The drive was… lively. Everyone was excited, especially Sky, which made me glad.

"I told him he wouldn't know fashion if it smacked him in the dick," someone said, and laughter ensued.

Despite the cheerful atmosphere, I felt gnawing anxiety. I wanted to roll down my window and stick my head out for fresh air. I tried to be happy for Sky and enjoy the moment, but I couldn't relax.

"Yeah, he is super hot. But I don't think he has ever made direct eye contact with me, and that is like a huge red flag," Peach said, and there was a chorus of agreement within the car.

I sighed.

When we finally arrived at the compound, I noticed the improved security: massive gates, an intercom, and a nearly indestructible door, upgrades since our last visit for my surgery. I was impressed; Alicia's reinforcements made me feel that this place really could be safe for us.

We parked inside a large, covered garage that didn't appear to connect to any immediate entrance, and there were no visible doors, just blank, concrete walls and silence. Everyone stepped out of the car.

"Alright, let's do this," Alicia said with a smirk, heading toward what looked like nothing more than a blank wall. She crouched slightly, tapped a small, raised bolt near the baseboard twice, then once more.

With a soft *click*, a narrow section of the wall slid open to reveal a hidden panel, sleek, black, and blinking softly.

"New trick," she said, winking as she typed in a code. The concrete wall beside it groaned, revealing a concealed elevator door. We followed her inside. The elevator doors slid shut, and with a soft chime, a mechanized voice filled the small space.

"Password verification."

"Alicia Marie Mack from the Mack clan," she replied smoothly.

"Access granted. Welcome back, Alicia."

Well, holy shit.

I kept my reaction to myself, though inwardly, I was impressed. It was reassuring to see all the security measures in action, but I wasn't about to let my guard down just yet. Beside me, Sky radiated excitement, her eyes wide with wonder — and as much as I loved seeing that, it also made one thing clear: whatever barriers she'd built were now gone. That meant I had to stay alert for both of us.

"O.M.G., Alicia! Did you see all those cars?" Peach's eyes were wide, clearly taking everything in with a thrill that suggested this was her first time at a gathering like this in a while.

Alicia chuckled. "Yeah, looks like we might be the last ones to arrive."

Chapter 18

Dayken

I was fully prepared to confront Aurora and Alicia the moment they arrived. They were almost an hour late, and I was beginning to lose patience. I checked my phone for the hundredth time and paced back and forth in the former conference room, now dining hall, because apparently pacing had become my new hobby. My mind raced with all sorts of scenarios about what could have happened to them. None of it was rational, but knowing that didn't help settle me down.

Just as I was about to reach my breaking point, one of Alicia's clan members grabbed the microphone and turned toward the entrance.

"Ladies and gentlemen," he began. "May I have your attention, please."

Finally.

The room fell silent. The entire crowd was on edge, eagerly waiting for the arrival of the two sisters. When Alicia, Aurora, and Peach entered, they stepped aside to clear the doorway. I strained to catch a glimpse of Onyx and Sky through the doors, but they closed again before I saw anything.

"It brings me great honor to finally present the Ravensfield sisters. Please rise and join me in welcoming home the lovely Onyxiana Beatrice Ravensfield and Skylar Anastasia Ravensfield."

The doors opened, and two breathtaking figures emerged, both so stunning that I almost forgot how to breathe.

Sky entered first, wearing a silky, floor-length ivory gown with a thick black sash around her small waist. Her hair was down, smooth and sleek, with a crystal hairpiece that glimmered against her black hair. She looked like she'd just stepped off a red carpet, poised and graceful, as if she were born to be admired.

Then Onyx entered, and it took every ounce of self-control I had to stay where I was. The urge to shield her, to claim her as off-limits to everyone else in this room, was overwhelming. She was… magnificent in a way that forced me to remember to breathe.

Her skintight, floor-length black dress had a high slit that revealed her flawless skin with every step. Every move looked deliberate and captivating, drawing everyone's attention, which I hated but couldn't ignore. Her long, black hair cascaded in shiny waves, framing a fiercely beautiful face, with deep red lips and dark-lined eyes. I couldn't look away. She seemed powerful and untouchable — she looked…

In that moment, a truth settled over me that I'd been trying to understand since she returned to my life: I felt deeply for her, more than duty or instinct.

Our bond was one thing, but this was different. She was more than my Sacar. She was a storm I'd gladly weather — lightning, thunder, and all. I realized I wasn't just bound to her; I was falling for her. I didn't know what she'd do if she knew — what I'd do — but I knew I'd do anything to earn her trust and see where this could go if she'd let it.

Maybe, just maybe, we could reach some understanding.

As the applause faded and lines formed to greet the sisters, I headed straight for Onyx. It felt like an eternity, navigating through the crowd, pushing past people who were either too slow or too distracted to notice. Finally, I broke through, close enough to see her face as she finished an introduction to the man in front of me.

Then, she looked up, and our eyes locked.

My breath hitched. She just stared, her expression unreadable, and I couldn't tell if she was surprised, annoyed, or something else entirely. If I had to guess, I'd say shock… maybe?

I stepped closer, taking her hand in mine and bringing it to my lips. She was so soft, and I fought back a groan when our skin touched. Placing a gentle kiss on her knuckles, I teased, "You're late." I grinned, bracing myself for the snarky comeback I was certain would follow. But, to my surprise, she didn't pull her hand away or roll her eyes.

Instead, she just kept looking at me, her silence almost unnerving.

"You look like a… *goddess*, Onyx," I added that word quietly. It wasn't just a compliment; it was the only word that felt right.

I half-expected her to snap at me, but she only said, "Thank you," in a soft tone.

That was it? No sarcasm, no eye roll, just… a thank you. What was going on with her? Had something happened on the way over? I felt the words, the urge to ask, rising on my tongue, but before I could say anything, the man behind me cleared his throat.

With a reluctant step to the side, I moved to stand just behind her to allow the welcome procession to begin. Tonight, I'd be her shadow. I wasn't letting her out of my sight — not for a second.

"I'll be right here, keeping an eye on everything. And I'll make sure they all keep their damn hands to themselves," I whispered into her ear, my voice rougher than intended. Jealousy dug its claws deep, rooting itself in my brain. There was no use fighting it. She was gorgeous, and she was mine….

As far as the bond goes.

My instinct to protect her was in overdrive — a lethal combination that was about to drive me insane.

But Onyx only nodded, turning back to the line. She moved through the pleasantries with grace. She was polite but distant, almost robotic. It was unnerving. I wanted a glare, a sarcastic comment, anything to show me that my fiery, quick-tempered Sacar was still in there, unharmed and unmistakably herself.

As a man from Alicia's clan approached, I couldn't ignore the way he sized Onyx up — his gaze lingering too long, his stance a little too confident. The way he gripped her hand was too firm, and his lips lingered on the back of it for far too long.

Mine.

Rage ignited in my blood, white-hot and uncontrollable. My wolf was already snapping at the edge of reason, demanding retribution.

A growl tore through my throat before I could stop it. "Release her hand and back away before I rip your arms from your body and shove them up your ass." I strode towards him, every step a promise.

Mine. She was *mine.*

His hands flew up in surrender, his face draining of color as he took a cautious step back, too afraid to turn his back on me.

I waited for Onyx to snap at me, to tell me she had it under control. But when that never came, unease gnawed at me.

Finally, I couldn't help myself. I reached out, brushing the back of her arm as I leaned in. "Are you doing alright, Sacar?" I whispered, my words barely more than a breath.

She just nodded, barely acknowledging me. She didn't pull her arm out of my grasp or hiss that she was a big girl.

That's it — enough of this.

Throwing my hand up, I announced, "The sisters are going to take a quick break and grab some refreshments. We'll be back shortly."

Ignoring the curious glances and murmurings, I took Onyx by the arm and guided her out of the room, heading down the hall until I was sure we were alone. I stopped, turning to her, and searched her expression.

"What's going on with you?" I demanded, my tone harsher than I intended.

"There doesn't appear to be any refreshments out here," she replied, crossing her arms over her chest, her eyes narrowing just enough to let me know she was fine — annoyed, even.

Lovely. Clearly, she's capable of being herself after all.

"Don't play coy with me. You're acting strange. Why?" I pressed, refusing to let it go.

"If by strange, you mean *polite,* I promised Sky I'd be on my best behavior tonight," she said, with a defiant tilt to her chin. "I even read a couple of books on etiquette, and I'm trying to follow suit, which, might I add, is damn near impossible while I'm standing in an empty hallway with *you.*" She jabbed her finger into my chest, her lips tightening in frustration. "Maybe you're the one who needs to read those damned books."

I couldn't help the laugh that slipped out. "You're something else, you know that?" I shook my head, more amused than anything. "Fine. If this is all for show, then by all means, go ahead. But my instincts don't lie. Something's off."

I stepped back, giving her room to brush past me in those stilettos that clicked like a countdown, each step echoing down the hallway. Just as she reached the doors, she hesitated. That one brief pause was so unlike her — a kind of self-consciousness I'd never seen in her before.

She turned back, her gaze shifting before it landed on me, her voice almost unsteady. "You… uh, you look very nice tonight."

Did she... compliment me? Yeah, I wasn't letting that slip by. As she turned to leave, I followed, catching her completely off guard when I grabbed her waist, pulling her away from the door, and gently pressing her back against the wall. A flash of surprise crossed her face, so briefly she almost managed to hide it. Almost.

"Are you crazy?" she barked, but her voice wavered slightly.

Possibly. No telling anymore, honestly.

I pressed closer, my body bracing her against the wall, my hands on either side of her, caging her in. I wanted her to know exactly how serious this was. Leaning in, I lowered my voice, a soft growl slipping out. "Say it again, goddess."

Her breath hitched, and I watched goosebumps spread across her bare shoulders. Her eyes widened, a blend of defiance and something else that made my pulse pound.

Chapter 19

Onyx

My head spun as I tried to get a handle on what was happening. Regaining control of the situation would have been much easier if Dayken hadn't looked so damn attractive right now. He looked like he stepped straight off the cover of one of those magazines Sky was always reading — fitted black tux that revealed his strong build, crisp white shirt, and a sleek, silky black tie. His hair was styled for once, highlighting his features beautifully, and he carried an intoxicating scent. It took everything I had not to close my eyes and breathe him in. And then there was the growl — that low, gentle rumble had pulsed through my entire body, tingling every nerve and lighting me up from the inside out. His pitch-black eyes were thrilling and made adrenaline surge through me.

No. I couldn't let him do this to me. Not now. I made a promise to Sky. I needed to be supportive, not distracted, and not alone in the hallway with Dayken.

I reached up, gripping the lapels of his tux, and spun us around so quickly that he probably thought the room shifted. The look of surprise on his face was almost satisfying as I slammed his back into the wall, not with full force, but enough to make him realize I was serious. Enough to show I was stronger, despite his larger size. I had to regain control. He made things confusing and disorienting, and I hated it. This unwanted attraction clashed with my logic. He was so beautiful, and I hated how much attention he drew to himself looking like that.

"Grab me like that one more time, Dayken, and I promise you'll regret it."

He had the audacity to smile, that annoyingly flawless side grin. His eyes were dark as night, filled with defiance. "I have zero regrets right now," he said, revealing a hint of his double fangs.

Watching him struggle to control his wolf made my stomach tighten and my skin tingle. That unexpected reaction stirred something deep and primal within me that I couldn't ignore. I'd experienced fear, anger, desperation, even rage — but this felt different. It was alien and unsettling, yet undeniably powerful. Before I could process the tumult of thoughts in my mind, I closed the distance and pressed my lips to his.

The response was instant. His arm locked firmly around my waist, yanking me closer, as if he couldn't stand the distance between our bodies. His other hand slid up the back of my neck, fingertips grazing my hairline, sending a shiver down my spine. Then his grip shifted, becoming rough, possessive. His fingers dug into the nape of my neck with enough force to remind me just how strong he was. Not that it mattered; I still had his lapels in a death grip. There was no way I'd let him pull back, though he didn't seem to have any intention of doing so.

His growl deepened, reverberating through me, and his hold tightened to a bruising intensity. He kissed me with a hunger that stole the air from my lungs, as though he'd been waiting his entire life for this moment. As if this was inevitable, like we'd always been meant to collide like this, all control shattered and left behind.

The thrill of seeing my gentle, protective wolf unravel sent a wave of pleasure through me, a sensation I'd never felt before. He wasn't holding back; he handled me with a raw intensity that left my body humming. A soft moan escaped my lips before I could stop it, and his fingers at my nape tightened in response, igniting something deep inside me.

His touch was rough, unrelenting, and somehow perfect. It felt like home.

Home.

Wait. Sky was my home, not him.

The thought hit me like a wave, snapping me back. My mind reeled, breaking through the fog he'd pulled me into. I'd left Sky alone in that room full of strangers. I suddenly couldn't breathe, quickly breaking the kiss.

What was *wrong* with me? My mind whirled with a dozen conflicting emotions. I swiped the back of my hand across my mouth, knowing my lipstick was smudged, as if I could erase what had just happened. I moved back toward the doors, and Dayken's eyes followed my every move. I could tell he was about to stop me.

"Wait, we should talk," his voice low, breathless but insistent.

"No, we shouldn't." I tossed the words over my shoulder, not even looking back.

With that, I pushed open the doors and walked back into the crowded room, trying to compose myself. My pulse was still racing, my mind a chaos of thoughts I didn't want to examine. I only came here to appease, not to play nice with him or his clan, but now I felt trapped. I waded through a sea of strangers with fake smiles and stiff clothes. Still, I kept walking, scanning the ocean of unfamiliar faces until I caught Sky's scent in the air. My senses guided me across the formal dining hall, where I found her still greeting a long line of eager clan members.

I must have approached Sky more aggressively than intended, because her first words were, "Are you alright?" I gave her a curt nod as I settled in next to her, reminding myself exactly where I belonged.

The greetings resumed, and as time passed, we were given more freedom to move about as we spoke with various clan members. It was impossible to tell who was wolf, bear, or falcon, but I was starting to pick up on subtle traits and scents.

I felt Dayken's presence behind me, but didn't dare look at him. I wanted to push that impulsive moment out of my mind for as long as I could.

Just as I was about to greet the next clan member, I heard Dayken's sharp, commanding voice: "Back. Up."

It was the harshest I had ever heard his tone — firm, authoritative, leaving no room for question. Then his hand slipped around my waist, pulling me firmly against his chest.

I tensed, my brain scrambling to process the sudden shift. But I didn't pull away. Letting him guide me, I felt myself melt into his embrace despite everything. I hated being touched… but somehow, with him, it was different. My thoughts fizzled, scattering in directions I did not want them to go. But Dayken was tense, anger radiating off him in waves. I needed to understand why.

"Oh, come on, buddy," the man in front of us drawled, his charming smile curling into a smug grin as his eyes locked on Dayken over my shoulder. "Is that any way to greet an old friend?"

The man remained calm and confident, completely unfazed by the angry wolf behind me. His short, golden hair was swept to the side in a sleek style. His sun-kissed skin glowed as if he'd just strolled in from the beach. His mocha eyes gleamed with composure, and his tall, warrior-like frame was accented with gold accessories that flashed on his wrists and fingers. He looked like money, and no doubt, plenty of women here would trip over themselves for a chance with him.

But me? Nothing. No spark, no thrill. He didn't make my heart race or my cheeks flush. Not like someone else did. Someone who was currently standing far too close, making me feel as though the only place I'd ever be safe again was in his arms.

The man's brow arched, his gaze taking on a subtle glint of challenge. Dayken's grip on me tightened, his silent warning impossible to miss.

"Friend my ass," Dayken growled, his voice low and dangerous. "Back up, or I'll take this as a direct insult to my clan." His arm flexed, barely holding himself back — a silent promise that nothing would slide.

To my surprise, the man stepped back, placing his hands in his pants pockets, as if we were discussing the weather. "Calm down, wolf. I was just admiring your vampire's beauty." His eyes slid back to me with a sneer. It didn't escape me that he said 'vampire' and not 'Sacar,' like everyone else. "Sweetheart," he added, his voice dripping with arrogance. "Why don't you let a real man protect you instead of this puppy?"

Dayken froze completely behind me. I let out a sigh. There went my promise to Sky about behaving. Without a second thought, I flicked my blade loose from its thigh holster. Keeping the blunt edge pressed snuggly against my wrist, I brought it up swiftly, pressing the cold steel to the man's throat.

Dayken loosened his grip on my waist, the silent gesture an unspoken approval; he was perfectly fine with this man's beheading tonight.

The golden-haired bastard froze, his arrogant expression faltering as his eyes widened. I leaned in slightly, my voice low and sharp as steel in my hand. "Insult my wolf again, and it'll be the last thing you ever say."

I felt, and even heard, the way Dayken reacted to my words. His heartbeat quickened at the word *my*, and the pride radiating from him was almost tangible as he watched me hold my ground. His silent support was steadying, a presence I hadn't realized I needed.

"Onyx, let me introduce you to Leonardo DeStephano from the DeStephano Clan," Dayken introduced, as if I didn't currently have a knife to the man's throat.

I didn't respond, holding my position. Leonardo remained frozen, his confidence momentarily shaken. Dayken's voice rumbled dangerously behind me, directed at him.

"Not only is she mine, but I'd love to see you try to look after her," he said, his tone dripping with menace. "It'd be hilarious, for the five seconds you'd last before she rips you apart." His hand lingered at my waist, possessive and grounding, as if silently telling Leonardo who I belonged to, whether I liked it or not.

Leonardo's grin returned as he took a small step back, giving my blade just a little more space. "Now that's more like it," he purred, his eyes gleaming with amusement. "I do enjoy a challenge. And since we're getting acquainted, call me Leo." He winked, and a fresh wave of anger surged through me. Between Leonardo's arrogance and Dayken's closeness clouding my thoughts, it was all I could do to stay in control.

"Listen closely," I snapped, my blade still poised. "If you're here just to stir up shit with me and my wolf, I'll slit your throat without a second thought. But if you have business, say it now."

Leo's expression barely shifted. "I didn't come to fight," he said with a dismissive shrug. "Curiosity got the best of me, that's all."

"Well, you know what they say — curiosity killed the cat," Dayken muttered, his voice low and edged with warning.

Leo's eyes sparked as he caught the meaning instantly. He gave a faint, amused nod. "Yes, well," he replied, his voice dripping with sarcasm. "We cats do have our ways." His gaze slid back to me, a silent dare lingering in his smirk.

"Consider your curiosity satisfied," I said coldly. "I am Onyxiana, and this is my Guardian, Dayken. Nice to meet you, now goodbye." I gestured toward the exit with a mocking flourish.

Leo's smile faltered, just a fraction, but he nodded, clearly aware he was outnumbered. As he turned to leave, he locked eyes with Dayken, a glint of dark promise in his expression.

"I'm rarely denied anything, and I always get what I want. Keep that in mind, friend." With a smirk, he strode off, confidence unshaken.

I watched him leave, still processing the encounter, and realized I'd relaxed into Dayken's chest. His proximity, his solid presence — it was undoing me, melting my tension. I lifted my head to meet his gaze, finding him already watching me. "Care to explain?" I deadpanned.

"He's an ass," Dayken replied, his voice rough with restrained anger. "I don't know who invited him. The clans will have to gather to figure it out." He shoved his hands in his pockets, trying to appear unaffected, then added, "Let's not let him ruin our night."

"Consider it ruined," I shot back, unamused. "I repeat, what was that all about?"

Dayken sighed. "Stubborn woman." He paused, tension tightening his jaw, then finally said, "I'm pretty sure he just declared war on my clan."

The words hit me hard, and I spun in his arms to face him fully.

Chapter 20

Her beautiful, eerie eyes were shadowed with confusion and concern, making her look even more irresistible. In her rush to turn, she forgot to step back, leaving her chest pressed against mine. I felt every curve as I kept my hand on her lower back, knowing she'd likely pull away once she realized how close we were. But for now? Heaven.

"Wait, what? Did you say *war?*" Her voice was urgent. "War meaning something other than the literal definition, correct?"

"No, war means exactly that, conflict, bloodshed." I held her gaze, knowing I'd have to elaborate. "Our kind has been at war with each other for years, Onyx. We've lost a lot of lives fighting over money, power, territory, and status. It's... not like the human world."

She looked confused, and I remembered she'd been confined for over twenty years. She couldn't really understand clan dynamics or the silent power plays in alliances. She didn't realize clans might fight each other, but when it came to humans? We'd close ranks every time. Keeping us hidden was the one thing we all agreed on.

"When a Sacar chooses a Guardian, it's the highest honor a clan can achieve. It also elevates the Guardian's status. But more importantly, it comes with..." I hesitated, searching for the right words. "Enhanced powers. Abilities, if you will."

My hand stayed on her back, feeling her steady breath, knowing she was absorbing this.

Her eyes sparkled with understanding, though still piecing things together. "Enhanced abilities?"

I nodded. "Clan leaders have a title: Primarc. They're already powerful, but when bonded… those abilities amplify. Being Primarc comes with responsibilities. They hold everything together, where the clan lives, trains, and raises children. The finances. They help everyone blend into the human world. Imagine a kid accidentally shifting in math class. Detention would be the least of his problems."

Her expression shifted as things began to fall into place. "So… bonded or not, these Primarcs battle for control and money with their clans at their back?"

I gave a small nod. "And with control and money comes…"

"Power," she finished, her voice barely above a whisper. Then her gaze sharpened. A glint of realization lit her eyes. "You're a Primarc."

I nodded slowly, watching as her eyes swept the room. Realization settled across her face; she understood now. I wasn't just part of this clan. I was responsible for it. But, just as quickly, something changed in her. She stiffened slightly, her gaze narrowing like she suddenly remembered exactly who she was talking to.

I wasn't sure what she was thinking, so I pressed forward. "So is Alicia. We're not all power-hungry like Leonardo. Derek and Chase's clan doesn't have a Primarc at the moment, so I help where I can. Eventually, they'll either share the title or choose who carries it."

Her eyes widened, like something just clicked, something important.

"I need to find Sky," she blurted.

"She's fine," I said, keeping my tone calm and grip firm, unwilling to let her slip away. "I've been listening for her. She's over by the stage, talking to Chase." I noticed a flicker of frustration cross her face, as if she was kicking herself for not doing the same, but before she could pull away, I leaned in to whisper in her ear. "I've got you," I said, my double meaning clear.

Her eyes narrowed, and her expression hardened. "Let go of me. You are making my brain all foggy," she said with a frown. "I don't like it." I chuckled and released her, amused by her irritation. So, she didn't enjoy it. I decided then and there to make it my life's mission to figure out how to make her.

"I do," I said, watching as a wave of goosebumps spread across her skin — a reaction she could not hide, and one I was quickly coming to adore.

"You two look… rather intimate," an older woman's voice interrupted. Onyx spun away from me, startled by the clan member's sudden appearance. The older woman looked familiar — one of Alicia's people, though I couldn't place her name. Her gaze was sharp as she added, "Might I remind you, Mr. Danielson, that your first duty is protection. Not fraternizing with your charge."

"Yes, ma'am, I'm aware," I said evenly, keeping my voice polite but firm. "And I kindly ask that you remember I serve as a Primarc. I take my duty seriously. Always." I kept my voice calm, not wanting to stir more gossip or suspicion. The last thing we needed was someone from within the clan questioning my judgment, especially with the DeStephano Clan already nosing around.

The woman quickly dipped her head, placing her hand over her heart in a gesture of respect. "Yes, of course, my apologies, Primarc. It's just been so long since we've had any new Sacar in our ranks. I'm only concerned for their well-being. And… it's such a shame about Kolton, too."

Onyx's voice cut in, cool and sharp. "Worry about yourself. I don't need anyone worrying about my 'well-being,'" she mocked for emphasis. The woman gasped, her eyes wide with shock as she clutched a hand to her chest like Onyx had struck her.

Nice one, Onyx.

"Now, if you'll excuse us…". I steered Onyx away, leading her over toward Sky. She shot me a look that was equal parts annoyance and curiosity, but I ignored it, keeping her close to avoid any further *conversations* with the wrong people. As I led her away, I glanced down, noting the fire simmering in her eyes.

She is pissed.

Once we reached Sky, I could tell Onyx wasn't about to let that interaction slide. She spun toward me, her expression dark.

"Fraternizing?" she snarled, her voice low and furious. Sky raised an eyebrow, while Chase suddenly found a great interest in the ceiling tiles.

And then, as if conjured by the universe's worst timing, Derek appeared beside us, grinning like he'd just hit the jackpot. "Oh, fantastic! Are we finally going to address the intense sexual tension between you two?" he asked, grinning around a mouthful of cheese he'd just snagged from a nearby plate, utterly unbothered by the agitation around him.

"There is no sexual tension!" Onyx hissed, her eyes flashing as her pupils narrowed to slits.

Derek tilted his head, unconvinced. "Hmm. Sounds like someone doesn't know what sexual tension means." He raised one finger, pointed toward the ceiling, then slowly brought it toward a circle formed by the fingers of his other hand. "Allow me to illustrate—"

"Derek!" Sky cut in quickly. "I've been dying to try champagne. Could you take me to find some?" She linked her arm through his, effectively steering him away before he could do any more damage. Chase trailed behind them, shooting daggers at Derek's back before glancing at us apologetically.

Onyx looked like she wanted to protest Sky's sudden departure, but was too fired up to let this go. "Explain," she demanded, crossing her arms and staring me down, fierce as ever. I held her gaze, captivated by that beautiful, stubborn fire of hers.

"I think she saw us together and ran with her own assumptions. Assumptions that, frankly, I couldn't care less about." I took a step closer, my voice steady. "I will protect you. And I'll probably keep looking at you like the goddess you are."

I gestured toward her, taking in every inch of that tight-fitting dress. "You can't blame me, Onyx. Even the Greeks couldn't sculpt this kind of perfection." Then I gave her a wink — part tease, part truth — hoping she caught on that beneath the calm, I was undeniably drawn to her.

Her eyes widened at my confession.

Her next words came out breathless, not entirely her own. "So, just from the way you were looking at me… that random woman assumed we were involved?"

She was trying to sound indifferent. But my words had affected her.

"Yes." It was all I could say. I wouldn't sugarcoat this. Onyx deserved the truth.

Her gaze flickered to the crowd, expression unreadable, but tension lingered in her shoulders. The weight of unsaid words hung between us, but pressing wouldn't get me anywhere right now.

"Let's get back to the others," she said briskly, as if what just happened hadn't affected her at all. She turned and walked towards Sky, who was now laughing at something Derek had said.

I followed, maintaining a respectable distance, and observed how she carried herself, always guarded, always in control. Yet, I could tell she was still holding something back.

As we rejoined the group, Alicia gave me a knowing look. I nearly rolled my eyes, but before anyone could comment, a loud chime sounded through the hall, signaling the evening's final announcement.

One of Alicia's clan members grabbed the mic. "Ladies and gentlemen, our evening is coming to an end. We're thankful to the Ravensfield sisters for their presence tonight. Let's raise a final toast to welcome them home."

Glasses lifted, and cheers rang out. I glanced at Onyx, her face framed in candlelight, her eyes still guarded — but softer — as she raised her glass. She met my gaze for the briefest moment. Something flickered there, a trace of acknowledgment.

Then the room broke into applause, and the crowd began to disperse.

"Shall we?" I asked, nodding toward the doors as Sky slipped her hand into Onyx's.

Onyx gave a faint nod.

As we left the ballroom, I couldn't shake the feeling that while the night was ending, this was only the beginning.

Chapter 21

In the days before the move, I shut myself away
from everyone, only surfacing occasionally to check on
Sky. I mostly stayed in my room, running through every
possible scenario in my mind. The thought of things
going sideways seemed almost inevitable. It gnawed at
me constantly.

I'd learned the hard way that if something felt too
good to be true, it probably was. As a child, living in
blissful ignorance, I was certain we were untouchable.
And ever since we were taken, I promised myself never
again. I wouldn't put my faith in a false sense of security.

Sky, on the other hand, was completely absorbed in
this dream of a new life. She kept updating me on clan
politics, breaking things down in a way that actually
made sense. She explained what it really took to form a
clan, not just strength, but structure, leadership, and
balance. I'd assumed a clan had to be made up of the
same species — all bears, all wolves — but that wasn't
necessarily the case.

For the most part, clans tended to stick with their
own kind. It was simpler that way, ensuring their
environment and resources were tailored to their specific
needs. Wolves thrived in packs, bears preferred solitude,
and falcons needed open skies. However, some species
could coexist, sharing territory and resources under a
single leader, as long as they obeyed their Primarc's
commands. It was about survival and hierarchy, not just
biology.

It deepened my understanding of Dayken, his demeanor, his authority, and the tensions that hinted at a clan war. Sky revealed a complex world of alliances and rivalries, much deeper than I ever expected.

When moving day finally arrived, a small, undeniable glimmer of relief blossomed within me as I took in the newly renovated compound. Sky and I had a new place, a place that was secure, safe, and isolated, just for the two of us.

Well, almost.

"Absolutely not, Dayken," I deadpanned, crossing my arms as I glared at him. He ignored me, continuing to haul boxes from the trunk to the loading dock.

"I'm sorry, but you're not stopping me," he replied, not even sparing me a glance. There was no trace of his usual smirk, which was honestly a little unsettling. He was serious.

Great.

"You two fight like an old married couple. It's kinda cute," Derek quipped, strolling over to the loading ramp with that obnoxious grin.

"SHUT UP, DEREK!" we both yelled in unison. To my amazement, he actually took the hint, spinning on his heel and heading back the way he came.

I refocused on Dayken, who still hadn't stopped unloading boxes. "Listen, this is not what I agreed to. I am fully capable of keeping the two of us safe, and so is the massive security center downstairs. There is *no* reason for you to stay here."

"Onyx, you won't even know I'm here." He hefted another box, placing it firmly on the dock. "I'll keep to myself, set up on ground level, while you and Sky have the basement."

He is *serious.*

I had been so close to being alone with Sky without anyone hovering. Now he was pulling *this*? Why couldn't he stay at his place? Why did he have to be so close? My mind scrambled, trying to figure out how to keep him out of here. How could I keep Sky safe with him here distracting me?

Damn him.

"Why? Why can't I break this damned bond and finally be *free*?" I muttered, defeated, hands dropping to my hips as I stared at the ground, desperately searching for a way out of this mess. I glanced up just in time to see the look on Dayken's face.

Hurt.

I'd hurt him. Damn it.

"Dayken, I'm sorry, I just meant—" He held up a hand, cutting me off.

"I know what you meant." His emerald eyes were full of pain, that beautiful gaze practically tearing me apart. Guilt hit me like a punch to the gut. "I'll be here," he continued, "unfortunately for you. And I was more or less preparing you, not asking for permission." With that, he turned and headed toward the main hall, leaving me standing there, stunned.

I clutched my chest as an unfamiliar feeling took root. What was wrong with me?

"You're probably just upset because he's mad at you," Derek said, strolling back with an armful of equipment. He glanced at me, eyes gleaming with mischief. "I mean, I *could* be wrong, but it kinda seems like, deep down, in that I-will-kick-your-ass-for-breathing-my-air heart of yours, you might actually care about him." He beamed, looking far too pleased with himself. "Oh, and by the way, we're living here too. Hope you like the smell of microwaved tuna." He grinned like he won a battle I didn't realize we were having, let alone one I just lost, as he turned to carry another box inside.

You've got to be fucking kidding me.
Oh, fuck this!

I stormed past Derek, throwing open the stairwell door so hard it slammed, then hurried down, taking two steps at a time, fists clenched. Why couldn't Dayken see my perspective? Sky was always my top priority. If he understood that, I wouldn't have shut him down so hard.

Once in the stairwell, memories flooded my mind. Sky's screams echoed through the facility's corridors, loud and relentless, as if they were alive in my head. My hands flew up to cover my ears, desperate to block out noises that weren't real. I felt hot, flushed, with damp palms pressed over my ears, tightening to stop the onslaught.

Stop.
Stop!
STOP!

The screaming in my head faded to a decrescendo as I fought to regain control of my thoughts. I reminded myself repeatedly that it was over. Just a memory. She was here, safe. No one could hurt her, no one ever would. Whatever it took, I'd make sure she would never scream like that again. *Never.*

I would burn the whole world down, and everyone in it, if it meant she was safe.

If Dayken knew this, maybe he'd give us space. He might let me protect Sky as I saw fit, but then I'd have to open up to him, reveal a darkness I didn't want him discovering. My demons were mine. I'd fought them my whole life, and fighting them with Dayken didn't seem possible.

Back in my new room, I was lost in thought, tearing tape off boxes full of things that weren't mine. I'd planned to unpack, but froze when I truly looked around the room. It felt like an office, with dreary wallpaper, dull paint color, and a simple bed where a receptionist's chair might've been. They'd tried to soften it with a lamp and linens, but the buzzing ceiling tiles and scent of paper and toner made it feel more like a workplace than home.

Dayken's hurt expression sliced through my thoughts again. Why?

Do I need to apologize or something?

Technically, I hadn't done anything wrong. Wanting my space wasn't a crime. The real issue was the guilt, a new, unwelcome feeling I couldn't shake. I made my choices with confidence; each action backed with clear intent. So why now, at this moment, was I so scattered and unsettled?

Without even realizing it, I found myself walking through the compound's corridors, thoughts swirling, and ended up outside Dayken's door, as if instinct drew me there.

"Come in," Dayken said before I even had a chance to knock.

I opened the door to find him sitting on his new bed, rummaging through a small box. And he wasn't wearing a shirt.

I paused, caught off guard. I felt like an idiot as my gaze lingered on his perfectly defined chest and shoulders for a second too long. So many hard lines… he was just so damn beautiful. His hair skimmed his brows, dangerously close to hiding those perfect green eyes — *and what a shame that would be.* The same eyes that were currently staring at me, waiting for me to speak.

Focus, Onyx.

"Are you okay? I felt a flicker of something through the bond, but it came and went so fast I wasn't sure if I imagined it," he said, then added, "I didn't want to come check on you immediately… figured I should give you some space."

Not wanting to disclose my little episode in the stairwell, I just nodded noncommittally. I stepped into his room and shut the door to make sure the others couldn't eavesdrop.

"Look, I'm sorry for what I said." My words tumbled out faster than I'd planned. "I didn't mean to upset you... Well, maybe I did…" This had sounded better in my head, but I kept going. "Who knows? I don't even understand my own feelings anymore."

Dayken froze, probably as stunned by my apology as I was. After a beat, he set down the box and shifted to face me fully, his gaze steady and focused, clearly waiting for me to continue.

He seemed to expect me to say more. But… what more was there to say? Also, his muscles were *very* distracting.

His patient look urged me on, and before I could stop myself, I blurted, "You get in my head, and it's confusing. Because I never know what's real and what's just the bond. I was looking forward to being away from you, you know? So I could get my head on straight."

The confession left my lips before I even realized I was saying it. "I kissed you, and now all I can think about is why… but also, when I can do it again." I let out a sharp breath, shaking my head. "And I don't understand why I'm thinking about that when there are much more important things to figure out."

I jabbed a finger toward my temple, as if that might somehow make him understand the chaos unraveling inside me.

Perfect. Great job, Onyx.

Dayken slowly rose from the bed, his eyes locked on mine, still silent. His full height was intimidating, and his bare chest was mesmerizing.

I watched as he prowled closer, each step deliberate and unhurried, testing me and my resolve. Instinctively, I took a step back for each step he took forward.

I had no idea what was going on in his head, what he was thinking. His face revealed nothing. No smirk, no hint of amusement. Just unwavering intensity. "Wha—"

Before I could finish, he reached out, grabbed the back of my neck roughly, and pulled me toward him, his grip firm and unyielding. Damn his reflexes. And those veins cording up his forearm. Damn *him*.

Holding me close, he murmured, "You get in my head, too. Difference is, I *enjoy* it." He pressed closer, and in doing so, I could feel the bulge in his pants as it hit my belly button. But somehow, I knew I needed that hard ridge to be pressed lower, much lower. I didn't have any experience in this department, but what my body craved was pure instinct.

How is he doing this to me?

"This… this scares me." I barely realized I'd spoken aloud.

Dayken leaned back just enough to meet my gaze, the intensity in his emerald eyes making fireworks ignite in my stomach, lighting me up from the inside. There was a knowing look in his eyes that told me he knew exactly what this was.

"There's nothing to be scared of," he murmured, his deep timbre wrapping around me like a promise. "I'll protect and cherish this." As he spoke, his grip shifted, and his hand lowered to my bonding mark. His fingers brushed the exposed skin above my tank top with deliberate care. The touch was soft, reverent, matching the weight of his words. The warmth of his palm against my mark sent a shiver through me, anchoring me to the moment, to *him*.

"You can trust me," he whispered, and for a moment, I just let myself *take him in.*

For years, I'd had no real point of comparison, no exposure to men beyond the ones who locked me away. And I didn't trust them. I didn't admire them. I didn't study their faces; I only learned their voices, so I knew who to brace for.

But after that ball, after seeing people, I was finally free to observe; I knew with certainty that he was the most beautiful man I'd ever laid eyes on. And not just outwardly either. There was something in the way he looked at me, steady and unflinching, that made me want to believe him.

And somehow, that made trusting him even harder.

As if sensing my hesitation — my undeniable pull — he moved. Without warning, he seized my lips like he'd been starving.

This kiss was different from the one before, deeper, all-consuming. It made me forget everything else. The threat, the potential for clan warfare, even my sister, faded from my mind, which should have been alarming.

But all I felt was the tension melting from my body as I surrendered to the moment, surrendered to him.

His lips were perfect. Full, insistent, owning every second. And I let him.

I lifted my hands, gripping the back of his neck, pulling him closer, locking him to me. One hand drifted up, fingers sliding through the shaggy lengths of his hair. It was so much softer than I expected, and I felt like I could lose myself in the simple act of running my fingers through it.

I couldn't get close enough, pressing myself against his hard, bare chest, trying to mold my body to his. This was reckless, but I didn't care. I was right where I wanted to be.

He broke the kiss, and before I could protest, he began nipping and kissing my jawline and then my neck. He stopped his pursuit and inhaled deeply against my skin, growling so loud it made my body reverberate from the sound. "You smell so fucking good," he rasped out, as if struggling for control.

Dayken resumed his fiery kisses down my neck, each one sending shockwaves through my body. Emotions I had never felt — possibly desire and pleasure — surged through me, settling in the sensitive area between my thighs. As he kissed lower, trailing down to my collarbone and over my heart, where my bond mark rested, I found myself rising on my toes to align my hips with his.

Before I knew it, I was shamelessly grinding myself against him. The almost roar of a moan that escaped him was all the encouragement I needed to know that the small movement felt as good for him as it did for me. And I wanted more. So much more.

"Tell me what you want," he murmured, his voice a low, rumbling command.

"I don't... I just... don't stop, please," I stammered, my voice barely above a whisper.

His answering growl sent shivers racing down my spine as his hands slid up my sides, grazing the sides of my breast with his thumbs, as if he already knew exactly what I needed. He began kissing me again, hard and desperate, as his huge hands began sliding the strap of my tank top off one shoulder and then the other. I untangled my fingers from his hair to help him, exposing the top swells of my breasts.

"Part of me doesn't want to ask," he murmured, resting his forehead against mine as he caught his breath, his tone carrying a dangerous edge. "But I have to know how gentle to be... and I'm feeling my control slip. Have you ever been touched like this before?"

"N-no," I managed to breathe out, my voice trembling and unfamiliar, even to me.

"Good," he growled, the single word dripping with raw, possessive satisfaction.

His hands continued their deliberate journey, igniting a fire within me I never knew possible. Each touch left me burning, aching for more.

"Wait," I said suddenly, my voice breaking through the haze of desire.

He froze instantly, his gaze locking onto mine with an intensity that made my pulse race even harder.

"Have you?" I asked, the question slipping out before I could stop myself.

Dayken stilled, his jaw tightening as though his answer might threaten the moment.

Suddenly, the fog that clouded my thoughts began to lift. I pulled back slightly, needing to know, even though part of me dreaded the truth.

"Is that why you make me feel this way?" I demanded, frustration cracking through my voice. "Because you've done this before?" The thought had never occurred to me, and a flood of emotions overwhelmed me, unraveling me. My mind spiraled, falling apart as I grasped for control. This — this connection, this tension — was probably nothing for him, just another fleeting dalliance.

And then the questions came, relentless and unforgiving.

When was the last time he kissed another woman?
When was the last time he touched someone like this?
Did he have a girlfriend before I came back into his life?
An arranged marriage?
Wait — does he even need to marry because of his status in the clan?

The onslaught hit me like a tidal wave, and I couldn't stop it. My thoughts tangled and splintered into one another, making it impossible to breathe, to focus.

I almost missed his voice cutting through the chaos.

"You feel this way," he said, his tone steady but low, "because we are attracted to one another, Onyx." His fingers brushed against my face, tucking a strand of hair behind my ear with deliberate care.

"And I don't have much experience with the opposite sex," he continued, his words holding a quiet vulnerability. "But I have enough to not be completely blind to what this is."

But he clearly has some experience.

The emotions roiled inside me, threatening to spill over: disappointment, jealousy, hurt, embarrassment. They wouldn't relent, no matter how hard I tried to suppress them.

And then a thought struck me, an idea I couldn't shake, no matter how much it hurt.

If I had never been captured... would I have been his first kiss instead of whoever it might have been while I was locked away?

I stepped back, lifting a hand to keep him at a distance. He must have caught the alarm in my expression, because he quickly said, "Talk to me, Onyx. I just want to be honest with you."

"I hate the idea of you with another woman," I blurted out, my voice unsteady. "It *hurts* for some reason."

Dayken's body tensed, his breath hitching slightly as if my words struck something deep inside him. His emerald eyes darkened, flashing black for the briefest second, his wolf pushing against his control. His jaw tightened, his fingers twitching like he was fighting the urge to pull me flush against him again.

"That, *my goddess*, is jealousy," he murmured, his voice rougher now, weighted with something primal. His hand lifted, slowly and deliberately, to cup my chin. "And I hate to break it to you, but that means you *care*. A lot." His voice dipped lower, raw and edged with possession as he whispered in the shell of my ear. "You hate it because I *belong* to you. Just like you belong to me."

I stayed silent, my heart hammering so hard that it echoed in my ears.

I didn't want to belong to anyone. I belonged to someone my whole life. I was treated like property for over twenty years.

But… why didn't the idea of belonging to *him* scare me the way it should? It was startling, jarring, but there was no cold dread, no suffocating fear. Instead, the words settled inside me. It was something I didn't understand but couldn't deny.

As if sensing the shift in my mood, Dayken exhaled sharply, his hands flexing before he forced himself to take a step back, giving me space. His eyes still burned into mine, the wolf within him still prowling just beneath the surface, unwilling to let me go too easily.

Finally, I managed to find my voice. "I, um, I've got to go find Sky," I mumbled, turning before I could think too hard about what just happened.

Without another glance, I pivoted and left his room, my pulse still racing, my mind in complete chaos.

Chapter 22

Onyx

My heart was lodged in my throat as I left Dayken's room, my stomach twisting like I'd swallowed something sharp, and it refused to settle.

I hit the stairs to the basement again, realizing I was essentially running away. But I needed space from Dayken and these intense, overwhelming feelings he stirred up. They clutched me too tightly, too suddenly, and I didn't know how to handle them.

Maybe running was cowardly, but I couldn't feel ashamed for needing some distance. Still, I didn't get far. Laughter echoed down the hallway, coming from the new security room. I paused, hearing Sky's soft giggles alongside the deeper voices of Chase and Derek.

"…and then I was like, 'Dude, where'd your pants go?'" Derek exclaimed, prompting another round of giggles from Sky.

"Hey, how was I supposed to know that transforming would shred my clothes like that?" came Chase's reply.

"Oh, the *best* part," Derek continued, "was the sequence of events! One second, he's screaming to let go of his precious Lego castle — '*My masterpiece!*' — and then *poof!* A bird is flapping around, and a split second later: one very naked Chase." I hear the dramatic snap of his fingers after every point, with Sky laughing harder each time. "I swear, it was like a perverted magic trick."

Chase's reply came quickly. "In my defense, you broke everything you touched. That castle took days, I had every right to be upset!"

I took that moment to slowly ease from the hallway into the security room with them.

"Right, sure, upset is fair," Derek said with a mock-serious nod. "But Chase, my guy, that transformation was Oscar-worthy. I'm still recovering. It was traumatizing, really."

Sky let out a laugh, covering her mouth as Chase threw his hands up in mock surrender. The glow from the monitors caught the metal rings in his face, making them glint as he shook his head with exaggerated exasperation.

"Alright, fine," Chase conceded, a sly grin tugging at his lips. "But if we're dredging up old memories, let's talk about *your* most embarrassing moment, Derek."

"Oh, hey, Ox!" Sky interrupted, hopping off the desk with excitement. "What do you think of all this?" She gestured broadly, motioning to the wall lined with floor-to-ceiling multi-screens. "I've never seen anything like it," she beamed.

I glanced at the monitors, brow furrowing as I took in the setup. Some screens were blank, but others showed detailed views of the trees outside and the underground parking garage. When a bird flew across one of the screens, I realized they weren't just pictures — they were live feeds.

"Is this real-time or recordings?" I asked myself more than anyone else.

"As live as you and me, baby," Derek replied, with a cockiness that was borderline annoying.

Before I could tell him to never call me 'baby' again, Sky cut in. "We're going to be so safe here."

Despite my best efforts, I was starting to agree with her. This place was beginning to feel pretty secure.

"Only time will tell." I then remembered my pathetic escape from Dayken's room and the distance I was seeking. "Hey, I was thinking we could head back to the farmhouse. I forgot a couple things, and I know you wanted to borrow some books from Aurora," I said, turning to Sky.

"Oh, perfect! Let me text her and let her know we're on our way."

"Great, where are the keys?" I glanced over at Derek and Chase, who exchanged a look, clearly reluctant to answer.

I extended my hand, and keeping my voice firm, demanded, "Keys." The idea of a drive with my sister, windows down, crisp winter air hitting my face, seemed like just what I needed to cool off. And I was not about to play clan hierarchy games with these two feather-headed pains in the ass.

Chase shifted, crossing his arms over his distressed-looking T-shirt as he spoke cautiously. "Uh, where's Dayken?"

Not. In. The. Mood.

My nostrils flared, a warning that didn't need words. "What do you mean, where's Dayken?"

"Dayken will kill us if we let you go alone," Chase stated matter-of-factly. His tone was even, but his eyes darted to Derek for backup.

"Yeah, and I like living," Derek added with a 'duh' expression, fumbling with the keys hooked to his belt. "You should really take him with you."

I clenched my jaw, stepping toward the twins. "We're perfectly capable of grabbing a few things from the house without him," I said, my tone sharp enough to cut through their hesitation. "Now, keys."

Derek glanced at Chase for support this time, but finally sighed and reluctantly handed them over. "Fine, but if Dayken kills us, I'm holding you responsible."

I grabbed the keys without another word and turned toward Sky, who was waiting by the stairs, her eyes bright with excitement.

"See?" I said as we headed up to the loading dock. "We don't need anyone to babysit us."

I gripped the wheel tightly, eyes on the winding path that led away from the compound. The car jolted over the uneven gravel, tires crunching through the quiet as night fell. Bare trees clawed at the darkening sky, and the cold air signaled nearby snow. Sky sat excitedly, face to the window, eager for the view.

A flicker of satisfaction stirred in my chest. This… *this* was what I wanted for us. A chance to breathe real air. To live outside the cold, clinical cells that had defined our existence for far too long.

"So, what are we grabbing first?" she asked, leaning forward with anticipation.

"Some more blankets and pillows, and a few things I left behind," I replied, keeping my tone casual. "Just whatever we need to make that place feel a little less like a bunker."

Sky nodded, leaning back. Her gaze wandered to the trees, illuminated by the headlights. "This is nice. Just you and me for once, no one standing watch over us."

"Exactly," I muttered, relieved she felt the same way I did. My grip on the wheel tightened further as I thought of Dayken and the twins' insistence on staying with us at the compound. But for this drive at least, it was just the two of us.

We were about 15 minutes into the drive when a sudden flash of headlights illuminated the rearview mirror, sharp and blinding. They were coming up on us way too fast. My muscles tensed, and an involuntary, 'fuck,' had Sky spinning in her seat, alarm flickering across her delicate features as she twisted to look behind us.

The other car swerved erratically, its aggressive movements making my pulse quicken. "What the hell—" Sky began, but her words were cut short.

I had no time to react before the vehicle slammed into our back bumper, the jarring impact sending a thunderous crack through the air. The steering wheel wrenched violently in my hands as our car spiraled out of control.

The world turned into a chaotic blur of trees, crushed metal, and shattered glass. Sky's scream cut through the chaos, and my instincts roared to life as I fought to regain control of the car. But it was too late, the tires skidded across the slick pavement, and we careened off the road.

The last thing I saw before everything went dark was Sky's terrified face and her hand reaching for mine.

***

I snapped to attention, unsure how much time had passed. I felt an inferno around me — thick and suffocating. My senses were spiraling out of control, the world a hazy heat. I looked around to see orange flames engulfing the wreckage, sparks flying. I pushed myself upright, patting out the flames on my clothes, feeling my burns already begin to heal. As I staggered forward, my vision began to blur, and I emerged from the fire with charred skin and the remnants of my clothes. I was mostly unharmed, except for a sharp pain in my chest. But that ache wasn't from an injury; it was from the sickening realization that I was completely *alone*.

"Sky?" My voice came out hoarse, panicked.

I scanned the darkness, feeling lost and disoriented. I was about fifty yards from the road, and I quickly turned, searching for her, but found nothing — no trail, tire marks, bodies, or signs of movement.

Only emptiness.

"SKY!" I screamed, my voice cracking as I poured every ounce of desperation into my shout.

No response.

Panic gnawed its way up from my stomach to my throat, bile gathering as fear clawed its way higher and higher. I was going to throw up.

Where is my sister?

"SKYYYYY!" I bellowed into the empty woods. But deep down, I knew, I couldn't feel her presence anywhere. My senses didn't lie. Sky wasn't here.

No, no, no.

This couldn't be happening. We had been so careful… until…

Suddenly, a car sped toward me. I patted myself down, checking for weapons. I drew the bulky hunting knife from my waistband, removed the sheath, and let it fall to the ground. I gripped the knife against my forearm, ready. But then I heard a familiar, rapid heartbeat and caught a scent I was quickly becoming familiar with.

Dayken.

He threw the car into park and leapt out, his shaggy hair bouncing as he ran toward me, a mix of bulk and speed. Without a thought, I launched myself at him, wrapping my arms around his torso and holding him tight. He pulled me close, one hand cupping the back of my head, the other firmly around my waist.

"I need help…" I croaked, my voice barely a whisper. "They took her." I felt Dayken's muscles tense beneath my hold.

"Fuck," was all he could muster, his voice low and seething with anger. Then he pulled back to scan me from head to toe, assessing my injuries.

"They took her," I repeated, hysteria rising in my voice. "They're going to hurt her… I-I didn't protect her!"

I felt his head turn, his body shifting as he looked around us, his hold on me tightening. "Shhh, shhh, don't talk like that," he murmured, his voice a soothing balm in the chaos. He gently tilted my chin up, forcing me to meet his eyes.

"Look over there." He nodded toward the twisted wreckage behind me. "With a crash like that... no one would expect survivors." He paused, eyes narrowing as he took in more of the scene, his jaw tightening. "And... see the silver on the ground? Silver can't hurt you, but it can slow you down." His gaze darkened as the pieces started falling into place. "They knew what they were doing. They knew to take Sky, not you."

His eyes searched mine, steady and intent. "Which means... they're trying to lure you in. Sky's probably safe, for now. They need her... to get to you." He ran his hands up and down my bare arms in soothing motions. "If I had to guess, they want you for an exchange. Your life for hers."

Shaking my head in denial, I stepped back from Dayken. His steadying hands reluctantly fell away as I tried to process what he said. His analytical mind missed nothing. The shiny, molten drops of silver dotted the scorched ground like scattered harbingers as the smoke from the wreck billowed into the dark sky, thick and acrid. My eyes drifted downward, catching sight of my newly healed bullet wounds, the faint marks barely visible against my skin.

Those bastards shot me with silver. My body ejected it and healed, but the knowledge burned hotter than the wreckage. They knew how to incapacitate me without killing me. The realization sank in, pressing into my chest like a vice.

Soon, the smoke would attract attention, and someone would call the fire department. We needed to leave, but my body refused to move. I was rooted to the spot, my mind racing over how to proceed. I couldn't decide where to go or what to do. I was torn between rage, fear, and the desperate need to find Sky.

"Can you smell anything?" I finally asked, barely keeping my voice steady.

Dayken shook his head, inhaling deeply for emphasis. "Your senses are better than mine. All I smell is burnt rubber and gasoline."

Panic crept into my voice as I glanced around again. "I can't catch a single trail of her. I can't even tell which direction they went." The world around us felt like it was closing in, thick and stifling, amplifying my helplessness.

As the moments stretched on, my anxiety shifted into trembling, uncontrollable waves. My thoughts scattered, slipping away before I could grasp them. I couldn't think or breathe; I couldn't make sense of anything.

A piercing screech snapped me out of my downward spiral. Both Dayken and I turned our gazes skyward, just in time to see an enormous bird soaring effortlessly above us, its wings stretched wide against the darkening sky. It let out another deathly shriek, and I heard Dayken's sigh of relief beside me.

"Is that…"

"Come on, let's go," he cut in. "They're headed south."

Another massive bird appeared to the east, equally intimidating but darker in color. Its chilling cry echoed through the air.

Derek and Chase.

My brain scrambled to process what I was seeing.

Why are they here?

Have they come to help?

"Quick, let's move," Dayken urged, already breaking into a run. "We'll be faster on foot. And harder to track."

Nodding, I followed, my senses sharp. As I ran, I kept glancing toward the sky, watching the falcons fly in wide arcs, guiding us each mile. The trees blurred past me in a rush of motion, but Dayken kept pace. His stride matched mine as if he were made for it. He shouldn't have been able to keep up. Not without effort. Not at the speed I was pushing.

Maybe it was the bond. Maybe it was just him.

"They've got eyes on the cars," he said, his voice strained but steady. "But they think stopping them will be tough."

"You can understand them?" I asked incredulously.

"It's a gift we inherit," he replied without missing a beat. "There are three cars, but they can't tell which one has Sky from this height."

"Leave that to me. Once I'm close, I'll sense her."

The forest blurred past as we moved parallel to the road, angling to cut them off before they reached the highway. If they made it that far, every car and bystander would see the fight, and it would draw more attention than we could risk. While a few government agents knew about us, the clans had worked diligently for centuries to keep our species hidden. Humans react violently to the unknown, so we had to reach Sky before they crossed into any populated areas.

"How much farther?" I asked, my voice tight with urgency.

As if in answer, both falcons let out another synchronized screech, closer this time, the sound reverberating through the trees.

"Getting close, be ready!" Dayken shouted, his eyes scanning the darkened road ahead.

Something felt off. My senses prickled as I picked up another heartbeat nearby, faint but distinct, on the other side of the road.

"Did you tell Aurora or Alicia to come as backup?" I asked, my breathing shallow as I adjusted the grip on my knife.

"No, I didn't have time." Dayken's voice was strained between breaths. "I sensed something was wrong and got to you as fast as I could."

Damn it.

Chapter 23

Onyx

Something was out there, but I focused on running, dodging trees and branches. I couldn't slow down or lose focus. I had to get to Sky.

The falcons descended slowly, wings silently slicing through the cold air. The tension was high, my every nerve eager for action. I could hear their calm and steady wings, as if the situation didn't weigh on them as much as it did me.

Chase was the first to shift back to human form. I saw him somehow change mid-air, curling into a tight ball to soften his landing before springing up into a runner's stance. Without missing a beat, he launched into a sprint, staying ahead of us. The entire action was smooth, seamless, like he'd done it a thousand times before.

I focused on the path, determined to rescue Sky, only fleetingly realizing that I was now running behind a naked man. I quickly brushed the thought away. There wasn't time for modesty.

"They're just a mile up ahead," Chase yelled over his shoulder. "We're gaining on them. Derek is going to stay up there until we stop the cars," he added, pointing to the sky, where his brother still circled overhead.

I nodded, pushing myself harder.

The rumble of engines grew louder as we sprinted along the shoulder, gaining ground. We approached at an angle, the pavement inching closer with every stride. Up ahead, the line of cars barreled down the road. Their headlights sliced through the dark, still unaware they were about to be ambushed.

Derek's shadow swept over the treetops, stretched long and sharp by the moonlight. With a powerful beat of his wings, he dove, landing heavily in front of the lead car. He didn't fully shift back to human; his enormous brown wings remained unfurled, casting a menacing silhouette across the road. The driver slammed on the brakes, tires screeching as the car skidded to a halt in a desperate attempt to avoid crashing into him.

Meanwhile, Dayken launched himself at the second car, barreling into it with terrifying strength and flipping it with a fierce shove. The vehicle crashed onto its side, leaving the stunned occupants too shocked to react. I made a mental note never to question Dayken's abilities again.

As Derek distracted the lead vehicle, Chase and I hurried to the back car. Chase forced open the front door to deal with the driver, while I tore off the back door, discovering Sky slumped across the seats.

"Sky!" I reached inside, my heart pounding. Her eyes were closed, her breathing faint but steady. Carefully, I slid her off the seat, moving quickly, yet gently, as I pulled her into my arms.

Derek, wings still outstretched, landed beside me. I was shocked to see he could have both wings and human arms, but I shook it off. His expression was fierce as he motioned to Sky.

"Hand her to me!" His arms opened, wings curving protectively as he prepared to carry her away.

I hesitated; the thought of handing her off to him felt *wrong*. I could do this myself. I could get her to safety. A single moment was all it took for my lack of trust to cost us. By the time I realized an airlift was her safest — and fastest — escape, it was already too late. The attack came from out of nowhere.

A massive shape burst from the trees on the other side of the road, an enormous animal launching itself at me with blinding speed. I barely had time to react before it slammed into me, knocking both me and Sky to the ground.

What the fuck?

I pushed myself onto my elbows, my vision swimming, only to lock eyes with a creature I never expected to come face-to-face with.

The tiger was massive, its muscular body towering over mine with a threatening stillness. Its yellow, slitted eyes drilled into mine, radiating an intense fury I felt deep in my bones. Before I could fully register the danger, it kicked off me, its powerful weight nearly breaking my ribs as it forced me back to the ground.

The tiger made a beeline for Sky's unconscious body, sending a jolt of terror straight through me. I scrambled forward, my hands digging into the earth as I pushed myself up.

"Don't you *fucking touch her!*" I roared, the sound tearing from my throat as I tried to throw myself between the tiger and my sister, refusing to let this beast near her.

The tiger didn't stop. Instead, it dipped its massive head and gently clamped its jaws around the back of Sky's jacket, lifting her like a mother might carry a cub. Her body hung limp, arms swaying, but the tiger's grip was sure: firm, yet careful not to hurt her. With a guttural growl, it bolted forward, carrying her away with powerful strides, as if she weighed nothing at all.

I didn't hesitate. I abandoned the agents still in the cars and gave chase. *Damn.* The animal was fast, but not faster than me.

"Onyx, wait!" Dayken's voice rang out from behind me, but I didn't stop.

I heard him run after us as Derek and Chase stayed to finish off the government operatives. More falcons dove from the sky, their wings slicing through the night with talons and beaks, turning the road bloody. Good. Let them handle that; I had my own target.

I'd always admired tigers, in pictures, but this one was about to lose its head.

Let's see how beautiful it looks on my wall.

Dayken's voice cut through my murderous thoughts. "Kolton! Stop!"

Kolton?

The tiger slowed to a jog, then stopped, turning to face us before carefully laying Sky on a pile of leaves. I halted, visibly shocked as the tiger's form shifted — fur receding, muscles reforming until a tall, lean man with yellow eyes was there, crouching protectively over Sky.

Although my heart was racing, I remained calm, refusing to let him intimidate me.

That was *my* sister.

He growled, low in his throat. The sound resonated with an animalistic power; his gaze locked on me.

He *growled* at me.

"I will kill you," I said, my voice steady. Because, regardless of the circumstances, I would do anything if it meant protecting Sky.

Dayken quickly moved to stand between us, one hand raised toward me, the other stretched out to calm Kolton. "Let's just take a second here," he said firmly. "Kolton, this is Sky's sister, Onyx. Take a deep breath. We've managed to get both of our Sacars out of harm's way, so let's take a moment and calm down."

Kolton's gaze flickered between us as he processed Dayken's words, struggling to regain control. He took a deep, shuddering breath, his lean chest expanding as he wrestled with maintaining his human form. His forearms and legs, striped with orange and black hair, indicated his difficulty.

He was fit, no question, but his build was lean and agile, a stark contrast to Dayken's sheer bulk. Tiger and wolf — two animals that couldn't be more different. And yet here we were, stuck in the middle of this mess.

Also, was anyone planning on telling us that Kolton was a *fucking tiger*, not a wolf? That seemed like an important detail. I would need to ream Dayken out about it later, because I had questions — lots of them.

"Back away from my sister," I demanded, my tone unyielding.

"No." His response was short. His voice was deep and unsettling, like a barely restrained force of nature. His eyes held a wildness that hinted at an inability to be tamed or controlled, no matter who tried.

A disturbing thought flickered through my mind: *maybe I should just put him down.* But before I could act on it, Sky stirred.

Kolton's expression shifted instantly, his fierce gaze softening as he knelt beside her. His hands hovered over her, unsure where to touch, yet clearly desperate to do something.

"Dayken, get that naked animal away from my sister *now*. Or I will," I growled, my frustration redirected at him.

"Onyx, hear me out for one second," Dayken said, his tone calm but insistent. "Sky has never been safer than she is right now. She has you, standing ten feet away, ready to tear down any threat to her," he said, nodding in my direction. "And she has her chosen Guardian by her side. Plus, I'm here. She's safe. Kolton can't hurt her, even if he wanted to. Look at him. His only concern is making sure she's alright."

I slowly processed what he said, while my mind raced. It was a lot to take in. A part of me felt like Dayken was betraying me, but my rational side knew he was right.

Without a word, Dayken shrugged off his jacket and tossed it to Kolton, who caught it without looking up, his attention firmly fixed on Sky, before tying it around his waist.

That's better. I guess.

Chapter 24

Dayken

The tension in Onyx's shoulders eased slightly. Maybe, just maybe, I was getting through to her.

"I need to get her out of here — take her somewhere safe," Kolton said, his tone firm. His eyes were still fixed on Sky's semi-unconscious form.

Onyx responded with a hiss, baring her fangs at him.

Okay…. Well, maybe not.

Also… I've never seen her do that before.

Time for me to step in.

"Kolt, glad to see you're alive," I began, trying to keep my voice steady. "Look, we have a secure compound north of here, where Sky and Onyx are staying. We'll get her back there safely, no problem."

Kolton's gaze, wild and intense, didn't waver. He looked ready to bolt, all feral instinct. "Safe? How the fuck did this happen if she was so safe there? She's coming with me." Not a question — a statement.

"LIKE HELL SHE IS!" Onyx's voice rang out; her words laced with vitriol. I could tell by the look in her eyes that she was seconds away from ripping Kolton apart. Once she set her mind to something, stopping her was next to impossible.

FUCKING HELL.

This was going to be harder than I thought. Explaining what worked for one Guardian's Sacar to another was tricky enough, but Kolton wasn't just a Guardian. He was powerful, and he was bonded. That changed everything.

Not that Onyx knew the difference yet.

She'd never seen how clans treated a bonded Primarc, how that kind of connection elevated a leader from respected to revered, sometimes even feared. Bonded Primarcs didn't just hold power; they were seen as touched by something sacred. Chosen.

Kolton wasn't a Primarc… not officially. But the fact that he was bonded and had survived it as an infant put him in rare company. Dangerous company.

And whatever was happening between Onyx and me? Our bond was still unfolding.

Still undefined.

Still… mine to protect.

Kolton's gaze was steely as he moved to scoop Sky up, carefully sliding his hands under her back. But before Kolton got Sky fully off the ground, Onyx became a blur of fury.

One moment she was behind me — the next she had Kolton pinned to the ground by his neck, her hand raised to land a punch. But before she could strike, Kolton shifted, his tiger exploding out, raw and powerful. With a fluid movement, he rolled her to the ground, catching her fist in his mouth and clamping down, a warning growl rumbling through his chest.

A surge of protective instinct rose inside me. Onyx was hurt, and my wolf clawed for control, overwhelming reason in my need to defend her. But wars were started when protection overrode logic. Kolton's duty was to protect Sky, while mine was to protect Onyx. Neither of us had authority over the other's Sacar, despite Kolton being in my clan and me being Primarc.

Yet, none of that mattered. I'd go to war with anyone if it meant keeping Onyx safe.

"Enough!" I yelled, trying to break through the chaos. But my voice fell on deaf ears; neither of them was listening.

So, like any rational wolf, I leapt into the fray, dodging punches and swipes as best I could. Mid-scramble, a thought crossed my mind. I was in over my head, and this was going nowhere. Maybe it was time for a different approach…

"Sky is being left unprotected while the three of us fight one another." That got their attention.

They both froze. Onyx had one hand gripped on Kolton's bottom jaw, the other clamped around his top, poised to tear them apart. Kolton's massive paw was buried deep in her thigh, his claws sinking into flesh. Blood dripped down her leg in crimson streaks. The sight made my vision sharpen. My wolf surged forward, fangs elongating in response.

And I was in the middle of it all, straining to pry them apart before one of them did something neither could take back.

Finally, Onyx released her grip just as Kolton withdrew his claws.

"You can't have her," Onyx said, not even winded from her clash with a full-grown tiger shifter. The wound on her leg began healing before my eyes.

Damn, she is incredible.

Kolton shifted back to human form, grabbed the jacket, and looked at Onyx with an unreadable expression. "She is mine," he said flatly. He stated it as a fact, without emotion or hostility.

"No, she is not," Onyx said, her voice low and laced with venom.

Kolton didn't blink. "She chose me," he said, smacking the back of his neck where the mark sat. "Not you. You can't protect her like I can." He wasn't loud. He didn't have to be. His certainty landed like the sharp end of a blade.

Onyx stilled, her silence sharp, coiled, electric.

And I felt it… the shift. The kind that splits a room. Because no Guardian had ever spoken to a Primarc's Sacar like that.

Not unless the bond gave them the right.

And Sky had given him exactly that.

Chapter 25

Onyx

How fucking dare he...

Rage coursed through me, boiling over as I stepped closer.

If he wants to play dirty, then let's go.

"Oh yeah? If you're so good at protecting her, then where the hell were you while she was being tortured for twenty *fucking* years? Huh, asshole?"

My words hit him like a slap. His face twisted in pain, darkening as his brows drew tight. I wondered if he was about to cry. "Tortured..." he murmured, gaze turning vacant, as if he couldn't process its meaning.

"Yes, tortured. And you can't even begin to understand the things I had to do to get us out of there." My voice was steady, but my hands curled into fists at my sides. "I will protect her. Not you. That is *my* right — mine alone."

I stepped closer. My breath was steady, but my pulse was a raging storm. "I'll give you a choice: one, yield now, and I will let you follow us back to the compound. I'm sure Sky will want to talk to you when she wakes up. Or, two, you can die." My gaze was locked onto his, daring him to argue. "But you don't get to just waltz in out of nowhere, demanding to take the one thing I love in this world."

I hope he chooses the second option, 'cause I really want to stab him.

My words snapped him out of his trance, and his expression narrowed. Sensing the tension, Dayken stepped in. As Kolton opened his mouth to argue, Dayken held up a hand, cutting him off. I jumped at the opportunity, grabbing Sky and running back to Dayken's car. I caught a quick, muffled exchange between Kolton and Dayken but kept going.

Moments later, I could feel that damn tiger right on my heels. His presence loomed like a shadow. But he couldn't catch me.

Speed was *my* thing, not his. So, I ran faster.

Once in the car, I placed Sky in the back seat, slid in with her, and gently rested her head in my lap, brushing away debris and stray hairs from her face. The tiger jumped into the front, twisting in the passenger seat to face backward, eyes on Sky. I was about to snap at him for staring, but saw no improper gaze — he looked at her with concern. If I didn't despise him so much, I might have found it almost endearing.

Dayken climbed into the driver's seat. He caught my annoyance with that quiet awareness I was starting to rely on and shifted Kolton's attention. "Where have you been, man?" he asked, his voice steady but curious as he started the car.

"California," was the tiger's short, clipped response. He was clearly not in the mood for a chat.

"Michigan weather must ha—"

A loud screech filled the sky, followed by another one further away. I was beginning to recognize the sound now.

"Threat's gone," Kolton said before Dayken could even finish his sentence.

I owe those twins more than they could ever realize.

Which was a slightly jarring thought as far as Derek was concerned.

The car ride back to the compound was quiet. The silence was only broken by Dayken's attempts to draw Kolton into conversation, which were met with short, one-word replies. I couldn't help but sneak glances at Dayken's face as he drove. His calm expression and steady energy stood out sharply against the chaotic presence beside him in the passenger seat.

There was something about Dayken, an air of authority that was both alluring and commanding. It left me wanting to peel back his layers, to uncover the other sides of him. Like the rough edge I'd glimpsed in his room, the one that made my pulse race.

Lost in thought, I barely noticed how quickly the scenery blurred past. Before I knew it, we were pulling up to the compound. The facility agents had gotten much closer than I'd realized.

Too close.

I carefully tugged Sky's limp body from the back seat, cradling her as if she were made of glass. Her weight was negligible, but the emotional weight of her condition pressed down on me like a ton of bricks. My movements were deliberate as I carried her through the corridors, my senses prickling as Kolton's presence trailed behind me like a restless shadow. His energy, wild and barely contained, was unsettling. I didn't pause until I reached Derek's makeshift operating room. Compared to what they had for my surgery, this space was cleaner, better organized, and equipped with more advanced technology — a recent upgrade that gave it a professional edge. It was a small comfort, but one I clung to.

Derek stood waiting, already scrubbed in and with gloves on, his sharp eyes assessing Sky the moment I crossed the threshold. Then, as Kolton followed behind me, Derek's gaze flicked to him, his brow arching in silent question.

He recovered quickly, though, refocusing on Sky. "Lay your precious cargo here," he said briskly, gesturing to the exam table.

I carefully set Sky down, stepping back as Derek immediately got to work. His hands moved with the steady confidence of someone who knew exactly what he was doing. His touch was methodical, his focus unshakable, and for the first time since the crash, I felt a flicker of hope.

I stood at her side, watchful, while Kolton paced and growled from across the room. His growl was different from Dayken's — deeper, raw, and wild. It had an edge that made my skin crawl. The animosity radiating from him was clearly directed at Derek for touching Sky, even if it was to help her. If my temper wasn't already frayed, I might have appreciated Kolton's protective reaction. But as things stood, I wanted him gone.

In an effort to distract Kolton, Dayken handed him a sterile gown with a low murmur about getting dressed.

"The only thing I can conclude is that there's some internal bleeding, which her body's struggling to heal," Derek finally said, his voice steady but tense. "When was the last time she fed?"

"Two weeks ago," I replied, the memory coming back to me — it had been on our drive to Michigan. A wave of guilt crashed over me, thinking I hadn't done enough to make sure she fed regularly. But then I caught myself. Two weeks was recent enough. We were typically fine going months between feeds.

"She's going to need more blood," Derek continued. "That should speed up her healing."

"I'll give her mine," Kolton said from the corner. He had finally stopped pacing to focus on the conversation.

Derek just nodded. I wanted to stop Kolton from getting close to her, but I knew this was best for Sky. My judgment had allowed the facility to take her again — even if it was just momentarily. I needed to take a step back, even if it went against every instinct I possessed. I clenched and unclenched my fists as I watched him approach, each step testing my patience. Since I couldn't feed her myself, I had to set my personal feelings aside.

At least he had clothes now, a small but necessary win.

Dayken gently rested his hand on my back, snapping me out of my thoughts. "Can I speak with you for a moment?" he asked softly.

I didn't really want to leave Sky, but she was safe enough with the stray cat and bird brain watching over her. I nodded and followed him into the corridor, casting one final glance back. Kolton was staring at my sister as if she were some precious, long-lost treasure.

I really don't like this.

Once we were in the hallway, Dayken grabbed me and pulled me close, the possessive look in his eyes sending goosebumps down my arms. He looked at me like a starving man at a feast, as if I were the answer to all his unspoken hunger. He cupped my face with both of his massive hands, tilting my head to meet his gaze. "Are you alright?" he asked, his words rushed and breathless.

I nodded, unable to speak.

Without warning, he pulled me into his chest, his hand cradling the back of my head. He exhaled slowly, grounding himself, his grip steady but desperate. "You scared the hell out of me," he confessed, voice raw.

Guilt twisted in my chest. I didn't want to make him feel that way. I opened my mouth to respond, but I was at a loss for words, unsure if he was comforting me or if I was meant to comfort him. We stayed silent for a moment until he finally spoke.

"I've been thinking a lot about this," he said, his voice low but firm. "I want to step up our security and bring in some outside help — a potential ally."

Was he asking for permission or just warning me? So far, everyone he'd introduced me to outside of the ball had been reliable, so I didn't see a reason to doubt him. Still, it felt odd to ignore my gut, which told me to refuse the extra help. But I gave a slight nod and said, "Alright."

If he was surprised by my willingness, he didn't let it show. I waited for the conversation to pivot, fully expecting a lecture about running off without him. But it never came.

"There's a fox clan that my pack and others affiliate with sometimes," Dayken began. "They're allied with the DeStephano clan, the arrogant lion from the ball." He grimaced, clearly sharing my distaste.

I remembered that lion, and I remembered what Dayken warned me about — warring clans. It was easy to assume that if this fox clan agreed to an alliance with us, it would probably increase Leo's implied threat.

"With enough persuasion, I think I can get their Primarc to consider my offer," Dayken explained, his tone calculated. "They've wanted a property of ours near the water for years, because of how secluded it is. If I offer it to them, they might be more inclined to help us with what I have in mind."

"And what exactly do you have in mind?" I asked, my curiosity piqued. His focused, confident manner made it difficult to keep my thoughts straight. He seemed born for this role, and when he took charge, it was irresistible, distracting enough to make me lose my train of thought. Suddenly, the sharp, metallic scent of blood filled my nose, snapping me back to reality. Sky was being fed, and the tiger was the one providing the blood.

I need to be in there.

But Dayken's voice pulled me back.

"I want an arsenal," he said, clear and decisive.

Now that was an idea I could get behind. "Go on," I prompted.

"I've generally stayed away from arms dealing," he admitted. "But I believe it's time to bring in the Sharp Clan, the foxes. Time to meet with their Primarc: Titus."

The idea of a clan full of foxes struck me as oddly entertaining for a moment. Images of sly, fluffy creatures darted through my mind, tails puffed up and playful. But then his words hit me, *arms dealing.*

My thoughts snapped back to reality. These weren't the cute, cunning foxes you see in pictures; these were dangerous, likely deadly, foxes. And now Dayken was planning on forming an alliance with them.

"Just don't let your guard down," I said firmly, meeting his gaze and pushing aside the fleeting humor. "And I want to be involved in every single decision concerning my sister's safety."

"Of course," he agreed easily, without hesitation. Like he wouldn't have it any other way. For a moment, something shifted in me, an unexpected spark. A sense that we were really becoming a team… a true partnership.

My words felt stuck, like they were trying to find their way out, but couldn't. "You know… I've been waiting for you to lecture me about leaving without you," I began awkwardly, a rush of nerves prickling at the edge of my voice. "I… I realize I made a mistake. It's not easy for me to admit when I'm wrong, and — look, my intentions felt right in the moment." I trailed off, searching his face. "I just want you to know that I'm… learning. Navigating this. And I'm going to keep trying, okay?"

Dayken's expression softened as he moved closer. He gently ran his finger from the top of my shoulder and down to my elbow before stopping at my wrist, as if he needed to touch me, to ground himself, before speaking. It was a tender moment that filled me with warmth.

"I'm not here to control you, Onyx. You're free to do what you think is best — it's not my place to lecture," he said softly, his voice warm but firm. "But don't expect me ever to feel comfortable being apart from you." Then, to shred any lingering doubts about his feelings, he added, "Bonds be damned."

My heart raced at his words, locking eyes with his intense green ones. He was perfect. I fought the urge to close the distance between us. Instead, I took a breath and nodded. "I should check on Sky."

I pivoted to leave, but a firm yank on my forearm spun me back toward him. His grip was commanding, and his voice was low, edged with promise. "Don't think for one second that we're not revisiting that conversation from my room… among other things."

Shivers shot down my spine at his words, and as he released me, my pulse thundered in my ears. With one last look at Dayken, I stepped into the room, taking in the scene before me. Kolton held his wrist to Sky's mouth, his other hand supporting her head to angle it correctly. Derek stood close, watching Sky's throat for signs that she was swallowing.

Kolton watched Derek, who shook his head, and I saw a quiet defeat on Kolton's face. I stepped forward to intervene, but noticed Sky's finger twitch. Derek tapped Kolton on the shoulder, pointing to Sky's throat. Relief washed over us. She was swallowing the blood.

Sky's hands quickly moved to grip Kolton's forearm, holding his wrist tightly to her mouth. Derek looked at him, a silent question in his eyes, but Kolton waved him off, too focused on Sky. Despite the cuts, bruises, and tangled hair from the crash, she still looked so beautiful.

Eventually, Sky released her grip and opened her eyes. My sister and I had been through so much trauma together, survived things that would destroy most people. Yet it was still shocking to see her and Kolton share a silent, private look. It made me feel like an intruder.

Kolton hesitated, wanting to reach out but holding back. Sky stared, wide-eyed, not in fear but almost entranced. The tension in the room was suffocating, and the discomfort crept up on me until, finally, Sky broke the silence.

"Who are you…" she whispered, her voice soft, barely audible.

"Your Guardian," Kolton replied, his deep, unsettling voice vibrating through the room.

Sky's smile was angelic. She radiated genuine happiness and relief as her hand moved to rest on her bonding mark. Her torn shirt revealed the dark petals beneath, which seemed to visibly affect Kolton. He raised his hand to the back of his neck, but suddenly her smile faded. Her eyes closed, and her head went limp in Kolton's hand. His face turned frantic, and he hissed fiercely as he turned to glare at Derek.

Derek raised his hands in surrender. "She's just exhausted, dude, chill," he said, unfazed. Then, muttering under his breath, he added, "Tigers, not exactly known for their intelligence. Geez."

"Alright, get your hands off her," I snapped, stepping forward to take Sky. But the damn tiger growled at me, his yellow eyes blazing. I cocked my fist back, ready to knock that look off his face, but Dayken's hand shot out of nowhere, catching my wrist in midair.

Did I consider this a partnership earlier? More like a betrayal-ship.

That's all I felt as I glared at Dayken, fangs bared. I hissed at Kolton, low and venomous, since I'd lost the opportunity to punch him. Kolton hissed right back, his impressive canines flashing.

Mine are sharper.

Derek nervously smirked as he took in the scene. "Shit, Dayken, looks like you've got your work cut out for you," he deadpanned.

I yanked my hand free from Dayken's grip, raising it to flip off the tiger before I scooped Sky up and carried her toward her room. Kolton was right on my heels, stalking us like the uncivilized animal he was.

As I laid Sky's limp, exhausted body on her bed, I half-expected to confront the tiger about stepping foot in her room. But he didn't even cross the threshold. Instead, he paced back and forth in the hallway, looking like he was diseased or something.

Maybe he has rabies?

I'd have to tell Dayken that we needed to put him down immediately.

It didn't make sense that he insisted on staying so close to her yet didn't dare enter her personal space. Not that I was complaining — his presence alone was pissing me off. I didn't know how I'd react if he actually tried to put his filthy paws on her.

But his behavior was… odd. He didn't act like Dayken did around me. Dayken was steady, respectful, and always honorable. This thing outside my sister's door was unstable and savage, like he'd been cut off from society for far too long and was barely holding himself together.

As if conjured by my thoughts, Dayken rapped his knuckles softly on the doorframe before stepping in. He moved to stand beside me. His presence grounded me as we both watched over Sky in silence.

"Is he just going to pace out there until she wakes up?" I muttered, casting an annoyed glance at the door.

"I don't know," Dayken said, running a hand through his hair. "I'll talk to him. Something's definitely going on." He hesitated, then added, "There's an unspoken rule: don't stay in your animal form for too long. The rumor is, if you do… you lose yourself. No one in the surrounding clans ever dared test it. And since I never heard about a tiger roaming free across the states, I figured he knew better than to risk it.

"The animal inside us is powerful, dominating, untamed," Dayken continued, his voice lowered. "We're taught how to control it, how to work with it. But if you were to become it completely… to stop thinking like a man…" He trailed off, his gaze distant. "Looking at him now… I'm starting to think there might be something to those old rumors after all."

Well, that's unnerving, but at least Dayken recognizes his behavior as odd.

Dayken placed a hand on my elbow, gently drawing my attention back to him. "I want to talk with you about our next move." He must have read the hesitation on my face because he added, "Kolton physically can't hurt Sky. He would die for her, so it's okay to leave him with her."

That did little to calm my nerves, but I nodded. My room wasn't far from my sister's, anyway. And if the tiger so much as looked at her the wrong way, he'd have to answer to me — possibly two dumb birds and a loyal wolf too.

Chapter 26

Onyx

The next morning, I woke early for a run around the compound. Feeling safe behind the gates, I enjoyed the fresh air without needing to look over my shoulder. It felt right to set my pace and feel the gravel and grass beneath my shoes, burning off my restless energy. Especially today.

Titus would arrive soon. I felt like I was in a chess match, making a move the opponent didn't expect — an alliance with a fox— but still the smart play.

By my fourth lap, movement near the tree line caught my eye. There were a few trees inside the compound, but beyond the fence, Michigan's dense forest stretched out.

I slowed to a walk, heading to the entrance where Dayken was waiting with a towel. His smile warmed something in my chest as I climbed the stairs toward him.

I pointed over my shoulder, about to ask about the movement I saw, but before I could, Dayken — always one step ahead — answered, "That's Sean, a clan member on patrol. Good kid."

I nodded as I took the towel from Dayken, wrapping it around my neck. Wanting to avoid the conversation he all but promised we would have, I steered the topic toward today's game plan as we walked inside the main entrance, heading toward the stairwell.

"About yesterday, in my room—"

"Dayken, don't you think this is a bad time?" I cut in.

"No, actually, I think it's the *perfect* time," he countered smoothly. "I have you to myself for a few minutes, and I need to get something off my chest."

I sighed but stopped walking, crossing my arms as I waited for him to speak. He ran a hand through his hair, making his shaggy locks even more disheveled. "You're irresistible, standing there like that, arms crossed, sweat covering your skin. Just looking at you makes every noble, gentlemanly thing I was about to say go straight out the window."

My heart fluttered at the confession. The way he saw me sent thrills through me, awakening a part of myself I didn't fully understand yet. And *hell*, I wanted to see what else I could do to tempt him.

But now wasn't the time.

"Dayken, I don't need you to be noble or a gentleman," I said, shaking my head. "I just need time to sort out my feelings. I've never felt this way, which makes me feel at a disadvantage — not just in life but also with the good-looking man I'm bonded to." I touched my mark for emphasis.

His lips twitched. "You think I'm good-looking?"

I groaned. "Seriously, wolf. That's *all* you heard?" I narrowed my eyes at him. "And you *know* you are. Those women at the party were practically drooling over any *tiny* scrap of attention you gave them."

Dayken stepped closer, a mischievous glint in his eyes.

"Stop right there," I warned, holding up a hand.

He halted but didn't wipe that damn smirk off his face.

"We don't have time for this. I need to shower and get ready," I said, turning to leave.

As I walked away, his voice rang out behind me. "If you need *assistance*, just let me know!"

I shook my head, but I couldn't stop the small smile that tugged at my lips as I disappeared down the stairs.

After a quick rinse and towel dry, I ran my fingers through my damp hair, trying to shake the lingering energy buzzing under my skin. I was restless by the time Chase's voice finally crackled over the PA system, announcing that our guest had arrived at the gates.

Game time. Hopefully, this will give us the advantage we need.

Talking about advantages, I saw the perfect chance to take down the tiger who was lying outside my sister's room, sleeping like a guard. The poor beast had turned down Dayken's offer of a room and had spent the night on the hard floor. I almost had to respect him for his dedication. I resisted the urge to act on the intrusive thought and chose to step around him as I headed to the conference room.

Despite the guilt gnawing at me over her injuries, I knew Sky was healing and safe, thanks to Kolton's presence… even if it irked me to admit it. It had been a close call. I'd come far too close to losing her to those monsters again. This meeting with the fox clan had to go perfectly.

Which means, no distractions. I reminded myself.

No kicking the tiger, no kissing the wolf, and no second-guessing myself. I walked straight to the center of the compound and into the conference room, ready for our next move.

Chase and Derek were leaning against the wall, almost statue-like. Their expressions were neutral, but their sharp eyes saw everything. Despite their stillness, they radiated a preparedness, a quiet intensity that made it clear they could act at a moment's notice. Their alertness was a silent testament to their skill, watchful, loyal, and deadly.

I was the last to arrive. Our guest was already seated at the head of the table, with Dayken to his right. The chair to his left remained open, waiting for me.

I didn't know what to expect from this meeting, but one thing was clear: Titus was captivating. As he stood up, I faced a man who looked like he had come out of a movie. He was tall and slender, moving with a sleek, deliberate grace that radiated effortless command.

His deep, flawless skin was dark and rich, and every feature was sculpted with clean lines and impossible symmetry, unfairly exquisite. Not a blemish, not a stray hair — he was perfect in a way that felt almost unnatural. But it was his eyes that held me. Light brown, nearly golden, they shimmered with a mischievous energy that was both a warning and an invitation, a risk and a reward. The longer I looked, the more I recognized the danger in them, yet I couldn't deny the strange pull they exerted.

Even though I was on high alert, every instinct screaming to be cautious, I still found myself intrigued, drawn into the aura he carried like an unspoken challenge.

His full lips, perfectly shaped, held a subtle, knowing smile. It hinted that he was reading every thought that flickered across my mind. I didn't know what I expected an arms dealer to look like, but it sure wasn't *this*.

While the others wore jeans and T-shirts, Titus's understated style stood out with his crisp olive-green and beige attire, enhancing his captivating presence. His gaze was confident as he extended his neatly manicured hand, effortlessly commanding attention. I couldn't help but lower my guard as I instinctively reached out, obeying his unspoken command.

Once our hands connected, I sensed Dayken's energy shift beside me.

Did I do something wrong?

Hardly. There was no doubt in my mind that I could easily take Titus down if he stepped out of line.

"You must be the famous Onyx that all the Guardians are talking about," Titus said smoothly as he released my hand, his voice carrying that same mysterious air as his gaze.

Titus wasted no time waiting for a response. He reseated himself and dove straight into business. His sharp eyes assessed us with a look that said he was there for a reason, and he intended to make the most of it.

"You must imagine my shock, Dayken, to hear that you wanted to meet with me," Titus began, his voice smooth but edged with challenge. "Especially after years of refusing to even acknowledge my clan."

"It wasn't a refusal to recognize the Sharp Clan, Titus," Dayken replied with a calm authority, like he'd anticipated this. "It was a refusal to hand over land you couldn't afford or control."

Titus raised a dark brow, his gaze steely. "Ah, how the tables have turned, then," he said, a subtle smirk tugging at his lips. "I now have wealth, and I have land. So, tell me, Dayken, what do you need from me?"

The tension in the room was thick. So sharp it almost stung.

Dayken… refusing anyone anything?

This strategic, political side of Dayken was something I hadn't seen before.

Dayken remained unfazed, his voice steady as he answered. "I want to broker an alliance between our clans. The Danielson Clan and the Sharp Clan, together. I want to—"

"No."

The silence that followed his short refusal was palpable, thick, and uncomfortable. Titus's response was swift and final, leaving no room for negotiation, at least, not without difficulty.

"I'm allied with the DeStephano Clan," Titus said. "Who supported me when others refused, including you. They gave me the resources to start my clan. I owe them my loyalty," he finished proudly, his gaze hardening. I didn't expect this. I wanted to help but knew little about clan politics. What could I add?

Dayken didn't miss a beat. "But at what cost, Titus?" he said as he crossed his arms over his chest, his tone measured but insistent. "I know Leo. The interest on his loans is notorious — and not always in the form of money. He expects favors and influence over your clan's governance. He's forced your people to relocate so he can leverage your land for his profit, without a second thought to what uprooting an entire clan entails. And I know he demands tech and weapons from you regularly, at no cost. That doesn't sound like someone deserving of your loyalty."

Dayken leaned in, his voice dropping. "What I'm offering you comes with no strings, no interest, no debt. Just a one-for-one deal. That's it."

Silence. Titus's handsome face lost its smug smirk, replaced by an unreadable indifference. Others might see disinterest, but I knew we had his attention.

"What exactly are you proposing?" Titus asked calmly.

"I'll give you Muskegon and the coastal lands extending north to Ludington. Free of charge. I'll sign the deed over to you right now," Dayken replied, his tone unwavering. "In return, you supply me with a truckload of weapons, enough for an arsenal. I have a list of what I need. They need to be of the highest quality, newest and best. None of the ancient stuff. I want new tech."

Titus raised a brow, his expression skeptical. "And what makes you think I need that kind of land anymore?"

Dayken didn't hesitate. "Because I know how challenging it's been for you to trade across into Canada and Wisconsin. Coastal waters and ferry operations will allow you better access for transportation and connection to the fox clans already established in those territories. It strengthens your clan and reduces your dependency on DeStephano."

Titus was quiet, his features still masked. His voice betrayed nothing when he finally spoke. "Well, Dayken, it appears I've severely underestimated how much you know about my business dealings. Foolish of me, but it won't happen again." He stood up, as if to leave.

"Wait," I blurted. "Do you have a vampire under your protection?"

Beside me, I heard Dayken let out a barely audible sigh, but I ignored it, my eyes locked on Titus.

Titus paused, his gaze steely as he glanced back. "You know I don't," he replied, his tone clipped, guarded.

I swallowed, feeling the weight of all my past trauma and pain press down on me. I hadn't planned on revealing any of it, but I knew that for Titus to truly understand, I had to be honest.

"Actually, I didn't know," I said calmly. "But I do know that you never experienced what I had to. You need to understand... I was taken and held captive for over twenty years. More than two decades of pure hell." His eyes narrowed, and I noticed a flicker, perhaps curiosity, maybe even empathy.

"They took me and my sister. Captured us. We were children." My voice was steady, but my hands felt cold. "They locked us away like animals, kept us in cells so we couldn't escape. It was a facility, buried in darkness, where the walls dripped with the smell of chemicals, blood, and decay."

The mood in the room shifted at my words. Titus's eyes softened slightly, but I pressed on, not allowing myself to waver.

"They didn't just lock us up," I said, my voice tight and low — *controlled* — despite the memories clawing their way to the surface. "They experimented on us. Sliced us open, tore us apart, *forced* us to regenerate… over and over again."

I swallowed hard. "They strapped me down, conscious, cut me open, *watched* as my organs regrew, scribbling notes while I screamed. To them, I was just a test subject. My pain was background noise."

My hands began to tremble, but I pressed on. "They pushed our bodies past their limits. Chained me up, made me run until I collapsed, only to drag me to my feet and make me do it all over again. They broke me — turned me into raw wounds and exhaustion, barely able to stand."

I forced myself to continue. "And then there was *Sky*. They did the same to her. *Worse*. Even though she was younger. Even though she *should've* been spared, and through it all, she tried to keep me sane. *She* was the one whispering stories through the bars of her cell, humming to me through the pain.

Titus's face was unreadable, but I knew he was listening.

"I overheard their plans one day," I said, my voice hoarse. "They had something *big* in store for Sky. A new experiment, one that involved dismemberment, then sewing *pieces* of her back together in the *wrong places*." I swallowed back bile. "They wanted to see if her body would naturally split apart again… or if it would *mend together permanently*."

A shudder rippled through me, but I kept going.

"I had to get us out. I *had* to." I clenched my fists. "I slaughtered so many in our escape. And I regret *none* of it." The guilt was a permanent balm, but I would never regret what I did.

I met his gaze, my own burning with something cold and unshakable. "They'll never understand what they did to us, but it *changed* me. I don't just want freedom. I want to make sure we're *never* taken back to that place again... that nobody is. If they come for us again, I want vengeance."

I exhaled shakily, my skin damp with sweat from even *speaking* about it. But he had to understand.

"Maybe... if we have the right resources, we can stop others from suffering the same fate."

Titus remained silent for a long moment, his eyes searching mine, expression conflicted. He didn't say anything, but I could tell he understood — maybe not fully, but enough. I had laid everything bare, hoping that somehow it would make a difference.

"I... I don't know what to say to all that," Titus stammered, his usual confidence shaken. The vulnerability in his voice was startling, a crack in his polished armor that I hadn't thought him capable of. For the first time, he seemed uncertain.

Only then did I break eye contact, letting my gaze drift to the others in the room. Their expressions mirrored his, stunned, horrified. The weight of my words pressed down on them like heavy fog. In that moment, I realized what I had done. I'd exposed a part of myself that could never be hidden again.

"I didn't tell you this for you to offer me empty words of comfort," I said, shaking my head. My voice evened out, firm, unwavering. "I don't need that. What I need is protection. Weapons. And that... that's something only you can give." I held his gaze. "But if I'm going to ask you for that, you deserve to understand exactly what we're dealing with."

Titus's gaze flicked briefly to Chase and Derek, as if measuring their reactions, before returning to me. His guarded expression softened just enough to reveal a flicker of something else, curiosity, maybe respect. He inhaled slowly, running a hand over his mouth, as if to buy time to gather himself.

"Well…" He cleared his throat. "This *is* an interesting offer and opportunity," he said at last, his tone measured but edged with intrigue.

Chase stepped forward. "The Avery Clan would like to offer our medical assistance — a separate alliance that includes our specialized avian support. It would be handled with the utmost discretion. Whatever you need, we're prepared to provide it," he said, his tone calm and respectful. His voice carried a quiet authority, born of experience, the kind that came from handling crises most couldn't even imagine.

Derek gave a small, assured nod, his demeanor steady and resolute as he added, "We're the best at what we do."

Titus's eyes glinted with intrigue as he considered the offer, weighing its benefits. It was more than a written alliance; it was a chance to strengthen his clan with loyal, skilled allies, especially vampires.

From what I had learned, a Primarc alone was powerful; two were nearly unstoppable; and one that was bonded to a Sacar: their power *surged*. Yet, everyone knew an alliance with the Danielson Clan had a cost, and Leo's reaction would be unpredictable.

Titus turned back to Dayken, respect clear in his eyes. "I see you came prepared," he said with admiration. "I'm inclined to listen." Titus's guarded demeanor softened. His earlier indifference shifted as he looked between Dayken and the twins.

"You're offering an alliance without strings, a straightforward trade of resources and support," he said, testing the offer's simplicity. After a moment, he extended his hand to Dayken. "Weapons and technology in exchange for Muskegon land and your team's medical expertise, discreetly, of course."

Dayken clasped Titus's hand in a firm shake, sealing the deal. "Agreed. Consider it a step toward mutual protection," Dayken replied. The weight of the handshake settled over us all, as heavy and certain as any spoken oath. "We will all be stronger because of it."

With the negotiations complete, a quiet fell over the room. The echoes of my past lingered, unspoken but undeniably present. The rawness of my story had left an imprint on everyone, a gravity that no one could ignore. They slowly drifted out of the room, each wrapped in their own thoughts.

Dayken walked Titus toward the exit, discussing the logistics of securing and transferring the property. Chase and Derek exchanged a brief nod, then headed toward the security room, their postures tense but professional, as they resumed their duties.

I remained still, staring off into nothingness.

I hope I don't regret exposing so much.

With that thought, I finally rose from the table and left the conference room, heading down the hall to check on Sky.

Chapter 27

Dayken

As I closed the door behind Titus and returned to the main floor, my thoughts raced, trying to process what had just happened. I should've felt relieved, the meeting was successful, but Onyx's words left a lingering ache. Her pain echoed in my mind, each syllable cutting deep. The conflict followed me through the dull corridors. I was torn between gratitude that her vulnerability secured Titus's agreement and sorrow for the raw pieces she had to reveal.

Upon reaching the stairwell to the basement, I heard raised voices. Kolton's coarse bellow echoed from the stairs, growing louder with each word. Tension filled the air, and I hurried down, taking the stairs two at a time, sensing something was wrong.

"Well, I'd rather be a rabid animal than a cold-hearted, selfish bitch!" Kolton's voice rang out, raw and unrestrained.

I entered the hallway to find him facing Onyx, his stance coiled, muscles taut. His orange, unkempt hair framed his face, his yellow eyes burning with anger. Tall and lean, his entire body was braced, ready to pounce. His gaze was wild with a barely contained fury that made my instincts flare in warning.

"Enough!" I growled, my tone sharp. "You will not speak to my Sacar like that." I stepped closer, blocking Onyx from his line of sight. "I don't give a fuck who you're bonded to, I will throw your ass out of here."

Kolton's jaw clenched as he turned his frustration on me. "How can you defend her?" he demanded, voice shaking with bitter resentment. He swept his hand out, gesturing to the compound. "Has she ever once shown you any appreciation for any of this? You did this all for her. Every single day, you think about how to protect her, to keep her safe, right? I know you do. And has she ever shown you an ounce of gratitude? Any thanks?" His gaze flickered with a hard edge, then he spun back toward Onyx. He pointed at her, his voice dripping with venom. "You are nothing but a—"

"Stop!"

The sudden interruption didn't come from either of us. We turned to see Sky standing weakly in her doorway, holding herself up with one hand braced on the doorframe. She looked pale, her face drawn with exhaustion, but her eyes were steady and piercing.

"This stops now," she said firmly, her voice quiet but demanding. "I won't stand here and listen to another word from any of you." She straightened, summoning strength from somewhere deep within. "And yes, I heard everything."

Kolton tensed at Sky's words. His fury softened, replaced with hesitation. His yellow eyes darted between Sky and the floor, anger fading as he struggled to control himself. He stayed firm, energy bristling, but his tension drained away, like a leash reining him in.

"Skylar..." he murmured, his voice was still a growl, but unmistakably subdued, like he was caught between defiance and submission. He looked like he was fighting some inner urge, a battle between his feral instincts and respect for her.

Sky's gaze didn't waver. "This stops now, Kolton," she repeated, her voice steady but gentle.

Kolton's fists unclenched, and he stepped back. He glanced at Sky with a softer expression, either guilt or regret, her reprimand turning his rage into reluctant obedience.

Then, Sky turned her sharp gaze to Onyx, a flicker of disappointment and frustration tightening her expression. Her tone was firmer, almost scolding. "And you," she said, her voice harsher than I'd ever heard her use. "I expect this from you, Onyx. But that doesn't make it right. We're supposed to be safe here, together. This isn't helping anyone."

Onyx opened her mouth to argue, but Sky cut her off, her gaze unwavering. "I know you're protective. I know you think you have to do everything on your own. But we're a family now — dysfunctional as it may be — and if you keep pushing everyone away, it'll destroy us."

Her words hung heavily, visibly affecting Onyx. Sky, fragile but determined, was the only one capable of calming Kolton and confronting Onyx simultaneously. Onyx crossed her arms, glaring at Kolton, still angry. "I just want to know one thing," she said coldly. "How did you know where to find the cars that took Sky?"

Kolton's jaw tightened, his face becoming unreadable, his silence only deepening the tension. I let out a frustrated sigh, stepping forward. "Trust me, I've already tried getting answers out of him. He's been a real pain in the ass about it," I said, eyeing Kolton, trying to read what was going on in that reclusive mind of his. "He just shuts down every time I ask him to explain."

Kolton's shoulders slumped, clearly uncomfortable being the topic of discussion. His gaze darted to the floor, evading our stares, and I could feel his reluctance, his instinct to remain quiet. Silence stretched between us, thick and charged.

Sky's voice cut through the tension, soft but steady. "Kolton, please. I need to understand. You wouldn't have followed them without a reason." She looked at him, her eyes softening. I watched Kolton's face shift, visibly torn. "If you were tracking them… then maybe it means you've been trying to watch over me for longer than I realized?" she asked, with such hope it was adorable, really.

Kolton's posture sagged slightly, like her words had broken down all his resistance. I watched as he ran a hand through his unkempt hair, his frustration clear in the way he fidgeted. "I've always tried to find you, to be close to you, but it wasn't enough," he admitted, his voice rough with regret. "I was always one step behind them."

He paused, gathering himself. His voice dropped lower, turning sincere. "I've been tracking those assholes for months. Ever since I left California. I've been keeping tabs on their operations. They have facilities everywhere — scattered, hidden — but I managed to follow their trail from California to Missouri."

Kolton's words settled over us, heavy and loaded. Curiosity gnawed at me, and I leaned forward. I was wary but wanted answers. "So, you were just… following them?"

Kolton nodded, his gaze still averted. "Yes. And when a large group abruptly left the Missouri location, I knew something was going on. I followed them here because…" He hesitated, glancing at Sky before continuing. "Because the closer I got to Michigan, the stronger my connection to her felt. I could sense she was here."

Sky's head dropped as she absorbed his words. Her face softened, touched. "So, you followed that instinct," she murmured, as if piecing together the trail he had followed.

"Yes," Kolton replied, his voice quiet, almost resigned. "It was the only thing that made sense. I knew you were close. I couldn't just… leave you. Not when they were clearly up to something."

The hallway fell silent as I looked at Kolton, whose hesitation and arrogance had melted away. I understood just how much he had risked, his safety and life, to pursue a faint connection to Sky. His loyalty went deeper than his well-being or pride, forged in something raw and unbreakable.

Sky finally broke the silence, her voice gentle. "Why don't you come in, Kolton? We can talk about what you learned while you were following them." She gestured toward her room, a modest space with a bed, a small desk, and a makeshift seating area with two chairs and a small table.

Kolton's immediate reaction was to shake his head and step back, as if the thought of being too close to her made him uncomfortable. His head dropped again, avoiding her gaze as his discomfort returned. The tension was thick; something about being near her seemed to make him painfully aware of an invisible boundary he was unwilling to cross: a line none of us fully understood.

I picked up on it immediately and cleared my throat, placing a steady hand on Onyx's shoulder before she could interject. "Come on, Onyx," I said softly, guiding her down the hallway. "Let's give them a moment. They've both been through enough. I think they deserve a bit of privacy." I nudged Onyx to move with me. She resisted, her gaze lingering on Sky, concern in her eyes. But eventually, she allowed me to steer her away. As we walked down the hall, I couldn't shake the strange feeling Kolton's behavior stirred in me. Whatever was happening between him and Sky ran deeper than I could grasp, a connection beyond reason or even pride. Something raw, primal, and powerful that I couldn't quite define.

"I want to hear what he knows, though," Onyx said quietly as I ushered her along.

I nodded, glancing back toward Sky's door. "I know. Trust me, I do too. But something is going on between them that I can't ignore. I know I told you this already, but they bonded as babies. That's... well, it's not normal, and I think it might have something to do with why he went feral."

Her eyes widened. "So, he is *feral*?! I knew it."

"Well... I'm pretty sure. His erratic behavior isn't normal, even for a bonded Guardian," I admitted. "But one thing's certain: I'll be having a word with him about the way he spoke to you. That's not acceptable, no matter how much the animal side takes over."

Chapter 28

Dayken's protectiveness sent a thrill through me that I couldn't ignore. The fact that some random insult to me could get under his skin meant more than I wanted to admit. I'd love nothing more than to smash Kolton's nose so hard it kissed his skull, but unfortunately for me, he had a point.

I hadn't shown Dayken a shred of appreciation for everything he'd done.

Not once.

I walked out without warning, left him in the dark, and still, he came for me. He didn't hesitate. He never did.

It was who he was, his influence behind security, the fortified compound, every layer of protection. Now, he was risking his clan to forge an alliance solely to protect me. All of it for a cause he was required to take on, because of me. And what have I given him in return? Nothing. Throughout everything, I never once showed how grateful I was, not for his loyalty, patience, or faith in me. Maybe because I never allowed myself to feel that kind of gratitude for anyone.

I had been alone for so long that I'd forgotten what it's like to lean on someone. To have someone support me without question.

But I wondered, if he knew how I escaped the facility, would he still stand by me? The real truth, not just what I told Titus. Would he see me the same way, knowing the choice I made? Regardless, I owed him, and he deserved to know how I felt.

I stopped suddenly, yanking open the first door I saw. It could have been a supply closet or an empty office; it didn't matter. My heart was pounding as I grabbed Dayken by the sleeve and pulled him inside. I slammed the door with a loud bang, probably harder than I intended. But at that moment, I didn't care.

"Wha—" Dayken started, but I cut him off, pressing my hands to his chest and pushing him back against the door. A surprised breath escaped him as he hit the door a little too hard.

Oops. That was definitely unintentional.

I felt my cheeks flush, but I didn't step back. Instead, I let my hands move from his chest to his sides, steadying myself as I wrapped my arms around his waist. Pressing my face to his chest, just below his collarbone, I felt his warmth sink into me, something I'd been missing without even realizing it.

"Onyx…" he whispered my name, soft and full of something I couldn't quite define. His arms came around me in a heartbeat, pulling me even closer. His hold was so strong it made my rough grip on him feel almost delicate. We stayed that way, holding each other, the silence thick with unspoken words.

In his arms, all the gratitude, the trust, everything I'd been too stubborn to say, was there, right between us. And for once, I let it be enough.

After what felt like an eternity, I finally loosened my hold on Dayken, drawing in a steady breath before stepping back.

"I know I struggle with understanding what the bond makes us feel versus how we actually feel about each other," I admitted, my voice uneven.

I cleared my throat — buying myself a second before exposing this uncomfortable truth.

"But that damned tiger made me realize it doesn't matter." My fingers curled at my sides, the words strange on my tongue. "You're looking out for me, and I am grateful."

Before I could overthink it, I rose onto my toes and pressed a quick kiss to his cheek. "I'm just sorry it took an unhinged psychopath to make me realize it."

Dayken's gaze softened. Something deep and unreadable flickered in his eyes.

"I've stopped caring about defining the bond or my feelings," he murmured. "I just am who I am, your Guardian, your provider, your protector." His fingers traced a slow path down my exposed arms, leaving a trail of warmth in their wake. "I never want you to feel like you owe me anything," he said softly. "It's an honor to be here for you."

I smiled, a genuine smile. I couldn't help it. He was just perfect, and I was so grateful.

Instead of smiling back at me, he just looked stunned. Surely, I'd smiled at him before… but as he stared at my expression, he was awestruck. I let my smile fade and cleared my throat, trying to compose myself.

"Right. I, uh… really need to check on those security… feeds." I could feel the heat rising in my cheeks, but forced myself to look calm. This was awkward, and I didn't know how to process it.

Dayken smirked, his green eyes glinting with a mix of warmth and amusement. "I'm getting used to you running away by now, no need to make excuses."

I didn't respond. I just pulled open the door and found Derek standing there, arms crossed, eyebrows raised, looking as if he'd won the lottery.

"HELLLOOOO," he sang, looking so fricking happy to have discovered us — *damn it* — his grin ever widening. "Oh, don't let me interrupt. Just emerging from a dark, empty room together… on a completely unrelated, definitely 'security feed' related mission, I'm sure?"

I scowled, but Derek only leaned casually against the doorframe, eyes twinkling with humor. "Please, do go on. Those security feeds won't check themselves." Then he pretended to ponder. "Unless… do you think we need a camera in here? Good thinking, Onyx," he mocked, craning his neck to inspect the corners of the room. His smile was bigger than I had ever seen.

"Derek…." I retorted, trying to keep a straight face. "Don't start."

"Sure, sure, I wouldn't dare." He nodded, sarcasm practically dripping from his voice. "Not with the infamous Onyx, champion of rational, tactical decision making, queen of storage room closed-circuit video feeds."

Dayken chuckled behind me.

I rolled my eyes, fighting a smile. "I swear, Derek, if I hear one word of this around the compound—"

He raised his hands in feigned innocence, the smirk still glued to his face. "Oh, don't worry. I'll be as quiet as a mouse." Then, he gave an exaggerated wink. "For a small feed — I mean fee."

I marched away from them toward the security room, determined to commit to my ridiculous claim of 'needing to check things out.' As I opened the door, the room greeted me with silence, aside from the gentle hum of the computers. At first glance, it looked empty — until I noticed a quiet figure sitting in a chair, browsing through the feeds. The slight tilt of his head told me he'd seen me and acknowledged my presence without speaking. That was one of the things I liked about Chase: he was perfectly happy to sit in complete silence.

With just the two of us in the room, I explored the setup, which was breathtaking. Every inch showed Chase's hard work and attention to detail, deserving of admiration.

As if sensing my unspoken praise, Chase casually propped his black boots on the desk, laced his fingers behind his head, and refocused on the monitors. The movement flexed the muscles in his arms just slightly, and I found myself pausing, unable to ignore how much time these animals must spend in the gym.

I bet Chase had no shortage of admirers. For a fleeting moment, I even felt the urge to ask him about his love life — but I quickly squashed it. Showing interest in another man felt wrong, even if it was just idle curiosity. As impressive as Chase looked, his fit frame was nothing compared to the hulking, massive wolf who dominated my thoughts.

My gaze fell to Chase's boots, and I blinked before doing a double-take.

"What are those?" I asked, breaking the silence.

"Boots," he replied quietly. His tone was nonchalant, as though it were an everyday occurrence for someone not to recognize footwear. Then again, considering Derek was his brother, that actually tracked.

"No, smartass," I shot back, narrowing my eyes. "What kind? Like, how do I get some for myself?"

Chase tilted his head, his black hair slightly askew, surprised by the question. It was amusing — my curiosity confused him, as if it made more sense for me to be unaware of what boots were.

After a beat, he answered, "I can put it in the expense report for Dayken."

Interesting.

I tucked that tidbit away, filing it under 'useful information.' The ease with which Chase brushed it off made me wonder just how simple it was to get Dayken to approve purchases.

Dayken was the king of this castle, and I realized how much it took to make the compound function. Every detail ran smoothly, like a machine built on his authority. Maybe Kolton was onto something.

But I'll never tell him that.

Chapter 29

Onyx

As the days passed while we waited for Titus's return, a sense of normalcy started to settle over the compound — at least, as normal as things could get under the circumstances. My room was set up and unpacked, and we'd fallen into a routine of gathering each night in the makeshift cafeteria. Even though Sky and I didn't need to eat, we joined the others as a social effort, a small attempt at fostering connection amidst the chaos. The round picnic-style tables were uncomfortable, but it was interesting to hear about the clan's political drama and the events of the day.

Although there was a lot of administrative work to transition the land's ownership, I believed it finally belonged to Dayken. Kolton spent most of his time lurking in the shadows, his gaze constantly on Sky. Derek and Chase kept watch over the compound, flew surveillance routes, exchanged intel with other Avery Clan members, and monitored the live feeds. They also regularly rotated access codes as an extra precaution.

Alicia had placed Mack Clan members on the first floor, some sharing rooms. She had explained that bears were skittish unless cornered, making them suitable protectors. Though I didn't know their names, they were respectful. Alicia often wandered around the compound with Peach, who insisted on staying over as often as she could, saying it was more fun to be around her own kind — Sky and myself — instead of bears all the time.

Aurora dropped in now and then — sometimes with urgent updates, other times with a tray of baked goods, fresh from the oven. No matter what she brought, she always looked polished and put-together, which struck me as oddly formal for baking. Still, I could tell Dayken appreciated having her around. It was obvious they were close, and living apart was new territory for them.

And then there was Dayken.

Always near but never hovering. He was a presence I couldn't block out, not with logic, reason, or distance. He didn't push or pry, but he kept getting under my skin in ways I wasn't ready to explore. Every look, every interaction, felt like we were on the edge of something I refused to acknowledge. I told myself I was just staying on guard, but the more time passed, the harder it became to believe that lie.

Despite living here for days, I hadn't checked out the training room Alicia had mentioned. With things quiet this afternoon, I decided it was time. Maybe burning off some steam would ease my tension.

Exiting my room, I saw Kolton against the wall across the hall, watching Sky's open door. I ignored him, though his presence unsettled me, a constant reminder of his unpredictability.

Pausing at Sky's door, I leaned in. "Hey, Sky, I'm heading to the training room. Any interest in joining?"

She looked up from her spot on the bed, holding a vampire romance novel, her face lighting up with excitement. "No, I'm good! I'm at the climax of the story. They're playing baseball, and I have to know if Jasper scores," she said, waving the book in the air like it was her lifeline.

A small smile tugged at the corner of my lips despite myself. "Enjoy," I said, stepping back.

Although I hated giving my back to the tiger, I kept moving down the hall, trying to ignore his unyielding stare. His presence constantly ate at me, like an itch I couldn't scratch. For Sky's sake, I suppressed my frustration and kept going.

When I finally reached the training room, I stepped inside and looked around. The space was clean and efficient, featuring rows of weights, punching bags, and mats for sparring, everything a person could ever need to train.

And then my eyes landed on it.

That vile machine. The one they made me run on for hours, maybe even days, without end. The memories hit me like a tidal wave, slamming into my consciousness. I staggered backward. My hand shot out, gripping the nearest surface, trying to keep myself upright as the past bled into the present.

"Ph-lea-se," I begged, barely able to breathe. They ignored me. "I'm… gonha-cal-laps…" I heaved. Still, they ignored me. Then, my blood-soaked foot gave out, and I slipped on the rubber belt. My face smashed on impact, sending me flying off the back. I felt the instant my jaw broke, and the burn across my forehead and cheek where the friction of the moving belt hit me.
"Up," that haunting voice commanded.
"No, please no. I can't."
"Again," he demanded. He always demanded. More. More… more.
"No, please don't."

It was just a memory, just a reaction. But I could *feel* it—

My legs burned, my feet slipping on the rubber belt as I ran, and ran, and ran. Snot dripped from my nose, my breath ragged and gasping, every muscle screaming for relief that never came.

I smashed the heels of my palms into my eyes, trying to stop the visions, but they just kept coming.

"Again."

Tears, sweat — what was the difference anymore? They blurred together, streaking down my face as I choked out desperate pleas. My throat burned from the effort, hoarse from begging for mercy that never came. My lungs screamed with every step, muscles seizing, my body trembling on the edge of collapse, but still, they made me run.

"Again, or it's Sky's turn," He taunted this time.

The treadmill's unyielding hum became a cruel symphony of my torment, its belt grinding relentlessly beneath my feet, threatening to swallow me whole if I dared falter. Now, every stumble earned me a jolt of electricity, a paralyzing and punishing reminder that I couldn't stop. My cries echoed off empty walls. Cold, unfeeling stares were my only audience.

Before I knew it, I was on my knees, jolted back to the present again. My hands dug into the rubber mats beneath me. My breathing was erratic, shallow and uneven, no matter how hard I tried to regain control. The room spun, the memories relentless. The overwhelming weight of them was crushing me. Air. I needed air.

Suddenly, the onslaught of visions started to fade away.

I felt gentle strokes run down my back, steady and soothing, grounding me in the present. A voice murmured something I didn't quite catch, but it broke through the storm of memories, its warmth chasing away the cold grip of my fear.

I inhaled deeply, air finally rushing into my lungs.

And I knew.

Dayken.

"Are you okay?"

I shook my head, my voice caught somewhere between my chest and throat.

Dayken's jaw tightened, his entire demeanor altering, turning lethal. "What did this?" he asked, his voice low and dangerous. He was ready to tear flesh from bone of whatever dared to hurt me.

The joke was on him, though. There was nothing here, no enemy to pursue, no living being to blame. Only a cold, emotionless machine that had inadvertently brought me to my knees.

I couldn't speak, couldn't find the words. So I just raised a trembling hand and pointed.

His eyes landed on the treadmill, and his brow furrowed. Confusion flickered across his face for a moment before understanding dawned. "The treadmill?" he asked, his voice softening.

I nodded, unable to trust my voice. Embarrassment started clawing its way up my chest now, replacing the much worse onslaught of emotions I was feeling.

Before I could process what was happening, Dayken effortlessly scooped me up. At five nine and muscular, I wasn't delicate, but in his arms, I felt small. He wrapped one arm securely around my waist, holding me steady, while the other slid beneath my knees. He held me as if I were weightless.

His grip was firm, yet careful, every move deliberate, as if he feared I might break. My mind raced, fragments from the past crashing into the present. My breath hitched, shallow and uneven, as I clung to him. I wasn't used to being held or relying on anyone. But now, I just wanted out of that room, away from the memories that left me feeling trapped.

I buried my face in his shoulder and wrapped my arms tightly around his neck, as if letting go would pull me back into the nightmare. If I was squeezing too tight, he didn't say a word. He was warm, steady, and grounding, and I could feel the rhythm of his heartbeat against me, a stark contrast to my irregular pulse. He started walking, his steps confident and purposeful. I let the motion soothe me, trying to match my breathing to the calm strength emanating from him.

The door slammed shut behind us with a bang, and I flinched at the sound. I felt Dayken pause, adjusting his hold on me just enough to tighten his grip. He nuzzled his jaw over the top of my head, reassuring me without speaking. His chest rose and fell in a steady rhythm. I tried to mimic it, forcing each breath deeper than the last.

I didn't know how much time had passed before I heard him speak, low and commanding. "Chase."

There was a shuffle, then the sound of a door creaking open. Dayken's tone shifted, laced with steel and an edge of protectiveness that sent a chill down my spine. "Get the treadmills out of the training room. Immediately."

Chase didn't hesitate. "Okay. Roger that," he replied, no questions, no trace of judgment, just quiet understanding.

The strength of Dayken's arms, his confident voice, and Chase's quick acceptance felt like a lifeline. My body trembled, but I could feel the storm inside me begin to settle. Embarrassment faded into gratitude.

I think they truly care about me.

The next thing I knew, I was being placed down gently. The luxurious softness of Dayken's bed surrounded me, engulfing me. Dayken moved with careful precision, his grip loosening as he slowly extricated himself from my hold. My arms, which had been wrapped tightly around his neck, fell to my side as I realized where I was.

He didn't pull back far, just enough for our faces to be inches apart, his green eyes locked onto mine. The silence between us was thick, unspoken words filling the space we shared. Somehow, he understood. He understood the weight of the trauma I carried, how it lingered in every corner of my mind, following me, threatening me wherever I went.

The words *I'm sorry* hovered on the tip of my tongue, but they wouldn't come. What did I have to be sorry for? I hadn't chosen that life. I hadn't chosen to be tortured. But in that moment, I felt like a burden he shouldn't have to carry.

I opened my mouth, but before I could find the words, Dayken reached up and tucked a stray piece of hair behind my ear. His touch was so gentle that it sent a shiver down my spine.

"Shhh," he murmured, his voice low and steady, grounding me. His gaze softened as he continued. "You don't owe me anything, Onyx. Not an explanation, not a reason. Nothing."

His hand lingered for a moment before it fell back to his side. His gaze stayed locked on mine, unflinching and sure, as he spoke in a quiet voice, full of conviction. "I'm yours, Onyx. Whatever you need, whenever you need it. If you want something gone, it's gone. If you want me to leave, I'll leave. And if you want me to stay..." He hesitated, just for a heartbeat, his emerald eyes burning with a raw, unyielding intensity. "Then I'll stay. Always."

He leaned in slowly, his forehead coming to gently rest against mine. The closeness was electrifying yet comforting, his presence both a shield and a balm. When he spoke again, his voice softened, becoming intimate. "I see you. All of you. And I'm here."

I swallowed audibly, emotions getting stuck in my throat.

"Thank you, Dayken… thank you." My breath trembled, but I didn't move from our position. Our foreheads remained connected, a quiet, intimate touch. I breathed again, the words slipping out once more. "Thank you… just thank you."

I kept repeating it because it felt like the only fitting response, the only words that conveyed my feelings, gratitude, intense and overwhelming. For him, for his unwavering presence, for the bond I had resented but now recognized as the anchor I needed.

Slowly, he sank onto the soft pillows beside me. Our faces were so close that I could feel his breath on my lips. One of my hands, still resting on his shoulder where I had wrapped my arms earlier, stayed there, a soft point of contact. His fingers found their way into my hair, threading through it with a steady, soothing rhythm. Each pass was like its own unique melody, lullabies to calm the storms that had been raging inside me for so long.

We didn't need to speak. In that quiet — that stillness — words felt unnecessary. The silence between us wasn't empty; it was full of understanding, of a connection that ran deeper than anything I had ever allowed myself to feel.

Chapter 30

Dayken

Derek and Chase hauled the treadmills to the loading dock that evening. Onyx would never see them again; I made sure of that. She needed rest, not another reminder of her shattered past.

They hadn't even complained about the effort, which, for Derek, was quite something. But even as I stood there, knowing I'd done all I could for her at the moment, the guilt gnawed at me. I knew all those years locked away had been horrible, but I hadn't truly realized how bad until I saw it in her eyes.

When I felt her panic through the bond, I knew she was in distress. I should have understood then. I should have known it ran deeper. That whatever she was reliving wasn't just painful; it was breaking her.

I had underestimated it. Now, I can't forget the image of her unraveling before me, watching a strong, unshakeable vampire like Onyx being brought to her knees was hard to erase. She had faced everything alone so far, but how much was she bottling up? How long before she broke?

I caught Chase near the security room, and he said, "We're done. The bears are loading them onto a truck headed to a clan den up north."

"Thanks for taking care of that," I said with a nod.

Chase nodded back, but his usual indifference was absent, replaced by something else. His gaze flicked to the monitor behind me, a faint crease forming between his brows. "Something's been bothering me," he said, his tone quieter than usual.

"What is it?" I asked, following his gaze to the screen.

He rubbed the back of his neck, hesitating. "It's probably nothing, but one of the perimeter cameras tripped this afternoon. There was no sign of movement on the footage when we checked; it could've been an animal, maybe. Still…" He trailed off, his unease clear.

I stiffened. "And you're just now telling me this?"

Chase raised a hand in defense. "Relax. I double-checked the entire perimeter afterward, and there wasn't a damn thing out of place. Could've been a glitch. But with everything that's happened lately…" He shrugged, clearly not wanting to push the subject further.

The thought unsettled me, but I pushed it away. If Chase wasn't concerned enough to sound the alarm, I would let it go. For now.

He paused, then added, "It really hit me… after hearing her tell her story to Titus," he said quietly. "It's easy to judge or assume I know their experiences, but the truth is, I have no idea. None of us do. It was unfair to think I could understand. Or empathize."

He shifted his weight, rubbing the back of his neck again, his gaze thoughtful. "I just… I want to do whatever I can to help them. Both of them. Onyx, Sky, it doesn't matter. They've been through enough. They deserve it."

His words caught me off guard. Chase rarely opened up, and it was clear how much Onyx and Sky's past affected him. I roughly clapped his shoulder. "I know. And they do too. What you and Derek did for them… that kind of loyalty isn't cheap." Chase nodded slightly, almost smiling.

Then Derek came over, grinning. "Chase, look up the treadmill's weight. That must be a new lift record," he said.

I laughed off his enthusiasm, saying, "Good work today." I meant it. Their support extended beyond security and medical; they helped in ways I couldn't, and I was immensely grateful. "I'm going to check on Onyx," I added, heading toward the corridor. Chase waved me off, his face thoughtful as he turned back to his post.

Onyx was resting in the same spot I'd left her, completely oblivious to the world around her. Her senses were relaxed in a way I'd rarely seen: calm, but only because she instinctively knew who was near. She'd never realize it was me — the reason she could rest peacefully, unaware. I knew because I constantly checked on her, ensuring nothing threatened her while she slept. Our bond gave her this trust and contentment, making my pride swell so intensely that I wanted to pound my fists against my chest.

I couldn't help myself. I reached my hand out, fingers lightly brushing along her arm. Her skin was soft, impossibly smooth. She was pale, like the white petals of a poisonous flower, beautiful and dangerous, crafted to lure you in. I knew she could kill; she was lethal in every way. But that didn't stop me. If she truly were poisonous, I'd still consume as much as I could, until I was intoxicated with her very being. My obsession with her knew no bounds.

At my touch, she stirred, her body shifting ever so slightly.

"Dayken," she murmured, her voice thick with sleep. It was the sexiest, groggiest sound I'd ever heard. Hearing my name on her lips was enough to undo me. But I held it together, forcing myself to be supportive, to not climb into bed with her and pull her against me for the rest of time.

I crouched down, bringing us to eye level. She cracked her eyes open, those icy blues already alert, despite her exhaustion. I tentatively slid my hand across the mattress, waiting. Would she take it? As if our minds were connected, she reached forward, her fingers brushing mine before tangling together in a simple, grounding hold.

"Hi," I said.

"Hi," she whispered back.

"Are you okay?"

She nodded.

"Do you want to be alone?"

She shook her head, then gave my hand a quick tug. It was a small gesture, but it said everything. She wanted me close. She wanted me in bed with her.

My wolf howled inside me. Pride, happiness, and something deeper slammed into me all at once.

I pushed up from my crouch, untangling our hands just long enough to slip under the covers beside her. We were side by side again, eyes locked, taking in everything about each other.

A shift in the blankets caught my attention. Her hand was moving. I didn't dare react, just waited.

I knew how hard it was for Onyx to be vulnerable, how easily she looked for a reason to shut down and flee. I wouldn't risk breaking this moment.

Seconds later, soft fingers brushed a stray strand of hair from my forehead. They drifted down, tracing my cheekbone, the line of my jaw, then lower, skimming my throat. My breath hitched. Her hand traced lower still.

Her touch slowed as she mapped the planes of my chest over my shirt. A low rumble escaped me. It was meant to be a gentle warning, a reminder that if she kept this up, it could quickly escalate beyond my control.

But she didn't stop.

Her touch firmed as her hand slid lower, passing over my pectoral, then across my nipple.

The growl came deeper this time, involuntary. My eyes snapped to hers, no longer watching her wandering hand but instead searching her face.

And the second I did, I knew. Her eyes were hooded, lips slightly parted. Her pulse was hammering, and her eyes were molten with desire.

She wanted me. By all that was holy, she could have me.

I fought the instinct to rip my shirt off, to press her hands to my bare skin, and speed this up. But I knew this was important, letting her lead, letting her set the pace.

At some point, my wolf would need to take over.

But that could wait.

For now, I would savor her quiet exploration, her touch, her curiosity.

When her hand slid down my stomach to the hem of my shirt, her fingers trailed my waistband, and I knew I was done for. She slipped her hand beneath my shirt, then went back up my abs, tracing each muscle and lifting the fabric as she went.

"Onyx…" I warned, testing to see if she knew what she was doing. Her gentle hum in response let me know she was aware.

"You are playing with a wolf right now, and that is very dangerous."

"Hmmm." Her fingers dug into my sides, pulling me closer to her. "I think I like dangerous."

My self-control snapped. I pinned her to the bed and slid over her. I took both her hands in one of mine, lifting them above her head. Fuck she looked so good like that. Exposed, wanting, *mine*.

"Are you sure?" I asked, giving her one last chance to run away.

"Yes." And before she could even finish the word, I closed the distance.

Chapter 31

Dayken kissed me like he was starving, like I was his salvation. I loved the thrill of it. I loved the feeling of him on top of me. His weight, his desperation, his growls. His eyes had gone completely black, and his teeth started to elongate. I couldn't help but wonder if he was aware that he shifted slightly when he looked at me like that — the wolf shining through his eyes.

His kisses were searing, hard, and perfect. He coaxed my mouth open with his tongue, and when I met his with my own, I moaned. I became frenzied. His grip tightened on my wrists, which were still locked above my head. I pressed my breasts into his chest to create some friction, and when that wasn't enough, I released a whimper.

"My greedy little goddess needs something, doesn't she?" he rasped against my mouth. I nodded. I didn't know what I needed, but I *wanted it*, and I wanted it now. He began kissing down my neck, nipping and claiming every inch of exposed skin. He finally released my wrists, and my hands shot to his hair, tugging it and pulling him back to my mouth. His perfect grin was there, and a knowing look was in his eyes.

As he kissed me, he ran his hand under my shirt, sliding it up my stomach. He inched higher until his fingers toyed with my bra.

"This needs to go," he growled. Before I could lift to reach the clasp, he snaked a hand behind my back, unhooking it for me. Then he slid my shirt off, allowing me to toss my bra onto the floor. When I looked up at Dayken to see why he wasn't kissing me again, his wild, predatory stare froze me in place.

"Fuck," he ground out, like he was in pain. I was frozen. I felt like a rabbit caught in a snare. He looked positively unhinged as he took in my exposed chest. And then, without warning, he lunged. He started at my collarbone and nipped his way down until he sucked a nipple into his mouth. I moaned. Pleasure shot through me. Hot, almost painful. I needed *more*.

"You are fucking perfect," he murmured against my breast. "I knew you had perfect tits, but these were fucking made for me," he said possessively as he roughly squeezed one breast while teasing the nipple of the other with his lips.

"These." He sucked, creating a pop. "Are." A pinch, and I moaned. "Mine," he nipped.

The onslaught sent me into a frenzy. I wasn't aware that any words had left my mouth, but I must have said something about more because he responded, "I'll give you everything, but I don't think you're ready yet."

I disagreed, but before I could protest, he ground his hips into mine, sending a shock of pleasure through my core as I felt his hard erection against my clit. I released another moan.

"Please, Dayken."

"Never in my wildest dreams did I expect you to beg for me. Now I think I could cum from that alone." He ground his bulge against me once more. "Say it again."

"Please.... Please"

"Ahh fuck Onyx." He started undoing my pants. They were tight, and he could barely contain his frustration as he removed them. Once he forcibly threw them to the floor, he was back on top of me, pushing his erection against my core again. Removing one barrier heightened the intensity, but it still wasn't enough. I fumbled to remove his shirt so I could feel his skin on mine. Once I got it over his head, he tossed it to the floor, and I ran my nails down the tight skin on his chest. No give, just solid, honed muscle. He ground into my center again, letting me know he liked it.

"More," I demanded. But instead, he lifted his hips and shifted to lie beside me. I whined. *Fucking whined.* Only to feel the pressure of his hand at my core instead of his bulge. His low chuckle blew breathy air across my nipples. The feel of his fingers on the fabric of my panties, sliding over my sensitive area, had me moaning so loud it very well could have been a scream.

"Is this what you want? Hmmm?" He growled into my neck before licking and kissing it.

"Yes, more… Please." And he delivered. He slipped his hand under my panties and plunged a finger inside me. At first, it felt like an odd intrusion until he started moving it in and out while also applying pressure to my clit with his palm. This time, I knew I screamed.

"That's right, Onyx. Fuck you are so wet. You are coating my finger." I wasn't sure what that meant, but it sounded like praise, and I immediately wanted more. He began kissing me again, and I was frantic as I kissed him back. The combination of his finger inside me and our tongues tangling together was intense. It caused something to build inside me. His forearms were flexed tight, veins and cords pulsing from the force he was using with his hand, bringing on a whole new surge of pleasure.

"Dayken… I… oh fuck."

"That's right, just like that. Be a good girl and let go." So, I did. I threw my head back on the pillow and let my legs fall open. I stopped overthinking and just let myself *feel.* He rewarded me with searing nips and kisses along the exposed column of my throat.

Heat enveloped me — pulsing through my veins, seizing my muscles. The noises escaping my mouth were loud, incoherent, and completely out of my control. Then, before I could even register what was happening, stars exploded behind my eyes. I slammed them shut, my body trembling and shaking with the most overwhelming, satisfying sensation I'd ever experienced.

His hand slowed, easing me through it. I suddenly didn't know if I wanted more or if I couldn't take another second. I forced my eyes open and locked onto him.

He was already staring at me.

His eyes were blown wide, pitch black, and his fangs peeked out from between his parted lips. He looked stunned. Awed. Possessive.

"What... was that?" I asked, breathless and amazed.

He blinked slowly, then withdrew his hand. "Wait. Have you seriously never had an orgasm before?"

I shook my head, heart still racing. "No... how would I have?"

"I mean, true," he muttered, his brows drawing together. "But, no privacy at all?"

"No," I said softly, shame creeping in despite myself. He caught it immediately. His expression softened as he leaned in, brushing my hair behind my ear.

"Well, I'm honored to be the one who gave you your first." His voice was low, reverent. "And I plan on giving you many, many more. The way you looked just now... That's for me. Only me. Do you understand?"

I think I did. I think I knew exactly what he meant. So, I nodded.

"Only you," I whispered, wrapping my arms around his neck and pulling him into a kiss, which he immediately deepened. He splayed his hand across my stomach, sliding it up in a slow, torturous way, like he was taking his time, feeling every inch of my exposed skin. I felt the press of his chest, the heat of him, and for a moment, something stirred inside me, uncertain but instinctual. I shifted, reaching for him. I wasn't even sure what I was offering. I only knew I wanted to give him something back.

But he stilled me with a touch, his gentle fingers wrapping around my wrist.

"Hey," he whispered, pulling back just enough to look me in the eyes. "This wasn't about that. It's not a trade."

My breath caught.

"You don't owe me anything, Onyx. I just wanted to give you something that was yours. Something no one could take from you. Ever."

Emotion tightened my throat. I didn't know what to say, so I leaned into him instead, resting my head against his shoulder, letting the steady beat of his heart relax me.

He gathered me into his arms like I was something to be protected, not possessed.

And there, in the quiet that followed, wrapped in his strength and warmth, the exhaustion finally caught up to me. My body melted into his. His arms tightened once, protectively, and then we both drifted to sleep, tangled together.

Exactly where we belonged.

Chapter 32

Dayken

The rumble of an approaching truck vibrated through the air as I stood on the loading dock, watching its headlights cut through the night. Titus was punctual. The truck stopped, the engine hummed, then fell silent. The door swung open, and Titus stepped out. Dressed in a tailored, earth-toned suit, he looked like a man who answered to no one. Moonlight caught his features, highlighting the sharp lines of his face. His light brown eyes surveyed us briefly, taking stock. Every move was deliberate, radiating confidence.

"Well, well," he said smoothly as he descended the truck steps. "Quite the welcoming committee. I'd almost think you didn't trust me." His gaze briefly landed on Peach, who sat on a nearby crate, calmly flipping through a magazine and seemingly oblivious to everyone gathered. Her light hair shimmered under the harsh lights as she ignored his stare.

He scanned the rest of us. Onyx stood in the shadows with arms crossed and a stern gaze. Alicia leaned against a support beam, watching quietly. The twins whispered loudly to each other, arguing over who would open the first crate.

"Trust isn't the issue," I replied, stepping forward. "The issue is ensuring the bargain is met. I don't make blind deals with anyone, Titus."

A smirk tugged at the corner of Titus's mouth, subtle but amused. "Pragmatic as ever, I see. Shall we?" He gestured to the back of the truck where his men were unloading the crates.

As Chase and Derek inspected the goods, Titus's gaze flicked back to Peach with curiosity but quickly returned to me, as if catching himself.

Derek popped the lid off the first box with exaggerated enthusiasm. "Ooh," he said loudly, lifting one of the weapons like it was the Holy Grail. "Ahh," he added, spinning it theatrically in his hands. He shot Titus a sideways glance. "It's like Christmas morning, but Santa finally got tired of my wish list and said, 'Fine, here's a bazooka.'"

Titus arched a brow, smirking. "Not only are my weapons top of the line, but their presentation and style are a statement in themselves. You should try it sometime, Derek."

"Oh, trust me," Derek quipped, grinning as he leaned toward Chase. "If I start dressing like that," he waved a hand at Titus, "people might expect me to have class."

Peach let out a soft laugh, finally glancing up from her magazine. "Oh, and we can't have that," she said, her purple eyes locking on Titus briefly before returning to her pages. Alicia chuckled, the sound light, easing some of the tension from the air.

Chase ignored them, pulling out a rifle and inspecting it intently. "It's all here. Exactly what you requested."

"Of course it is," Titus said smoothly. "I'm a man of my word."

I kept my gaze steady. "You'll forgive me if I take no one's word at face value."

Titus's smirk faltered briefly before he recovered. "You're thorough, Dayken. I'll give you that."

"Chase?" I prompted.

Chase inspected another weapon, nodding. "Quality's impeccable. It's solid."

"Great," I told Titus. "The Muskegon and coastal areas are yours. I've already signed; now you just need to do the same."

Titus nodded, showing his genuine respect. "Dayken, I admire your steadfastness more each moment."

"He's too smooth. He's probably planning a 'world domination' speech," Derek whispered to Chase.

"Shut up, Derek," Chase retorted, smiling faintly.

Alicia rolled her eyes. "If you two are done, maybe we can finish up here?" she asked.

Titus let out a quiet chuckle, shaking his head. "A pleasure doing business with you," he said, his tone blending charm and candidness. His gaze drifted to Peach one last time, his smirk softening, as if debating whether to say more. Peach responded with a slight smile, her expression guarded but amused.

"Get out of here before Derek tries to steal your jacket," I said, breaking the moment.

Titus's chuckle echoed as he climbed back into the truck. "Till next time, Danielson," he said before driving away into the darkness.

I turned to Chase and Derek. "Inventory check tonight. I want a full report by morning."

"Yes, boss," Derek said, giving me a mock salute before slinging an arm over Chase's shoulders. "Come on, bird boy. Let's not get fired for playing with the new toys."

I rolled my eyes and started back toward the compound entrance. Let them crack jokes. Humor wouldn't last forever, but for now, it was one thing that kept us grounded as the world edged closer to chaos.

As I crossed the dock, Alicia's voice caught my attention. "Did you see the way he kept looking at you?" she asked Peach in a teasing tone. "You had that fox rattled, Peach."

Peach flipped a page without glancing up. "Hmm. Didn't notice," she said playfully. I shook my head, suppressing a grin.

When I reached the back of the dock, I went to Onyx, who still watched from the shadows. I approached her, leaned in, and inhaled deeply. "You smell so fucking good," I murmured in her ear. I saw her pulse quicken, and goosebumps appeared.

"Good thing your pillow smells like me then," she purred. "Because that's the closest you're getting tonight. We have work to do." She was right. Our makeshift armory wouldn't build itself.

She kicked off the wall, putting distance between us, but my wolf loved the chase. She could run, but I knew firsthand how her body responded to me, and this was just the beginning.

Chapter 33

Onyx

The rhythmic thud of my fists hitting the training dummy filled the air as I worked through my drills. My breath came quick, muscles burning with exertion, but I welcomed the challenge. Each strike was a release, sharpening the edge I refused to dull. Dayken observed, advising me to tighten my timing and maintain momentum. I adjusted, throwing a rapid combo — jab, cross, hook — absorbing the impact, focused on movement and control.

"Alright, enough." Dayken's voice cut through my thoughts. "Let's see how you handle a real opponent."

I turned, wiping the hair from my forehead as he stepped onto the mat, rolling his shoulders. His green eyes held a challenge, a silent promise not to go easy on me. I welcomed it. The first exchange was a test. I feinted then struck, but he dodged easily, shifting as if predicting my moves. He was quick, but I was faster. I swept my leg low, making him hop back.

"Better," he said with a grin, sweat on his brow.

I nearly smiled, but was interrupted by a deafening screech that sliced through the room. My ears throbbed, and I instantly moved to cover them.

Dayken grabbed my arm. "We've got to move," he said, tone sharp.

Then Derek's voice blared over the PA, shouting, "Everyone, get to the security room! Now!" Realizing it was the alarm, the twins' alert system, made my stomach tighten.

"Oh no," I whispered, assuming the worst.

Dayken's eyes shot me a frantic look, but his tight jaw assured confidence as he gave me a firm nod. "Come on."

The training room door slammed open as we bolted out. My adrenaline surged, fueling every step as we sprinted down the hall, the pounding soles of my new boots echoing like a second heartbeat. The hallway was alive with activity. Figures darted past as clan members raced to their positions. It felt like the alarm had woken the Mack Clan bears out of hibernation.

We rounded the corner, and Alicia emerged from another hallway. She fell into step beside us without a word, her presence reassuring. Her towering frame and focused expression radiated a calm authority, even in the chaos around us.

The screeching alarm continued to claw at my ears, but I pushed it aside. I was laser-focused on one thing: reaching the security room and figuring out who — or what — had triggered the alarm.

By the time we arrived, the twins were already deep into the emergency response protocol. Chase sat at the controls, his fingers flying over the keyboard with practiced precision. The monitors cast an eerie glow over his focused expression as the rhythmic tapping of keys filled the room. Derek stood behind him, arms crossed, his dark, calculating eyes scanning the screens intently. Whatever they saw had stripped away all humor, leaving behind a grim atmosphere that was impossible to ignore, affirming the gravity of the situation.

Sky and Peach were the next to arrive. Peach hovered nervously near the entrance, her hands fidgeting as she glanced uneasily at the glowing screens. Sky stepped in beside her, her petite frame calm and composed. Her blue eyes sharpened with determination as they flicked to the monitors, already assessing the situation.

Kolton followed closely behind Sky, his presence impossible to miss. His orange hair was as chaotic as ever, sticking out in all directions, and his expression was tense as he started pacing. He lingered near Sky, his body protective and alert as his yellow eyes darted between the twins and the monitors, ready for anything.

The air in the room seemed to compress as everyone gathered, the unspoken apprehension pressing down on us. Derek finally moved, spinning to face us with an urgency that sent a chill racing down my spine.

He'd finally found what he was searching for. Pointing aggressively at the screen, he barked, "We've got company en route!" His voice was razor-edged, cutting through the silence. "And a lot of it!"

Murmurs erupted across the room, nervous energy spreading like wildfire, but Chase didn't falter. His hands flew over the controls with practiced ease, his voice calm and measured as he said, "Activating the emergency notification system to all surrounding clans."

The monitors flickered, and a red alert symbol pulsed on the main screen, casting an ominous glow over the room. Despite the chaos brewing around us, Chase remained steady, his focus unwavering as he worked to sound the alarm.

A loud ping echoed through the compound as the signal went live, the sharp sound bouncing off the walls like a warning bell. The pre-arranged alert had been sent, but it was a small comfort. Reinforcements might come — but we'd have to hold out long enough for them to arrive.

"Where are they?" I called. My voice was tight, matching the knot of anxiety in my chest. Every second felt like an eternity.

Derek's dark eyes flicked toward me, his expression grim. "They're on Route 67," he said, turning back to the monitors. "The highway camera picked them up about a mile and a half out. They tripped the motion sensors right around here." He pointed to a spot on the satellite map.

Then his hands gestured to the screen, where grainy footage showed shadowy shapes moving in our direction with unnerving purpose. I swallowed hard, a cold dread creeping into my stomach as the size of the approaching force became clearer on the screen.

Chase's knitted cap sat haphazardly over his black hair, as if he'd shoved it on without second thought. He seemed entirely unbothered by it, his focus unshakable as his fingers moved deftly over the controls. With a few precise keystrokes, the grainy feed came into focus, enhancing the footage until the screen displayed an unmistakable image: black SUVs tearing down the desolate highway. Their headlights sliced through the darkness, stark and unforgiving, like a cluster of beady eyes glaring at us from the void.

"They're moving fast," Derek added, leaning over Chase's shoulder, his gaze unrelenting as he analyzed every inch of the feed. His tone was clipped as he continued, "Convoy style. No attempt to cover their tracks. They want us to know they're coming."

A heavy silence settled over the room as the full weight of that information sank in. Kolton's insistent pacing slowed, his low growl finally ceasing, though the tension in his body remained palpable. The stark black vehicles slicing through the snow-dusted road on the screen weren't just a sign of their approach; they were a statement, a silent challenge we were more than ready to meet.

"Agreed. They're not being subtle," Alicia muttered from her spot by the door, her arms crossed tightly. "They're making sure we see them."

"Arrogant," Dayken said, his voice cold. His eyes stayed locked on the screen, taking in every detail of the convoy. "And it will be their downfall." He turned his gaze to me, his green eyes burning with determination. "It's a mistake to underestimate us."

Before I could respond, Derek jerked his head toward the door. "Armory. Let's go."

I turned to the main hall, still alive with activity. It was a short run to the makeshift weapons depot. Dayken burst through the doors, and I was right on his heels. Moments later, our companions filled the space, their expressions resolute. The muffled shuffle of boots and the metallic clang of weapons echoed off the walls, each sound charged with urgency.

Peach appeared amidst the commotion, slipping through the crowd with surprising grace as she passed out loaded magazines like Halloween candy, each placed into waiting hands. Her purple eyes gleamed, brighter and more determined than I'd ever seen. Her calm, focused demeanor was a stark contrast to the mayhem around her. She didn't need to speak; her silent efficiency said everything.

Dayken's commanding voice rose above the commotion, cutting through the noise like a blade. "Alright, everyone, just like we planned. We've been over this before, so stick to your zones! Mack, lead the first-floor team in the north. Derek and Chase, take the second floor and the roof — keep me updated on their movements."

He clipped a tablet to his belt with practiced ease. The twins mirrored his action, perfectly in sync. "When the rest of the Mack Clan gets here, we'll have them set up suppressive fire at the south entrance. Until then, Onyx, Sky, Kolton, and I will secure the south."

Alicia nodded, methodically strapping weapons to her chest, waist, and thigh. "They should arrive quickly. Until then, I've got a few bears roaming the forest nearby. I'll call them in," she said, pulling her unruly curls into a low ponytail. "But I need these two to let them in fast."

The twins nodded in unison once more, their synchronicity as uncanny as ever, despite their stark physical differences.

The clan members fell into line, their movements like a well-oiled machine. My rifle felt heavier than it should have when Dayken handed it to me. His green eyes locked onto mine with an intensity that steadied me more than I cared to admit.

"They think they've got us pinned," he said, his voice low but brimming with quiet determination. He checked the magazine on his rifle; his massive frame made the weapon look like a toothpick. "Let's prove them wrong."

I nodded, swallowing hard to push down the lump in my throat. "How many are we talking?"

Dayken glanced at the tablet in his hand, jaw tightening. "Enough to make this messy," he muttered. Despite his attempt to mask it, his concern hit me like a freight train. He forced a grim smile, resolve shining through. "They're confident. Probably think we'll scatter. But they're wrong."

Sky appeared silently at my side, her hand light on my arm. Her presence was steady, a quiet anchor amidst the approaching hurricane, but her words carried an undeniable urgency. "We'll hold the southwest corridor," she said, voice firm as she gestured toward Kolton, who stood near one of the many walls of weapons. He was rifling through the options with his usual single-minded intensity, his frantic energy matching the scene. "You stay with Dayken on the main south line."

"Like hell we're splitting up," I snapped, the words spilling out before I could stop them. But Sky's calm, steady gaze held me in place.

"Onyx," she said, her tone gentle yet unyielding, something only Sky could pull off. "You'll hold the line. We need you there. There's no reason for the four of us to be that close to the loading dock, and you know it."

I clenched my jaw, ready to argue, but before I could, Kolton came barreling to Sky's side. His expression was a storm of dismay. Clearly, he was upset that she had slipped away from him for all of two seconds, which had gone unnoticed.

And in his hands… were grenades.

Grenades. That's what he chose?!

He should absolutely *not* be allowed to have grenades.

I pushed the thought away, forcing myself to focus. If anyone could keep Sky out of harm's way, it was this maniac. The grenades, however, were a problem for another time.

I hadn't even realized Derek had left until his voice boomed over the intercom. "They're about ten minutes out if they maintain this speed. Keep them together, and don't let them scatter. Get ready."

Ten minutes. Just enough time to wrap up here and get into position. The hum of energy in the compound was so tense, the approaching threat pressing down like its own tangible force.

Dayken's voice sliced through the tension as he placed a tender hand under my chin, tilting my head up until his green eyes locked with mine, steady and reassuring. "I've got you. Don't worry," he said, his tone low and confident. Then he nodded toward my sister. "Stay sharp, Sky, Kolton. Let's make them regret ever coming for us."

I forced a tight grin, gripping my rifle until my knuckles turned white. Whatever was coming, we weren't going down without a fight.

Chapter 34

Dayken handed me a tablet to hook to my belt before we left the armory and headed toward the south entrance. I couldn't shake the feeling that the building had become a pressure cooker. The walls felt too tight, the air too still, pressing in from all sides.

I moved quickly; my steps urgent as I made my way down the dimly lit corridor toward the nearest stairwell. The soft hum of the compound filled the space, but a faint prickling sensation crept up my spine, a subtle warning that I couldn't ignore. I paused mid-stride, my ears straining for any sound out of place. Dayken stopped beside me, trusting my instincts.

Raised voices drifted from somewhere behind me, harsh and cutting through the stillness. My muscles tensed until I recognized Kolton's low, growling tone. It was unmistakable, and a second later, Sky's response followed, steady but laced with vexation. I homed in and directed my hearing toward their conversation.

"You're staying here, underground, where it's safe!" Kolton barked, his voice bouncing off the metal walls like a physical blow.

When I realized what was happening, I motioned for Dayken to continue to the loading dock without me. Not having time to argue, he forged ahead, knowing I'd follow as soon as I could.

I quickly switched directions, sprinting back the way we came. I rounded the corner just in time to catch the scene. Kolton was pacing, his movements wild and erratic, his hands clenched in tight fists at his sides. His yellow eyes blazed with frustration, the feral edge to his glare practically burning a hole through Sky.

Sky, in stark contrast, stood perfectly still. Her petite frame exuded a calm resolve that only seemed to infuriate Kolton all the more. Her light blue eyes tracked his every movement, steady and unwavering, as if she were weathering a storm. It was clear she wasn't backing down, and that calm defiance was pouring fuel onto Kolton's fire.

"Kolton, I'm not hiding away while everyone else fights," she said, her tone unyielding.

I felt my own irritation rise as Kolton's pacing became more frantic. His agitation wasn't helping anyone, not Sky, not him, and definitely not my fraying patience. When he stopped pacing and advanced on her, his voice rose to a near-snarl, and I instinctively inched toward them.

"You don't understand — they'll kill you. It's my job to protect you. Let me do my job!" he snapped, his large frame towering over her.

Sky didn't even flinch. Her expression stayed calm, but there was steel in her voice. "And I'm telling you: it's my decision to make, not yours."

I'd seen enough. I stepped forward, my voice harsh. "Kolton, back off."

Before I could get any closer, Sky's hand shot up, palm facing me in a silent command. Her eyes flicked to me for only a second, but the message was clear: *I've got this.* I stopped in my tracks, my jaw tightening as I forced myself to trust her to manage her Guardian. She always had to handle things her own way, even if it made me want to shake her sometimes.

Kolton, of course, didn't notice — or didn't care. His focus was entirely on Sky. He let out a frustrated growl, raking his hands through his disheveled orange hair. "Damn it, Sky!" His voice cracked, his emotions spilling out like water through broken glass. "You don't get it. I've already failed you once. Do you know what that did to me? I'm not letting it happen again!"

Sky tilted her head slightly, her gaze icy. "Do you think this is all about you?" she shot back, her tone sharp. "Your guilt doesn't give you the right to make decisions for me."

Kolton froze for a second, his chest heaving as he searched for a response. When he finally spoke, his voice was low, almost a growl. "If I have to, I'll tie you up and throw you in the supply closet to keep you down here."

He's serious.

That did it. I pushed forward again, ready to intervene, but Sky's hand was back up before I could say a word. She took a step closer to Kolton, her composure unbroken even as her voice dropped to a dangerous level.

"You will *not*," she said, her tone like ice. "Think about what you just said. Really think about it."

Kolton's yellow eyes flickered, but instead of stepping back, he doubled down. His voice was desperate and trembling as he said, "I'll do whatever it takes to keep you safe. Even if I have to restrain—"

The slap came out of nowhere. Sky's hand cut through the air and connected with Kolton's cheek. A sharp, echoing crack reverberated through the hallway, freezing everything. I blinked, stunned. So did Kolton. His head had turned from the force of the strike, his body going still as he processed what had just happened.

Sky's voice, sharp and unrelenting, filled the silence. "You are my Guardian, Kolton, and your job is to guard. Now is your chance. Fight for me up there, *please*. But you will not hold me prisoner to keep me out of this. This is my fight."

Kolton didn't respond. He didn't even move. The fire in his eyes was gone, replaced with something softer — shock, maybe, or guilt. Whatever it was, it kept him rooted to the spot as Sky turned on her heel and strode past him with the kind of grace and confidence only she could exude.

As she passed me, I fell into step beside her. I said, in a voice low enough that only she could hear, "I swear, Sky, sometimes you're terrifying."

Her lips twitched, but she didn't respond. When I glanced over my shoulder, Kolton was still standing there, staring at the wall like it held all the answers. Good. Maybe he needed a minute to cool off and reconsider his role as a Guardian.

With the loading dock attached to the compound, I didn't have to go far. When I got there, I reached down and rolled one of the metal doors up into the ceiling, discovering Dayken on the other side. Open air rushed in, but we were still shielded by the wide overhang, its weight supported by thick concrete beams and heavy columns that framed the dock. A row of raised platforms stretched along the structure, each with its own blue dock plate, sturdy metal ramp, and tall roll-up door. There were five bays in total, but we only opened one of them. Even with the breeze cutting through, the space felt controlled — built for movement, for function, and ready for whatever bloodshed was about to spill in.

As we stepped onto the nearest platform, Derek's voice crackled over the comm on my shoulder. "They're breaching the perimeter!"

Dayken glanced down at his tablet, his jaw tightening at what he saw. I looked at the screen just in time to see two SUVs smash through the first gate, brutal and deliberate. Once inside, they swerved to make way for two more vehicles, which were equipped with thick metal bars welded to their hoods. My chest constricted as they rammed the second set of gates, one car on each side, breaking through with terrifying force.

A falcon's cry echoed overhead, piercing and frantic, cutting through the chaos. My stomach churned as the SUVs spilled onto the compound's main grounds, their charge relentless and efficient.

"Here they come," I murmured, dread pooling in my chest. Panic seized me as my thoughts turned to Sky. I wished I could see her, confirm her safety, but I had to trust that orange-haired, feral beast. I knew he had calmed himself and took his place at her side; I could smell his odd, earthy tone. But it still left me uneasy. Sky and I had always fought together. It felt wrong to be separated like this.

"They won't get far," Dayken growled as we reached one of the metal ramps and stepped off the loading dock. The distant echo of shouts and the rumble of approaching engines made the space feel tense, charged with the promise of bloodshed.

He paused, hand on the railing. His eyes swept our surroundings, assessing every shadow. Then, his gaze locked onto mine. His rugged face, one I'd fantasized about more times than I'd admit, softened. For a moment, the hard edge I'd come to rely on melted away, revealing something raw and unguarded, a storm of emotions beneath the surface.

"Onyx," he began, his voice low but urgent. The words spilled out like he feared he wouldn't get another chance. "I need you to know something — something I should've said a long time ago. No matter what happens, you've always had my respect, my admiration, my loyalty. Every choice I've made, every thought in my head, somehow comes back to you. I'm completely consumed by you, Onyx. And it's not because of the bo—"

I didn't let him finish. Before I could stop myself, I closed the space between us. He was perfect, so good, so steady, everything I wasn't. I didn't deserve him. Gods, I knew it. And yet again, I found myself relying on actions to say what words never could.

Toe to toe, I raised my hand to his cheek. My hand was trembling, but my touch was tender. I reached up, and I slammed my mouth to his, fierce and unyielding, desperate to convey everything I couldn't say.

"Tell me when this is over," I whispered against his lips, my voice weighted with emotion. Then I pivoted, breaking away, and sprinted toward the nearest concrete beam. Pressing my back against the cool, solid structure, I strained my ears, listening for the footsteps I knew would arrive at any second.

Our comms buzzed in our ears, Derek's voice crackling through. "Well, if you two lovebirds are done making out, you've got incoming." *Damn it, I forgot about the cameras.* "As predicted, it looks like they thought the back was the best place to start. Bears are here — I can smell them. Alicia will probably send them your way any moment now."

I ignored his initial remark, focusing instead on the present, straining my ears to pick out the sound of heavy bear steps mixed with human ones.

"Who would've thought a little death and carnage would get you two all hot and bothered?" Derek continued over the comm. I took a deep breath, trying to summon patience, but he wasn't done.

"Kinky," he added with a smug lilt in his tone.

I rolled my eyes, the corner of my mouth twitching despite myself. I shot a glance at Dayken, who was already looking at me, shaking his head with a grin plastered on his face. As annoying as Derek was, I couldn't deny that his humor was a comforting distraction with the convoy approaching.

The sound of footsteps grew louder, mingling with the low murmur of voices and the faint clinking of gear and packs as they rustled from movement. I pressed my rigid back harder against the cold concrete, every muscle coiled, waiting — another glance at Dayken, and he gave me a subtle nod. We didn't need words. And the thought that we probably never would was a quiet reassurance I didn't realize I needed.

Shoving the thought aside, I locked my focus on the figure entering the loading bay. His rifle swept the area, hunting for movement. He wouldn't find any — not from Dayken or me. We were shadows, waiting for the perfect moment.

I was patient, letting him take a few more steps, making him think he was undetected. Then I moved. In one fluid motion, I lunged, grabbing the barrel of his rifle and wrenching it sideways. I drove my knee into his stomach, hard enough to make him fold over like paper. Before he could hit the ground, I yanked him back upright, using his body as a shield.

Dayken emerged from his spot, taking advantage of the moment. His rifle cracked three times in rapid succession as he fired at the men spilling inside.

Gunfire erupted, echoing through the open bay, but nothing came close to hitting me. I pitched the body in my hands to the side, ready to move again, when a deafening roar shook the air. The unmistakable crunch of paws on snow echoed from behind the soldiers. The Mack Clan burst out of the frozen landscape onto the concrete. The strategy completely blindsided the remaining humans. The bears' guttural growls ripped through the mayhem as they charged.

I didn't hesitate. While the enemy faltered, I shifted my grip, pulling my rifle into position. One of the bears had a soldier by the leg, thrashing him violently. My sights locked on the soldier's head. One precise shot, and he went limp, my forced training coming back to me instinctively.

Dayken moved in beside me, his aim clean and deliberate. I didn't have to check; I knew he'd take care of my blind spots.

Another soldier rounded the corner; his weapon aimed directly at me. I dropped low, grabbing the knife from the belt of the man I'd just dispatched. The blade left my hand effortlessly, sinking into the soldier's shoulder from sheer muscle memory. He staggered back, screaming, and Dayken's shot finished him before he could recover.

We moved like a storm, unrelenting and unstoppable. Another soldier charged me, thinking he caught me by surprise. He didn't. I pivoted, using his momentum against him, and drove my elbow through his jaw into the back of his skull, the crack of bone reverberating through my arm. The man slumped to the ground, silent and lifeless. Behind me, Dayken fired again, the consistent rhythm of his rifle sounding off like a drum, keeping the beat of war.

And just as quickly as it started, the gunfire slowed. The surviving soldiers scrambled back the way they'd come, their shouts fading into the distance. I watched as the bears chased after them, their massive frames disappearing into the snow.

Beside me, Dayken reloaded his weapon, his focus sharp as his eyes swept the corridor. I pulled my comm to my mouth. "Loading dock clear. For now."

Our comms buzzed with a response, Derek's voice breaking through. "Roger that." Then, after a pause, his tone shifted. "Second wave of backup just arrived. You're going to want to see this."

I glanced down at the tablet strapped to my belt, unhooked it, and brought it up to see what Derek meant. But first, I needed to check on Sky. With a quick toggle to a different camera view, I spotted her alongside Kolton as they held their position in the southwest corridor. They moved with precision, picking off stragglers who had unfortunately stumbled straight into the belly of the beast. If those men thought that section of the compound was a weak spot, my little sister and her pet tiger showed them they were sorely mistaken.

Chapter 35

Dayken

I watched as Onyx monitored her tablet. Her pale blue irises stood stark against her pupils, dilated to thin slits from the firefight. The lingering edge of battle clung to her, sharpening her focus as she scanned the feed intently. Her hair was pulled back for once, secured in a tight ponytail that trailed down her back, leaving her profile fully exposed. The sight was striking, too striking.

I snapped myself out of the unintentional trance she put on me and took advantage of the lull in movement, forcing my attention back on our surroundings.

If any footsteps drew near, I knew Onyx would hear them immediately. Her ability to detect the slightest sound or pick up the faintest scent was uncanny, a rare skill among her kind, and a crucial edge in the situation at hand. I crouched beside the nearest body, rifling through pockets and pouches for any useful intel, identification, or even a hint of their objective. Any scrap of information could bring us closer to understanding who these monsters were and what this agency wanted. Right now, we were fighting blind, at a clear disadvantage, and I needed something — anything — to start piecing together a motive.

All I knew was that they wanted Onyx back, but I couldn't understand why they were so hell-bent on returning her to the facility, back to the hands of her torturer. What was their main objective? Research and development didn't seem like a strong enough justification.

Suddenly, the air shifted. A deep, rhythmic whooshing sound filled the bay, vibrating in my chest. The moonlight dimmed, the shadows around us shifting. The tall industrial lights outside were blotted out completely, leaving us in true darkness.

Onyx was already moving, stepping out from under the awning and onto the snow-covered ground. Her boots crunched against the icy surface as she strode into the open. I pushed myself to my feet and followed, pausing just under the edge of the bay's overhang.

Outside, the shadows over the snow deepened, and I saw what had darkened the sky.

The Avery Clan had arrived.

They came in like a swarm, massive wings outstretched, screeches filling the air. We stared in awe as they flew over us, towards the front of the compound. Onyx pulled her tablet out again. We watched through the feed as they descended on the humans like a wave crashing against the shore. At the center of the attack was Derek, his form half-human, half-bird. His powerful, brown-feathered wings extended from his back, moving with calculated precision to propel him into the air in sharp bursts. He still had human arms, his rifle steady in his grasp as he fired with ruthless accuracy, and his legs carried him with inhuman agility as he landed a brutal kick before soaring upward again.

"Don't blink!" Derek's voice rang out through the comms, laced with excitement. "You'll miss the show!"

"As thrilled as I am by his arrogance, I think we should let Sky and Kolton know we abandoned our posts," Onyx said, her gaze still fixed on the tablet screen. "They can handle the back. I think we'll be more useful up front."

I smirked, unable to resist. "You just want in on the action. Can't stand the idea of Derek hogging all the glory for himself," I said with a wink.

Onyx scoffed, her eyes rolling and then sparkling with mischief as she tore her gaze from the tablet and turned it on me. Gods, she was beautiful.

Her fingers moved deftly as she returned to the camera feeds, toggling and searching for Sky and Kolton. The moment she located them, she reached for her comm.

"Sky," she said, her fangs flashing as she spoke. Her voice was steady but clipped. "We're abandoning the loading dock. Derek needs our help up front. You and Kolton will have to hold the entire south now. The Mack Clan is still here for backup if you need them."

Sky's voice came through, clear and calm. "Got it. Be careful."

Kolton's unhinged growl followed, rumbling through the comm before it cut out.

Onyx inhaled deeply as she snapped the tablet back onto her belt. I couldn't tell if the steadying breath was because of Kolton's antics or in preparation for the battle out front. But when she looked at me, determination radiated off her, cutting through any lingering doubt.

Without another word, we raced off at a sprint, boots crunching through the snow as we rounded the building toward the front entrance. The sounds of chaos and death hit us before we even got a visual of the scene — gunfire cracked through the air, shouts tangled with the harsh cries of the falcons as they danced through the sky, and the guttural growls of Mack's bears rumbled like a storm, filling the air with raw power.

We barely had time to slow before we were in the thick of it. More SUVs were pulling in, their doors swinging open as agents spilled out, six to eight bodies per vehicle, weapons at the ready.

The bears, massive and relentless, tore through the advancing men with brutal efficiency. One agent let out a strangled scream as a grizzly swiped him aside like he was nothing more than a rag doll, his body flung through the air before crashing limply to the ground. Blood splattered the dirt and snow, mingling with the scent of sweat and gunpowder.

Through the chaos, my eyes locked onto a massive grizzly, its brown coat streaked red with the enemy's blood. Recognition hit instantly.

Alicia.

Fighting side by side with her people. Like a true Primarc.

Above, the falcons dominated the skies. They moved with terrifying precision, their wings slicing through the icy air as they swooped down, ripping weapons from the hands of unsuspecting agents. Talons slashed across faces, leaving eye sockets empty and hollow in their wake. One agent fumbled for his rifle, only to have it snatched away as a falcon's talons raked across his arm, leaving him defenseless.

The moon, barely visible through the gray clouds, glinted off Derek's wings as he descended, his rifle firing in controlled bursts. He moved like a shadow, landing for a split second to take down an enemy before launching back into the air.

Raising my rifle, I aimed at the first agent who came into view, his focus locked on the bears. He never saw it coming.

Onyx was already ahead of me, moving with deadly grace. She took cover behind a giant cement planter near the front door, her eyes scanning the battlefield as she fired off a shot that sent another agent sprawling. Her movements were precise and efficient, with no wasted energy.

"Dayken!" she called over her shoulder, nodding toward a group of agents trying to load what looked like an RPG near one of the SUVs. "Cover me!"

I was already moving, laying down fire to pin them in place as Onyx broke into a sprint. Her form blurred against the snowy backdrop, a force of nature tearing through the mayhem with ruthless efficiency, a beautiful wraith amongst the bloody havoc.

But my protective instincts — my wolf — were stronger than I anticipated. The need to abandon my cover and act as her personal shield gnawed at me, building with every step she took. My pulse thundered in my ears as I fought against the wolf inside me, the primal urge demanding that I shift and put myself between her and every danger ahead.

I clenched my fists. The battle raging within me was almost unbearable. Onyx advanced, oblivious to my inner turmoil, her movements unfaltering and deadly as she carved a path through the thickest fog of battle. I followed close behind, acting as her shadow. But all I wanted was to be in front of her, to shield her from the awaiting storm.

Her destination was clear: the front gate. She was heading for a bottleneck, likely intending to choke off their reinforcements and trap them. The closer she got, the thicker the frenzy became, and the harder it was for me to hold myself back.

My vision shifted, narrowing unnaturally as my wolf clawed its way to the surface. I felt the telltale prick of fur sprouting on my arms, the pressure of my teeth elongating. Every instinct screamed to shift, to protect her no matter the cost. And then—

It happened.

Chapter 36

Onyx

I twisted and cut down another nearby enemy, adrenaline surging through me. An arrow suddenly whistled past, hitting my next opponent square in the neck. I froze, spun around, and saw a blonde figure on the rooftop with a bow: Peach.

"There's no way Peach is using a freaking bow and arrow," I muttered under my breath, disbelief threatening to cloud my focus. But my eyes did not lie.

Sweet, innocent Peach was confident amid the chaos, seemingly born for this. Her golden hair caught the dim light as she knocked another arrow, movements graceful and fluid. Arrow after arrow hit its mark with deadly accuracy.

I tightened my grip on my blade, tearing my gaze away from her. Peach's unexpected skill was a surprising comfort, but it wasn't enough to pull my focus away from the fight. Who knew what other surprises she was hiding?

When I turned to look for Dayken, I was unprepared for what I saw. The wolf was a blur of dark fur and muscle, a force of carnage. Firing a weapon was one thing — ripping throats, shattering bones, and dismembering limbs was another. That was exactly what Dayken was doing.

Massive paws pinned a man to the ground while Dayken's powerful jaws tore through another's jugular, leaving nothing but shredded uniforms and crimson pools in his wake. My stomach churned for half a second before another arrow zipped by, snapping me out of my stupor. This was no time to gape at the blood dripping from Dayken's muzzle.

Peach landed another hit from the rooftop, her aim impeccable. As if she could sense my startled thoughts, her voice buzzed through the comms, singsong and with a small giggle — utterly unbothered.

"I've always loved archery."

That was enough to remind me why there wasn't time to process the wolf's carnage or Peach's random skill set. Pivoting, I headed toward the SUVs at the front gate. If I could stop their access and bottleneck them at the fence, it would give us the advantage.

The fence had been built deliberately high, far too tall to scale without exposing yourself. And if anyone tried? The falcons circling above would pick them off before their feet even hit the ground. It was a simple tactic, but it was the best shot we had to keep the fight from spilling into the main compound.

Dodging a strike, my blade flashed as I dropped another attacker. My focus snapped back to the SUVs. Slowly but surely, they were being forced to retreat — either rammed backward, abandoned, or cracked open as a Guardian ripped someone straight out of the driver's seat. Whatever the method, it was working. That choke point was doing its job, forcing our enemies to slow down and funnel them into predictable lines of attack.

Now it was just a matter of keeping them there.

My body ached, every muscle screaming from the relentless barrage of raising my rifle, dodging, punching, kicking, and the endless swing of my blade. My arms felt like lead, my legs heavier with each step, but I wasn't done. Not even close. We were holding the line, forcing them back, bit by bit, when something else caught my attention, a vehicle that didn't belong.

Among the all-black SUVs, a new car approached. The silver SUV stood out with gleaming crossbars and roof lights in the haze. It looked reinforced and meant to carry something, or someone, important. A cold knot tightened in my gut as warning bells rang.

And then another one appeared.

And another.

"You guys seeing this?" Chase's voice rang out over our comms.

"What's happening?" Sky asked with a hint of panic, her normally calm demeanor gone.

Fuck, something is very wrong.

Panic started to wrap around my chest like a vice, threatening to choke the air out of me. My grip on my blade tightened until my knuckles screamed in protest, but I forced myself to stay grounded. They hadn't broken through to the rear of the compound yet. They weren't spilling into the forest or scattering through our defenses. They definitely couldn't cut through the thick fence. That meant Sky was still safe, for now, with that tiger guarding her.

A flash of orange fur darted past my leg. Barely reaching my knee, it wasn't big enough to be a wolf. I blinked, and another streak of black fur followed, then white, then another blur of orange.

I barely had time to register what was happening before one of the creatures launched itself at a man directly in front of me, jaws locking onto his throat with terrifying accuracy. Blood sprayed in a hot arc as the man crumpled, his gurgled scream lost in the chaos. The creature didn't hesitate, moving with lithe efficiency, already seeking its next target.

"Sharp Clan at your service, ma'am!" an unfamiliar voice called out from across the battlefield, clear, cool, and almost amused.

I turned just in time to see a well-armed man firing a handgun with lethal accuracy. Each shot was fired casually, like he was punching in for another shift at work. He appeared to enjoy this.

This was madness.

This was war.

And somehow, it was *wildly* impressive.

Titus and his clan had arrived, and they weren't holding back. More foxes darted and weaved through the battlefield, their movements precise and deadly, causing ripples of panic among the enemy ranks.

I couldn't help but wonder, was Titus one of these massive foxes? Did he come here himself? Or better yet, was he somewhere in the chaos, orchestrating the bloodbath with that calculating mind of his?

The arrival of the new SUVs was almost forgotten in the fray, until I heard the dull *thunk* of their doors slamming shut. More reinforcements. The foxes didn't hesitate; they immediately responded to the new threat.

These men were covered head to toe in SWAT-style riot gear, forcing their attackers to work harder for a clean hit. Dayken remained at my side, tearing through bodies like a force of nature. I barely flinched when he dislodged an arm from a man's body, blood oozing onto the ground.

The foxes noticed Dayken's method and quickly changed tactics. One man. Four foxes. Each grabbed a limb and pulled, causing a sickening pop as they dropped their trophies.

"Dayken," I called out as I drove my elbow into the ribs of the man in front of me, spinning to slash my knife across another's throat. Blood gushed, hot and fast, as the body crumpled. I barely had time to wipe the sweat from my brow before another enemy lunged at me.

I faced him head-on, twisting as he swung and ramming my knee into his stomach. He gasped, doubling over, and I finished him with a clean strike to the back of his neck. "Remind me," I panted, brushing a bloody strand of hair from my face, "to never underestimate any of these foxes again." My breath was heavy, and my muscles burned from the brutal fight.

Dayken, still in his wolf form, tore through an enemy just a few feet away, his massive jaws snapping down on the man's shoulder with a sickening *crack*. He tossed the limp body aside like a rag doll, his dark eyes flicking toward me.

His only response was a low, guttural growl — deep, rough, and vibrating through the air. It was as close to an 'Okay' as I was going to get.

Good enough.

Chapter 37

Onyx

I didn't have enough time to appreciate the Guardians' thoroughness as more gunshots echoed through the chaos. One shot had a higher pitch, accompanied by a distant whistling sound, indicating that they had deployed a sniper.

"Avery Clan — I hear something up in the trees. I think they are trying to snipe us," I yelled into my comm.

Silence… everyone was too busy to respond. I would have to trust that they heard me and would take the direction. Then my thoughts went to our own "sniper." I grabbed the comm again while simultaneously disarming a man, firing his weapon into his chest. "Peach, you'll be exposed to the sniper up there. Take cover."

I didn't hear a response before another car door slammed. This one was louder than any of the previous, indicating it was reinforced. A figure appeared, his polished boots crunching over debris as sounds of the battle seemed to fade in his presence, and bullets whizzed by without alarming him.

He moved with a predator's grace, unhurried, effortless. His posture was deceptively relaxed, arms spread wide, no weapon in hand. Untouchable.

Then his voice sliced through the pandemonium like a blade of ice, cold, deliberate, and laced with venom.

"Behold your pale-skinned monsters. You think they're this way because they were born like this?"

His voice carried effortlessly over the battlefield, slicing through the chaos and commanding silence from those closest to him. He wasn't speaking to anyone in particular; perhaps he was talking to everyone.

He let out a dry, humorless laugh. "Hah." The sound scraped against my skin, eerily familiar, a ghost of something I hoped to never hear again.

"No." His voice dropped lower, each syllable sharp as a scalpel. "They are this way because of me."

I froze.

A sudden, suffocating pressure crushed the air from my lungs. That voice—

No.

No. No!

My gaze snapped to him, my stomach twisting violently as my worst nightmare stepped into the light.

It was *him.*

I had never seen his face, but I would know that voice until my death. That voice had been there through every second of my suffering.

"Again."

"More."

"Not done yet."

The memories crashed upon me, vicious and unrelenting, every unseen scar burning with phantom pain. I struggled to quell my body's natural response — panic— the same way I reacted to seeing the treadmills. I tried to cover my ears, to rip the sound out of existence, but I couldn't.

I wouldn't.

I wouldn't show weakness. Not to him. Not to the monster who tried to break me.

Not while I was still standing.

His dark coat billowed in the wind. He looked smug as his gaze swept over the carnage like a king surveying his newly conquered realm. He gestured grandly, as if unveiling his masterpiece.

"Me," he repeated, his grin stretching wider. "And me alone."

Then his eyes landed on me.

He didn't hesitate.

He approached me with icy confidence, every step deliberate and inevitable. My muscles stiffened, my breath froze, caught in a moment I couldn't escape. But before I could even process the terror gripping my ribs, Dayken moved.

He must have sensed exactly what was happening through the bond, the effect this man had on me, because in a blur of movement, he jumped in front of me.

The man's hand darted into his pocket, so fast it barely registered, then a muffled crack split the air.

A shot was fired.

He fired from inside his coat, not even bothering to pull the weapon free. The bullet struck Dayken square in the chest, and the force sent him staggering backward, into me.

"No!" I screamed, catching his weight as he stumbled.

Panic surged through me, but then — out of nowhere — the memory of what he told me when we first met echoed through my mind:

"That won't kill me, you know. It'll hurt like hell, but it won't kill me."

"Dayken, please," I begged, barely holding myself together.

He just nodded, steady and unwavering, as if he already knew what I was about to ask.

Thank fuck.

Now it was time to kill that son of a bitch for shooting my wolf.

Before I could move, Sky chose that exact moment to enter the fray. She surged forward, as if each step fueled her determination — she was done holding back. Her tiger prowled at her side, muscles coiled, eyes locked on the threat before us.

The monster's smile twisted, turning more amused and viler — a sick sort of glee dancing in his eyes. "And look at you now," he sneered, taking a slow, measured step forward. "Two ungrateful brats, pretending to be warriors."

His voice dripped with derision, but beneath it, something sharper lurked… something unhinged. "Do you have any idea what you've been given?" His tone rose, cutting through the air like shattered glass. "No, of course not."

His lips curled in disgust.

"Gifts." He spat the word like it tasted rotten. "I gave you gifts, and you dare to squander them."

What the fuck is he going on about?

Then he turned — casual, unbothered, like a man at a dinner party, not one on a battlefield.

I didn't hesitate. I took the opening, raising my gun and aiming dead center at the back of his head.

But before I could fire, pain exploded through my shoulder.

The force knocked me back, my arm falling limp at my side. For a second, my brain scrambled to catch up, to piece together what the hell had just happened. Then the tangy scent of metal filled my nose.

My blood.

Shot. I'd been shot.

Son of a bitch. That fucking hurt.

Through the haze of pain, I barely registered the psycho's retreating form. He didn't falter. Didn't so much as glance back. As if nothing had happened, he reached for the car door and opened it with a soft, deliberate click.

He reached into the back seat and yanked Aurora out by her throat. She struggled, gasping, her feet kicking against empty air as he held her aloft with effortless strength.

Dayken let out a furious snarl at the sight of his sister in that monster's hands.

"*Tsk tsk* Onyxiana. Relax that trigger finger. You wouldn't want to hurt this lovely lady," he drawled, holding Aurora as though she were nothing more than a sack of grain. "Who has been such an *immense help*." His tone dripped with mockery, his smile twisting into a cruel sneer. The words made my stomach twist, each syllable leaving behind a stain of doubt and dread.

What does that mean? Did she help him? Intentionally? Unintentionally?

My thoughts raced. Flashes of doubt and suspicion tore through my mind. Had Aurora betrayed us? Had she given something away, some secret, some advantage? Or was this just another one of his tricks? So many questions clawed at my mind, but the answers didn't come.

"But alas..." He shrugged and sighed theatrically, as though truly lamenting her supposed usefulness, lips curling into a foul grin. Then, his expression changed; gone was the faux sympathy. His eyes went cold — dead — devoid of any pretense of humanity as he looked at Aurora. "I am no longer in need of her assistance." He stared at Aurora with an almost clinical disinterest, like she was a tool he had finished using and was ready to discard.

And then he did.

Without warning, he threw her to the ground with a sickening thud. The sound of her body hitting the earth was dull and hollow, like a discarded, broken doll. I felt my knees weaken. The rage and helplessness inside me collided in a dizzying storm. I surged forward, every muscle in my body prepared to strike, but his voice stopped me cold.

"Ah, ah, ah," he chided, wagging a finger at me like a parent scolding a wayward child. "Don't be so hasty." There was no urgency in his tone, no hint of fear at what I might do. He spoke as though I were predictable, manageable — a mere pawn moving exactly as he'd planned.

"I don't need her, or you, anymore," he added, his words slamming into me. He tilted his head, a slow smile creeping across his face, every inch more sinister than the last. A chill prickled down my spine as his voice dropped, each word deliberate and pointed, almost intimate. "I'm here for someone else."

My chest tightened. A vise squeezed my ribs as a surge of emotions almost overwhelmed me. Fury bubbled to the surface, raw and unchecked, threatening to spill over.

This had to be another one of his twisted games. If he thought he could just waltz in and take the most precious thing in my life away from me — again — he was dead wrong.

"You bastard—" I snarled, my voice cracking under the weight of my rage.

"Ah, there it is!" he interrupted, clapping sharply. "That fire! I gave you that, too." He stepped closer, whispering, "Tell me, Onyxiana, does it burn? That rage inside you? Does it make you feel alive?" His grin widened, teeth gleaming. "It should, because I made you that way. You're mine, my little weapon. Every drop of blood you spill is a tribute to my design."

"She belongs to no one but *me*," said a voice that stopped everything. It was raw and raspy, distorted like an audio feed gone wrong. Gasps and murmurs rippled through the gathered crowd, raising alarm bells in my head. The sound was unnatural, foreign, but somehow it rang with a strange familiarity. It wasn't a threat to me, I knew that much instinctively.

I risked glancing away from the madman toward the source of the voice. My eyes locked on Dayken, standing tall in his wolf form. He looked menacing and radiated lethal power. The surrounding foxes, bears, falcons, and wolves backed away in deference. Then it hit me, the voice had come from him. My wolf. My protector. Somehow, impossibly, he had spoken.

The man gave a soft, contempt-filled laugh, the sound grating. "Oh, this is rich," he sneered. His attention shifted to Dayken, ignoring me entirely now. "Look at what I've created. I've strengthened your bond so much, it can speak!" His evil laugh was piercing and maniacal.

He turned his back to me, spreading his arms wide as if presenting himself for attack, or taunting me to try. It was deliberate, calculated, a move meant to humiliate me and assert his control.

When I didn't move, he glanced over his shoulder, his smile never faltering. His voice dripped with smug satisfaction as he said, "No attack while I'm unarmed? A pity."

His eyes narrowed, the mockery giving way to sharp, gleaming malice. "You'll regret that hesitation, my dear. Because when this is over..." He turned to fully face me, his voice dropping to a lethal hiss. "You'll wish you'd killed me when you had the chance."

I tapped into every shred of resolve and strength I had left, chanting to myself: *This needs to be done. This is the final piece.* My heart screamed at me to move, and this time, I didn't hesitate. I moved so fast it shocked even me. New energy surged through my body, a power that felt like it had been lying dormant, waiting for me to reach for it.

Too quick for anyone to track, I closed the distance. My knife was at the sadistic bastard's throat so quickly that no one had a chance to even flinch. It was like the world was on a delay, stuck processing what had just happened.

"I made you," his voice was low, his gaze fixed on mine. His words were a taunt, meant to shake me, but they only strengthened my resolve. "And I will unmake you."

He moved fast, unnervingly so. My knife registered the movement late — almost too late.

Keyword: almost.

I twisted, removing the blade from his throat just in time, but not before driving my fist squarely into his nose. The crack was satisfying, and he staggered back with a hiss, blood streaming down his face. I quickly moved to reclaim my position, the knife once again pressed against his throat.

His dead eyes studied me, calculating, as if considering he might finally be out of his depth. Yet, he kept that maddening confidence, his smile still lingering.

I felt Sky behind me, too close for comfort. Her energy vibrated with tension, and I knew she was reading the situation just as clearly as I was.

The needle moved faster than I could track, straight into my hand. The liquid silver was a familiar sight as it sloshed around in the syringe. His thumb hit the plunger, starting to administer the poison before Sky popped into my peripheral and smashed the bones in his hand, causing him to let out a bellow of rage. And then Dayken lunged.

Chapter 38

Dayken

I watched as Onyx pressed a hunting knife to his throat, her grip steady, her intent lethal. The man didn't flinch. His dark eyes, unreadable yet calm, flicked down to the blade, then back up to Onyx's face — more curious than concerned.

I guessed he was in his mid-fifties — clean-cut but with unruly dark hair streaked with gray, giving him an ironic mad scientist look.

Off to the side, my sister lay crumpled on the ground, unmoving. The depth of his words hadn't fully settled, my mind unable to grasp what he had revealed about my own flesh and blood.

I glanced back at him. His posture was loose, almost indifferent, as his coat gently shifted in the breeze. He didn't move or step back, seemingly patient, waiting to see what Onyx would do.

I took my eyes off them to scan the scene. Most of the clans stood behind me, waiting. SUVs had stopped arriving, and the fighting had slowed. There were snipers in the trees, but I knew the falcons had been picking them off. Onyx would end this bastard, and we would walk away victorious.

Sky stood at Onyx's back, a silent support in the storm. Kolton, still in tiger form, reached out a paw, brushing against Sky's leg, as if trying to pull her back to safety.

In a blink, a syringe came out of nowhere. A flash of silver liquid, and then, Onyx began to lose her balance. All I could do was watch as it unfolded before me.

Sky lunged. Her fingers snapped around his hand, breaking bones as the syringe clattered to the ground. Then, she spun and drove a brutal roundhouse kick into the side of his head.

Onyx collapsed to the ground.

A bullet whizzed past.

Somehow, either by instinct or sheer luck, Sky twisted at the last second, and it landed harmlessly into the SUV instead.

As soon as that bastard hit the ground, Kolton lunged forward. His razor-sharp teeth bit into his throat, a menacing snarl echoing through the air.

I quickly joined Kolton, latching onto his hand with my jaws and crushing it with brutal strength, savoring the sickening crunch of bones shattering beneath my teeth.

I didn't need Onyx to tell me who this man was. I already knew. He was the one who had tortured her.

Mutilated her.

Broken her.

He was the reason she found it difficult to let anyone in, and the reason she had constructed thick walls around herself, keeping even those closest to her at a distance.

Yes. I would enjoy every single snap of his bones.

"Don't kill him." Sky's voice cut through my rage, firm, unwavering.

Kolton froze, his fangs still buried deep. A fox gnawed at the man's fingers, tearing flesh from bone — a gruesome sight, but fitting.

"We still need answers," Sky added.

The bastard lay there, unconscious. Whether from blood loss, sheer agony, or both, it didn't matter.

Good.

I turned to Onyx's limp body, immediately shifting back into my human form. My hands trembled as I ran them over her body, searching for wounds, the injection site, anything that would tell me what he did to her.

My heart shattered.

Her beautiful, lifeless form would haunt me for the rest of my days. If not for the faint rise and fall of her chest, I would have ripped that man's heart out and painted the compound with it.

Instead, I brushed her hair from her face and gently lifted her into my arms, cradling her close.

"I assume everyone else can take it from here," I said, my voice harsher than intended.

Bears, wolves, and foxes scattered. Heads dipped in silent acknowledgment.

Yes, they had it.

And I had her.

Chapter 39

Onyx

I slowly came to. The world around me was blurred and hazy, with voices murmuring somewhere nearby.

"That was a nasty concoction, my man. I've been studying it for hours. He combined fentanyl and silver. Honestly? I'm shocked she even has a heartbeat."

"Thanks for the confidence," Dayken replied with an annoyed, flippant tone.

"I'm not underestimating your Sacar — I'm just saying that it should have killed her. And I don't understand how it didn't."

Panic slammed into me like a freight train.

I snapped to attention, the haze instantly dissipating from groggy to sheer terror. My body jerked upright, breath ragged, heart pounding against my ribs as if it were trying to break free. The pungent scent of antiseptic stung my nose, and the stiff sheets beneath me only confirmed what I already suspected — I was in Derek's medical room. The overly clean, chemical-laden air was nearly unbearable due to my heightened senses.

I did a quick scan of the room and spotted Dayken sitting in a chair beside my bed. He blinked, almost startled, as he straightened.

"You're awake," he murmured.

"Sky?" My voice came out hoarse, strained.

"She's safe," he reassured me. "In her room, with a tiger in the hallway." He offered a small smile, but it didn't reach his eyes. The usual crinkle at the corners was missing.

Something was wrong.

"What happened?" I asked, even though the memories were already pushing their way forward, disjointed and jagged.

"I'm going to get back to studying this thing," Derek said, nodding towards the exit. "Glad to see you're up," he told me as parting words.

I couldn't respond. His words barely landed before something inside me cracked open — memories flooding in, too fast to brace against.

The fight.
The wolf.
The betrayal.
The syringe.

My pulse pounded in my ears, and I barely registered the door clicking shut behind him.

Then Dayken's voice cut through the static.

"We got him." He ran a hand through his hair, tone stiff. "He says his name is Dr. Alistair Crowe. Chase has been investigating his background. The man is like a ghost."

He got up from his chair to stand next to my bed, eyes scanning me with a tenderness I wasn't ready for. "He's being held at Alicia's place. They have holding cells, which we don't. He's talking — telling us everything. Almost too much…. like he's proud of it." He hesitated, his voice catching on some unknown emotion. When he spoke again, it was rougher.

"And my sister…" He cleared his throat, jaw tightening. "She's in a holding cell across from him."

"Fuck," I breathed. The memory hit me like a wrecking ball. It all came flooding back, her questions, the way she always seemed to know where we were.

"It's worse than I thought," he said, dragging me back to the present. "She was in direct communication with him from the moment you arrived at the farmhouse. He reached out to her, had her watching you, watching us. Since day one. I'm so sorry."

The words were a slap to the face. I fucked up. I should have never let my guard down. Should have never allowed myself to trust. I knew this had been too good to be true.

"I knew it," I choked out, my voice breaking as emotion clawed at my throat.

Confusion flashed across Dayken's face so quickly it was as if I'd smacked him. "Knew what?" he asked.

"I knew it. I knew I should have trusted my instincts, but instead, I suppressed them for this stupid, misguided feeling of belonging with you." My voice rose as I threw the words at him. "Because of these *feelings*, I made a mistake. A huge mistake. The enemy was so close — this entire time, and I was blind, naïve, and selfish. And now, look at this." I stretched my arms out, and motioned to myself in a fucking hospital bed.

"Wait a minute. Are you — you're seriously blaming *me* for my sister's betrayal?" Dayken asked, his voice tight with disbelief.

"I'm blaming myself for trusting this situation," I shot back.

"No, you're blaming yourself for trusting *me*." The distress on his beautiful face cut deeper than I expected. He ran a hand through his hair, frustration crackling around him. "Damn it, Onyx. I had no idea… she's my sister, I never could have imagined…" he said, stepping closer.

"Don't," I warned, putting my hands up to stop him. He halted at once, his frustration turning into something rawer, more painful, as if my refusal had physically wounded him.

"I need to think. I need to get out of here. I want to question that asshole myself." I began ripping the wires off me and pulling the blanket down off my lap. But Dayken wasn't letting this go.

"If I'd known she was capable of this kind of deception, I never would have let her in," he said, his voice bordering on frantic. "You have to believe me. I would choose you over my own flesh and blood — any day, any moment. *You.* I choose you, Onyx," he pleaded.

His words cracked something deep inside my chest, but it didn't matter. There was no coming back from this. I was done letting him distract me from what should have always been my number one priority: protecting Sky.

I had tricked myself into thinking I could do both, protect her and have feelings for someone at the same time. But I knew better. I knew from experience that if something felt too good to be true, it probably was. Or worse… Just because they stop torturing you, doesn't mean it's over. It only means you get a moment to breathe before the next wave hits. It means you will still suffer; you just don't know when. I should have known better.

That was my mindset now. Forever. It had to be.

Because it was safer to expect pain than to believe in the lie that this forced bond was anything more than a cruel trick of fate.

"I'm not asking you to choose me. I never have," I said coldly, my words sharp and unforgiving. "I understand history forced me to choose you as a child, but we're adults now, Dayken. Let's get over it."

Each word hit him like a physical blow, but I didn't stop.

"Don't you get it? I knew Aurora was acting weird. I noticed her odd questions, how pointed they always were. And on the way to that party, I almost told you something felt off. Almost."

I let out a harsh breath, my chest tight. "But I didn't say anything. Do you know why?" I didn't give him the chance to answer. "Because I didn't want to upset you. I couldn't stand the thought of hurting you by accusing your sister of something malicious. And look where that got us, we were in danger this entire fucking time, and I ignored it because of these unwanted, fucking feelings."

I shook my head, frustration boiling over. "This is a complication I don't need, and sure as hell don't want."

He pressed his lips together, forming a thin, rigid line. His eyebrows furrowed, deepening the lines of his face, as if he were in physical pain. He began nodding slowly, almost imperceptibly, as if agreeing with me.

Wait. Why is he agreeing with me?

"You're right," he said, his voice low, raw. He took a step back, widening the distance between us. "I've been holding on to the past. And I can now see just how unwanted I am."

His throwing my own words back at me felt like a slap to the face, but he wasn't finished.

"You can stay here as long as you need," he continued, his tone cold and distant — though his eyes betrayed the storm raging beneath. "But since this place is compromised, I get it if you want to leave. I won't stop you. Not that I ever really would have."

He let out a breath, shaking his head. "We were supposed to be a team. *A team.* But you know what? I'm done. Do what you want."

And with that, he turned on his heel, his steps measured but heavy, each one feeling like another crack that could never be mended.

I just sat there. Frozen.

Watching him walk away.

My heart shattered into pieces, and yet I couldn't understand why. This is what I wanted. Wasn't it? To be rid of him. To push him away. To protect myself. And now he was giving me exactly what I demanded. He was going to let me go.

So, why did my chest ache as if it were collapsing in on itself? Why were my feet rooted to the ground, refusing to move?

I looked down at my forearms, taking in the cuts and bruises as they slowly healed. The scars would fade. But not really.

Not the real ones.

Not the one that now felt permanently embedded in my soul.

Just when I started to believe I could get better, I was shattered all over again, beaten black and blue, as if it were meant to be a permanent mark.

Maybe my soul was never meant to heal.

Maybe I was never meant to be *loved*.

I vowed to remember this pain. It was different from what I was used to, and I would use it to shield myself from ever being vulnerable again. I needed a plan to leave; I always had a plan. This was no different. Yet, my mind wouldn't cooperate. It felt like my heart and brain were at war.

Sky, I needed to check in with Sky. The plan was, first Sky, then question that piece of shit, then figure out how to get out of here.

I descended the stairs to the basement, feeling the air grow cooler. My chest ached, and everything felt off. I ignored the unease and kept going until faint voices drifted from down the hall, tingling my senses. The dim light cast long shadows on the stone walls, and the quiet hum of conversation was broken only by a sudden, irritated voice.

"I asked — what are you doing?"

I paused at the bottom of the stairs, just out of sight, catching the faint scuffle of feet across the concrete floor.

"Well," a familiar voice retorted, the dry edge of exasperation unmistakable. "Like I said, if you're going to refuse to come into my room and talk to me, then I'll just come out here and talk to you."

There was a pause, a beat of silence that felt heavy in the musty air.

"The way we were talking before was just fine."

"No. It. Wasn't."

Oh wow. That was Sky's angry voice, which was rare to hear and made me pause. I shouldn't eavesdrop, but curiosity got the better of me. Her tone made me expect another slap.

There was a low, guttural inhale — definitely Kolton — deep and rumbling from his chest. "What is it then — wait. Do not sit on the ground out here—"

I peeked around to see Sky sitting defiantly on the cold concrete floor, her petite frame dwarfed by Kolton's as she sat beside him. Her icy gaze was locked onto Kolton, and despite her delicate appearance, her stubborn jaw showed she was ready to fight.

"Skylar! Why are—"

"Oh, hush," she cut him off with an eye roll, waving a dismissive hand. "You're being so dramatic. See? Isn't this nice?" She leaned back, her calm demeanor a stark contrast to Kolton's wild, restless energy.

"You need to get off the ground."

"Well, if you're going to sit on the ground constantly, then I will too."

"I'm different—" Kolton growled, his voice low and rough, like it always was when he was agitated.

This was getting too personal, and I didn't need to witness whatever this was becoming. I cleared my throat and made my footsteps louder as I approached, deliberately scuffing my boots against the steps. It wouldn't fool Sky, but it was the thought that counted.

"Hey!" Sky said cheerfully from her perch on the floor. "I was just about to tell Kolton we should head up soon and check on you."

My gaze met Sky's, and her face immediately brightened, eyes sparkling with excitement. The tension I'd been carrying melted away instantly, replaced by a warm, genuine love, the kind that made you forget everything else for a moment.

"I thought you'd be out for at least a few more hours," she added, her voice light and full of concern. The warmth in her expression was a balm to the lingering tension in the hallway. "How are you feeling?"

"I'm okay," I assured her. "A little overwhelmed and still processing everything, but otherwise okay." A lie. But I wasn't about to lay out the details of how I just left things with Dayken.

Before I could say more, she sprang up and pulled me into a tight hug, her small arms strong as she squeezed me close. I hugged her back, my chest tightening at the simple comfort of her presence. Sky was amazing like that, effortlessly grounding, a constant in a world that often felt chaotic and uncertain.

"Speaking of processing," I pulled back, just enough to look at her. "I want to go question that Crowe bastard. Want to come?"

"Of course!" she said, without a hint of hesitation. "We'll face this together, okay? I don't want you feeling like you have to tackle this all by yourself."

I nodded, feeling a flicker of hope in the midst of all the chaos. With Sky by my side, I could manage whatever came next.

"I'm sure if we give Kolton some catnip, he'll snap out of his grumpy mood and join us without too much fuss."

My eyes bulged as I slapped a hand over my mouth to hold back a guffaw. Did Sky just roast her own Guardian?

Kolton didn't respond; he just exhaled sharply and let his head thunk back against the concrete wall, eyes closing as he pinched the bridge of his nose.

"Isn't that right, Kolty-Wolty?" she cooed at him in a taunting way.

"Skylar…" he warned, but the threat held no real weight, especially with the smirk twitching at the corner of his mouth, fighting for an appearance on his otherwise brooding face.

Their relationship was so odd, and I suddenly felt like I was intruding on something I had no business with.

"Well, I'll be in my room," I said, taking a step back. "Just want a quick shower and a change of clothes. Catch you in, what, thirty, forty minutes?"

"Sounds great! See you soon!" Sky chirped, completely unbothered.

And with that, we parted ways.

Chapter 40

Onyx

When we arrived at Alicia's place, we were greeted by two women and a man who escorted us inside. I followed along until we came to a set of stairs leading to the basement, and I glanced over my shoulder at Dayken.

He shoved his hands into his pockets, avoiding my gaze. "Don't worry, I'm staying up here," he said, pivoting away.

I wanted to tell him he could come, that I didn't mind. But we were already drawing attention, and I was the one who insisted on putting distance between us.

Sky, Kolton, and I descended the brightly lit stairs. When I reached the bottom, I nearly collided with Titus Sharp's striking frame. Beside him stood a white-haired woman I didn't recognize.

"Onyx, Sky, what a pleasu—" Titus began, but then sighed and cut himself off. "Kolton."

That was all he said in acknowledgment. It seemed no one — other than Sky — ever enjoyed the tiger's company.

"What are you doing here?" I asked curiously. My gaze flicked to the woman as she turned to face us. She was wearing sunglasses... in an underground prison.

Interesting.

Titus rubbed a hand over the trimmed stubble on his chin. "I was curious about the weapons and ammunition they were using. Seemed like some new tech, especially the snipers'." He pulled a bullet casing from his suit pocket. "Thought I might be able to pry some details out of the prisoner." He nodded towards the cell down the hall. "Only to find out that *prying* wasn't necessary. He was very forthcoming."

Was that why Titus showed up to help us fight? Because he wanted to get a good measure of the enemy and their weapons? I thought maybe it was because he was developing a kinship with Dayken, but that must have been my weak, hopeless optimism at play again. Sky approached the woman. Both of them were nearly identical in height.

"Hi, I'm Sky," she said, extending her hand.

"Nessalay Sharp, of the Sharp Clan," she replied.

I must have been staring, because Titus added, "This is my younger sister, Ness. She oversees all our shipments and inventory — our resident quartermaster, if you will."

They looked nothing alike. I would not have guessed they were related if he hadn't declared as much.

Nessalay dipped her head toward me in a low, respectful greeting. It caught me off guard. Made her… endearing in a way I wasn't used to.

"Mind if we have a turn?" I asked, gesturing toward the cell.

"By all means," Titus said, stepping aside.

We moved past the Sharps down the illuminated corridor. Their footsteps followed behind us, indicating they were curious to hear our interrogation. There was a row of cells on each side. They were modern, with thick plexiglass barriers, and offered no privacy to the occupants.

I approached his cell, arms crossed, and observed his pitiful appearance. He still wore his clothes from the night of the battle, now covered in dirt, and he was held by metal chains. I noticed he had gauze wrapped around his neck and a hand covered by what I could only assume was a cast. He looked simultaneously weak and menacing, and I hated that I couldn't just see him as weak. His cold, dead eyes locked onto mine, unmoving and unfeeling. So, I matched him.

"Why?" No pleasantries. No restraint. I spat the word like venom.

This man, who stole two decades of my life — my childhood, my humanity — tilted his head with a kind of lazy arrogance that made my blood boil. His smile split slowly, a mix of amusement and mockery.

"That's the question, isn't it?" he said, his voice like silk over razorblades. "Everyone wants to know *why*…. Why? Why? Why? It really should be obvious."

He leaned forward, chains dragging against the floor like an omen. "So, I'll give you the same answer I gave the others: Because *you*," he raised his chained hands together, gesturing at me, "and *you*," now pointing to Sky, "shouldn't exist."

He spoke as if that were the end of a morbid bedtime story, a fictional tale meant to send a child to sleep with a moral lesson. As if our existence were inconsequential, not meant to be taken seriously.

I focused on his heartbeat. It was steady, too steady. This asshole believed every word he said.

"No," I said, my voice cold. "It's more than that." I stepped closer, forcing him to feel my presence, to know I wasn't the same girl he locked in a cage all those years ago.

"The tests. The experiments. The screams. That wasn't just research. That was pleasure for you." I didn't blink. "This wasn't clinical. It was personal."

He chuckled, like what I said was cute. Titus, whose presence I had nearly forgotten about, cuffed like the chuckle made him want to punch Crowe. I felt that sentiment deep in my bones.

"Ah, Onyxiana. You were always the clever one." Then Crowe turned his gaze toward Sky. "And your sister... Well, she had potential, too."

Kolton released a low growl, feral and deadly, instinctively stepping forward. The tiger looked ready to punch through the glass and tear Crowe's throat out.

"Sky," the man continued. "We tried to fix you. Remember? The electricity, the shocks... to activate the unused parts of your brain." His voice dropped into something almost reverent. "So much potential locked away in that skull."

Sky didn't flinch. "Oh, please. Shut the fuck up," she said, voice like steel wrapped in ice.

That's my sister.

"Tell us why," I demanded. "The real reason this time. Spare us the theatrics. You're not here to lecture, not anymore — or I swear, we'll rip it out of you."

He sighed dramatically. "Fine. But I want something in return. I want to speak with the *other* vampire."

A flicker of something passed through Sky, recognition. Dread.

Peach.

I didn't give him the satisfaction of reacting. "Get fucked."

He only smiled wider. "I suppose it doesn't matter. I already have everything I need." He tapped one of his unmauled fingers against his chin. "What is her name again? Ah, that's right, Peachabelle Clarisse Vaughn."

My heart sank. I heard growling, but I couldn't focus enough to determine where it came from. He shouldn't have that information.

"You motherfu—" I started.

"Oh, and the clans? Crumbling from the inside out. You think the war hasn't started yet? It's been happening for years — quietly. While you all slept."

My stomach clenched.

Then he dropped a bomb.

"Your parents were never civilians. They were government agents, assigned to you. Embedded from the start. Their mission was simple: monitor the anomaly. Report every change. Every symptom. Every sign of the unnatural."

He smiled, soft yet savage. "But after your bond… they went quiet. Started asking questions. Got attached. So, we eliminated the variable. It was their own fault, really… letting something as useless as feelings cloud their objective."

The words hit like a knife to my heart. Sky buckled, her hand covering her mouth like she could swallow the truth out of existence. Kolton moved closer. Protective. Ready. But he didn't touch her. Didn't know how.

I felt a stab of jealousy. I missed my own Guardian with a suffocating regret. I forced it down. I had to. Never. Again.

"That still doesn't explain why," I hissed, fire rising in my throat.

Crowe exhaled through his nose, amused. "Because you're not like the rest of them. You weren't turned. You were *born*. Direct descendants of Lunce himself."

Shock spread through the room like a virus.

"You're the last of the true line," he went on, reverent now. "The only living evidence that the origin story wasn't a myth. That real vampires — pure ones — still exist."

He leaned forward, voice turning bitter. "We tried to recreate you. Blood. Tissue. Even embryonic cloning. But your genes refused. Every cell is encoded with that cursed flower. Cosmos atrosanguineus. Non-native cloned cells cannibalized themselves as soon as they were exposed to a host that, well, wasn't *you*." His face twisted, venomous now.

"We burned your blood under microscopes. Injected your DNA into a thousand failed embryos and watched it reject everything we gave it. But you? You wouldn't break. You wouldn't *die*." His gaze locked onto mine, unblinking. "Do you know why? Do you know why you are impervious to death despite endless torture and despair?"

I stayed silent.

"Because you are immortal," he whispered. "Truly, irreversibly immortal. The only thing that could kill you, according to our research, is… beheading."

The word echoed through me, merciless and final.

Then he looked up at the ceiling, almost thoughtful, like he was remembering something mildly inconvenient. "So, I suppose, after enough failed attempts… After the government threatened to shut us down and defund the entire program… After I sacrificed my entire life trying to understand you…" He smiled faintly, as if the memory amused him. "I may have taken it a little personally.

"*But* why tell you this now?" he said as he leaned back, a slow, serpentine smile spreading across his face. "Because even in chains, I've already won. My research lives on. There are others. Watching. Testing. Perfecting what I started. They don't need you to be alive anymore. Just… usable tissue, with or without a head." His eyes slid lazily toward Sky. "Now we just have to confirm if there are more of you. That blonde, Peachabelle? She's next. We've seen enough to know she'll be perfect."

Titus moved before I could blink. He slammed a fist into the glass, pointed teeth bared — lethal, gleaming, and furious. His eyes were wild as he growled, "Go ahead. I dare you. But understand — once you do, no power in this world, no deal, can save you from me."

He pointed at the bastard, his finger radiating unspoken wrath, and he lifted his fist to slam against the glass again. Nessalay darted in to pull him back, but it was like trying to stop an explosion after ignition. His elbow struck her face, knocking her sunglasses to the floor.

And when they landed…

Everything stilled.

Her eyes glowed with a piercing red light — unnatural, inhuman. White lashes. White brows. They contrasted her dark skin, giving her a terrifying kind of beauty.

"Enough, my brother," she said, her voice smooth and glacially cold. She exuded grace and willed obedience.

Sky knelt to retrieve her fallen sunglasses, offering them with a hand that barely trembled. Nessalay smiled, composed as ever, one hand still braced on Titus's arm.

"I think that's enough for today," I said, knowing how much this psycho enjoyed inflicting anger and pain. We were playing right into his game.

But Crowe wasn't finished. His voice was almost wistful as he said, "We tried everything. Forced ovulation. Gene manipulation. We even removed your reproductive organs to see what would happen."

I went cold. My stomach hollowed out.

"But there were no eggs," he said, eyes bright with awe. "You're too pure. Too close to the source. Nature itself refuses to replicate you."

His gaze flicked back to Titus. "That's why the blonde is perfect. So pretty. So pliable. So…. willing to take part?" He leveled a wry, goading smile at Titus, perfectly hitting its mark.

Titus thrashed in his sister's arms like an animal in a cage. Wild. Beyond words. It was a miracle Nessalay held him at all.

"I said that's enough!" I barked, stepping between Titus and the cell. "We're done here."

"Onyx? What about Aurora?" Sky asked.

"What about her? Let's get the fuck out of here."

Sky looked disappointed as we turned and headed back toward the stairs, but she didn't push. Crowe's laughter echoed behind us as we climbed to the main floor. We got the information we needed, but at what cost? I wasn't sure it was worth his unending glee at watching our reactions.

I had expected Dayken to be waiting for us at the top of the stairs. But he wasn't.

He stood near the front entrance, talking to someone, barely sparing a glance at me.

This is for the best. I reminded myself. Never. Again.

"All set?" Dayken asked.

But not to me. To Sky.

"He said they've infiltrated the clans here in Michigan," she told him.

That got his attention. His eyes snapped to mine, worry tightening his jaw.

"I'll need to call a meeting with the Primarcs. Everyone needs to be informed, and I want to find out who already knows," he said, looking back at Sky and Kolton, as if he remembered that he didn't need my agreement anymore.

Sky looked between us, clearly trying to figure out what was happening with me and Dayken. I wasn't trying to hide it, but I didn't want to talk about it either. Sky was incredibly smart. I'm sure she already realized that I had pushed him away. His refusal to look at me made it even more obvious.

"Did you want a moment to speak with your sister?" Sky asked him.

Dayken's hand was already on the front door, just starting to push it open, when her question made him freeze. His spine stiffened. A slow breath filled his lungs. Then he shook his head.

"No," he said. Just one word — but the way he said it gutted me.

I should have said something. Should have told him it was okay. Talking to her might help. Maybe he could find answers. Closure.

But how could I, when I didn't even want that for myself?

I was still pissed. Aurora had nearly killed Sky. Hell — she'd almost gotten all of us killed with her selfish recklessness. And for what? What the hell was worth all of that?

I was mad. Furious. And I deserved to be.

But I couldn't tell if Dayken's refusal came from the same rage I felt, or if he was just trying to protect me.

He'd seen what happened; he had been there, but he didn't feel it like I did. He didn't carry the guilt, the fear, and the fury of Sky nearly dying because of Aurora. That lived under my skin, not his. Or so I thought. Maybe he was angry; maybe he wasn't. I wasn't sure which would hurt more. I should have told him to talk to her. But I didn't.

Once in the car, I sat in the back seat with Sky, listening to her replay everything that fucking psychopath said.

A pure vampire.

I didn't fully understand it. Crowe clearly did; he probably kept us ignorant on purpose. I wish I had paid more attention when Sky read those history books in Dayken's library. I didn't remember much about Lunce, just that he had a wife and children. That's it.

"Explains why you guys can go so long without blood, though," Kolton said, snapping me out of my thoughts. "Practically unheard of until you two came along."

"Aw, are you calling me special?" Sky teased, nudging his arm.

Kolton shut down immediately, crossing his arms over his chest like a sulking guard dog. I could practically *hear* the grumble he didn't let out.

Sky just snickered to herself.

I would have smiled at her antics, usually did — but it only made me miss the playful rhythm Dayken and I had fallen into.

Now he wouldn't even look at me. He had even tilted the rearview mirror away from me. Not down or up — *away*. Like, even an accidental glance at me would be too much.

Can I blame him?

Chapter 41

Onyx

I sat in a chair near the main entrance, taking in my surroundings. The once decrepit room now looked like a hotel lobby, plush couches and cushioned chairs arranged intentionally, almost inviting. The only difference? No glass doors. No revolving entryway. Instead, a massive, fortified metal slab stood in their place, locked with a code that still rotated every twelve hours. Security here was absolute, but whoever styled the space had done a damn good job at making it seem… cozy. The rugs were a nice touch, softening the otherwise heavy atmosphere of steel and concrete. Still, it wasn't enough to ease the tension.

I sat there, deep in thought, trying to process recent events, when I saw Chase and Derek in the hallway, walking from the cafeteria with coffee. Both were left-handed and unconsciously mirrored each other. Chase was dressed in black jeans and a black shirt, the faint glint of his facial piercings barely visible against the way he seemed to blend into the shadows, as if he belonged there. Derek, on the other hand, wore blue jeans and a graphic T-shirt with a slogan about T-Rexes disliking push-ups.

Whatever that meant.

They caught me looking with a quick glance from the corner of their eyes, but they didn't pause. No nods, smiles, or waves, just their consistent stride toward the basement, on their way back to the security room. As if I weren't even there.

Fine by me.

I was never here to make friends. Focusing on my job was easier without distractions like friendship.

Left alone, my thoughts returned to what I had just learned: Dayken was at the Primarcs meeting and never told me about it. The only reason I knew was because I overheard it in the cafeteria, casual chatter from a couple of wolves in the clan. Not from him.

I didn't understand why that bothered me, but it did. I needed to move past these feelings, but I was stuck wondering if I made the right choice in pushing him away. It felt good when we worked as partners, when he trusted me, shared ideas, and talked through details. It made me feel included and respected. Now?

Now, he wouldn't tell me what was going on or even look at me. I had to overhear news of an important meeting through random, low-ranking clan members. It hurt. But at the end of the day, I had hurt him too.

I couldn't keep living like this… trapped in an endless war with myself. I wanted more, but I'd pull away the second I got too close. It wasn't fair to me or Dayken. It wasn't healthy. And it sure as hell wasn't something I wanted constantly consuming my thoughts. This wasn't solitude. This was exile. And the worst part? I'd done it to myself because that's just how it had to be.

I promised myself to cut out all distractions.

And that meant leaving the compound. I needed to get back on my own two feet. Be independent and provide for myself.

That was the thought I held onto like a blade, sharp and unyielding.

A new plan began forming.

I would leave, but first I would train. I would gather the things I couldn't afford to borrow — strength, discipline, and an exit strategy. Then Sky and I would be gone.

My ears caught a strange sound from the loading dock that snapped me out of my mission plan. I composed myself and headed down the corridor toward the noise. The sound of metal crates clattering against the ground echoed through the courtyard as I exited the loading dock's main door. The air remained thick with the scent of smoke and gunpowder — lingering effects from the recent battle.

Titus stood near the loading dock, overseeing a delivery as his crew unloaded crates of ammo, blades, and other weapons to restock everything we had used while defending the compound... defending me. His light brown eyes flicked to me the moment I stepped outside, and before I could pass, he called out—

"Hey, Onyx. Is it just you?"

It was obvious he was looking for Peach, as his eyes scanned over my shoulder. Titus wasn't as sly as he thought, and I, the sadistic asshole I was becoming, enjoyed dragging out his torture. I leaned against a crate, arms crossed, and let the silence stretch, making him squirm.

"At the moment. Why?" was my only reply.

Titus kept his expression neutral, but the flicker of something — disappointment? Frustration? — crossed his face before he smoothed it away.

"No reason."

I didn't buy it, but I let it go, mainly because of my own troubled thoughts.

Dayken should've told me about the meeting. A few days ago, he wouldn't have let me out of his sight. He would've been hovering too close, stealing glances like they were oxygen. Now? It was like a thread between us had gone slack. Not cut, not broken. Just... limp.

My chest tightened before I could stop it.

"What's going on with you and Dayken?" Titus asked, reading my silence like a map.

"Nothing. Why?"

Titus arched a brow, knowing he struck a nerve.
Touche, Titus.

"Because you two went from being unable to take your eyes off each other to seemingly incapable of even being in the same room together. First, you went to question Crowe without him. Now he's at the Primarc meeting without you." He paused, pondering his next words. "I find the suddenness of it odd."

I shut my eyes and rubbed the bridge of my nose. If I could get headaches, this would be the moment. These animals were too damn nosy.

"Titus… did you ever consider that maybe… I don't know… it's complicated. And speaking of which, why aren't *you* at the meeting?"

He grinned, entirely unbothered. "Leo will represent my territory. And sure, it's complicated. That doesn't mean I'm not going to ask, though."

I exhaled, shaking my head.

He tilted his head slightly and said, "How about this? I can sense that something's going on, and you look ready to break out of your skin. Why don't you check out my weapons hub? It's nearby, and there's even a forge. I think you'll enjoy it."

I narrowed my eyes at him. He was either offering because he wanted gossip… or because he wanted more information on Peach.

Either way… I didn't hate the idea of getting out of here.

"Give me the address, and I'll think about it."

Despite being told it was safe to have a phone, I still didn't feel right about owning one. Unfortunately, that made exchanging contact information… awkward. Titus said I could reach him through Chase or just show up at his place; either way, he'd make himself available. I found his eagerness to distract me both suspicious and oddly endearing.

When Titus left, I made my way down to Sky's room, intending to see if she had any interest in checking out his weapons foundry.

She wasn't in her usual reading spot. I tracked her scent down the corridor and realized she was in the training room. I headed back upstairs, intent on finding her. As I approached the training room, I heard heavy breathing and pounding heartbeats. I opened the doors and saw Sky and Peach lifting weights together, while Kolton strained his muscles as he flipped a tire. Sky paused, noticing me in the mirror's reflection mid-lift.

"Hey!" she beamed, setting the weights down.

Her energy, her light, hit me like a shock to the system, cutting through the ache in my chest, making me instantly feel better. I hadn't realized how quiet my world had gotten until I heard her voice.

Dayken leaving without telling me suddenly seemed less important.

But then, just as quickly, something dull and unwelcome twisted in my gut. They'd been here together. Training. Laughing. And no one had thought to invite me. Not Sky. Not Peach. And definitely not Kolton.

I wasn't sure why it bothered me so much. I had been keeping distant on purpose, hadn't I? This was what I wanted: less attachment, fewer distractions.

So why did I dislike the feeling of being on the outside, looking in?

"Oh, hi!" Peach chirped, pulling out a small earbud like she'd only just noticed me.

I crossed my arms. "Titus extended an invitation for me to check out his weapons depot nearby. Figured it might be nice to get out of here for a bit."

The heaving, breathy growl that came from Kolton was instant.

"Remember what happened the last time you thought it was a good idea to go on an *adventure*?" He spat the last word like a curse.

Dear gods, it was going to take every ounce of patience I had not to choke him.

I cracked my neck, buying myself a second to respond — but Sky beat me to it.

"Our enemy is literally sitting in a cell, Kolton. It's fine."

"Yeah, but you heard what he said. He's infiltrated the clans. They could be anywhere. They could be here for all we know."

She *tsked* him like a mother would a child. "We have no proof that any of that was true. He could have just been trying to scare us. Don't let your anxiety cloud your judgment."

He said nothing in response, but his eyes flashed bright yellow for a second before he returned to his task a little more aggressively, if I do say so myself.

"As for checking it out, I'd love to," Sky said. Then she turned to Peach. "Would you like to come?"

I was hoping it could just be me and Sky, but it looked like our party of two turned into a party of three. Well, four, if the tiger's manic mannerisms were any sign.

I bit the inside of my cheek. I hadn't asked Peach. Sky had. And now it was just… assumed.

Typical. I tried to do something with just her, but apparently even that was too much to ask. Maybe this was why I didn't try.

"I'll have to check with Alicia. She's been playing Mother Hen ever since that creep said he wants to meet me or whatever. But I'm sure it'll be fine if we have Day with us," Peach said with a shrug.

I felt a prickle of unease at the way she casually used a nickname for Dayken.

Day? Is that their thing or something?

"There will be no Dayken," I said — too forcefully.

Silence.

Kolton paused mid-task again. The tire landed with a dull thud.

Sky sighed through her nose.

Peach blinked at me like I'd just suggested burning down the building.

Awesome.

I was the problem again.

"That's fine. I'll go," she said at last, voice soft but steady.

Sky gave a quiet nod. "It's a date, then."

Even Kolton seemed ready as he stepped forward. "Let's make it quick."

I blinked. That... wasn't what I expected.

Alright, fine. Let's go then.

***

Titus's operation was tucked on the edge of a crumbling industrial block — one of those clan-held spaces that technically didn't exist on any city records. Still, everyone knew it belonged to someone dangerous. I've learned that most clans had places like this. Hidden in plain sight. Fortresses that were disguised as storage units.

The inside was bigger than I expected — steel beams, scorched concrete, and the permanent scent of metal and ash. Half the space was dedicated to forging — an anvil, a press, a furnace, and the works — while the other half resembled a modern tactical gun range. Mismatched, but intentional. It was so Titus — one foot in the old world, one foot three steps into the future, and one finger always on the trigger.

Kolton didn't like being here. He made that clear on the drive over, and again when we pulled up.

"Just keep your eyes open," he muttered as we stepped out of the car. "Titus still has DeStephano ties, whether he acts like it or not."

I arched a brow at him. "You think Leo DeStephano is gonna crash through the roof?"

"No," Kolton said. "But it was his grandfather who murdered Dayken's parents. Doesn't take much to reopen old blood feuds."

Point taken.

Also… how had I not known that?

The light thought drifted in. A passing detail I should've clocked before — but didn't. I blinked, letting it roll around in my head like a loose screw. Just a fact. A background note.

Then came the other thought.

Why didn't I know that?

I hadn't known Dayken long — not really. But I'd slept beside him. Fought beside him. Kissed him. Let him see parts of me I didn't even know how to name.

So, how had I never asked about his parents?

My chest subtly tightened, a quiet squeeze like a hand around my ribs. I'd assumed they were gone — casualties of war, politics, or something vague enough to shrug off. But memories from that night at the ball sharpened — the look in Dayken's eyes, the edge in his voice, and the crack in his armor when he spoke of Leo DeStephano — it all made sense now.

His parents were not merely *gone.*

Someone had murdered them. And I never asked.

The guilt didn't slam into me. It slid in quietly, coiling around my spine, tightening slowly until I couldn't quite breathe right.

Voices broke through the fog, bickering between Titus and Peach. It wasn't enough to snap me out of it, but enough to redirect my eyes. They argued over something trivial, probably her heeled boots or whether his vest matched her mood. It should've been funny, the way she rolled her eyes, him bumping her shoulder like he was trying to be gentle but didn't know how. It made something inside me ache — the way he let his guard down around her, her touching him without hesitation. It was a language I once spoke, but now it felt foreign.

Still, Titus waved me over when he noticed me standing awkwardly in the doorway.

"You ever forged a sword before?" he asked, already heading toward the stacks of raw iron.

I rolled my eyes. "No. They preferred to stab me with them at the facility — *testing my reflexes*," I said, complete with air quotes. "Pretty sure it was just an excuse for creative torture."

"Righhhht. Well... let's flip the script," he said with a grin.

The next hour was filled with heat, sweat, and sparks as Titus taught me how to shape the metal by listening and balancing force with finesse. The guilt softened, but it didn't vanish; however, this did serve as a welcome distraction.

Later, Titus handed me a custom-built 9mm I helped design, with the aid of one of the Sharp Clan's weapons engineers. It was a combination of new technology and old power.

"This one's yours," he said. "Built from the scraps we pulled after the last ambush. There's virtually no recoil, and it has micro-laser marking that your vision should have no problem tracing."

It felt solid in my grip. Heavy. Real. *Mine.* "Thank you, Titus."

Peach and Sky were also browsing weapons. Peach insisted that hers have color. When Titus told her that was ridiculous. She countered with, "Then I don't want a gun." Which naturally led to the two of them arguing before they arranged a future time to create a custom piece.

Kolton lingered in the far corner, arms crossed, silent but steady. Watching. His eyes never left Sky.

And me? I didn't know how I kept ending up alone, but there I was again. Somehow, even in a crowd, I found the edges. Titus noticed, and he wandered over, gaze assessing but not invasive.

"You seem in your element," he noted.

I glanced at the floor, then back at him. "Not sure I'd call it that. Just easier to think when no one's around."

He nodded, like he understood more than he let on. Then, almost offhandedly, he said, "You know… I'd pay you. If you wanted to keep this up."

The offer caught me off guard. Not because of the money, but because he didn't make it sound like a transaction. It sounded like kindness. Like permanence.

I didn't say yes.

But I didn't say no, either. And on the drive back to the compound, all I could think about was the next time I could go back.

And eventually, I did.

One visit turned into two. Then three. And before I realized it, I'd slipped into a routine, quiet, steady, unexpected.

Weapons-making was an art that required patience, precision, and material knowledge. It was strangely satisfying to shape deadly things myself, especially now. Titus had scavenged abandoned weapons and materials from the enemy's failed attack: warped rifles, broken casings, melted scraps. He gave them to me to turn into something stronger, something ours.

With Dayken no longer watching me, questioning me, or even caring when I came and went, I stopped driving and started running to Titus's property. Twenty miles there. Twenty miles back.

I ran through dense forests, along winding roads, over hills that burned my legs until the pain became just another sensation to push through. Michigan was beautiful — vast lakes, open land, rolling hills, and forests. It was peaceful, and the exhaustion felt good. The ache in my muscles signaled I was getting stronger. And the work? That felt even better.

At Titus's forge, my hands grew skilled and steady. I learned how to balance a blade and sharpen edges until they could cut through bone. I discovered how to mold a weapon into something personal, lethal.

Every strike of the hammer, every run through the trees, every second spent honing my skills — it all brought me closer to what I needed to become.

Untouchable. Unstoppable. Free.

Chapter 42

Onyx

I stood in Sky's room, taking in all the decorations she had added since we moved in. It was all crafted from items she'd been given, but it was the placement and design that made it so… Sky.

"So let me get this straight — you're planning to keep working for Titus until you can afford a place of your own?" she asked, her tone careful.

I nodded.

"And then I'll come with you to this new home?"

I nodded again.

Her brow furrowed as she gestured toward the hallway where her tiger was usually stationed. "And what about Kolton?"

I blinked, caught off guard. "What about him?" I asked, shrugging. I had just assumed he would stay here.

"He's my Guardian, Onyx," she said with such hurt, as if I suggested they permanently separate. Okay, so I hadn't given him much thought, but I also didn't think she would care that much about leaving him. I mean, she did slap the shit out of him not too long ago.

"So?" I countered, not willing to let her know that I hadn't considered him at all.

"So, just because you're willing to leave your Guardian behind doesn't mean that I'm okay with leaving mine." She stood up from her reading chair to face me with the full force of her ire.

I huffed, crossing my arms. *I'm not taking that bait, Sky.* "Fine, then he can come too. Problem solved."

Sky let out a frustrated sigh, her hands falling to her sides. "Onyx, you can't stand each other. Could you please just stop and think? This isn't something you can bulldoze your way through."

I turned away, pacing the room, tension bubbling under my skin. "I don't see the problem. If you want Kolton to come, he'll come. He's your Guardian; it's his job."

"It's not that simple," she said quietly, her voice cutting through my defenses. "You're asking me to uproot his life because you want to leave. Do you even care how that might affect him? He just started acclimating to being in a clan again."

'Acclimating' was a strong word for the tiger, but I closed my eyes, jaw tightening as I gathered patience. "It's not like I'm forcing him to come, Sky. He can stay here if he wants."

Her eyes softened, but a hint of disappointment still lingered. "And what about you?" she asked, her voice barely above a whisper. "You're acting like Dayken doesn't matter. Like what you're leaving behind doesn't matter. Are you really okay with that?"

The mention of Dayken's name sent a pang through my chest, but I pushed it aside. I didn't know how to figure that out yet. His words rattled around in my head nonstop. It was maddening.

"This isn't about him. This is about what's best for us, for you."

Sky shook her head slowly. "No, Onyx. This is about what's best for *you*. And you're dragging me and Kolton into it without even thinking about how we feel."

Her words stung, and I didn't know how to respond. She was right, I hadn't thought about that. About any of that. All I knew was that staying here wasn't an option.

"I'm just trying to protect you," I finally said, my voice quieter now, less certain.

Sky's expression turned gentle, but there was sadness in her eyes that I didn't know how to fix. "I know, Onyx. But maybe, just this once, you need to let us protect you."

She suddenly tilted her head, struck by a thought. "Do you have a hobby?"

I frowned at the sudden shift in topic. "A hobby? Why would I need or want something like that?"

"Because it's a natural, healthy thing," she said patiently. "Something that brings you joy. Happiness."

I crossed my arms and leaned back against the wall. "I don't believe in those things. But I do find a certain peace in making weapons."

Her lips twitched like she was holding back a smile. "See? That counts. I enjoy reading. It's fun and exciting. What's your favorite color?"

I already knew she liked reading. The whole exchange felt odd. "I don't have one."

She gave me a long look, unblinking, like she was trying to peel layers off me that didn't exist. "Okay. Would you say you're more of a morning person or a night person?"

"I'm the same all day," I said flatly.

Sky exhaled, exasperated, though warmth still lingered in her eyes. "Onyx, you're missing the point. Figure yourself out. Enjoy this time. Learn things about yourself."

Her words lingered long after she stopped speaking, irritating in the way only Sky could manage because she meant well. I shifted my weight, refusing to squirm under her gaze. She wanted me to dig, expose parts of myself that weren't there.

But what unsettled me most wasn't Sky's stare. It was the fear that if I ever started peeling back those layers, I would expose a darkness I didn't want anyone to see.

Chapter 43

Dayken

It had only been fourteen days, but it felt like a full year had passed since I'd last been here.

I had spent the last two weeks with the other Primarcs in Petoskey, dissecting every word out of Crowe's mouth. Two weeks straight of meetings and logistics. But no one flagged anything suspicious. No odd behavior. No signs of infiltration.

Which left us with two possibilities: either Crowe was lying, or his spies were so deeply embedded that we'd never find them. Either way, there was still a threat... a threat aimed directly at us.

Through it all, I couldn't stop thinking about Onyx. The need to protect her from this, keep her safe, had become more urgent than anything else. I know I'd left without a word. She probably didn't care. But I did. And it gnawed at me for fourteen damn days.

The moment I stepped back into the compound, the smell of concrete, sweat, and clan life hit me, and beneath it, something more familiar. Her scent. Distant. Faint. But still there.

Thank fuck.

My wolf surged as we crossed the threshold, ears up, claws ready, desperate to find her. I reined him in, unable to barge in on her after everything that happened. I took a steady, focused breath, then went to the security room.

Chase sat reclined in one of the rolling chairs, feet up, watching the monitors with monotonous boredom. Derek was typing something into the system, but they both looked up when I entered.

"You're back early," Derek said, standing. "Thought you were staying another day?"

"Changed my mind."

Chase raised an eyebrow but didn't press. "Everything go smoothly at the meetings?"

"Define smooth. Crowe kept his cards close. We're left with two scenarios — either he lied about spies in the ranks, or they're buried too deep to detect," I said, shaking my head.

Derek swore under his breath. "Either way, it's a problem."

"Exactly. A calculated lie is dangerous. But so is a truth we can't see."

Chase turned to one of the screens and tapped a few keys. Footage of the outer training field flickered up. "She's been steady," he said casually, not looking at me. "Running drills. Keeping to herself."

My chest tightened. "Any trouble?"

"Not from her," Derek said. "Though… she hasn't exactly been warm. She's been hanging out with Titus. At his place."

"What do you mean?" The words barely made it past my teeth, rage building fast and sharp under my skin.

Derek, oblivious to my reaction, kept going, "Yeah, he offered her a job or something. She heads over there almost daily and sometimes returns with weapons. I peeked into her room — she's stockpiling some good gear. I even thought about swiping a few for myself."

"I want every detail of that arrangement," I said as I turned fully toward him, voice low and dangerous. "Titus is not a male I trust getting close to my Sacar. Not without oversight."

I hadn't expected her to become close to someone else. The thought ignited a fire in my chest, burning through every rational part of me.

A deep-seated instinct rose up, demanding I remind everyone she was mine — mine alone.

Chase finally glanced my way. "She knows you're back?"

"Not yet."

"You want us to—"

"No," I said quickly. "Don't do anything. Just… keep eyes on her."

They exchanged a look but nodded. I lingered a few minutes longer, watching her on the screen. She moved alone. Efficient. Unbothered.

Or at least pretending to be.

I had left her without saying a damn thing. No warning, no note. I just vanished, telling myself it was the most strategic choice. The meeting was critical, and she needed space. But that didn't make it right.

I thought about her every second I was gone. In every room I entered, every political landmine I tried to avoid, she still consumed my thoughts. I thought about what she'd say. What she'd do. What she'd smell like standing next to me. It was pathetic.

And still… I couldn't stop.

I left the security room with my stomach twisted and my wolf pacing under my skin. I told myself I wouldn't look for her — that I'd give her time. Then I saw her down the hallway. She was moving with purpose. Chin up. Eyes forward. Like she hadn't been cracked wide open weeks ago. Like I didn't still live inside every scar she refused to show.

She hadn't seen me yet, but I slowed anyway, giving her space. Letting the air shift. When her gaze finally locked with mine, she froze just a beat too long. Then her spine straightened, and her expression sharpened. Distant.

That wall was up again. Clearly built just for me.
She passed by without saying a word.
And I let her.
But my wolf didn't. He detected something — a scent.

Fox.

I turned slowly, breathing it in. It was faint… but fresh. Too fresh. My jaw clenched. My hands curled into fists. But I didn't follow her. Didn't press her against the wall the way my instinct demanded.

Not this time. She could have her space. Her secrets.
But she was still mine.
Even if she hadn't figured that out yet.

Chapter 44

Onyx

Dayken had been back for three days. Three days of tension. Three days of silence. And now, I was starting to doubt every decision I'd made. I didn't know what I wanted anymore. I didn't have any answers. Everything felt like a trap with no escape, like an anvil had taken up permanent residence on my chest. My hands were shaking. I probably needed to feed.

But instead, I went to the one place where I still felt like myself. The gym had become my last refuge. No politics. No whispers. No Dayken. Just sweat, solitude, and the illusion of control. Or so I thought. I was halfway through my last set when the door creaked open, and my stomach dropped. His scent hit me first — pine, ozone, something raw and wolfish. Then I saw him in the mirror. Dayken. He was only wearing gym shorts and sneakers.

His bare, broad chest was carved like stone, every muscle defined. I hated how my eyes tracked its subtle movements as he breathed, firm, powerful. I hated how my body responded.

He paused in the doorway, as if entering took effort. His expression remained steady, but I saw the flicker, the near-flinch.

And gods help me, it gutted me.

I kept curling the weight like I hadn't noticed him enter. Like my body hadn't just gone tense. Like I wasn't suddenly hyper-aware of every inch of our exposed skin. This was my space. My hour. My silence.

He crossed the room quietly, heading to the far end. Every step felt louder than it should have, as if the floor itself wanted to remind me that he was here.

I didn't look towards him.

But I saw his reflection in the mirror. I noticed the set of his jaw as he settled into his stance. Saw the way his gaze, dark and intense, drifted over and caught me staring.

It hit me like static shock — charged and sharp.

A single drop of sweat slid down my neck. I watched it trail past my collarbone in the mirror, disappearing beneath my tank top.

When I glanced up, his eyes were locked on my chest.

For a heartbeat, his irises flashed black. Just a flicker. Just enough to let me know the wolf was close to the surface. Watching. Wanting.

My pulse spiked, traitorously loud in my ears.

But still, he didn't say a word.

And neither did I.

He turned away a second later, picked up a weight, and started his own set as if nothing had happened. As if we weren't standing on a fault line waiting to split open. But I felt him.

I felt the heat of his gaze, even when it wasn't on me. Felt the electricity in the air shift every time I moved. The tension stretched so tightly, it was a miracle that neither of us snapped.

I quietly set the dumbbell down, wiped my palms on a towel, and turned to leave without looking back. I sensed him watching me, like he wanted to stop me but didn't dare.

I kept going until I got to the hallway. His scent was so thick in the air, I could almost feel it on my skin. I was so distracted that I ran right into Chase. He grunted, steadying me with a hand on my arm. "Whoa. You alright?"

I couldn't answer. My heart was pounding, Dayken's presence still with me. But Chase didn't need my response to start talking.

"Listen… I probably shouldn't say anything, but I think you should know, Dayken never stopped watching over you."

I blinked. "What?"

Chase scratched the back of his neck, suddenly looking younger. Uneasy. "When he left for Petoskey, he made me and Derek check in on you. Every day. He wanted updates. Nightly."

I stared at him. "Why are you telling me this?"

"Because I saw the look in your eyes," Chase said gently. "You looked like you thought he gave up on you. He didn't." He hesitated. "Honestly? I think leaving killed him. But he did it anyway. For you."

I shook my head. "He didn't say goodbye."

"No," Chase said, softer now. "He didn't. But that wasn't indifference. That was self-preservation. For both of you."

He glanced down the hall, then back at me with a lopsided smile. "Also... he's been very *not chill* about the Titus thing."

My brows lifted. "What thing?"

"The weapons. The training. You heading out to Titus's place every day. Dayken's been pretending he doesn't care, but—" Chase gave a low whistle "—he's feral. You should've seen his face when Derek told him."

Something cracked inside me at Chase's admission. Not big. Not loud. Just enough to steal the breath from my lungs.

I turned and walked away without another word.

"Onyx—?" Chase called after me, but I was already gone.

At first, I didn't know where to go. My feet just moved: down the hallway, out the back door, across the compound, and into the trees. Then, suddenly, I knew. I needed somewhere quiet, far from the noise in my head, the guilt clawing at my ribs, and the weight of Dayken's gaze. Somewhere I could finally breathe.

The air outside was crisp and cold. I knew I was technically running away. *Again.* I knew I was lost. Completely, utterly lost. And yet, this still felt different. Important. A chapter of my story that needed to be written. I didn't know what to do or how to fix the mess unraveling around me. So instead, I went to the only other place I knew, the farmhouse.

Alicia was still holding Aurora, so I didn't have to worry about confronting her. The facility agents would have no reason to think we'd come back to a house with no security and no protection. It was the perfect plan.

Or maybe it was just desperation.

Inside, the house was a disaster, ransacked, with cabinets left open, furniture upended, and glass shattered. The stale air carried muted scents. No one had been here for a while, and I wondered why Dayken hadn't cleaned it. Perhaps it was too painful, dealing with a loved one's betrayal. I even wondered if he might have marked the house for demolition.

Moving cautiously, I cleared each room. I saved Dayken's for last, knowing it would be the hardest. His scent was everywhere. It wrapped around me like a ghost I couldn't touch or escape. Despite the chaos, it was still *his*.

Books, photos, and clothes lay scattered across the floor, remnants of a life abruptly interrupted. The chests that once held his weapons, knives, and small daggers had been dumped out, their contents carelessly strewn about.

My stomach tightened.

What were they looking for?

I began picking up books when a thin, almost paper-like magazine caught my eye. I turned it over and read the cover: Class of 2005.

Flipping it open, I found rows of small, square pictures — kids with bright, eager smiles, with their names printed neatly beneath each photo. There were only five or six children per page, followed by an image of an adult.

Then, I saw it.

Dayken Danielson

He was adorable.

My fingers traced over his photo, my heart melting at the innocence in his toothy grin. His hair — unruly even back then — fell into his eyes like a wild mess.

I kept flipping. The numbers at the top of the pages increased — second grade, third, fourth… Then, another name stopped me.

Aurora Danielson

She, too, looked so innocent, so untouched by the cruelty of the world. Nothing about this girl — this smiling, bright-eyed child — hinted at what she would become.

A woman who betrayed her only family. Her clan.

How did Aurora become someone willing to sacrifice others for her own selfish interests? I questioned whether I had reacted too quickly by insisting she remain at Alicia's encampment, and whether I should have been willing to seek answers.

As I kept flipping, I was greeted with images of children sitting at tables, learning and laughing. So, this was what school looked like for him. Small, intimate. Normal.

They had been raised in a world so different from my own. Even before Sky and I were taken, when we lived in this town, my — apparently fake — parents had home-schooled me.

Suddenly, a folded piece of paper slipped out of the yearbook, fluttering to the floor.

I picked it up, and the moment my eyes landed on the messy handwriting, I began reading.

> *Dear Mr. and Mrs. Danielson,*
> *I'm writing to inform you that Dayken has, yet again, escaped school grounds. This time, we had to enlist the help of the mountain lion clan, Clan Brownell, to track him down and return him. He missed a full day of classes and will need to make up the time after school over the next two weeks.*
> *I am also writing to update you on my conversation with him. He remains insistent that his Sacar is still alive and is determined to find her. When I gently reminded him of the girl's sudden and heartbreaking death, he lost control, destroying my classroom, cracking the chalkboard wall, snapping three chairs, and breaking five desks.*
> *While this type of behavior is not unusual for children his age as they develop their strength, I strongly believe it is crucial for him to process his grief rather than remain in denial. Convincing himself that she is still alive is not only unhealthy, but it also affects his ability to learn and move forward.*

My vision blurred, the words disappearing as my eyes watered.

A sob tore through me, raw and unstoppable, as I clutched my mouth, trying in vain to hold it in. The image of a young, shaggy-haired boy desperately looking for me smashed into my mind.

Desperation clawed at my chest as I scrambled for more yearbooks, shaking them aggressively, violently, hoping more letters would fall out.

They did. Three more. Each one marking the years as he got older.

I unfolded them with trembling hands, my pulse pounding in my ears.

> *...if he continues down this path, the clans won't be able to help him. We can't understand why he still believes she is alive...*

> *...as you are aware, with Dayken having been gone for two days this time...*

Two days.

He never stopped looking for me.

He never stopped.

I had been so quick to dismiss him, so quick to assume his life moved on without me. And yet, here I was, smacked with the truth of it.

He never stopped.

And gods, it shattered me.

Chapter 45

Dayken

She left again.

I watched her on the cameras from the security room. The mongoose I hired wasn't far behind. Those little guys were fierce, loyal, and very tiny. Holding a conversation with one was a nightmare, but if you managed it, they were worth their weight in gold.

I didn't have an official alliance with them, but their Primarc didn't seem to mind lending a hand in exchange for protection over their cottages in Port Austin, on the other side of the state. Fair trade.

I watched Onyx pass the last highway camera we installed. After that, she was off the grid.

No way to track her. And not knowing where she was going? It tore me apart.

But knowing she'd be safe… that was the only thing holding me together.

"I'm sure she'll be alright, man," Chase said beside me, trying to sound reassuring.

"I know," I muttered. "I just feel bad for anyone dumb enough to get in her way. She's ruthless enough not to make it quick."

Chase chuckled. "Fair."

I stared at the blank monitor a few seconds longer, watching the timer at the bottom corner tick like a heartbeat I couldn't reach.

I didn't know how long she'd be gone. But that didn't matter. She could take as long as she needed.

Because she didn't know that I'd be right here —
waiting for her. I'd wait forever if needed. But I'd never
ask her to carry that knowledge. That truth... it would
overwhelm her. She couldn't bear that weight right now,
not after everything. Yet, it remained within me. Calm.
Constant. Unwavering. Hidden beneath her walls, harsh
words, and silence, I was there, willing to wait, regardless
of the distance or her time away. She was everything.
And I'd wait for as long as she needed to find her way
back to me.

Chase leaned back to look at a different monitor.

"Where's your brother?" I finally asked, recalling why
I came in here.

Chase furrowed his brows. "Why does everyone
assume we always know where the other is? Just because
we're twins doesn't mean we have built-in brother
trackers." He huffed, but it lacked any real frustration.

"Well, you two are together all the time. I figured he
might've mentioned if he was in the gym or something."

He sighed. "He's grabbing a cup of coffee."

I stared at the back of his head, completely
flabbergasted. "What? Then why—"

"You still shouldn't assume," he cut in.

I groaned. "Jesus, I can't with you right now."

And I hadn't even dealt with the more obnoxious
twin yet.

Chapter 46

Onyx

I ran. I ran hard. I couldn't stop. It felt like deja vu, only this time, no enemy was chasing me. This time, it was my past, and it was gaining on me. In fact, it caught me completely off guard. I needed to fix this, and fast.

So, I ran.

The gates opened on their own accord; clearly, one of the twins was watching the cameras. But when I got through the main entrance, I was met with silence. Dayken's room was on the main floor, which meant I didn't have to descend the stairs to the basement. I marched down the hallway and stopped right outside his door. I didn't detect any traces of his scent or hear his familiar heartbeat. Regardless, I opened the door, slipped inside quietly, and shut it behind me.

I went over to his bed, pulled back the covers, and slid inside to wait for him. The need to be wrapped in his scent overwhelmed every other part of my rational brain, the smell of him a comforting balm on my over-sensitive nerves.

I lay on my side, staring at the wall. Minutes, maybe hours, slipped by; I couldn't tell. My mind kept turning over every word from the letters, each one digging deeper. Guilt tangled with excitement, and something bitter twisted in my gut. Nausea, maybe. Or that quiet, creeping dread that comes when you know everything's about to change.

"Onyx?"

As soon as I heard his beautiful, deep voice, it eased all my nerves. The door creaked open, and a thin beam of light filled the room. He approached the bed and stood there with a questioning look in his eyes. I remained quiet and simply pulled back the blankets in a silent invitation.

After not talking for so long, it astonished me how he seamlessly slipped beside me without a word, his eyes alert as he settled in. We remained quiet; yet somehow, words were unnecessary.

"You never stopped looking for me," I croaked, placing my hand on his side, feeling the solid muscle beneath my palm.

"I told you I didn't."

"Dayken, I'm so sorry."

He pulled me to him, sliding me across the mattress until I was nestled against his chest. His warmth, his presence — him — felt like something I should have never gone without.

"I don't know what happened," he murmured against the top of my head. "But you sneaking into my bed after leaving the compound feels like some kind of dream."

"I think I found the answers I was looking for."

"Yeah?" His voice was low, measured. "And what did you find?"

"I found that… I love you," I confessed, the words tumbling out before I could stop them. "And maybe I've loved you all along, but I was too afraid to see it." My throat tightened, my grip on him turning desperate. "You're everything I never let myself believe in, good, strong, loyal to a fault. And I know I don't deserve that kind of devotion. But if you'll forgive me for pushing you away, for all the times I fought this… I swear, I won't fight it anymore. I won't fight *you*. I'll be yours, if you'll still have me."

"Say it again."

"I'll be yours."

He smirked. "Not that part."

I exhaled a shaky breath. "I love you. So fucking much. And I'm so sorry."

"There's nothing to be sorry for, Onyx. I'm yours. Always have been." Then he kissed me — rough and unyielding, his control finally slipping.

He growled, low in his throat. The sound was deep and dangerous, vibrating through his chest as he pressed me back. His hands gripped my hips like he meant to stake a claim, like his body had decided it was done asking for permission.

And then I was under him.

His body pressed into mine, his weight grounded me, and the kiss deepened. The urgency in his touch made my pulse race. It was a hunger neither of us could deny.

And gods, did I love it when he lost control.

"Say it again," he demanded as he stripped off my shirt, then hastily unclasped my bra.

"I love you." My breath hitched as his large palms explored my bare skin.

"Again."

"I love yo—" A moan cut through the words as he captured my nipple between his teeth. Heat radiated off him, his impatience clear with each touch as his hand slid down my stomach, fumbling with the button of my pants.

The moment it gave, his hand slipped inside, rough, warm, and searching.

"I fell hard," he murmured against my skin, dragging his mouth across my breast. "And I have no regrets."

He found the ache between my thighs immediately, circling his thumb over the sensitive bundle of nerves through my underwear. The onslaught of pleasure between his lips on my nipple and his hand between my legs was more than I could take. Yet I still wanted more.

"Dayken, please."

"There it is — my undoing," he growled in a rasping tone that signaled his wolf was taking over. He released my breast and, with sudden urgency, slid my pants and underwear down so quickly that they barely cleared my ankles before I began tearing at his shirt.

Everything happened quickly, as if we both knew this moment was inevitable, and we had already wasted too much time. He finished removing his shirt, and I was greeted by his perfect chest, sculpted shoulders, and the cords of muscle running down his arms. His chest was pure beauty — a deep line ran through it, dividing his massive pecs. I ran my hands over it, marveling at every inch.

"Keep looking at me like that, and we'll never leave this room," he purred.

"I'm okay with that. You're perfection, and I've spent too long admiring you from afar. I want to take you all in," I replied.

He leaned over me, eyes burning with untamed hunger. "That will have to wait, because I *need* to be inside you, and it's tearing me apart," he murmured.

I couldn't help but smile at his impatience. He paused, taking in my smile, then lowered himself against me. His pants were still on, while I was completely bare and exposed. But the feel of his hard chest pressing against my breasts was enough to send me over the edge. He kissed me and murmured, "beautiful," against my lips. The kiss turned frenzied, tongues clashing with fervor. I ran my nails down the planes of his back as he pressed into my naked core.

"Dayken…. Your pants," I breathed between kisses.

"Are you sure? Because, once I remove these, I don't believe we can return to how things were."

"Off. Now, Dayken."

"Yes, my goddess. But say stop and I will."

There would be no stopping. I needed him like I needed air. Like I needed blood to survive. He was my new *need*. But I nodded anyway, just to get him to resume removing his clothes.

He worked quickly, tossing his pants and then his boxers to the floor, and before I knew it, his weight was back on top of me. I could feel the warmth of his hard erection against my wet folds.

He groaned out a slew of curses. "I could cum just from resting my dick here," he said before grinding against my sensitive bud. I almost screamed. I dug my nails into his back on instinct, not wanting him to pull away. I wanted him locked to me. The friction he was creating felt so good, but it still wasn't enough.

"Are you ready for me to be inside you?"

"Yes," I breathed.

"It might hurt a little," he warned, and I shook my head 'no,' as if I knew it wouldn't. He lowered his lips to mine in a searing kiss. He reached down to grip himself, lining the head of his cock with my entrance. He rubbed the tip up and down just enough to make me buck with need.

"Lay still, my goddess," he murmured. He leaned back and pressed his hand to my abdomen, using the other to ease the tip of his cock inside my slick center.

Little by little, he filled me. When he was confident I would stop squirming, he removed his hands from my stomach and his shaft, lowering his weight back onto me. He nipped at my neck as he rested his elbows on either side of my head. I was moaning even though he was barely inside me. Losing my patience, I wrapped my legs around him and squeezed. The motion caused his hips to flex forward, and we both swore in pleasure as he slammed fully into me.

"Fuck. Dayken," I cried. "You are so big. I think..." I didn't know what to think.

"Shhh, shh. You are taking me so good." But he wasn't moving, as if he was giving me a second to adjust to him. I unlocked my legs, and he pulled his hips back, then rocked forward.

"Yes. Again."

"Fuck you are so tight. I'm not going to last long."

He rocked back into me again. It felt so fucking good. Every thrust, every kiss, every breath was mine. It was all for me.

I clawed at him recklessly. I felt like I couldn't get him close enough, and he praised me for it.

"You like it like this, don't you?" he growled as he thrust hard into me. I nodded yes, unable to speak as the blinding heat built. "Mmm, you like it hard. Then hard is what you will get." With that, he pushed himself up, grabbed my thigh, and spread me wide. Slamming into me with such intensity, I had to brace my hands against the headboard to meet his thrusts.

"Fuck…. Yes. I'm going to…" And as if he knew what I was going to say next, he took his thumb and started circling my clit. I screamed — the pressure rising unexpectedly fast.

"Good girl. Let this whole place know you're mine."

And then I saw stars.

Heat exploded through me, and I felt him begin to pulse inside me. His thrusts slowed as I came back to reality. Or maybe I never really left. This was it. He was it.

I reached up and pulled him to me so I could capture his perfect lips.

"That was amazing," I breathed. "I want more."

He chuckled against my lips, melting my heart. "Who am I to deny you anything?"

He was still inside me when I felt him swell again — thick, ready. I shifted my hips, urging him on.

"Now, Dayken."

He pulled out, but before I could protest, he flipped me onto my stomach.

"Yes, ma'am," he murmured against the shell of my ear. His hard length pressed along the curve of my ass. The shift in position sent a thrill through me, sharp and immediate.

Dayken was relentless in giving me pleasure. He drove into me with a pace that blurred the edges of time. He fucked me again and again until my throat was hoarse from screaming his name, until I was wrung out and trembling, our hunger finally — if only temporarily — sated.

We lay there in silence, our legs tangled together, my head resting on his chest while his fingers traced idle, thoughtless patterns along my spine. I slowly ran my hand up and down the ridges of his abdomen, letting the motion distract me, hard muscle beneath warm skin, rising and falling with each steady breath.

It should have calmed me, anchored me. But despite overwhelmingly embracing and admitting that I was in love with Dayken, something gnawed at me, low and constant. A fear I couldn't shake.

Because maybe… maybe if Dayken knew what I had done to get out of that facility… Maybe he'd feel differently. He said he fell hard, but what if he didn't know he fell for a monster?

"I killed someone who helped us." I hadn't meant to say it. But the words clawed their way out before I could stop them.

Dayken didn't flinch. Not even the slightest twitch of a muscle beneath my fingers. No shift in his breathing.

I looked up to see him watching me like he always did, calm, quiet, maddeningly patient.

"Her name was Elena. She was a nurse. Brought extra blood when she knew they were intentionally starving us. Whispered warnings when the scientists were coming. She was kind." I swallowed. My voice was starting to crack, and I hated it.

"I'd figured out that I was building a tolerance to the silver. I sat on that knowledge for a while, kept testing, kept planning. I mulled over how I might get out of my restraints.

"Once I had enough strength, I ripped through one and slipped it just far enough around my wrist to make it *look* like it was still secure. But I didn't think it would be Elena who walked in.

"I didn't have time to think. I didn't see another chance. Not with the cameras always watching us. I just... reacted." I let the silence hang there. I waited for him to speak. To judge me. To tell me I was right to hate myself.

But he didn't. He just kept running those slow, methodical strokes up and down my spine.

I broke eye contact and turned away, choking on everything else I felt compelled to confess.

"She looked... so confused. Not betrayed. Just... confused. Like — why was I hurting *her*? Her, the one who helped us." I swallowed thickly.

"And, um... it–it didn't stop there. There was a kid waiting for Elena. Some intern. He was going to hit the panic button.

"He was shaking, terrified, and I ended him. I had to. I had to get out. I had to get to Sky. It was too important." My voice cracked beneath the weight of my confession. "He was just a kid, Dayken."

I felt him wrap his hand securely around mine. Steady. Warm. Unshakable.

"You want me to be horrified?" he finally asked, his voice low, resolute. "Because I'm not."

I looked up at him then, as something raw and ugly in my chest threatened to split me open.

"You could burn the whole goddamn world down, Onyx," he said, his green eyes blazing like wildfire. "And I would only care that you didn't hurt yourself in the process."

I stared at him, feeling like he'd just broken something open inside me.

"You think I care if your hands are clean? I care that you're here. That you're breathing. That you still feel this deeply after everything they did to you." He held me closer, arm tightening around me, as he lifted my hand to press it against his chest. "I don't need a perfect version of you. I never did."

And for the first time in a long time, I didn't feel like a monster. I didn't feel like someone who needed fixing.

I just felt... *seen.*

He pulled me on top of his chest and kissed me.

"I just need you," he whispered against my lips.

Chapter 47

Onyx

I stirred awake, warmth engulfing me. The steady heartbeat at my back told me exactly where that warmth was coming from... my wolf. My protector. My Guardian.

"Dayken?" I whispered into the darkness, my voice barely audible. His bicep flexed around me in response, tightening gently, a silent confirmation.

I didn't want to do what I had to next.

Fuck. This feels too perfect. Too right.

And, just for a second, I let myself wonder — what would it feel like to stay like this forever?

"Hmm?" he murmured groggily, his breath warm against my neck, making my skin shiver with his every exhale.

Damn it. I really didn't want to move. But this, this was the balance I'd been looking for. Enjoying the moment... while never losing sight of the big picture.

I exhaled slowly and whispered, "I have an idea."

***

I gathered everyone in the security room. No one questioned the middle-of-the-night wake-up call. I'm pretty sure Chase didn't require sleep, because he was already at his post — alert, focused, and unbothered. His coffee intake was truly impressive.

Derek, however, burst in like he owned the place, wearing fluffy pink pajama bottoms covered in bright yellow bananas, mismatched fuzzy socks, and a satin sleep mask pushed up onto his forehead like a tiara.

No shirt. All Derek.

He yawned, stretching dramatically before plopping into a chair like this was the most normal thing in the world.

Sky and Kolton entered next. Sky was in a tank top and sleeping shorts. Kolton… was fully dressed. Jeans. T-shirt. Boots.

I raised an eyebrow but said nothing.

Kolton definitely noticed Sky's lack of clothing. His pupils thinned the second he looked at her, turning razor-sharp, his yellow eyes practically glowing. His nostrils flared, and his jaw tightened like he had to force himself to look away.

He failed. Miserably.

Actually, he wasn't even trying anymore.

His gaze drifted over her bare legs and up the curve of her waist, where it settled with shameless focus. To his credit, he did try to appear casual, but his fingers twitched at his sides, his shoulders were too tense, and his breathing was a little too controlled.

Yeah. He was suffering. And I was just morbid enough to enjoy it.

Alicia and Peach were already patched into the audio system, their voices crackling through the speakers as the last of us settled in. The room was quiet, waiting to hear why we had gathered them.

"I've been thinking," I began.

Derek let out a dramatic gasp, clutching at invisible pearls. "No way! I didn't know you could do that!" he exclaimed, looking around like he expected the apocalypse to begin.

I ignored his outburst. "I think—" I emphasized, shooting daggers at Derek. His grin widened, but I powered through. "We should go to them. I've been crafting enough weapons to arm the entire U.S. Military, and I'm sick of living in constant fear. If we take them head-on, we might actually have the element of surprise."

"Well, I'm relieved to hear you say that," Chase said, surprising me and already pulling up data on his tablet. "Because while they were here, I may or may not have taken the liberty of upgrading the gate's security system. Specifically, I installed software that scans for active IP addresses within a five-mile radius. The system flags any device sending out signals, phones, laptops, or anything with a network connection. The problem was that there were a lot of hits, and sorting through raw data like that is a nightmare. But I ran some correlation algorithms, cross-referenced connection pings, and filtered out irrelevant data, such as nearby civilians ordering overpriced coffee. Eventually, the highest recurring signal came from a concentrated location in Missouri," Chase said, like he wasn't casually pulling off high-level cyber warfare.

"Translation," Derek cut in, smirking. "We're pretty damn confident we tracked their asses."

"Where in Missouri?" Alicia asked over the speaker.

"Sainte Genevieve."

A realization struck me, and I glanced at the others. "Wait... didn't Kolton mention Missouri before, too?" Yes, I was talking about the tiger like he wasn't in the room, but he didn't seem to care. He just stared at the screen, nodded once, and said nothing. That had to be the spot then.

"Do you remember crossing the river when you escaped?" Chase asked me.

"The river?"

"The Mississippi River? Giant body of water. Goes north and south through the whole country. Still nothing? Big wawa go uppy and downy?" Derek explained.

Patience, Onyx.

"No, we never crossed a giant body of water. Little ones, but nothing that big."

"Hmm, maybe that's not the location then," Chase contemplated.

"Well, we can still check it out, see how it's connected," Dayken added. Everyone nodded in agreement. "We're going to need a lot of bodies for a mission like this," he said with finality.

"Actually, I disagree—" I started.

"Shocker," Derek huffed, not so quietly, under his breath.

I was not going to punch him. He was just tired and extra sassy today. That's all.

Just let his jabs go, Onyx.

That was the mantra I kept repeating to myself.

"I believe we can pull this off with a small stealth team," I said. "If we travel there with an army, they will see us coming and have time to prepare. We need the element of surprise for this to work.

"Whose giant trucks are those in the underground garage?" I asked suddenly. "I saw a black one and a gray one."

"They're both mine," Dayken said. "Being this close to Motor City, it's practically mandatory to own at least one truck with 4-wheel drive."

Derek snorted. "Yeah, but those are F-250s with double rear axles. Practically monsters. You way overdid it, my man."

Dayken just shrugged, like owning a fleet of oversized trucks was completely normal.

"They're big, sure," I mused. "But they're casual enough not to look suspicious when we roll into Missouri."

Everyone nodded in unison, and Alicia's voice crackled over the phone, signaling her agreement.

Alright, transportation was set.

Now, it was time to figure out which weapons to bring: silencers, edged weapons, hollow-point ammunition, and, according to Derek, black ski masks. The conversation continued around me, plans forming, strategies being laid out, but my mind drifted.

I had pushed them all away and kept my distance. Shut them out. And yet, here they were. Backing me up. Believing in me.

I swallowed hard, my chest tight with something I couldn't quite name. Guilt? Yeah, definitely. But there was something else too, something even more dangerous.

Belonging.

I used to think I could survive on my own; I felt like I needed to. But it turns out I didn't. I just needed Dayken.

I needed the whole package deal that came with him, too.

His loyalty, his clan, and this ridiculous, dysfunctional, completely unwavering team.

For so long, I convinced myself I was better off alone. Safer that way. Easier. But if that were really true, then why did this moment feel like a missing piece clicking into place?

Why did it feel… right?

I refocused on the mission, holding tightly to what I knew best: action, strategy, and control.

A sharp voice cut through my thoughts.

"Fine, but Sky stays back with the Mack Clan."

Kolton.

His tone was final, but his body told a different story. His shoulders were rolled back, muscles coiled like a predator scenting a threat. His fingers flexed at his sides, not quite into fists, but itching for it, claws unsheathing from his nail beds. Sharp. Brutal.

Most telling of all? His head was tilted slightly, eyes narrowing with a calculated intensity that sent a chill through the room.

It was a blatant challenge for dominance.

Sky didn't take the bait. Instead, she stepped right into his space.

"Don't start this shit again, Kolton."

Wow. He actually managed to make Sky swear.

There was no way anyone in the room missed his gaze flicking down — sharp, heated — to the exposed bonding mark over her chest. His eyes flashed yellow, wild and primal, before he forced them back up. When he met her eyes again, his expression was controlled, but barely.

"It's not worth the risk." His voice was measured, clipped. "We," he gestured to the room, "can handle this just fine."

"You probably could. But you won't." Sky's voice didn't waver. "I'm ending this, and you are not going to take that away from me."

Kolton's jaw locked. He inhaled a deep, steady breath. "Stubborn goddamn woman," he muttered, voice low, dangerous. Then he turned and stormed out, his heavy footsteps echoing down the corridor.

Now that I thought about it… that might be the farthest I'd ever seen him walk away from her.

They had a lot of shit to figure out.

Dayken was protective, but nothing like Kolton.

At the end of the day, though, the only thing that mattered to me was that my sister was safe.

And Kolton? He cared about that a lot.

As the conversation wrapped up and the details were finalized, exhaustion tugged at my limbs, but my mind refused to slow down. I convinced Dayken to come to my room, since it was closer. We slipped inside, shutting out the rest of the world.

Only, neither of us fell asleep. We lay there, side by side, lost in thought. The silence between us was thick but not uncomfortable, heavy with everything we had yet to say.

We were strategizing, planning, and preparing — reviewing every angle and risk. We were about to enter enemy territory, and failure wasn't an option. No casualties. No mistakes. We had to get this right.

"We're gonna finish this." My voice was steady, full of certainty.

Dayken turned his head toward me, his dark eyes unwavering. Slowly, he reached over, his thumb lightly touching my bottom lip, as if checking to make sure the words I'd said were real.

"Yes, we are." He closed the gap, kissing me with a perfect mix of force and tenderness, grounding us in what truly mattered. "Together."

Time was short. We both knew it. Neither of us knew how many days or moments we had left.

So, I pushed him back onto the bed, straddling him, deepening the kiss. His massive hands gripped my thighs, fingers digging in just enough to send a shiver down my spine. He rocked up into me, his body answering mine without hesitation.

"Together," I breathed against his mouth. Then I nipped my way down his thick neck, feeling his muscles tense beneath my lips. My fangs descended — sharp, aching, desperate.

I wanted to bite him. Needed to. The idea of his blood hitting my tongue sent a whole new thrill through me. But I wanted him inside me more.

Could I have both?

I pulled back just enough to meet his eyes, to let him see the sharp glint of my fangs.

"Fuck, you are sexy," he growled, voice low.

"I think I might have trouble controlling myself this time, Dayken," I warned.

"My goddess," he rasped, his eyes black and wild. "There is no need for control with me. Ever. Bite me. Fuck me. Ruin me. I am yours." His hands slid up my body, palms rough as they cupped my breasts, squeezing hard enough to make me gasp. I bucked against his groin, and he groaned, deep and filthy.

"I think I'll take both then," I whispered.

His pupils blew wide. "Fuck..."

I slid my hand down and wrapped my fingers around him. He cursed and grabbed my wrist, hard.

"Did I hurt you?" I asked, startled.

"What? No. Gods, no," he panted. "I just don't want to come in your hand. Take your fucking pants off. Now." His tone left no room for argument, but I found myself hesitating, just to see what he'd do. His eyes darkened further. "Don't make me repeat myself, sweetheart."

But he was already stripping my pants off, his own shoved low around his hips as he gripped my waist and pulled me over him.

"I'm going to come inside your tight little pussy," he growled, voice like thunder and sin. "And then I'm going to fuck you again — hard — and come all over your stomach and these perfect tits so my wolf knows exactly who you belong to."

I nodded, my core clenching at the picture he painted. "Yes," I breathed. "I want that."

"Good girl," he snarled, voice feral. "I was too damn impatient last time. This time? No holding back."

He grabbed my ass with both hands, lifting me slightly. Using one hand to grip himself, he aligned his cock between my folds, and I felt the pulsing ache. I dropped down onto him so fast he barely got his hand out of the way.

"Fuck!" he barked, his head snapping back into the pillow. "You're so wet. You were made for me."

I started moving, bouncing, grinding, and finding a rhythm that sent sparks up my spine.

His black eyes locked onto mine, hungry and raw. "Mine," he growled, double fangs bared, claiming me like he had every right to.

"Yours," I moaned, the word ripped from my throat. "I'm going to—"

But I couldn't finish. He sat up, wrapped one massive arm around my waist, and took over. He lifted me effortlessly, slamming me back down onto him again and again until I shattered.

I screamed, stars exploding behind my eyes, and without thinking, I leaned forward and sank my fangs into his neck. His body jerked. A string of curse words left his lips, but he didn't stop me. Didn't flinch. Instead, I felt him throb inside me, his rhythm stuttering, his orgasm crashing into him as I bit down.

His taste was unreal, power and heat and something so darkly addictive I almost couldn't stop.

"Take whatever you need," he whispered, one hand stroking down my back as I fed. "It's yours. I'm yours."

Eventually, I pulled back and licked the puncture wounds, staring at the small, already healing marks.

"I've never done that before," I admitted, stunned.

"Which part?" he asked, smirking lazily.

"All of it," I said, the smile hitting my face before I could stop it.

His grin deepened. "Good. You'll only drink from me from now on. And just so we're clear..." He grabbed my chin, holding my gaze. "You'll only ever fuck *me*."

I nodded, breathless. But that wasn't good enough for him.

"No, no, my goddess. Say it. My wolf needs to hear the words."

"Only you," I whispered.

"Only you what?"

I had never been so uncomfortable — and so turned on — in my life.

Is this a power exchange?

Whatever it was, it was sexy as hell watching him claim every inch of me — mind, body, and soul.

"I will only ever drink from you and have sex with you," I vowed, my voice shaking with the intensity.

"Forever," he said.

"Forever," I echoed.

"Good girl," he growled, giving me a smirk that was pure sin.

I leaned forward and nipped his lower lip. "Mmm... my feisty little vixen," he murmured, grip tightening on my hips. "Round four?"

I didn't answer. I didn't have to.

He flipped me over and pinned me to the bed, already hard again.

He was huge, and heavy, and perfect, slotting between my legs as I wrapped them around him, locking him in.

We weren't going anywhere.

And sleep? Please.

The man of my dreams had fangs, claws, and a filthy mouth — and he was mine.

And right now?

I had *a lot* of needs.

Chapter 48

Onyx

It felt like everything depended on this moment — it would either make or break us. In order to spare others from the same torture and brutality, we had to eradicate the source. Destroy their entire operation. Wipe out their influence. Leave nothing but ruin. If we let their relentless pursuit continue, we'd never truly have peace. We'd never escape the constant cycle of running, packing up our lives, and exchanging one safe place for another. I wasn't willing to live like that anymore. It stopped now. We just had to finish our final briefing before heading out.

"I've had our scouts fly overhead," Chase began. "They dropped an echo-device on the roof of the building we believe is our target. My system scanned for any cloud signals or consistent power sources. We found multiple cameras and motion sensors."

He pointed to a satellite map on one of the large monitors, his finger tracing a line along a massive river. "If you follow this path here, you'll avoid the motion sensors — but you *will* be caught on camera. I can only pause the feed for twenty seconds at a time. Anything longer will raise suspicion."

I listened carefully as Chase outlined the terrain — where we could use trees for cover, and where we'd be dangerously exposed. I would never take the falcons for granted again. Their aerial scouting skills were unmatched.

While the others discussed who would drive, I kept my eyes on Chase. He looked exhausted after spending the last few days buried in screens, data, and computer code, working diligently to keep us safe. But who was taking care of *him*? He wasn't just security; he was invaluable. But that was something I'd have to deal with later. For now, we had a mission.

As the meeting ended, we said our goodbyes. Alicia hugged Peach tightly, a gesture more than words. She held her close, with her cheek on Peach's hair. When she stepped back, her hand stayed on Peach's arm.

"You don't leave that room unless you have to," Alicia said. "And if something feels off, you listen to your gut — no hero shit."

"You're the one going full tank mode into enemy territory," Peach replied, trying to keep her voice light. But it cracked, just a little.

Alicia didn't smile. "Exactly. You stay safe. I mean it."

She had brought more Mack Clan members to the compound to put her mind at ease, but I noticed her hesitance; she was only leaving because Peach was okay with it.

Chase was quietly saying goodbye to his brother, their silent display reflecting a deep bond. Derek clasped Chase's neck, their foreheads together, an unspoken connection. This was not some one-time act but a long-standing tradition, a moment of brotherly unity.

It was almost heartwarming.

Almost.

"Listen to me," Derek said, pulling back just enough to meet his brother's gaze — dark brown clashing with pitch black. "If I don't make it back... I need you to promise me something."

Chase nodded solemnly.

"You'll clear my browser history. No questions asked."

Chase smirked, and I groaned, disappointed in myself for expecting more than ten seconds of seriousness from Derek.

We left the security room and headed to the armory, footsteps echoing as fluorescent lights cast shadows on the concrete walls. Peach perched herself on a counter as soon as we entered the room, sliding aside anytime someone needed to access the drawers for magazines and ammo.

"We have a guest." Chase's voice crackled over the PA.

I arched a brow at Dayken. He just shrugged, his expression saying, *'Don't look at me.'*

"Should we head up and see what's going on?" Alicia asked, almost rhetorically. I nodded anyway, and Peach jumped down from the counter to follow us out.

We quickly moved back down the hallway and up the stairs. Stopping abruptly at the main entrance, we were all surprised by who we found waiting there. He looked as polished as usual. His olive-green, custom-fit outfit, with perfectly coordinated earth tone accents, radiated refinement and luxury. He looked as if he'd just stepped off a runway — again.

"Titus?" Dayken asked, voice tinged with confusion and frustration.

Titus let out a dramatic sigh. "What's this I hear about an out-of-state trip? I may be stunning, but I'm not an idiot. This can only mean one thing, and frankly, I'm deeply offended I wasn't invited."

"How did you even hear about it?" I asked, narrowing my eyes.

"He called me," Alicia said, stepping in. "Just checking on a shipment. I mentioned we'd be out of town for a few days. Told him not to worry about it."

Titus raised a manicured brow. "Imagine my surprise — hearing you were leaving *again*. From a place that's *designed* to never require leaving," he scoffed. "I want in."

His eyes suddenly settled on Peach, unmistakably intense — smoldering and focused, deliberate. "Is she going?" he asked.

Peach stepped forward before anyone could reply, pointing a delicate, pink-painted nail at him. "She can speak for herself," she said coolly. "And not that it's any of your business, but no. I'm staying here. Helping Chase with security."

Titus tilted his head slightly, considering her. Then simply said, "Good."

Just *good*.

I turned to Alicia. "Who else did you tell?"

She frowned. "No one. I barely told him."

This was risky. Given Titus's connection to the DeStephano Clan, none of us fully trusted him. I even worked for him and still had reservations about his motives. He was constantly involved in shady stuff and holding secret meetings. But the fact was, we could use the extra muscle. And let's be honest, despite being a fox, Titus had plenty of it.

With a defeated sigh, I looked at Sky, then Dayken. Both wore the same expression: *'Why not?'*

I groaned. "Okay, fine. But you can't come dressed like that. And you need to bring your own damn weapons, I know you've got plenty."

Chapter 49

Onyx

Once we were on the road, my impatience began to build, fast and furious.

Kolton sat in the backseat with Sky, while Dayken drove, and I rode shotgun. My mind buzzed with anticipation. I wanted answers. Needed them. But I forced my body to stay relaxed, to stay steady. I didn't want to appear as rattled as I felt.

The car was tense, thick with unspoken apprehension, but beneath it, there was excitement. We were finally getting close to ending this. Kolton had unknowingly tracked Sky for years, always ending up at the river, but on different sides, sometimes Missouri, sometimes Illinois. Not only different states, but different clan territories, and all the muddled politics that went along with it.

With Chase's latest tech — half science, half sorcery, if you asked me — we had narrowed it down to a precise location.

We weren't stuck on the defensive anymore. We could finally bring the fight to them.

Guided by Kolton's instincts and Chase's innovative designs, we were journeying to the one place I vowed Sky and I would never return. The place that shattered our entire world, tortured us, broke us, and transformed our lives into a living nightmare. Now, we were heading back to the facility, but this time, there would be no running — only pursuing answers and seeking justice. My anxiety twisted at the thought, but I maintained a calm expression.

I looked at Sky, the only person in this world who I would willingly risk my life for. She sat quietly, but the tension in her jaw and the way her fingers curled into her hoodie showed me everything.

She was scared.

So was I.

As the hours passed, the landscape shifted from farms to cityscapes, limestone cliffs to winding riverbanks. Memories flooded in — certain smells, distant sights, flashbacks of running and bleeding, of hiding in darkness. A reminder of our escape and what we once again faced. I leaned my head against the window, closing my eyes to steady my nerves.

A moment later, Dayken reached over, intertwining his fingers with mine. I cracked one eye open, glancing down at our hands. His hand was big and strong, the calluses of a fighter worn into every inch. Mine was smaller, paler, almost delicate by comparison. The contrast was sharp. And yet... we fit. Perfectly. I squeezed back — a quiet reassurance: *I'm okay.*

From the backseat, Sky reached forward and rested her hand on my shoulder, tracing gentle circles with her thumb. Her touch — always soft, always grounding — eased something jagged in my chest. I exhaled, tension leaving me in slow waves.

I am so fucking lucky.

How had it taken me this long to realize?

After crossing the river from Illinois into Missouri, we still had an hour left to drive before reaching Sainte Genevieve. We pulled into a quiet rest stop outside of the city limits, and the second truck rolled in behind us. As soon as we stepped out, Dayken started stripping down to shift. Despite the serious situation, I couldn't help but stare — the way his abs flexed as he peeled off his shirt, the slow, confident roll of his hips as he kicked his pants aside. He wasn't rushing — he never did — and maybe that's what made it worse.

Like he *knew* I was watching.

I tried not to stare shamelessly. I even thought I was being subtle, until I saw the unmistakable jut of his erection. His green gaze met mine, and I could practically feel how much he enjoyed having my eyes on him. He didn't speak, just grinned like the devil before shifting into his wolf form. Smooth, effortless, unbothered. I stood there too long, my mind drifting to places it shouldn't go… not now, not here. But gods help me... I wanted to go there.

I looked over my shoulder, hoping no one saw my gawking. Sky was talking to Kolton, and Alicia had already shifted into her bear form. The others soon followed. Taking animal form would allow them to move quickly and quietly through the forest. Titus turned into a sleek black fox and vanished into the trees, while Derek soared into the sky, wings cutting through the night.

Kolton didn't shift. Not because he didn't want to — he *always* wanted to — but because he refused to let Sky move without someone guarding her back. So, he stayed human. Alert. Protective. Orange hairs dusted his arms, streaked with black. His yellow eyes flickered, feral and on edge.

While the others were shifting, Kolton, Sky, and I shouldered heavy packs filled with clothes, ammo, and gear. Once we were loaded up, we pushed forward, winding through dense forest and staying clear of any houses.

Even in the dark, this place whispered its history — weathered cobblestone, grand old homes, long-forgotten paths running alongside the river. It was beautiful in the way haunted places always are.

But I barely registered it.

My mind was somewhere else, on the mission. On the pain. On what lay hidden in this place.

We reached a densely wooded area. My wolf appeared silently beside me, massive paws barely making a sound. Derek dove from a branch, shifting before hitting the ground. The others followed, grabbing clothes from our packs and changing quickly.

"We're close now," Sky said, reaching for a small black plastic case. Inside were eight sleek earpieces. "Time to switch to comms."

She handed them out as she spoke. "Chase showed me how to use them. You can leave them on, so we're always connected. Avoid any side conversations, though, or it'll get confusing."

She slipped hers into place. Kolton followed, but his brow furrowed. "When were you with Chase?"

Before she could answer, Chase's voice crackled into our ears. "Hey, everyone, can you hear me?"

"Brother!" Derek shouted.

Everyone winced, clutching their ears.

"Shhh!" we hissed in unison, but Derek just shrugged his shoulders as if pleading ignorance. Alicia looked like she was seconds away from tackling him.

"Okay," Chase said calmly. "I've got your location and a lock on the target. Keep heading southeast toward the river. You'll come upon what appears to be a large residential area, but that's just a façade. None of those houses are occupied. If my intel's correct, the best entry point is the random mansion sitting on the western side of the grounds."

We exchanged glances. Nodded.

Titus led the way, slipping into the brush. From this point on, we'd be exposed, no more trees, no more cover. We had to move quickly, quietly, and as a unit. We continued silently until we reached the last row of eastern red cedars. The sharp, resinous scent hit me, triggering a memory. I recalled the night Sky and I escaped, and my blood started boiling with rage. The memory sparked anger rather than fear. I took that as a good sign.

We paused together, perfectly coordinated — one breath held, one shared rhythm — ready to charge forward. On Chase's, 'go,' we bolted from the clearing. Alicia was on my left. Sky on my right.

The moment my feet hit open ground, adrenaline surged as my senses sharpened. The wind whipped my hair back. The air felt cool on my skin. Darkness surrounded us, a fragile veil. We ran hard over uneven dirt and rocks, no hesitation, just forward momentum.

The mansion came into view, with a basic security guard stationed at the entrance. He was an older man in slacks and a jacket, who seemed harmless. But I knew better: those who looked the least threatening were often the most dangerous. Even if they didn't do the torture and maiming themselves, they certainly had no qualms about alerting the sadists who did.

I tensed, ready to strike.

But Dayken moved before I could. He was swift. Silent. Precise.

One moment, the man was standing. The next, he was in a sleeper hold — feebly gripping Dayken's arm, face turning purple before he went limp. Dayken let him drop to the pavement, unconscious, like trash alongside the highway.

Chase's voice came through my earpiece, steady and focused. "You're clear. Move."

We approached the entrance, our steps light, controlled. The silence that greeted us was deafening. Almost unnatural.

"We're just gonna waltz right through the front door?" Derek whisper-yelled, and we all shot him a look.

"Yes," Chase replied flatly.

Three of us took up positions on one side of the door, the other three mirroring us on the opposite side. Dayken pressed a hand to the doorknob. Twisting it slowly, he tilted his head, listening.

Nothing.

Then, with one sharp motion, he flung the door open. We moved as one, emerging from cover with weapons drawn.

Still nothing.

No movement. No heartbeats. No scent.

The silence clung to the air, thick, oppressive.

We stepped over the threshold together.

At first glance, the house looked exactly like what it pretended to be: an extravagant estate. Expensive. Curated. A legacy of refined wealth, elegant on the surface, rotten underneath.

Gold-trimmed mirrors caught the dim glow from the chandelier. Massive oil paintings stretched across the walls in gilded frames. Plush, embroidered furniture and heavy velvet drapes created an illusion of comfort.

But it was staged; the details were plainly meant to distract and mislead. A beautifully constructed lie.

We moved deeper inside, and I stopped at the second door on the left. My hand hovered over the handle, hesitating.

Then it hit me… *the scent.*

Concrete. Metal. Bleach.

It crashed into me like a fist to the face, dragging me backward in time.

My stomach twisted. My pulse spiked.

I knew that smell too well.

I jerked my hand from the doorknob, already certain the scent wasn't coming from behind the door.

This is the place.

I was back where it all began, I could feel it, smell it... but I couldn't *see* it.

I inhaled again, deeper this time, even though it made me want to puke. Nausea from the past rose in me, but then I *placed* it — the source.

It wasn't in front of us.

It was below us.

My gaze dropped to the thick, ornate rug under our feet. The entrance had to be beneath it. I started to point, but Alicia was already watching me, tracking every movement. Without a word, she motioned for everyone to step back and kicked the rug aside, revealing a trap door.

Sky stepped forward and crouched down, her fingers finding the handle almost instinctively. With a firm tug, the door creaked open, revealing a narrow shaft of stairs to the darkness below.

I listened for movement, but there was nothing. No shuffle. No breath.

"It's quiet down there," I whispered. "No signs of life."

"Let's check it out," Alicia replied, already moving.

We followed silently, slipping into the perfectly concealed nightmare beneath the floorboards.

Titus and Derek stayed up top, guarding our escape route. Their presence was a tether, a last line of defense if everything went sideways.

The air became cooler as we descended the makeshift wooden steps. There was a narrow tunnel at the bottom, where we encountered our first obstacle.

A thick metal door, a complete contrast to the wooden planks around us. No hinges. No handle. Just a solid, seamless slab of reinforced steel with a keypad embedded into the wall beside it. It was clear this door wasn't meant to be opened easily, maybe not at all. Or perhaps it was intended to keep something in.

"Tell me what you see," Chase said through our earpiece. When Dayken finished explaining it, Chase replied, "One second," followed by the rapid clack of his keyboard in the background. "Let me know when it flashes red."

Seconds dragged. Time stretched. Nervous silence filled the damp space. Then—

A soft pulse. The red light blinked on the keypad.

"It's red," Dayken confirmed.

"Okay. Punch in one–zero–three–one–one–one–four, then hit star," Chase instructed through the earpiece.

I exhaled, fingers tightening around my weapon. Each button sounded with a loud, grating beep, like the tick of a bomb before it explodes. When Dayken pressed the final number, there was a hiss, followed by a low, mechanical groan.

Then the door slid open.

We raised our weapons, braced for the worst.

But no one waited for us.

No ambush. No guards.

Just... a lab.

Flooded with harsh fluorescent light, the room stretched before us in sterile perfection. Cold. Wide. White walls and chrome surfaces gleamed like they'd been scrubbed just hours ago.

Machines rotated slowly. Robotic arms glided on rails. Test tubes spun inside glowing centrifuges. A low hum filled the air, punctuated by the soft, mechanical *clicks* of unseen functions, continuing without supervision.

It was operational. *Active.*

But there wasn't a single heartbeat.

On a desk nearby, a pair of goggles lay abandoned. A metal chair was pushed back at an odd angle, a lab coat still draped over its back. The laptop at the desk blinked an error code:

ID CARD REMOVED WITHOUT PROPER LOGOUT.

Someone had just been here.

A gentle hand brushed my back. "Does any of this look familiar?" Dayken's voice was soft. Grounding. He leaned in, a steady presence in a place that had once been hell for us.

I shook my head. "No." The word felt like a failure.

Sky stood nearby, scanning the room. She paused and looked at me. No words. Her expression said it all: she didn't recognize this place either.

Alicia pointed toward a corridor on the right. "Looks like there's more this way."

Dayken tapped his comm. "All clear… for now. But someone was here recently."

Moments later, Titus and Derek entered the lab, quiet and watchful.

We kept moving.

Deeper into the facility.

Alicia stayed close to Sky, but her eyes kept drifting to every corner, checking shadows, watching exits. She wasn't just being tactical. She was wired. Tightly coiled.

I could have said something and told her to ease up, that we had her back. But the mission was everything.

I hadn't realized until that moment that she was carrying more than gear and anger. She was carrying the responsibility of someone relying on her for protection back home. But as a unit, we pressed on.

We moved like professionals. Like we'd done this a hundred times. No one spoke, but hand signals passed between us like second nature. Unrehearsed. Understood.

The silence was thick, but we were solid. Tension hummed through our bones, but trust in each other held us together.

Chapter 50

Dayken

As we navigated the corridor, we entered another wide-open space and halted, listening. The room resembled the other lab, with white walls, humming machines, and cooling systems built into the floor. Cold, clinical, and filled with data. No cover or obvious exits.

Suddenly, a large man burst through the far entrance with a handgun raised. Alicia was quick. She roared and shifted mid-sprint, transforming into her bear form, claws gouging into the concrete as she prepared to strike. A shot rang out, hitting its target. Hard.

She let out a guttural sound, stumbling back. Her paws scraped for traction, but whatever hit her had some real force behind it.

The man stepped forward, intent on finishing her off. He was calm, mercenary — like he had all the time in the world.

I didn't.

I fired twice. Then twice more.

The bullets struck his torso and sparked.

They bounced right off him.

What the hell?

Maybe it was some kind of reactive armor? Shock-absorbent plating? It didn't matter. I was already moving.

He reached behind his back, and the moment I saw what he grabbed, my blood turned to ice.

A sword.

Massive. Gleaming. And *wrong*. It pulsed with an eerie light, like a storm caged within the metal. Like Onyx's forge blades, but twisted and weaponized with malicious intent.

It was designed to kill someone like Alicia and me. A bonded Guardian. A Primarc.

"Alicia, run!" Onyx screamed, tearing forward into the chaos.

Derek was already sprinting toward her. So was I.

But we were too late.

Alicia was still trying to rise onto all fours. Whatever bullets the man used had slammed her hard enough to keep her off balance just long enough for the enemy to strike.

Then — out of nowhere — Titus.

He hit the man with full force, tackling him sideways with brutal precision.

But the sword still fell. It wasn't stopped, just slowed. And it landed a hit.

I couldn't see exactly where, not clearly. Everything moved too quickly. The sword clanged to the ground a second later, after Derek yanked it free from Alicia. But that didn't matter. Titus was already finishing the fight.

A sharp, sickening crack echoed off the walls as he snapped the bastard's neck.

Silence.

Then—

Then, Sky erupted. I turned to her, looking for the source of her hysteria.

Alicia.

Derek knelt close, his hands deep in her fur, exploring her neck. His breathing was shallow, uneasy as he worked. Then he paused, his head slightly tilted as he listened carefully. I mimicked him, ignoring all distractions, and solely concentrated on listening for the one sound that truly mattered right now.

There.

It was faint, but undeniably there.

Alicia's heartbeat.

"What happened?" Chase's voice cut through the comms, too sharp. He couldn't see; he could only listen. The uncertainty must be eating him alive.

"We have to get her out of here," I said, already moving.

"*Who?*" he asked, more forcefully this time.

Derek cursed, stripping off his shirt and using it to slow the bleeding. "How the fuck are we supposed to carry a bear out of here?"

"Fuck." Chase's voice was clipped, short. But I heard the pain behind it, the helplessness.

I couldn't bring myself to tell him that Alicia had almost been beheaded. It felt too surreal, and saying it aloud would make it real.

I scanned the corridor, watching for movement in the shadows. Blood was already pooling beneath Alicia, slick and dark against the concrete. We didn't have time.

The fluorescent lights flickered overhead, casting a sharper reflection into the blood — the smell of iron, sweat, and singed fur filled the air, thick and suffocating.

"It's getting weaker," Onyx said as she tried to comfort Sky. "Whatever we do, we have to do it now."

"Chase," I said, harsher than intended. "There's a coyote clan in Missouri. Can you contact their Primarc?"

He hesitated. Just a second. Just long enough to think. Then, "Yeah. Give me a minute."

I exhaled. That was our best shot. I'd only met them once, years ago. I couldn't remember names, just that they were fast and efficient.

"And until then?" Kolton asked, voice low, eyes bouncing between Sky and Alicia. "We just sit here?"

"No," I said. "We can't all wait. Who wants to scout?"

"I'll go," Titus offered, already yanking his shirt over his head.

Onyx turned away on instinct, like she did every time someone other than me stripped to shift.

Despite everything, I wasn't sure how I'd feel if she didn't.

Actually — scratch that.

If she *had* kept looking, I'd have killed him.

I let out a low growl under my breath. Just enough to make it known.

A second later, fabric rustled. Then a blur of black fur shot past me, vanishing into the shadows.

"Is it safe to send him alone?" Onyx asked, glancing at me.

"He knows what he's doing," I said, keeping my voice steady. Even if she didn't believe it, I needed her to *hear* certainty in my tone.

I stepped forward and raised my voice, projecting across the room. "Listen up. They're going for decapitation. That means kill orders. Stick to hand-to-hand. They're wearing body armor — use bullets only as a last resort."

The words settled like stone. No one argued.

Then Peaches' voice cut through the comms. Raw. Shaking.

"Tell me what happened to Alicia!"

It wasn't just fear. It was hysteria trying to mask as calm.

Sky answered first, her voice soft but steady. "A man with a sword tried to behead her. Derek's trying to close the wound… but Peach… I'm not going to lie… it's really deep."

We heard Peach's muffled cry choke through the comm.

Derek's voice followed. Frustrated. Tense. "That weapon cauterized most of the surface damage, but it tore through soft tissue on impact. Left chunks missing. It's not a clean slice, which makes regeneration… impossible."

"She was hit on the left side of her neck," I added quietly, giving Peach the truth. There was nothing else we could do right now — except hold her together and pray the coyotes arrived quickly.

"Peach, we're going to do everything we can, okay?" Sky added, softening my blunt update.

There was a shuffle over the comms, and then Chase's voice came through, "I've got it." We all waited. "Andrew Roseline. From the Roseline Clan. His grandfather is in our registry, but he isn't. It's got to be him, though. I've already sent out multiple alerts. My clan is in the sky right now, tracking him down. Shouldn't be much longer."

Derek cursed. "Fuck. She's bleeding out. I can't get it to stop." His voice was tight, desperate. "Search the room — anything that can help me close this."

We scattered. Ripping through every drawer, tearing apart cabinets, overturning furniture — nothing. So much equipment and machinery, but no supplies. No storage. No closets. Nothing.

I threw a panicked glance at Kolton, who looked just as frantic as the rest of us. At least he cared about someone other than Sky for the moment.

When we made eye contact, he pointed at the sword. I followed his gaze, eyes narrowing as I took in the discarded weapon.

"Derek, if the sword cauterized some of the wound, could we use it to close the rest of it?" Derek's head snapped toward me. Then to the sword.

Kolton moved first, cautiously stepping forward, but Derek didn't wait. He plucked it from Kolton's hands and started messing with the handle. A second later, it flared to life, that same eerie glow illuminating the edges.

He hesitated, just for a second, eyes flicking toward the ceiling as if weighing the risks. Then his gaze dropped back to Alicia.

"I know this is gonna hurt like hell, but I also know you'd rather bleed out than admit I saved your life. So, let's call this even, yeah?"

And with that, he pressed the flat of the sword to her neck.

A sickening sizzle filled the room. The stench of burning flesh was instant and awful.

"I'm going to be sick," Sky choked out. Kolton was at her side a second later, hovering like a mother hen, peppering her with questions, yet never touching her.

"Guys..." Titus panted, reemerging from the corridor. "This place goes on forever. The tunnel system is insane. I would've gotten lost if I couldn't track your scents back here. There aren't any other smells or sounds for miles. It's a damn maze down here."

"Like a bad game of Dungeons & Dragons... only there's no Dungeon Master," Derek said as he peered theatrically down a tunnel, keeping the sword pressed to Alicia's neck.

If Alicia were conscious, she'd be scolding him for his *terrible* timing.

Then suddenly — new sounds. New scents.

I stiffened, turning toward the entrance. Onyx was already moving, having sensed the threat before the rest of us. I watched as she pressed herself against the wall near the doorway, poised to catch whoever was about to step inside.

The first thing to emerge was a coyote. It slinked into the room with its head low, jaws wide, displaying sharp, deadly teeth. Its nose twitched, nostrils flaring as it caught the scent of blood, thick in the air.

Then three men followed. One had an earpiece. Another had a falcon perched on his shoulder, its talons digging into his shirt, leaving tiny tears in the fabric.

"Help should be there now," Chase said in our ears.

Help.

Finally.

Onyx stepped from her ambush position, voice firm and commanding. "Over there," she said, pointing toward Alicia.

They nodded, and two of them stepped forward, kneeling beside Derek to assist. I heard Derek bring them up to speed on Alicia's condition, bookending his report with a telling whisper, "She's a bonded Primarc."

Realization fell across the men's faces, and they glanced at each other nervously. The stakes just went up. The third man approached me, his expression dark with barely restrained anger.

"Our Primarc apologizes for not being here himself," he said, but his voice was clipped, his frustration bleeding through. "We were briefed on the situation, and I'll be frank — this facility's existence is a gross oversight by our clan. The fact that it has operated undetected within our territory for so long is… deeply concerning." I met his gaze, catching the fire burning in his eyes. This wasn't just about assisting another clan. This was personal.

He took a breath, reining in his emotions before placing a hand over his heart and bowing — a gesture of respect and submission. "There will be an investigation into how this place remained hidden for so long. Someone knew, and we intend to find out who."

His lowered head and respectful demeanor indicated that he recognized me for what I was: another bonded Primarc.

I nodded in acknowledgment. "I appreciate that. In the meantime, please get her out of here and put your best healers on her case."

The tension didn't dissipate. If anything, it thickened as the coyote beside him growled low, ears twitching, as if scenting the ghosts of whatever horrors had taken place here.

"We'll transport Alicia Mack, bonded Primarc of the Mack Clan, to our settlement, and we'll start digging into this immediately. If someone was complicit, either in allowing this operation to continue or intentionally misleading us, we'll find them."

Enlisting the help of a new clan was always a gamble, but I felt reassured by the respectful way he spoke of Alicia and their outrage about the facility, which closely mirrored our own.

We had expected to meet enemies today, which we did. However, we found allies as well.

We watched them carry Alicia's bear form out of the room. It was sobering and gut-wrenching to witness. But we had a mission to complete, and despite our immense loss, we needed to continue.

Derek picked up the sword again, inspecting it in earnest this time. "What the actual fuck have they been doing down here?"

"I don't know, but something tells me that is just the first of many surprises." I couldn't help but forebode.

✳✳✳

We walked for what felt like miles. Everyone was silent and on full alert. Then we heard it. Faint. Kolton inhaled deeply, then growled, soft and low. I shot him a look, and he stopped.

A man rounded the corner ahead of us, gun raised. I easily disarmed him and punched him in the face. He crumbled to the floor. We paused, waiting to see if more would come. When they didn't, I motioned to press on. But before we could, a groan came from the ground.

"I've got him," Derek said as the man slowly came to. Waving us ahead, he lowered himself to the ground, gun in hand. He pressed the barrel to the man's temple.

"Team Edward or team Jacob?" Derek asked, as if they were buds having a friendly chat. I didn't hear the response as we pressed forward. But the following sound — ***thump*** — let me know Derek didn't agree. Crazy bastard.

I heard shuffled footsteps coming from behind a bend in the corridor. I raised my hand, stopping our advance. I could smell the blood pumping through the bodies there, a lot of them.

Derek joined us seconds later, and I locked eyes with everyone. I wanted to confirm that everyone else picked up on what I was sensing. When I got nods in return, I lifted my hand and held up three fingers. Then, I made a countdown.

3

2

1

Go.

We burst around the corner into what appeared to be a staging area. Alarmed faces let us know that we caught them off guard, but they were otherwise prepared. Ten humans raised their weapons in unison.

They had pushed the tables and equipment against the walls, anticipating our arrival. They left the entire space open with no place to take cover.

Onyx was the first to get hit. Her pain immediately shot through our bond.

"NOOOO," I bellowed.

She clutched her abdomen, blood seeping between her fingers, but with her other hand, she waved me off. "I'm fine!"

In a blur, she lunged at the nearest agent, yanking off his helmet and pressing her gun to his temple. He fumbled for his sword, but she was faster. He fell instantly.

Then, so did she.

She collapsed, limbs splayed across the floor. Our bond went cold. I felt nothing.

Panic seized me. A roar tore from my throat, freezing everyone in their tracks.

Despite all my training, all the instincts that came with protecting my Sacar, *nothing* could have prepared me for this — the sheer, gut-wrenching *loss* that clawed through me. I felt sick.

I bellowed my rage.

Sky let out an equally ear-piercing screech.

"Don't you dare leave me, my goddess."

Chapter 51

I was at Onyx's side in an instant, dropping to my knees, clutching her to me. My fingers pressed desperately against her neck, looking for a pulse — *nothing*.

No. *No.*

I tore my attention away from her just long enough to flip a table. Glass shattered and objects tumbled around Onyx's head, but I needed a makeshift shield as the bullets whizzed past, bouncing off the concrete walls. I refocused on Onyx.

What did they do to her? Why is she out cold?

My mind scrambled for answers, but my thoughts were a mess, too many distractions, too much noise. I'd always been told I was a natural-born leader, that I thrived in chaos. But at this moment?

I felt *lost.*

"Get it out of her," Sky's voice snapped through my haze as she crouched next to me, using the table for cover as well. "Something's inside her, preventing her from healing."

I swallowed my fear and gently laid Onyx down, adjusting her arms and legs so she wasn't just a heap of limbs. The battle raged on around me, muffled sounds of our team hitting their mark, but it didn't matter — not to me. Nothing else did. Onyx was everything. She was all that mattered.

If I didn't leave with her, then I wasn't leaving at all.

My hands moved over her stomach, searching for the source of the bleeding. I tore at her clothing, barely registering the sound of ripping fabric. My breath caught when I saw it — a bullet wound, tearing through her otherwise flawless pale skin. I rolled her to her side and quickly checked for an exit wound. *Nothing.*

I exhaled sharply.

I know what I need to do.

Without hesitation, I shifted her onto her back and pressed two fingers into the wound. I explored the cavity, feeling for any foreign bodies.

She didn't flinch. She didn't move. She stayed completely unresponsive.

Blood coated my fingers, warm and slick, but there was *nothing.* My jaw clenched.

Where is it?

I pulled my hand out, adjusted my angle, and drove my fingers back inside, deeper this time.

I can't feel anything.

A growl ripped through me, frustration bleeding into every word. "I *can't* find it!"

I was about to tell Sky to try when — *there.*

Cold metal, lodged deep into her flesh.

I gripped it between my fingers, twisting, pulling, and finally yanking it free. The moment it left her body, a sharp, toxic stench filled my nose. My stomach turned.

Poison.

It wasn't just a bullet; it was *laced* with what smelled like the same shit that Derek found in Crowe's syringe. The same shit that took her down so quickly before.

Terror curled in my gut. I was so sick of these freaks and their psychopathic bioweapons.

"Don't get hit!" I roared to the others. "Their bullets are laced!"

We can't afford to lose anyone else.

Sky peeked over the edge of the table just as a bullet slammed into the aluminum plating, warping the metal with a dent that jutted toward us, proof that the cover was doing its job.

Her voice was steady, even amid the chaos. "Go. Fight. I'll watch over her."

I didn't hesitate. I turned, leapt over the table, and *got my vengeance.*

I dodged, disarmed, and destroyed — fast, efficient, ruthless. I even dismembered a few of them. But the urge to return to Onyx's side was unbearable.

The humans thought their technology and advanced weaponry would even the odds.

They were wrong.

Their tactics were clean. Clinical. But I had become pure chaos. I was rage, vengeance, and desperation made flesh.

My speed and strength won out.

No, *my love for this woman* is what won the battle.

That wild, unyielding devotion made me unstoppable.

By the time it was over, I was drenched in blood, panting, my fists still clenched.

But I was back at Onyx's side.

I watched the steady rise and fall of her chest, every breath more reassuring than the last.

Derek was there, updating me on her condition, his voice low but steady. Like I surmised, he suspected it was the same toxin that had taken her down at the compound.

Her body was fighting it, resiliently burning through the poison. She'd wake up soon, just like last time. Gods, she was strong. So powerful. So perfect.

Pride swelled in my chest as I crouched down and scooped her into my arms, cradling her against me.

"Let's keep moving," I barked, harsher than intended from the adrenaline still coursing through me.

Onyx stirred, her body shifting slightly in my hold. I slowed my steps, adjusting my grip so her head could rest on my shoulder. The movement made her moan, but it wasn't a sound of pain. No, she inhaled deeply, pressing her face closer to my neck, and moaned again.

Fuck.

Heat coiled low in my stomach as my body responded instinctively. This was not the time for such thoughts, but when she nuzzled against my neck again, I knew exactly what she needed.

Blood.

"You guys go on ahead. I think Onyx needs to feed."

No one questioned me. They nodded and continued forward, leaving us alone.

"Goddess?"

"Mmm?"

"You hungry?"

"Mmhmm."

Before I could tell her to go ahead, she sank her teeth into my neck. The pain lasted for only an instant, replaced by the deep, rhythmic pull of her feeding. She moaned softly, the sound vibrating against my skin.

I sank to the ground, holding her in my lap. She shifted, straddling me without breaking contact, her strength returning with every swallow. Her hands slid up my chest, fingers curling around the nape of my neck, gripping the hair there, positioning me exactly how she wanted.

I was hers. Putty in her hands.

Desire curled through me, dark and consuming. I wanted to take her right here, to let her drink until pleasure tore through her, and then fill her in a different way—

"Yes," she murmured against my skin, licking the wound she left behind.

Shit. I must have said that part out loud.

Her eyes gleamed with mischief, and relief flooded me at the sight. She was alert again. Strong.

I seized her mouth with mine, the kiss instantly turning fiery. She clung to me like I was the only thing keeping her grounded — and I held her just as tightly, unwilling to let her go.

"You scared the shit out of me," I rasped against her mouth.

"I'm sorry," she admitted, pulling back so I could see her dilated, icy eyes. "I thought if it were laced with anything, it would be similar to what they used during the attack, and that I would burn through the shit faster this time."

I nodded, biting back the argument I'd save for later. Apologies were new for her, and I didn't want to take away from that. But she wasn't getting away with brushing off my concern either.

"Come on. Let's catch up to the others." I pulled her to her feet, keeping her close. "And then we'll go home... so I can make good on my word."

I shot her a wink, lacing my fingers through hers.

Chapter 52

Onyx

The wound on my stomach felt sensitive, but thanks to Dayken's blood, it was now just pink, healing flesh. Nothing that would slow me down.

We quickly caught up with the others, arriving at a barely lit, concrete corridor. It was wider than the others, and Titus warned us that he hadn't scouted this far ahead. We would be going in blind.

Once we entered the corridor, I quickly noticed a strange scent, which the others seemed to pick up too. The further we went, the more pronounced it became. The air began to feel hot and dense, heavy with humidity.

We slowed as the corridor opened into a large space, bright enough to make me squint. The moisture created a foggy haze, thick as smoke. It clung to the glass walls in front of us, obscuring our view. However, it was clear that something was growing inside.

"Let's check it out," Kolton said before barreling inside like a bull in a damned China shop.

The greenhouse's lights hung low, casting a harsh glow over the rows of plants. I approached cautiously, caught off guard first by the scent, then the sight — eight brown petals.

"Son of a bitch," I muttered.

"Yup," Derek agreed.

"He lied," Sky said, her voice tight with restrained fury. "He must not have thought we'd actually come here. That whole story about planting his people in the clans? It was a distraction — just enough to keep us from looking closer."

I could see in her eyes as she connected the dots — that razor-sharp mind of hers firing through every fact we collected, every theory we discussed. Sky didn't need time to mull things over; her brain processed everything in a blink, and she looked ready for war.

"He fucked up when he came after us," I said, clenching my jaw. "Thinking he could round up more test subjects. Like we're nothing but lab rats." Silence enveloped us; everyone was lost in the implications of our discovery. My only thought: *we need explosives.*

"Should we take some?" Derek asked, looking between the eight-petaled flowers and the rest of us.

I hesitated. "I don't know. If they got into the wrong hands—"

"They are already in the wrong hands," Titus cut in.

"Okay, but if anyone finds out we have it," I countered, "then it's only a matter of time before someone tries to steal one, and they spread even further…"

A heavy pause followed.

"Clan wars like we've never seen," Dayken murmured, his voice grim.

The truth hung there, bitter and unrelenting. This wasn't just about shutting down one of Crowe's hidden facilities. This was about destroying something before it could upend clan life as we knew it.

I could practically hear Chase's frown through the earpiece. "Okay, hold on — what exactly are we looking at here?" he asked, and Derek described the greenhouse full of Sacar flowers. The sharp hiss Chase released showed he shared our concern. Crowe was trying to recreate the ancient ritual, and from the looks of it, he got damn close to accomplishing it.

So, the choice stood:

Destroy it all, and burn this place to the ground, leaving nothing behind.

Or take what we could, study it, understand it, and maybe, just maybe, keep it out of the wrong hands.

Both options were dangerous. Both had the potential to change everything.

I exhaled slowly, locking eyes with Dayken.

"What's the call?" he asked, leaving the decision to me. I looked at Sky, and once again, we didn't need words. Our energy spoke to each other like the immortal blood we shared.

"Burn it to the ground," we said in unison.

Titus smirked, holding up a small, sleek metallic disc and tossing it lightly in the air before catching it. "Lucky for us, I came prepared." He reached into his bag, pulled out several more discs, and handed them out. "Each of these is an incendiary directional charge, precision-made. Lightweight, no unnecessary boom, just controlled destruction. You're welcome."

Derek whistled low. "Damn, Fox, I knew you had tricks, but these? That's some next-level shit."

Titus gave a mock bow. "What can I say? I aim to please."

Sky smiled after throwing me a disc. I flipped the device over in my hand as the rest of the team set about placing charges around the greenhouse. "And I'm just supposed to trust that these won't blow my hand off?"

Titus rolled his eyes. "I made them. They're perfect. You should feel honored to even hold one."

Derek, checking his placement on a nearby support beam, glanced over. "Onyx, just stick it where I tell you — *that's what she said* — and if it kills us all, we can haunt Titus together."

Titus snorted. "I'd be a fantastic ghost."

When we were nearly done placing the devices in strategic spots around the greenhouse, I turned to watch Titus wipe his hands, admiring his work.

"Perfect placement," he said, pleased. "This will implode surgically, *exactly* the way I planned." He held up a small rectangular box with tiny buttons on it as he *not-so-subtly* moved into Derek's space to inspect his work.

Sky, flipping an extra explosive in her palm, grinned. "What's the radius on that detonator, Titus?"

"We could blow this place up from Aruba as we sip—"

A low whirring noise cut through the humid air. I heard it first, snapping my head toward the sound. It was faint, but the others soon noticed it too, their heads rising in unison.

Something was wrong.

Chase's voice suddenly spiked through the earpiece: "Guys, you've got company!"

"Sky—" I started.

A black drone swooped down from above. It was a blur, faster than any of us could react.

It barreled toward Titus, forcing him to stumble back, as he rose an arm to block it. The machine didn't slow, zeroing in on the detonator clutched in his hand and somehow latching on to him.

Titus's forearm flexed, fighting, his grip straining — but then, an electric current shot visibly down his arm. The smell of singed hair hit instantly. His fingers spasmed open, dropping the remote for the drone to cleanly snatch.

Titus had no time to recover before the drone banked hard, zipping away, the remote dangling beneath it in a mechanical claw.

Derek lunged, too slow.

Titus, absolutely furious, bellowed, "Are you *fucking* kidding me!?"

We scrambled, following the drone's path out of the greenhouse. It hovered above us, impossible to reach.

Sky drew her gun, lining up a shot. "I can take it down—"

But Kolton stopped her, shaking his head. "Too risky. If you miss, the detonator's gone for good. Or worse, it *goes off.*"

Titus glared toward the ceiling. "Who the hell sends a drone to steal explosives?"

My hands curled into fists. "Where's it going?"

Then—

A figure stepped from the shadows of a distant corridor, directly beneath the drone.

I recognized him. He always wore a surgical mask when he entered my cell, but I would never forget those cold, calculating eyes.

A sleek, black-gloved hand reached up, plucking the detonator from the drone's grip before it peeled away, disappearing just as quickly as it appeared.

The man grinned, flipping the detonator in his palm.

"Well, well. How convenient," he said as his eyes settled on me. "Welcome home, Onyx." Then his gaze shifted, a slow, deliberate sweep. He smiled at Sky. "*And* Skylar, lovely as ever."

Kolton snarled, his body half-shifting, bones snapping as stripes rippled beneath his skin.

Dayken's hand was at my back in an instant, his presence calming the ice in my veins.

Titus exhaled slowly, his posture relaxed but his tone murderous. "I *really* hate when people touch my things," he rasped, bluntly pointing at the detonator.

Chase's voice crackled in the earpiece. "Hold up, what just happened? Someone explain."

I gritted my teeth. "One of Crowe's lackeys is here, and he used a drone to snatch the detonator from us."

The man tilted his head. "Aw, I'm *flattered.*"

Through the comm, I heard Chase swear violently. "Titus, tell me you put a failsafe on those things."

Titus ground his teeth. "I *had* a failsafe. Someone stole it."

For dramatic effect, the man waved the detonator in front of him, his thumb hovering over the button.

Derek's face went white. "Oh, fuck." The man smiled in response.

"You know," he mused, admiring the detonator. "I wasn't sure I'd get here in time." He lifted his gaze to us. Smug. Relaxed. Knowing. "But Crowe? He didn't think you'd come." He chuckled. "He really thought he threw you off the trail. But *I* knew the second that bear left her territory."

How the hell has he been in communication with Crowe?

Sky's jaw tightened. "You *knew* we'd come here."

He shrugged. "Please. The moment you began heading south, I knew exactly where you were going."

A chill crept down my spine. They'd been watching us.

His smile sharpened. "But we'll have to cut this reunion short. We can't have you poking around down here." And with that, he lifted the detonator.

My heart twisted. He was really willing to do it. To blow up the greenhouse. The flowers. All of it. He would rather burn the facility to ash than let us anywhere near it.

And then—

He clicked the button.

The charges blinked red in unison.

The ground shuddered beneath our feet as everything detonated.

A violent bloom of glass, fire, and earth erupted around us, ripping out like a scream.

He didn't even flinch.

He smiled through the smoke, like torching the place was a message. Not preservation. Not caution. Just strategy.

Either the flowers meant nothing to him…Or…. Even worse… this wasn't the only site.

More labs. More hidden crops. Enough that he could reduce this one to cinders and not suffer the loss.

That terrified me more than the surrounding destruction ever could.

Then… there was nothing but darkness. A heavy, suffocating weight crushed my chest. My lungs strained for air, each breath dragging in dust and blood. My head pounded, the thick, grating ring in my ears making the world feel slow and distant.

I tried to move.

Nothing happened. Panic slammed into me, sudden and sharp. I was pinned. The realization clawed through the fog in my mind, snapping me awake in an instant. My fingers twitched, reaching and scraping at the dirt and debris around me.

Something large was on top of me.

No — someone.

My pulse spiked violently, heart hammering against my ribs.

I pushed weakly, but my arms wouldn't work. Pain ripped up my wrist like white-hot fire, and nausea twisted in my stomach as I realized it was broken.

I bit back the cry rising in my throat, forcing myself to cut through the panic.

Focus.

I shifted my fingers, brushing against fabric — broad shoulders, a solid frame.

Recognition slammed into me.

Dayken.

My chest tightened as the realization hit like a sledgehammer.

He wasn't moving.

No.

No, no, no.

"Dayken!" My voice was raw, broken. I could barely hear myself over the high-pitched ringing in my skull.

He didn't react.

My breath shattered, panic gripping me in a stranglehold.

He shielded me.

He took the brunt of the blast.

And now—

"Dayken!" I shoved him, my left hand gripping his shirt, shaking him hard enough to rattle my own injured body.

Nothing.

I pressed my fingers to his throat, desperately searching for his pulse.

It was there.

Faint.

Weak.

But there.

A strangled noise caught in my throat. I pressed my forehead to him, squeezing my eyes shut as relief and fear waged inside me.

I had to get him out of here.

And Sky…

Where's Sky?

"Sky?" I croaked.

"I'm here," she rasped from somewhere nearby.

A tear escaped, trailing down my cheek as my head fell back against the debris, a wave of relief crashing over me.

But we did not have time to rest.

My injured arm screamed as I planted my good hand against the ground and shoved. My breath hitched, pain splitting through my nerves like lightning, but I didn't stop.

I twisted, dragged, pushed — finally wriggling free from under him, my body shaking violently from the effort.

The moment I was out, I collapsed onto my back, gasping through clenched teeth. My bones were already mending, but the dull, deep ache of healing fractures lingered.

Dayken was still out cold.

I rolled onto my side, reaching for him, hands trembling as I pressed my palm to his cheek.

"Come on, come on," I whispered, voice wrecked.

A faint groan came from somewhere nearby, followed by shifting debris.

The others.

They were waking up.

I barely acknowledged it, my world narrowing to only Dayken.

I pressed my forehead to his, voice barely above a whisper. "Wake up, you stubborn bastard."

Nothing.

The bunker groaned, the concrete walls shifting.

We were running out of time.

A pained sigh echoed through the collapsed space.

Sky.

Before I could shout again, I spotted her — a figure amid the dense smoke, unsteady yet standing.

She was pulling someone.

Not just anyone, but Kolton.

His arm hung limply over her shoulder, blood smeared across her front. Kolton's body was slack, unconscious, and Sky's heaving sighs grew more prominent as she got closer. Regardless, I knew she had it handled. Meanwhile, Titus leaned against Derek, teeth gritted so hard it looked like his jaw might snap. His leg was mangled, twisted at a sickening angle, but he was moving. Of course, he was. His strength knew no bounds.

"Where the fuck is the exit?" Titus demanded, voice strained but sharp.

Derek struggled to keep him upright, scanning the debris around us. "I don't know, man — give me a second to get my bearings." A distant creaking sound echoed above us — the ceiling shifted. The entire bunker was collapsing.

"MOVE!" Sky shouted.

Titus, sweating and pale, waved Derek forward. "Find us a fucking exit — now!"

Derek pushed ahead, scanning the wreckage. "There!" He pointed to a section of the collapsed wall, a narrow gap leading to what appeared to be a stairwell.

Sky didn't hesitate. She hauled Kolton with her, her steps staggered but strong.

I threw Dayken's arm over my shoulder and gripped his waist tightly. My healing arm screamed in protest, but I ignored it.

Titus limped forward, practically dragging his injured leg. Derek kept him steady, both of them moving faster than they should have been able to.

We were getting close, but we were moving slowly, much too slowly. Above us, concrete fractured, and dust showered down as the structure caved in.

We ran for it.

Sky squeezed through the opening first, moving chunks of large rocks off the stairs and pulling Kolton up behind her.

I went next, dragging Dayken, each step a searing, painful effort.

I heard Titus curse harshly behind me as he tripped, his injured leg buckling.

"Come on, man, if you just turned into a fox, I could carry you," Derek shouted, tightening his hold.

Titus gritted his teeth, his face pale yet resolute, a silent defiance in his demeanor. "I'd rather be left here to die," he declared, his voice strained.

Derek scoffed, the mockery evident. "Oh, don't be—"

Suddenly, a thunderous **CRACK** reverberated through the air, the structure shattering around us.

I whipped around, just in time to witness the stairwell's ceiling give way — dust and debris cascaded down like a storm. A chunk of earth and concrete struck me on the head. Blood began dripping down my forehead, blocking my vision. I tried using my free hand to wipe it away while holding onto Dayken with my other, when I was suddenly met with… light.

Bright natural light flooded in, slicing through the chaos and illuminating the darkness that had enveloped us.

Chapter 53

We dragged ourselves and the others away from the crater we had no doubt just created. My pace slowed as I took a deep breath, familiarity creeping into my senses. The trees, the sounds, the smells… they all tugged at recognition. I knew this place. This was the exact spot where Sky and I escaped the facility, where I shattered my shackles… marking the cusp of a new chapter. The last time I stood on this dirt, my feet were bare and vulnerable. Now, I looked down at the thick, black leather boots I wore. The contrast was striking. Then and now. Captive and free.

I gently laid Dayken down and spun in a slow circle, taking it all in. The river flowed nearby, calm and steady, but there were no familiar signs of the route we'd taken in our escape. There was no worn path, no trail, and no cameras or motion sensors mounted to the trees. Nothing. As if this place was never meant to be found. As if it wasn't supposed to exist.

It was shocking to be here after all that time. And now, it was inconvenient, because I had no idea how to get back to the trucks we'd arrived in.

I ripped the comm from my ear and smacked it against my palm. "Chase?"

Silence. I hit it again.

"Yeah," Derek said dryly. "Every tech nerd ever will tell you that smacking it to bits will definitely fix it."

I shot him a glare. "Oh, shut up."

His expression turned serious. "Trust me, I'm more worried about losing contact with my brother than anyone here."

"He'll find us," I said softly. "I trust him."

And I did. We were here, alive, *because* of them. Because of Sky, because of Chase, because of Alicia and Kolton, and even Derek.

We were safe. And we blew that horrible place sky-high.

Because of my friends.

Yes — *friends*. Not colleagues. Not teammates. Not associates.

Friends.

Derek's brow lifted like he heard the shift in my tone. He clapped a hand to my shoulder and motioned toward our battered little group. "You can trust all of us, you know."

I opened my mouth to reply—

"Getttt. Your. Grim-y. Hand. Off." *Deep breath.* "Her." The voice was weak but unmistakable.

"Dayken!" I dropped to my knees where he lay, brushing the hair from his face. His eyes were barely open, but he smiled at me.

"Hi," he said, voice rough but tender.

"Hi," I whispered back, a smile spreading across my face before I could stop it.

"Where are we?"

I looked around again. "This might sound crazy… but I think we're on the other side of the river."

"We are," Sky said, rising from where she'd been checking on Kolton's still form. She tapped her earpiece. "Chase just confirmed — we made it across."

"Gimme, gimme, gimme," Derek muttered, snatching the earpiece like a child who never learned patience.

"Brother!" he shouted into it.

None of us had the heart to shush him this time.

Not after everything.

Not after *Alicia*.

Chase confirmed that help was on the way. Kolton lay crumpled near a fallen log, unconscious but breathing. Titus was worse off; blood seeped from his temple, his face slack. Derek knelt beside him, muttering something I couldn't catch.

Dayken, having recovered enough to be on his feet, stood guard near the tree line. His back was tense, scanning the woods for movement even though we were miles from any known patrols.

And Sky — Sky hadn't moved. Her hand rested over her heart like she was holding herself together from the inside out.

I forced myself to ask, "What about Alicia?"

Silence stretched across the clearing. Even the forest seemed to hush.

"The Missouri coyotes have her, right?" Sky asked, voice tight, knowing, but wanting confirmation.

"Chase says she is," Derek confirmed, grim. "He has her location. They've been responsive and helpful. But… it isn't good. She's alive, but barely. They're stabilizing her as well as they can."

"We can't just leave her there," Sky whispered.

I agreed. Everything in me screamed to bring her back with us, to see her with my own eyes. But we were barely standing. We couldn't move fast, not like this. Not with so many half-broken bodies.

"She won't make the trip to Michigan," Derek muttered. "And I trust that coyote medic," he continued, voice softer now. "Chase said she's already working on Alicia."

"She's Bear Clan," Dayken added, still watching the woods. "Coyotes don't trust easily, but they respect honor. Alicia's earned that, ten times over. Their territory is the best option for her. She'll be safe there — protected."

"But it's not what she would want," Sky said, looking at me. "She'd want to be with us. She'd want to get back to Peach."

"She'd want to live," I replied, my voice harder than I intended. "And right now, this is the only way that happens."

Derek swore under his breath, staring at the ground like it might give him a better answer. "So, we just… leave her?"

"No," I said. "We're going to see her. Then we let her rest and recover so she can survive this." The silence that followed was heavier than before, but no one argued. We owed her that much.

The silence persisted as we shuffled along the riverbank, following Chase's directions and the falcons circling overhead. Their occasional screeching call was the only sound to break the tension, warning us whenever we veered off course. Our steps were far less confident than when we first arrived. We took turns hauling Titus and Kolton through the unforgiving terrain. Despite how taxing the trek was, it was obvious that no one was in a hurry to say goodbye to Alicia.

Once in the trucks, the drive wasn't long. I could see even more clearly why the coyote who spoke with Dayken was so upset about this oversight; the enemy was literally right under their nose.

Before we knew it, we faced the all-too-familiar sight of an abandoned, rundown warehouse. This one sat just off the road from a busy downtown area, hidden in plain sight.

We entered through the back door, passed "danger" and "exit only" signs. I heard the beep of medical machines, letting me know that we hadn't been led astray. The closer we got to the sound, the more obvious it became that it was the soft rhythm of Alicia's fragile pulse.

Tubes and wires snaked from her arms and nose, connected to IV bags and oxygen. She was massive, still in her bear form, and yet in that bed, she appeared hollow, a shell of herself. I stood beside her, fingers curling around the rail as if I could hold her life there by sheer will.

The coyote medic moved with deliberate, calm precision, providing care I couldn't quite follow. Derek stayed close behind me, clearly fighting the urge to step in. I pulled my gaze away from Alicia to observe the rest of the room.

A group of coyotes were gathered against the wall. There was a vampire among them, silent and watchful. His pale skin mirrored mine, but his posture was different: composed and alert. I saw this as a good sign. Based on my limited knowledge of clan politics, his presence indicated strength, safety, and a place where Alicia could find healing and rest.

I turned to the medic. My voice came out sharper than intended when I asked, "Is she going to make it?"

She blinked and looked away, unable to meet my gaze. "I... I'm trying everything I can."

I narrowed my eyes. "That's not an answer."

Her voice was tight, almost pained. "Because I don't have the answer you're looking for," she said before turning her back to me.

Across the room, Dayken stood with their Primarc. I didn't catch their conversation, but I didn't need to. There were no harsh tones, no posturing — just a nod. Mutual understanding. Trust offered, not demanded.

We didn't want to leave her, but we had to. When we finally did, it felt like failure, like betrayal wrapped in duty.

As we walked back to the car, Sky wrapped her arm around my waist, and I, in response, wrapped my arm around her shoulder. "That first night in the library at Dayken's? I could tell you tuned out, but you missed something important. The fact they've got a male vampire in their ranks, that's huge." I arched a brow at that, because I hadn't realized she picked up on me not paying attention, and I didn't know anything about male vampires now that I thought about it, "There hasn't been a male vampire since Lunce."

Well, holy shit.

Gave her one more squeeze before letting go so we could get in the truck. Dayken opened the door for both of us, and once inside, Sky was overwhelmed with emotions. Kolton snapped awake at the sound of her sobs, and he awkwardly tried to comfort her.

No one said a word on the drive home, but the deafening silence felt loud. It raised questions we couldn't answer.

What about the flowers? Are there more? Are there others like us?

Did anyone survive that explosion? Will they find us again? Will we ever stop running? Will we ever be free?

What comes next?

None of us knew, and even worse, no one dared to ask, even though we were all thinking about it.

Still, we were alive. And for now… that had to be enough.

Epilogue

Onyx

Dayken's head rested on my stomach as I ran my hand through his hair, the ends curling ever so slightly around my fingertips.

"I love you," I said, breaking the quiet lull.

"I love you so much, my goddess," he replied, lifting his head to look at me.

We really should have been productive and made the most of our day off, but this felt so perfect. I didn't want to ruin it.

"Wanna hit the gym?" he asked. It was almost creepy how he always seemed to read my mind. I still hadn't figured out if it was from the bond or just him.

"Yeah, let me get dressed." I reluctantly unraveled myself from underneath him.

"I'm gonna see if Sky wants to join too," I said as I pulled on a sports bra.

I padded down the hallway to her room.

Knock, knock.

No response.

I didn't hear the shower running. Actually, I didn't hear anything at all.

"Sky?"

Silence.

A strange unease crept through me as I inhaled deeply, then flung her door open.

Empty.

From the corner of my eye, I caught movement down the hallway — Kolton was coming down the stairs, a cup of coffee in hand.

"Where's Sky?" I asked, my voice sharp.

Kolton frowned. "She said she was coming down to hang out with you."

That didn't sit right. My eyes scanned the hallway behind him. "She's not in the kitchen?"

"No," Kolton said, already turning on his heel. "I'll check the guest rooms."

"I'll try the gym," I said, moving fast.

We swept through the compound — hallways, common rooms, the back patio. Nothing.

By the time I got back to the stairs, my unease had already twisted into dread. When Kolton arrived without Sky, realization dawned on us. Without a word, we bolted toward the security room.

Inside, Chase was lounging in front of the monitors, casually watching some bears unload boxes at the loading dock.

Kolton didn't bother with pleasantries. "Chase, have you seen Sky pop up on the feeds?"

"No, why?" he asked, sitting up straighter.

Dayken must have sensed my panic through the bond because he was at my side instantly.

"We don't know where she is," I bit out.

Chase's face darkened. "That's not like her. One second." His fingers flew over the keyboard. A few commands later, and the footage rewound — seconds ticking back in sharp, grainy detail. And then, there it was.

A man.

A waiting truck.

A sack slung over his shoulder.

My world narrowed.

Kolton and I moved in unison, sprinting up the stairs and cutting through the main part of the compound, Dayken trailing behind us. We reached the entrance doors at full speed, just in time to see the truck barreling toward the exit.

Chase was already on it, slamming the security gates closed. The metal groaned as they slammed together.

The truck barreled through, just barely, its sides scraping against the gate with a screech of metal. The back bumper clipped the bars a split second before they slammed shut behind it with a deafening clang.

I screamed.

Kolton bellowed — the sound part broken man, part raging beast — and lunged for the fence. Clawed hands gripped the bars like he could tear them apart.

Dayken was already shouting at the nearest camera, barking orders he knew Chase would hear.

But the truck didn't slow.

It didn't stop.

By the time my eyes tracked it past the tree line, it was already disappearing down the road.

That's when it hit me.

Gone.

Sky was gone.

Keep Reading

Want to know more about the Facility and their
motives? Curious about Kolton and his past? Wondering
about the sacred flower and the secrets it still holds?

Good. I'm glad you are.

Because this story is just beginning.
Book II is coming soon — and it's all about
Sky and Kolton.

About the Author

S.M. Storm is a Michigan writer who loves all things dark, magical, and a little bit spooky. She's been writing her entire career, but her favorite experience has been this one, where she gets to weave together vampires, shifters, and the kind of slow-burn romance that makes you yell at the page.

When she's not writing, she's cheering on her son at soccer, rewatching her favorite comfort shows (with a fairy-tale ending, always), and dragging her husband into endless coffee shops.

Sacar is her debut novel and the start of **The Marked Bonds Series**, a paranormal romance and urban fantasy world full of secrets, bonds, and, most importantly, tension.

S_M_STORM